More praise for the novels of Leonard Goldberg

Deadly Exposure

"A lethal microbe, a brutal murder, and a sentient iceberg menace coolly competent forensic pathologist Joanna Blalock . . . salty . . . zingy." —*Kirkus Reviews*

"Compelling." —*Publishers Weekly*

"A riveting biological thriller . . . a nonstop thrill ride of medical suspense." —*Lincoln Journal Star* (NE)

Deadly Harvest

"Diabolical . . . a first-rate medical thriller."
—*Virginian Pilot*

"Excellent . . . a tangled web of a case. . . . Goldberg has the anatomy of ingenious murders down pat."
—*Kirkus Reviews*

"A page-turner with ample plot twists, medical realism, believable dialogue, and characters who command our sympathies."
—*Charleston Post and Courier*

"Goldberg certainly knows how to bring authenticity to his novels. The Joanna Blalock series is a good one to hand to readers of Patricia Cornwell."
—*Library Journal*

continued . . .

Deadly Care
A *USA Today* bestseller and *People* magazine
"Page-Turner of the Week"

"[Goldberg] has clearly hit his stride in this brainy nail-biter . . . *Deadly Care* offers not only fascinating forensics and insider insights into the health care system, but plenty of intriguing characters and a devilish plot—the perfect Rx for curing those reading blahs."
                                        —*People*

"A fascinating, fast-moving, thought-provoking thriller."
                                        —*Booklist*

"A scalpel-edged page-turner . . . cool cuttings by a sure hand."
                                        —*Kirkus Reviews*

"*Deadly Care* is fast-paced, gripping, and informative. . . . A wonderful forensic detective. . . . A book everyone should read."   —Michael Collins

"*Deadly Care* is a first-class medical thriller, loaded with suspense and believable characters."
                                        —T. Jefferson Parker

"Illuminating, entertaining, grips readers with its realism. . . . This is state-of-the-art forensic medicine and sharp social commentary."
                                        —*Liberty Journal* (FL)

A Deadly Practice

"Goldberg keeps Dr. Blalock in jeopardy and the culprit is well-concealed. . . . The sense of events happening in a real institution matches the work of other, longer-established doctors who write. The sights, sounds, smells, and routines of a great hospital become a character in the story."
—*Los Angeles Times Book Review*

"Terrific! Guarantees medical authenticity, non-stop enjoyment. . . . Joanna Blalock is a great character. . . . This is truly a gripping mystery, well-written and altogether an extremely satisfying read."
—*Affaire de Coeur*

Deadly Medicine

"A shuddery venture, worthy of Robin Cook or Michael Crichton, into the cold gray corridors of a hospital that confirms our very worst fears."
—Donald Stanwood

"A terrific thriller, with unflagging pace, a driving sense of urgency that keeps the reader turning the pages, great characters (Joanna Blalock is especially good) and the kind of medical authenticity that really rings true."
—Francis Roe

DEADLY EXPOSURE

Leonard Goldberg

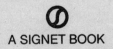

A SIGNET BOOK

SIGNET
Published by New American Library, a division of
Penguin Putnam Inc., 375 Hudson Street,
New York, New York 10014, U.S.A.
Penguin Books Ltd, 27 Wrights Lane,
London W8 5TZ, England
Penguin Books Australia Ltd, Ringwood,
Victoria, Australia
Penguin Books Canada Ltd, 10 Alcorn Avenue,
Toronto, Ontario, Canada M4V 3B2
Penguin Books (N.Z.) Ltd, 182–190 Wairau Road,
Auckland 10, New Zealand

Penguin Books Ltd, Registered Offices:
Harmondsworth, Middlesex, England

Published by Signet, an imprint of New American Library,
a division of Penguin Putnam Inc.
Previously published in a Dutton edition.

First Signet Printing, February 2000
10 9 8 7 6 5 4 3 2 1

PUBLISHER'S NOTE
This is a work of fiction. Names, characters, places, and incidents either are the
product of the author's imagination or are used fictitiously, and any resemblance to
actual persons, living or dead, business establishments, events, or locales is entirely
coincidental.

For B.K.G.

ACKNOWLEDGMENTS

Special thanks to Audrey LaFehr and John Paine, superb editors who always find the best novel in my manuscript.

And now there came both mist and snow,
And it grew wondrous cold:
And ice, mast-high, came floating by,
As green as emerald.

—COLERIDGE,
"The Ancient Mariner"

One

The baby girl had been dead for four hours.

Joanna Blalock glanced at the baby's face. It looked like a China doll with straight black hair and almond-shaped eyes that stared out into nothingness. The only sign of death was the bluish discoloration of the tiny hands and feet.

Joanna sighed to herself and went back to stitching up the incision that ran from the infant's sternum to its pubis. She carefully placed the sutures close together to minimize the disfigurement caused by the autopsy. Chances were the baby would be buried in a gown that would cover the incision. But Joanna knew the parents would look under the gown to see what had been done to their daughter.

"I hate doing autopsies on babies," Dr. Lori McKay commented. "Don't you?"

"Dead is dead," Joanna said evenly, though she really felt otherwise. As director of forensic pathology at Memorial Hospital, she had performed hundreds and hundreds of autopsies, but the babies always got to her. There was something so unfair about it.

The ventilation system switched itself on in the special room where autopsies on contaminated cases were done. The air began to stir, but Joanna barely felt it beneath her cap and gown and mask and gloves. She wiped the perspiration from her forehead with a sleeve and again glanced over the small body.

The infant seemed so tiny on the stainless steel table. But of course, she reminded herself, these tables were made for adults, not babies.

The intercom came on with a blast of static. A female voice said, "Dr. Blalock, Colonel Hawksworth is here to see you."

"Send him in," Joanna said, raising her voice.

"Would you like me to leave?" Lori asked.

"You stay put," Joanna told her. "We're not finished here yet."

"Is this guy really a colonel?"

"Yes."

"So why doesn't he wear a uniform?"

Because he's with the National Security Council, Joanna started to say, but she held her tongue as she was asked to. "He didn't say."

There was a brisk knock on the door.

"Yes?" Joanna called out.

Colonel Guy Hawksworth entered. He was tall and well built, in his early fifties, with narrow eyes and a square jaw. His gray hair was crew cut, his posture ramrod straight.

"Don't touch anything unless you want to get cholera," Joanna said.

If the word "cholera" bothered Hawksworth, he didn't show it. "You've received your security clearance. We have to leave as quickly as possible."

"I'll need a few minutes more," Joanna said, and turned to Lori. "Make sure you get the cultures on all the baby's fluids and organs. Tell the bacteriology lab they're looking for the *Vibrio cholerae* organism."

"Right," Lori said, making a note on her pad.

"I've dictated the gross findings on the baby. I want you to read the microscopic slides. Pay particular attention to the intestinal mucosa. That's where the abnormalities will be."

"Got it."

"While I'm away, you'll be in charge of forensics at Memorial. Be careful and take your time and you'll do fine."

Lori's eyes widened. She had never directed a division of forensic pathology. She had been out of her training only a year, with most of that time spent as a junior medical examiner for the County of Los Angeles. Lori had been invited to join the staff at Memorial less than two months ago.

"Is something wrong?" Joanna asked.

"Nope," Lori said, quickly gathering herself. She mentally repeated Joanna's advice. Be careful and take your time. *And don't fuck it up.* "How long will you be away?"

Hawksworth answered for Joanna. "For an undetermined length of time."

"What if I need to get in touch with you?" Lori asked.

"You won't be able to," Hawksworth answered for her again. "I'll leave my number with Dr. Blalock's secretary. If there's a true emergency, the call will be forwarded to Dr. Blalock."

Lori felt like telling the colonel to go screw himself with his hush-hush rules. But she knew it had to be something important, otherwise Joanna Blalock wouldn't stand for all this nonsense. She turned her back to the colonel and asked Joanna in a quiet voice, "Do you have any idea where you're going?"

"Someplace very, very cold. That's all I know."

Lori wrinkled her brow. "Someplace like Antarctica?"

"You'll have to ask Colonel Hawksworth."

Hawksworth's face was closed, his expression blank. "We need to move on, Dr. Blalock."

He watched the women leisurely stripping off their gloves and gowns. Now they were talking about the cholera organism and a toxin it produced—an adenyl cyclase inhibitor. Hawksworth glanced up at the wall clock.

It was 11:15 A.M. He wished they'd hurry it up. He was already behind schedule.

His gaze dropped to the baby on the stainless steel table. From where he stood, only one arm was visible, the fingers balled up into a tiny fist. Hawksworth stared at it, his mind flashing back to Vietnam.

The American forces had decided to pacify the villages in the Mekong Delta, an area controlled by the Viet Cong. They gave the people food and medicine, and even vaccinated the children. One hot August day Hawksworth led his platoon into a village where the vaccination program had just been started. It was deserted, everything and everybody gone. In the center of the village was a stack of children's arms that had been severed at the shoulder by the Viet Cong. On most of the tiny arms you could see the vaccination marks. Hawksworth still had nightmares about that. Not as often as before. But he still had them.

"Ready," Joanna said, breaking into his thoughts. She pushed through a set of swinging doors and led the way out.

They went down a long corridor with flickering fluorescent lighting. In places the paint on the walls was cracked and peeling off, and overhead there were water marks on the ceiling. The overall appearance was of chronic neglect.

They walked through another set of swinging doors and the corridor suddenly widened, its walls now covered with lime-colored grass cloth. The sound of Mozart's "A Little Night Music" came from behind a closed door.

"I didn't know we still had cholera in America," Hawksworth said.

"We don't," Joanna told him. "The baby you saw had just been adopted by an American couple. They picked the infant up in Shanghai and it became ill on the plane ride back to the States."

"So the baby caught it in China."

"Probably."

Hawksworth squinted an eye. "Why would this case require a forensic pathologist?"

"The baby died two hours after getting off the plane and nobody knew why. That makes it a homicide until proven otherwise." Joanna nodded to a group of approaching technicians and waited for them to pass by. "Of course, most babies who become ill on planes are not the victims of homicide."

Yeah, Hawksworth thought sourly, and most babies who receive vaccinations don't get their arms cut off because of it, either.

"Will I need to bring any equipment along for this project?" Joanna asked.

"No," Hawksworth said at once.

"You have microscopes and dissecting instruments?"

Hawksworth smiled thinly. "Everything. But if by chance you require anything from your laboratory, we can have it flown up to you in under six hours."

"I see," Joanna said slowly, her mind now calculating distances. She was going somewhere very cold and it was six hours away from Los Angeles by jet. That ruled out Europe, Antarctica, Greenland, and the North Pole. Joanna wetted her lips. "So we're going to Alaska, huh?"

Hawksworth didn't answer, but Joanna could tell from the tightening of his jaw muscles that she'd guessed right.

They walked into the reception area of Joanna's office. She pointed to a leather-covered chair for Hawksworth, but he remained standing. Joanna's secretary, Virginia Hand, held up a thick stack of phone messages.

Joanna waved them off. "They'll have to wait unless something is urgent."

"They can wait," Virginia said, sensing the seriousness in her boss's voice.

"I'll be away for a while working on a government project. Lori McKay will be in charge until I return."

"How long will you be away?"

"Weeks," Joanna answered before Hawksworth could. "Colonel Hawksworth will give you a number where I can be reached in case of a true emergency."

Hawksworth came over to the desk and looked at the secretary. "The number I give you is for your eyes only. Understood?"

"Understood."

Joanna went into her office and closed the door behind her. She hurried to her computer and logged on to the Internet. She searched for anything in Alaska that would require the government to bring in a forensic pathologist. Joanna was particularly interested in incidents on military bases, atomic weapons, exposure to radioactive materials, and toxic dump sites. There was nothing worthy of note.

Then she went to the Bering Sea which separated Alaska from Russia. Maybe the Soviets dumped some of their toxic junk into the sea and it had now made its way into American waters. But again the Internet came up with nothing. It was like looking for a needle in a haystack, she told herself. It could be anything.

She switched the computer off and quickly got out of her scrub suit and into a tweed skirt, white Oxford shirt, and blue blazer. She looked in the mirror and brushed her hair, then added new lipstick, all the while wondering where she was going and what the project was and why the need for so much secrecy.

She glanced over at her desk, seeing if there was anything that needed to be taken care of before she left. She saw stacks of letters to be answered, reports to be dictated, slides to be read. A hundred things, but nothing that couldn't wait.

Her gaze went to a framed photograph. It showed her and Jake Sinclair on a white sand beach in Hawaii. She studied the detective's face for a moment. He was so good-looking, and getting even better looking with time.

His hair was thick and brown and swept back, just covering the tops of his ears. But it was his eyes that were overpowering. They were deep-set and blue-gray, and they could look right through you or right into you, depending on how he felt. No, it was over between them, she reminded herself, and she planned to keep it that way. Joanna removed the photograph from its frame and crushed it into a small ball, then dropped it into the trash can. She grabbed her suitcase and left the office.

Hawksworth was standing in the exact same place as before. "Let's go, Colonel," she said.

Hawksworth took Joanna's suitcase and held the door for her. They hurried down the corridor to a bank of elevators and rode an empty car to the second floor. Quickly they headed down another corridor, passing through a pediatric wing, then an administrative area. Hawksworth was moving so fast that Joanna had to break into a half run to keep up. Now they were going up a short flight of stairs, then through a door and out onto a rooftop.

A helicopter with no markings was waiting for them. As soon as they were aboard, the engine whined to life and the rotor began to swing in wide circles overhead.

Moments later the helicopter was flying over West Los Angeles at an altitude of a thousand feet. Beneath them Joanna could see the vast expanse of Los Angeles, with the downtown area to the east and Santa Monica and the ocean to the west. She glanced over at Hawksworth, who was sitting in the cockpit next to the pilot, his face closed as ever. One thing was certain. She wasn't going to learn anything more from Hawksworth.

Joanna shifted in her seat and tried to find a comfortable position as her mind drifted over the past twenty-four hours. Everything had gone so quickly and smoothly, without a hitch. All of her duties and responsibilities at Memorial had been assigned to others and nobody said a word—not even Simon Murdock, the dean at the medical center, who usually insisted on being in control and knowing every detail. He didn't ask her who, what, where, or for how long. She didn't even have to fill out a leave-of-absence form. Someone had smoothed the way and taken care of everything for Joanna.

The helicopter abruptly began to descend. Joanna tightened her seat belt and looked out. Below them she saw Los Angeles International Airport. Commercial jets were lined up next to the runway, but none was moving or taking off. The helicopter circled over a larger hangar at the end of the tarmac, then landed scant yards from a Boeing 727 without markings or windows. As they scrambled from the helicopter and up the steps to the plane, the jet engines came to life. A young steward led them aft.

The 727 was divided into two sections by a wall with a closed door. A sign on the door read NO ADMITTANCE. The spacious first-class area had twelve seats, six on each side. In the center was a small conference table surrounded by swivel chairs that were bolted to the floor. A diminutive man rose from a chair and extended his hand. "Doctor Blalock, I presume."

Joanna recognized the famous astronomer from Cal Tech immediately. Benjamin Kagen was a small man, much smaller than he seemed on television, with thin gray hair, inquisitive eyes, and an oversized forehead. His television documentaries on the universe had made his face and name known all across America. "It's a pleasure to meet you, Professor Kagen," she said formally.

"Ben, please." Kagen's voice was soft and soothing and made you want to listen. He was wearing a corduroy suit with a black turtleneck sweater and highly polished penny loafers. "I'm delighted you've agreed to join our scientific team."

"I am too," Joanna said, liking the man instantly. "But I have no idea what I've gotten myself into."

"You've gotten yourself into what might well turn out

to be the most fascinating project of your life." Kagen
signaled to the steward. "Would you care for a martini?"

Joanna nodded. "Two olives."

With a jerk the giant jet began to taxi. Then it slowly
turned and stopped. Since the plane was windowless,
Joanna had no idea where they were. At the end of a long
line, she guessed, remembering the aircraft that were
stacked up waiting to take off.

Suddenly the engines roared and the jet was zooming
down the runway. Joanna leaned back, now recalling her
phone conversation with Peter Allen Weir. He had said
that Hawksworth had authority from the very highest
level. The power Hawksworth must have, Joanna was
thinking, the incredible power. One phone call and he
could put an entire international airport on hold.

With a smooth rise the plane was airborne.

Joanna had no sense of motion because there was no
reference point. She felt as if she were in a tube or a submerged submarine. Even the noise of the plane seemed
subdued.

"Why no windows?" Joanna asked.

"Most large military jets are used to transport materiel,
not people," Kagen explained. He waved his hand around
the cabin. "All of this could be removed in minutes and
the plane would revert to its original use—moving
cargo."

The steward brought two martinis on a tray and served
them. Now he was wearing white gloves.

"Cheers," Kagen said, sipping his drink while he studied Joanna. She was so young, he thought—too young.
Her curriculum vitae stated she was in her late thirties,
but she didn't look it. She was strikingly attractive, her
face unlined except for delicate crow's-feet that only
showed when she smiled. Her sandy blond hair was
drawn back in a simple barrette, and this seemed to ac-
centuate her high cheekbones and patrician features. So
young, he thought again. Youth meant inexperience and

poor judgment, and with those qualities you couldn't be a good scientist. Shit, Kagen cursed to himself, keeping his expression bland as he chewed on his olive. He needed a scientist with wisdom and years of experience on this project. He needed a Peter Allen Weir, not a Joanna Blalock. But Weir was unavailable because of a badly broken leg suffered in an automobile accident.

Hawksworth unbuckled his seat belt and stood. "If you require anything, let me know." He walked to the rear of the cabin and through the door, shutting it behind him.

Joanna tried to see in, but the door closed too quickly. "What's in the back of the plane?"

"The next section contains rest rooms and lounge areas."

"Why the no-admittance sign?"

"To keep people from wandering in, I would guess," Kagen told her. "There's a third section which is strictly off limits, however."

"What's there?"

"A special telecommunications room," Kagen said, and signaled to the steward. "Would you care for another martini?"

Joanna shook her head. "How much longer are you going to keep me in suspense?"

"I waited intentionally," Kagen said. "I wanted Hawksworth out of here."

"I thought Hawksworth knew everything."

"He does. The problem is, he keeps interrupting conversations with statements like 'Don't mention that' or 'That's classified' and other such nonsense."

Kagen reached for a sheet of paper with a lot of small print on it. "This is a standard nondisclosure form in which you agree not to reveal any information about this project without first receiving appropriate authorization. I'd like you to sign it."

Joanna quickly read the form. It contained dire

threats of prosecution for any disclosure. "Is this really enforceable?"

"Probably not. According to my lawyer, you can disclose just about anything you want as long as it doesn't involve spying for a foreign country. This form is more of a formality than anything else."

Joanna signed the paper and pushed it back to Kagen.

Kagen's second martini arrived. He sampled it slowly. Satisfied, he nodded to the steward and waited for him to disappear. "Dr. Blalock, have you ever heard the term ETOXAT?"

"No."

"Most people haven't. It stands for Extraterrestrial Toxic Agent Team. Its abbreviated name is ETOX. In the late nineteen-sixties, President Nixon signed an executive order authorizing the formation of ETOX. It consisted of a group of distinguished scientists whose function was to investigate extraterrestrial toxins. In particular, ETOX was formed to carefully study the astronauts who landed on the moon and the lunar rock samples they brought back to earth. After all, we had no idea what they might bring back with them. A major concern was that there might be some strange microorganisms on the moon that were highly toxic and transmissible. Just think if Neil Armstrong had brought back some terrible infectious plague for which there was no treatment. It would have been one small step for man, one giant disaster for mankind. So we studied the astronauts and their space suits and the rocks, and fortunately found nothing. After that, ETOX was kept intact, just in case. But you'd be amazed at how hard we had to fight to keep our funding. No one seems to believe that there's a real possibility of life in outer space."

"Even after the findings on ALH?"

Kagen nodded. ALH 84001 was the name of a Martian meteorite that had been extensively studied by NASA. "What do you know about the Alan Hills meteorite?"

"Only that it came from Mars and showed some evidence for the presence of bacterial life there." Joanna paused, thinking back to the article she'd read in the *Los Angeles Times*. "It contained polyaromatic hydrocarbons, and there were fossilized findings as well."

"Exactly," Kagen said, impressed. "They also found a carbon isotope, carbon-12, in it. This form of carbon is present in methane, which of course is produced by bacteria."

"Are we dealing with extraterrestrial life in the project?"

"I'm getting ahead of myself," Kagen said, now doodling on Joanna's signed disclosure form. He was drawing an iceberg. "Let's go back to ETOX. Our team meets once a year to review various projects and studies, particularly those being done on newly discovered meteorites. We've never had to deal with a toxic agent before—not until ten days ago. At that time the Coast Guard was patrolling an area west of Juneau called Icy Strait. It's just south of Glacier Bay. They came upon a charter fishing boat that was tethered to an iceberg by grappling lines."

Joanna's brow went up. "Isn't that kind of dangerous?"

"To say the least. One shift in the wind and that boat would have been turned into splinters. Anyone who knows the sea stays as far away from icebergs as he can."

Kagen reached for his pipe and lit it. "Anyhow, there it was. A boat and an iceberg, hand in hand, drifting with the current. The Coast Guard came alongside and two seamen boarded the fishing boat. They found the deck covered with chunks of ice that were neatly stacked up. And atop the ice were pickaxes. For safety's sake they released the grappling lines. As they moved away, they noticed gouged-out areas on the iceberg. Someone on that fishing boat had used the pickaxes to rip off pieces from that iceberg."

Joanna gave him an inquiring look. "Why? Why would anyone do that?"

"The iceberg had some unusual colors that sparkled brilliantly in the sunlight. Gold and blue and flecks of green here and there. Our best guess is that the people on the boat thought they were looking at precious metals."

"Were they?"

"Yes and no," Kagen said evasively. "You'll understand my answer in just a moment."

Hawksworth reentered the cabin and came over to Kagen. "Dr. Neiderman is in Juneau, but he refuses to go to the site until he's assured the project will in no way endanger the environment."

"Give him my assurances," Kagen said. "Tell him that, if anything, the project will preserve the environment. Send him a fax under my name. Leave out all the specifics, of course."

Hawksworth nodded ever so slightly. "This colleague of yours is turning out to be very difficult."

"Brilliant people usually are."

Kagen drew on his pipe as Hawksworth disappeared behind the door. "So," he said and turned back to Joanna, "we have a fishing boat whose deck is covered with chunks of ice. The Coast Guard team search the entire deck and find nothing. One of them goes below and stays there for at least a minute but no more than two. Suddenly he comes back topside, choking and gasping and clutching his throat. He drops and dies on the spot. His partner, who is no fool, gets the hell out of there and returns to the Coast Guard vessel. He then reboards the fishing boat, now wearing a gas mask and protective clothing. Any guesses at this point?"

"I need to know more," Joanna said, but she was already listing the possibilities in her mind. It was most likely something in the air, she thought, something very toxic. But the same symptoms would have occurred if the man had aspirated a big wad of bubble gum and acutely closed off his airway.

"Our coastguardsman opens the door below," Kagen continued, "and finds a middle-aged couple dead on the floor of the cabin. There's a large piece of ice in a bowl, another almost melted piece in a pan on the stove."

"How was the stove powered?"

"By a portable generator. It was gasoline-powered."

Joanna nodded slowly. "What was the color of the victims' skin?"

"Blue."

"Then it's probably not carbon monoxide," Joanna said thoughtfully. Carbon monoxide killed by combining with hemoglobin to form carboxyhemoglobin, making the hemoglobin unavailable to transport oxygen. Carboxyhemoglobin had a cherry red color that was frequently seen in the victim's skin. "What happened next?"

"The coastguardsman grabbed the baby and got out of there."

Joanna's jaw dropped. "There was a baby?"

"More like a toddler," Kagen corrected himself. "Against the wall was a four-year-old sitting in a highchair. He was sucking for air as hard as he could, but he was still alive. And he still is."

Joanna leaned back in her swivel chair and tried to put the pieces of the puzzle together. It had to be a toxin, a deadly pollutant, something in the air. But what would kill three adults, one almost instantly, yet not kill a baby? She searched her mind for an answer, but couldn't find one. "I assume the toxin came from the melting ice."

"Correct. Samples of the ice aboard the boat and from the iceberg were tested in a toxicology laboratory at the NIH. It contained a very poisonous protein that can be transmitted in the air by droplets. Its molecular structure is unlike anything we've ever encountered. Preliminary studies indicate it's a polypeptide, which means it's organic in nature. But we have no idea if it's produced by plant or animal or something in between."

"Was it tested on laboratory animals?"

Kagen nodded. "It killed mice, rats, and guinea pigs in less than a minute. It's very, very lethal."

"It's got to be an enzyme inhibitor to kill that fast," Joanna said, thinking aloud.

"That's what the toxicologists think too. But they don't know which metabolic pathway it interrupts."

"Were the brilliant colors in the iceberg related in any way to this toxin?"

"Probably not. The blue and green colors were the result of embedded plankton. The gold flecks were caused by large sulfur crystals."

Kagen signaled to the steward for another martini. "There were also other things present in that iceberg," he continued. "They detected a fair amount of sulfur dioxide and trioxide and some sulfuric acid as well. And they then discovered the most astounding thing of all. It's the reason why you and I are on this plane and why other members of the ETOX team are now converging on Juneau."

Kagen wetted his lips, savoring the moment. "They detected an incredible amount of iridium in that iceberg."

"Iridium?" Joanna asked, puzzled.

"It's a precious metallic element resembling platinum. It occurs very rarely in nature. The high concentration of iridium in that iceberg has been found previously in only two sorts of places on earth. In the craters that asteroids make when they crash into our planet, and in the meteorites that are the remnants of such asteroids."

"Are you saying that the toxin and whatever produced it were brought to earth on an asteroid?"

"Beyond any doubt."

"Jesus!" Joanna uttered softly, now grasping the importance of the ETOX project. "Can we guess when the asteroid fell to earth?"

"Oh, we can do better than guess," Kagen said as his third martini arrived. "Using a potassium–argon dating technique, we determined precisely when it touched down."

"When?"

"Sixty-five million years ago."

TWO

In the autumnal late afternoon light, the helicopter skimmed along the coastline north of Juneau. The city and its suburbs had passed beneath them thirty minutes ago. Now they were flying over mountainous terrain that was covered with ice and snow.

Joanna looked down at the bleak desolation. There were no roads, no houses, no lights. She wondered where they were going, hoping the investigation wouldn't take place in Quonset huts. She hated those damn things. They gave her claustrophobia.

Joanna huddled up in her fur-lined parka and turned to the man seated next to her. He was a big, fat man with a double chin and wire-rimmed glasses. His name was Dr. Malcolm Neiderman. It was his laboratory at the NIH that had done the initial toxicology studies on the iceberg. Neiderman shifted in his seat and reached into the pocket of his parka for a small candy bar. Slowly he peeled the wrapping off and let it drop to the floor.

"How lethal is this toxin?" Joanna asked, trying to make conversation for the third time since they boarded the helicopter in Juneau.

"It's deadly as hell," Neiderman said, devouring the candy bar in an instant. When he swallowed, his double chin bounced.

"Compare it to some known poison."

"Are you familiar with ricin?"

Joanna nodded.

Neiderman nodded back, then licked the remaining chocolate from his fingers. He pulled his parka over his protuberant abdomen and let his head drop down on his chest. The conversation was over.

Joanna stared at him, wondering if Neiderman was being secretive or if he was just socially inept. "I'm intimately familiar with ricin," she said, starting the conversation again. "A few years ago I worked on a case in which people were being murdered with ricin."

Neiderman looked over out of the corner of his eye. "How was it being administered?"

"I really shouldn't talk about it. The murderer was found guilty, but the conviction is now under appeal."

With effort Neiderman turned toward her, straining against his seat belt. "It had to be injected."

"Nope."

"Then how?"

"The ricin was placed in implantable medical devices, like pacemakers and morphine pumps."

"Oh, yeah. Yeah," Neiderman said, remembering the newspaper reports on the HMO doctor who was killing his patients with ricin. "That was your case, huh?"

"I was the medical examiner, if that's what you mean."

"What method was used to detect the ricin?"

"A radioimmunoassay."

"Who performed the test?"

"An outside lab."

Neiderman waved his hand derisively. "If the murderer you're talking about is smart, he'll hire a good pharmacotoxicologist and blow your case right out of the water. There are only two labs I know of that can measure ricin reliably. The others are just jerk-offs."

"Is the lab the CIA uses a jerk-off?"

"How did you get to them?" Neiderman asked, impressed.

"Through a colleague," Joanna lied. She had sent the

specimen to the FBI and they forwarded it to the lab employed by the CIA.

Colonel Hawksworth glanced up at the mention of the CIA. He was about to say something, then decided not to and went back to his discussion with Ben Kagen. They were speaking in low voices about an absent member of the ETOX team.

The helicopter hit a small area of turbulence and bounced up and down, losing altitude briefly before smoothing out.

"So you think this toxin is similar to ricin?" Joanna probed gently.

"Only in potency," Neiderman said. "On a per-weight basis, it's every bit as toxic as ricin. Our preliminary studies indicate that one molecule of this toxin will kill a human cell."

Just like ricin, Joanna was thinking. Ricin was an extract from the common castor oil plant, and that made it sound innocuous. But it was one of the deadliest toxins on the face of the earth. "Is it a protein like ricin?"

"They're both proteins," Neiderman said carefully, "but their chemical structures have little in common. And to complicate matters, this new toxin is not a single entity. It seems to consist of at least two separate polypeptides that are lethal as hell. One good sniff and lab animals drop like flies."

"What changes do you see when the animals are examined postmortem?"

"Those studies were done in someone else's lab," Neiderman said, an edge to his voice. "You see, they parcel out small amounts of this toxin, just enough for one to do preliminary studies in a limited area. They never allow a single laboratory to do all the work. That way nobody knows too much." Neiderman turned and stared over at Kagen. "Right, Ben?"

"Exactly right." Kagen smiled benignly as he looked

up. "I always kept in mind that people who don't know very much usually don't talk very much."

"Forgive my naivete," Joanna said, "but I'm not certain I understand why this is such a sensitive project. So far, we have evidence that an asteroid fell to earth sixty-five million years ago and brought with it a very lethal toxin. And some of this material somehow got caught up in an iceberg." Joanna shrugged her shoulders. "Why does this require so much secrecy and security?"

"Games," Neiderman said mockingly. "It makes everybody feel important."

Kagen glared at Neiderman. Taking a deep breath, he turned to Joanna.

"Your question is a good one. It has several answers. First, all ETOX projects are kept confidential because our mandate requires us to do so. Remember that ETOX was formed just prior to the Apollo moon walk. It was essential to have tight security for ETOX in case the astronauts brought something terrible back with them. Anything was possible. People were speculating that there might be microorganisms on the moon that could cause diseases for which there was no cure. Or maybe these organisms could infect plants and kill off the earth's vegetation. Well, none of these things happened then, but they could still happen now. And the last thing we want is for this to leak out to the news media, who would in short order panic the public with rumors and half-truths. So it's best for now that we keep everything under a tight lid until we know exactly what we're dealing with."

Kagen turned to Hawksworth. "There's yet another important reason for tight security. I'll let the colonel explain it, since it's in his area of expertise."

Neiderman yawned, uninterested.

If Hawksworth saw the rude gesture, he didn't change expression. "The government's major concern—from a security overview—is that this toxin could represent the perfect biologic weapon. One whiff and you're choking, dead within a minute. Swallow a tiny drop and you get terrible cramps and diarrhea, followed by shock and death. A thimbleful could wipe out a battalion."

Neiderman blinked rapidly. "We didn't do any studies on the toxin's effect on the gastrointestinal tract."

"That was done elsewhere," Hawksworth said, not bothering to look at Neiderman. "The toxin can be frozen and thawed a dozen times and not lose an iota of its potency. And it's remarkably resistant to heat. Put it in water and boil it and it doesn't affect the toxin one bit. It always clings to the vapor and hangs in the air, waiting for someone to inhale it. From the standpoint of biologic warfare, you couldn't ask for a better weapon. It's—"

"If you're going to use this to develop some sort of weapon," Neiderman interrupted, "count me out."

"That's not our intent." Hawksworth spoke evenly, but a vein on his forehead bulged. "Nevertheless, you are free to leave this project whenever you wish."

"I'll play it by ear for now," Neiderman said coyly.

"Good." Hawksworth nodded agreeably. "Just let me know when you decide to leave, so I can have all of the ETOX and NSC projects transferred out of your laboratory. Of course, the funds we gave you for these projects will go elsewhere as well."

Neiderman's face went pale. His lips moved but made no sound.

Joanna watched Neiderman's reaction to Hawksworth's threat. Like all research laboratories at the NIH, Neiderman's lab was entirely dependent on federal grants and contracts. If his funding was cut off, Neiderman would have no lab to go back to.

Hawksworth's gaze came back to Joanna. "I think you can imagine what the consequences would be if this agent and what produced it were put in the hands of the Libyans or North Koreans. Worse yet, think what might happen if terrorist groups got hold of the toxin. Those bastards don't hesitate for a moment to blow up a bus-load of people in Tel Aviv or unleash a canister of sarin nerve gas in a Tokyo subway. Think what they might do with a truckload of this toxin. They could wipe out a country."

"You're assuming there's a great deal of this toxin or whatever produced it still floating around," Joanna said.

"I assume nothing. My mission is to find out what the toxin is and what produced it and to gather every last drop of both and make certain they stay in safe hands. And my instructions are to do so as quickly and as quietly as possible."

Neiderman wiped his nose with his sleeve. "You can't keep something like this quiet in Washington."

The helicopter began to circle. Below it was dark, everything gray except for a few red streaks from the setting sun. Joanna could see a bay and its ice-covered shores. But still there were no roads or houses or buildings. Then she saw the ship, huge and black, its lights twinkling. Amidships there were two large cranes which towered over the pilothouse at the stern.

The helicopter was suddenly buffeted by crosswinds.

"Hold on, folks," the pilot yelled back. "It's going to be a little rough going in."

Joanna tightened her seat belt as the helicopter began to descend. It rocked back and forth, but the pilot kept it on course.

The air was turning misty, and now Joanna had trouble seeing the ship. All she could make out was a circle of flashing lights. The helicopter rapidly descended and Joanna felt her stomach come up to her throat. The wind gusted again, but the pilot corrected for it as the aircraft touched down on the helipad.

The noise from the rotor slowly faded and died away.

A marine wearing a sidearm ran up to the helicopter and opened the door. He saluted sharply as Hawksworth stepped off. "Welcome aboard, sir."

The marine led the way across the vast deck to the pilothouse. Joanna had expected the ship to be big, but not this big. It was considerably longer than a football field and rose at least ten stories above the waterline, not counting the height of the cranes. She glanced back at the helicopter. It seemed so tiny now, like a fly on a horse.

The wind picked up, howling and bitterly cold. A light rain started to fall.

They hurried into the superstructure at the rear of the ship and walked down a short passageway to a closed elevator. The marine inserted a key and turned it. The elevator door opened and a pinging sound began. Stepping aside, the marine waited until the visitors were aboard, then turned the key back. The pinging sound stopped as the door closed.

The elevator was small, the four passengers crowded together and involuntarily touching. Everything was silent. Even the elevator made no noise. It had no floor indicator, only a panel of buttons lettered A through D.

With a sudden jerk the car stopped, and the door opened.

They walked out onto a metal scaffold that seemed to wind around a huge Plexiglas cylinder. Holding on to a rail, Joanna moved closer and looked in. At first all she could see was something white and ill-defined. But as her eyes accommodated, she saw the blue ice and the frost and the steepled top. Joanna suddenly realized she was looking at an iceberg.

Neiderman was at her side, staring and breathing heavily. "Holy shit!"

Joanna was speechless, mesmerized by the iceberg's size and beauty. There was something dominating and majestic about it. She reached out and carefully touched the Plexiglas. It was cool, but not nearly as cold as she had expected.

"There are two layers of Plexiglas with a sealed air pocket between them," Hawksworth told her. "The insulation is excellent."

Joanna slowly walked around the cylinder, still staring at the gigantic mass of ice. It had to be sixty feet tall and at least that wide at its base. Large metal struts and cables supported the iceberg and kept it anchored in place. "It's so huge."

"Not really," Kagen said. "As icebergs go, this one is relatively small. Some icebergs, such as those in Antarctica, are a hundred miles long and weigh millions of tons. Even in the Arctic, icebergs are frequently twice the size of this one."

"Perhaps this one is only part of an iceberg," Joanna suggested, now studying the jagged front edge. "Maybe it split apart from its mother."

"That's a possibility," Kagen conceded, hoping it wasn't the case. If this iceberg was just a splinter of another, that would mean there was at least one more poisonous mountain of ice floating around. And God knew how big that one might be.

They walked down the scaffold, everyone stepping carefully and holding on to the railing. Hawksworth watched them, knowing that heights did this to people, particularly when they were going down scaffolding. But it was also the close presence of the ice that made the group cautious. They expected things to be wet and slippery, though they weren't. The inside of the ship was actually dry and warm, the temperature maintained at a comfortable sixty-eight degrees Fahrenheit.

At the bottom of the steps Joanna looked up to the steeple of the iceberg. "How did you manage to get this thing aboard and in one piece?"

"This ship is capable of doing a lot of things," Hawksworth said. "She was patterned after the *Global Explorer*. As you may recall, that was the ship that plucked that Soviet submarine from the floor of the Pacific during the Cold War."

Joanna nodded, recalling the event. "That was from a depth of five thousand feet."

"More," Hawksworth said matter-of-factly.

Neiderman shrugged, unimpressed. "But you didn't bring it up intact. It fell apart and most of it just sank back down."

Hawksworth smiled thinly. That was the story they had given the news media to keep the Russians guessing. They had raised the submarine intact and were able to study every screw and bolt of it.

"In any event," Hawksworth continued, "this ship can not only explore the ocean floor, it can also serve as a floating laboratory in case of biologic warfare. There are labs set up for toxicology, pathology, biochemistry, microbiology, and a dozen other sciences. All have the newest and most sophisticated equipment. In case of an attack with biologic weapons, this ship is designed to quickly identify the gas or toxic organism that's being used against our troops. We don't have to transport specimens or bodies thousands of miles back to the States for study. And time is obviously important. The faster the biologic agent is identified, the faster we can come up with an antidote."

Kagen said, "So this ship was constructed for a just-in-case scenario."

"Almost all weapons systems are," Hawksworth said tonelessly. He thought for a moment, then added, "You might be interested to know this ship was positioned fifty miles off the coast of Kuwait when the Gulf War broke out—just in case Saddam Hussein decided to use biologic weapons."

"Great," Neiderman droned sarcastically. Then he saw the others staring at him and he tried to quickly make amends. "I mean, it's great Saddam didn't use biologic weapons."

"I'm not sure he didn't," Hawksworth said, thinking of the Gulf War Syndrome so many of the troops suffered from.

He led them over to a large console where technicians

were seated, watching monitors and dials. "We keep everything within the cylinder constant. This includes temperature, humidity, barometric pressure, as well as O-two and C-O-two levels. It has its own ventilation system, and within the cylinder there is a strong negative pressure. If a leak occurs, air is sucked in and not let out."

Hawksworth stood back as the scientists gathered around the monitors. He was glad they were distracted and not asking any more questions about the Plexiglas cylinder. It had been constructed the year before when the *Global Explorer II* was first sent to Alaskan waters to find out why the sea life was dying off so mysteriously. Something was killing whales, sharks, dolphins, seals, and fish. A toxic agent was obviously in the food chain.

Initially they thought it was something the Russians had dumped into the sea, accidentally or perhaps on purpose. The Russians could be incredibly sloppy when it came to toxic disposal, not giving a damn about the environment. The experts on the *Global Explorer II* searched and searched for a cause, studying everything that had died. Even a dead whale—a sixty-five-foot bowhead—was lifted from the sea and placed in the refrigerated cylinder while it was studied. No pathogen or poison or toxin was ever discovered, and the epidemic of death in Alaskan waters stopped as mysteriously as it had started. Everybody thought it was a one-time event.

But then the couple and the coastguardsman suddenly died aboard the fishing vessel, killed by a toxic iceberg, and new questions arose. *Was the toxin in the iceberg the same one that had killed all the sea life? Was the toxin spreading over the entire Gulf of Alaska and perhaps beyond, now on the verge of causing a global catastrophe?* Hawksworth shivered to himself. Christ!

"This way," Hawksworth said, guiding the group away from the brightly lit console and past a large stainless-steel door. On the door was a sign.

> MORGUE
> AUTHORIZED PERSONNEL ONLY

Joanna pointed to the door. "Occupied?"

"Yes." Hawksworth inserted a key and a light above turned from red to green. He opened the door.

Inside was a casket on a gurney, an American flag draped over it. It contained the body of the coastguardsman who had died along with the couple on the fishing boat.

Three

The autopsy room was small and designed for contaminated cases. There were no windows to the outside world and only one door. Everything was done in stainless steel. Joanna and her assistant wore caps, gowns, goggles, masks, and gloves for protection against infectious agents. Past experience had told them there was no danger from any toxin that still might be in the corpse. None of the Coast Guard crew who handled the bodies nor the Juneau coroner or his assistants had become ill.

"Sorry I'm late," Kagen said over the intercom. "I'm afraid I overslept this morning."

"No problem," Joanna said. "We're just going into the coastguardsman's chest."

"Have you uncovered anything important?"

"Not so far," Joanna reported. "By the way, when I finish here I want to reautopsy the Kincaid couple."

"I'm afraid that won't be possible."

"Why not?"

"Because they've been cremated."

"Cremated?" Joanna asked incredulously. "How could you let that happen?"

"We had no say," Kagen said. "The dead couple were turned over to the Juneau medical examiner. He performed the autopsies and found no obvious cause of death. The bodies were cremated as per the instructions

in their wills. Of course, this all happened before we
knew about the contents of the iceberg."

"Jesus," Joanna groaned. In all likelihood, the Kincaids had been exposed to the toxin longer than the
coastguardsman, giving them a higher tissue level of
toxin and perhaps inducing more abnormalities. "Well,
at least I want to look at the microscopic slides on those
two autopsies."

"You'll have them by this evening."

Joanna went back to the postmortem examination on
James Whitten. The coastguardsman had been a lanky,
good-looking kid with a square jaw and a crew cut. And
thus far, his body showed no real abnormalities. A healed
appendectomy scar, mild acne, a tattoo on his upper arm
that consisted of an eagle holding arrows in its talons.
Below the tattoo was the word FOREVER. Forever stopped
at age twenty-four for James Whitten, Joanna thought
somberly.

She removed the heart and lungs from the thoracic
cavity en bloc and carefully examined them. There were
no gross abnormalities. No fluid buildup, no inflammation, no pus. But then, Joanna expected none. Nasty toxins like this one acted at the subcellular level where they
interrupted critical metabolic pathways and killed the
cell almost instantly. Those events couldn't be seen with
an electron microscope, much less the human eye.

Joanna decided to examine the entire airway system
once more. That was the route by which the toxin had
entered the body. Perhaps it had left some sign behind.
Using a speculum, she inspected the nasal passages. The
mucous membranes were clear, with no discharge of
inflammation or necrosis. Next she went to the oral
cavity. Again the mucosa was clean except for a trau-
matic abrasion on the hard palate. The tongue was rolled
back and Joanna forcibly straightened it. On the back of
the tongue were several dime-sized black spots. Joanna

took a cotton swab and gently rubbed at the spots. Some of the black came off.

She quickly looked over at Kagen, who was observing from the next room through a large Plexiglas window. "Was this man taking antibiotics?"

"I don't think so," Kagen said. He opened a thick folder. "But let me check."

Joanna motioned to the female technician assisting her. "We need to culture this, particularly for fungus." She used a small instrument to scrape off the black substance and handed it to the technician.

Quickly and expertly the technician placed the material in three separate tubes containing nutrient-rich culture media. Joanna closely watched the technician, still not sure of her. Her name was Ann Cormier and she was a pathology technician from Bethesda assigned to ETOX. She seemed bright enough, but she was young and inexperienced when it came to forensics. And she talked too much, particularly about men. Joanna found the technician's chattiness distracting. She would speak to her about it later.

"Let's do a biopsy as well," Joanna said.

Kagen's voice came over the intercom. "He wasn't taking antibiotics. May I ask why that's important?"

"Because he has several black spots on his tongue," Joanna told him. "When some people take antibiotics, the drug suppresses the normal bacterial flora in the GI tract, and fungal organisms begin to proliferate. Clinically, the fungus appears as discolored spots on the surface of the tongue."

"But our man wasn't taking antibiotics."

"Exactly."

"Then what caused the black spots?"

Joanna shrugged. "I don't know. All I know is that the black spots were there and shouldn't be."

"Maybe he was eating licorice," Ann Cormier suggested.

Joanna thought for a moment, then shook her head. "If it was due to licorice, there'd be stains on his teeth and the spots on his tongue wouldn't be circular. But nice try."

"What was that?" Kagen asked, not catching every word.

"Nothing," Joanna said. "What time does our conference start?"

"Right after lunch. But we can delay it if you wish."

"That won't be necessary." Joanna turned to the technician. "Have you closed before?"

"More times than I can count."

"Make it as neat as you possibly can."

Ann Cormier watched Joanna leave, then reached for a large suturing needle. Using a big hemostat, she grasped the needle and pushed it through skin and muscle. As she jerked the needle upward, it severed a blood vessel. A small dark clot of blood flew up and hit Ann's mask. Quickly she pulled her mask off and examined its inner surface. She could see a faint red spot, but it didn't appear to have soaked through. Ann tasted her lips for blood and couldn't detect any. Nothing had really penetrated the mask, she thought hopefully. Just to make sure, she picked up an alcohol swab and ran it over her lips and chin. Her lower lip stung a little, but there was no blood on the cotton. She breathed a sign of relief. There had been no penetration. No blood had gotten through.

Ann put on a new mask and resumed suturing up the body of James Whitten. She kept telling herself there was no danger, none at all.

The door opened and Bobby Shea, a young orderly, entered the room. He was wearing a scrub suit with cap and mask, but he didn't have gloves on.

"How much longer are you going to be?" Shea asked.

"About five minutes," Ann said, watching the orderly scratch at the pimples on his forehead with a bare hand. "If you want to stay in here, put gloves on."

Shea continued to scratch at the small bump, then looked at his fingernail to see if he'd removed the head. "I'll put gloves on when I have to touch the body."

"Get them on now or get out," Ann said sharply.

Shea shrugged and left the autopsy room.

Ann went back to suturing up the corpse, carefully avoiding any exposed blood vessels. She could still taste the alcohol she'd rubbed over her face, and her lower lip was still stinging a little. She hoped she wasn't getting another fever blister. She hated those damn things.

Four

A nn Cormier pulled down the bill of her baseball cap to shield her eyes from the brilliant afternoon sun. She quickly did some stretching exercises, then began to jog around the deck of the *Global Explorer II*. Someone had told her that eight laps around the ship was equal to one mile, but she knew she'd be lucky to run half that distance. She had to stop smoking those damn cigarettes. With effort she picked up the pace, her long ponytail now bouncing up and down on the back of her sleek warm-up outfit. Off to the left she saw a group of sailors busily winding a giant coil of cable. She smiled at them and they smiled back. She jogged on, feeling their eyes on her.

Up ahead a squad of marines were doing their daily calisthenics. They were performing pushups, counting them off. "And eighty-four! And eighty-five! And eighty-six!" Ann stopped to watch the wonderfully conditioned men. They all seemed so young and good-looking with crew cuts and muscles that bulged against their beige T-shirts. But one in particular caught Ann's eye. He had a small waist and a tight behind, and this accentuated his very broad shoulders. Mmm-hmm! she thought, watching him push up and down.

"One hundred!"

The marines jumped to their feet and began to run in place, sweating profusely through their shorts and T-shirts despite the chilly afternoon air. They ran faster and faster, making a mean growling sound. Then they abruptly stopped and let out an ear-splitting battle cry.

"Take five!" the squad leader barked.

Ann watched the Marines walk away from one another, stretching their arms and backs as they cooled down. The hunk she'd been looking at pulled up his T-shirt and used it to wipe the sweat from his forehead. The man's abdomen was so flat and heavily muscled that it looked like a washboard. There wasn't an ounce of fat anywhere.

Ann strolled over to him and said, "Every time I try to do pushups my back hurts."

"That's because you're not doing them right," the marine said. "You've got to keep your arms in close to your body and make sure your back stays straight."

"I think I do that, but my back still aches."

"Well, I can show you how to do it when I get some free time."

"That'd be great," Ann said softly, her eyes now on the marine's T-shirt. Stenciled on it was the name WALSH, E. She pointed at his chest. "What does the E stand for?"

"Eddie."

"I'm Ann."

"It's nice to meet you." Eddie was about to extend his hand, but he saw the squad leader eyeing him. He nodded instead. "I could show you how to do pushups now, but the squad leader would bust my butt."

"You have such a small butt, he'd probably have trouble finding it."

Eddie smiled broadly. He liked the woman a lot, although she was definitely older than he was. She was at least twenty-five. But everything about her was sexy. Her walk, her talk, her body. Her warm-ups were tight fitting, and he could tell she had nice legs and a great ass. And her face was cute as hell too. He envisioned her on top of him, her ponytail in his face. "I—I guess I could show you how here."

"I don't want to get you in trouble," Ann said, stealing a glance at the other marines. They were all watching intently, envious of Eddie Walsh and wishing they were in his place. She moved closer to Eddie. "When I get free time I go to the recreation room near the sickbay. Do you know where it is?"

"Oh, yeah," Eddie said, his voice husky.

"That's where I like to work out," Ann said quietly. "In the early evening around seven-thirty. There's usually nobody there."

"Yeah, that's a good time." Eddie knew the recreation room well. It was big, with rows of ping-pong and pool tables. Off to the side were chairs and couches. Large, soft couches. He grinned at her and she grinned back. "You go there a lot, huh?"

"A lot."

The squad leader put two fingers in his mouth and whistled loudly. "Fall in!"

Eddie winked at Ann and ran over to join the others. The marines quickly formed a straight line and snapped to attention. They stared directly ahead, not moving an inch.

"Down and dirty," the squad leader yelled out. "Give me twenty-five."

The marines dropped to the deck and started doing pushups again, counting them off. "One! And a two! And a three!"

Ann smiled to herself and walked away. She had never done a pushup in her life and didn't plan to do one anytime soon, although it might be fun to do a few with Eddie Walsh's hands around her waist and butt to make sure she kept her back straight. She thought again about the recreation room. It was by far the best place to meet up with Eddie. There was a strictly enforced schedule detailing who could use the facility and when. The civilians had their time slots, the marines and naval personnel theirs. But the civilians aboard the *Global Explorer II* never seemed to use the rec room. Ann had been in there a dozen times and never seen another person.

Ann neared the stern of the ship where a helicopter was being anchored with thick cables. She strolled over to the navy pilot who was supervising the procedure. The name on his flight jacket read CDR. MIKE MALLORY.

"Hi, Commander," Ann said pleasantly. "Do we have some rough seas coming in?"

Mallory nodded. "Tonight. We're supposed to have swells up to twelve feet."

"Why not just fly to shore and come back tomorrow?"

"That would be a consideration if it was going to be really rough." Mallory called out to one of the crew and pointed to the rear of the helicopter. "That cable is too taut. Give it some slack."

Ann glanced up at his hand and saw the wedding band on his finger. Her gaze went over to his face. He was stunningly handsome, with coal black hair, wide-set green eyes, and a firm jaw. She had to pry her eyes off him. "It's got to be a real bitch to land this thing on a moving ship."

Mallory shrugged. "If the weather is good, it's no problem."

"And what if the weather is awful?"

Mallory smiled thinly. "It can get kind of exciting."

"I'll bet." Ann glanced again at the handsome pilot's face, wondering what it would be like to have someone like that in your bed every night. "I'd love to go for a spin in your helicopter someday."

"That's against regulations."

Ann's eyes twinkled. "You look like a man who knows how to get around rules and regulations."

Mallory grinned. "I guess it's been known to happen."

"So what are my chances of going up in your helicopter?"

"That depends."

"On what?"

"On how you play your cards."

"I don't play cards," Ann said, turning to jog away. "I play much more interesting games."

Five

Joanna entered the conference room and sat across from Malcolm Neiderman. He nodded to her, then reached for a chocolate doughnut. Taking a huge bite, he turned back to Ben Kagen and spoke as he chewed. "The toxin consists of two big polypeptides that have about the same molecular weight."

"Can you separate them?" Kagen asked.

"I think so," Neiderman said as he finished the doughnut and licked his fingers. "They have different electrical charges, so we should be able to isolate them by electrophoresis."

"If they're polypeptides they're probably not from a plant source, right?"

Neiderman moved his head noncommittally. "Under ordinary circumstances you'd be correct. But remember, we're dealing with something sixty-five million years old. Who the hell knows what plants did back then?"

Joanna went to the coffeemaker and poured herself a cup. "But as a rule, plants don't make toxins this powerful, do they?"

"Plants can be pretty nasty. They evolve just as animals do, and they'll produce whatever is required to ensure their survival." Neiderman spoke authoritatively, but his voice was low and he tended to mumble.

"For now let's assume the toxin is nonplant in origin," Kagen said. "Do we know anything about its mode of action?"

"Nothing, nada," Neiderman said at once. "All we know is that it acts almost instantly and certainly affects the lungs in both man and animals."

Kagen looked over at Joanna. "Did the autopsy show any airway abnormalities?"

Joanna shook her head. "There was no inflammation, no fluid, no obstruction."

"But those were findings seen on gross examination," Kagen said and made a check mark on the legal pad in front of him. "Perhaps the microscopic slides will tell us more."

"Don't bet on it," Joanna said. "Powerful toxins don't leave much evidence behind. The pathologic changes are minimal because the toxin acts so rapidly at the molecular level. And that's what makes a lot of poisoning cases so difficult to solve. There's no trauma, no evidence, and no witnesses."

Kagen sighed to himself. In virtually all scientific investigations, the beginning was the most difficult part. Everything seemed so confused and ambiguous. "Let's go back to the basics for a moment. I'm told that most animal toxins share certain characteristics. Is that true?"

"Correct," Neiderman said.

"Go over them for us, would you?"

Neiderman had to use the chair arms to push his large frame erect. He picked up another doughnut and went over to the blackboard on the wall. "I'll use diagrams," he said, chewing as he reached for a piece of chalk.

Joanna felt a wave of fatigue coming over her and forced herself to keep her eyes open. The clock on the wall read 2:10 P.M., but it seemed like 2:10 A.M. to Joanna. Her body clock was out of kilter and she was having difficulty telling whether it was day or night. Hawksworth had advised them to go topside at least once a day to expose themselves to sunlight and fresh air so their metabolic rhythms would stay on schedule. Joanna had followed his instructions, but it hadn't helped very much. But then again, she reminded herself, this was only her first full day aboard the *Global Explorer II*. It would probably take a week for her body clock to adjust. And getting a good night's sleep wouldn't hurt. Her sleeping quarters were cramped, the bed hard and uncomfortable, the bathroom the size of a closet. Yet Joanna had been told that the scientists' quarters were luxurious when compared with those occupied by the hundred crewmen aboard ship. She could only imagine what their quarters were like. She stifled a yawn and promised herself to go topside again as soon as the meeting was over.

Neiderman was drawing a large *V* on the blackboard. He labeled one side *A*, the other side *B*. "All toxins are thought to have the A–B structure. That is, they are composed of two subunits, A and B. B is the binding portion of the toxin, which attaches it to a target cell. A is the enzymatic portion, which is responsible for the toxic effect on the cell. Toxins are usually classified by their cellular target or by their biologic effect. For example, the botulism toxin is called a neurotoxin because it attacks nerves."

Kagen asked, "And one organism produces one toxin?"

"Usually."

"But we have two toxins in our iceberg, two polypeptides. Does that mean there are two organisms in there?"

"Oh, no," Neiderman said promptly. "Sometimes one microbe makes multiple toxins that act in concert to exert a deadly action."

Kagen rubbed at his chin, now out of his depth. "How can we determine if these two toxins came from a single source?"

Neiderman shrugged. "That could prove very difficult."

"Maybe not," Joanna said. "If these two toxins are acting in concert to induce death, they must be coming from a single microbe, right?"

"Right," Kagen said slowly, trying to follow her line of reasoning.

"Well, then, prove that they're acting in concert and we'll know there's only one source of the toxin."

"And how would you go about proving this?" Neiderman asked, settling back into his chair. It groaned under his weight.

"First, separate the two toxins by electrophoresis," Joanna said. "Then expose experimental animals to each toxin individually. If the animals don't die, expose them to the two toxins together. If it takes both toxins to kill the animal, then we know they're working in concert and probably come from a single source."

"Excellent," Kagen pronounced. "It's a quick experiment and easy to perform."

Neiderman's face colored. He squirmed in his chair. "It's a crude measure at best. These kinds of sophomoric experiments never work out in toxicology. I can give you a hundred reasons why it won't work, but let's not waste any more time than we have to."

"Just do the damn experiment," Joanna said sharply, irritated by her fatigue and Neiderman's condescending manner. "If it doesn't work, you can give us your hundred reasons."

Neiderman gave her a hard look. "You take care of pathology and leave toxicology to me."

What a horse's ass, Joanna was thinking. It was such a simple experiment, and Neiderman was upset because he hadn't thought of it.

There was a discreet knock on the door.

"Yes?" Kagen called out.

A marine guard opened the door and stepped inside. In walked a tall man wearing a dark blue Armani suit.

Joanna stared, not believing what she saw. She continued to stare, making sure it was him. *Oh, Lord! After all these years.*

"Hello, Mark." Kagen pushed his chair back and stood to greet the man with a handshake. "It's good to have you aboard. Let me introduce you around. This is Mark Alexander, a very fine microbiologist who's going to help us determine if there are any odd microbes in our iceberg. The lady on my right is Jo—"

"Joanna!" Mark said. He smiled broadly. "What an unexpected pleasure."

"You two know each other?" Kagen asked.

Mark nodded. "We were at Johns Hopkins together."

Kagen introduced Mark to Neiderman, who was reaching for the last of the doughnuts. Neiderman grunted and didn't bother to shake hands.

"Hawksworth take good care of you?" Kagen asked.

"Everything's fine," Mark said. "But I'd love a cup of coffee. It's freezing up on that deck."

"We've just brewed up a fresh pot," Kagen told him.

Mark smiled at Joanna again. "Can I get you a refill?"

"Yes, thanks." Joanna tried not to smile back, but she did. Mark Alexander was charming and damn near irresistible, and he knew it. He was also very good-looking, with sharp features, thick brown hair, and pale blue eyes. She kept watching him as he poured coffee and chatted with Ben Kagen about the details of the project. Everything about Mark was class and money. The Armani suit, the Rolex watch, the Gucci loafers—all looked as if they had been made expressly for him.

Joanna's mind drifted back a dozen years. She was just beginning her residency in forensic pathology at Johns Hopkins and had taken a weekend off to ski in Vermont. On her first downhill run she hit a patch of ice and took a bad tumble, bruising her shoulder. Out of nowhere Mark appeared and helped her back to the lodge. They talked and touched and fell madly in love, each unable to get enough of the other. Everything went so smoothly, without any awkwardness. Initially, she didn't tell him she was a doctor, fearing that she might intimidate him. But soon she learned he too was a physician—a postdoctoral fellow in infectious diseases at Hopkins. It couldn't have been more perfect.

Then they returned to Hopkins and their work. They still saw one another often, but Mark made it clear he wasn't interested in a long-term relationship or marriage. There were too many things he had to do first. Joanna didn't really believe him. She thought surely she could change him with time. But six months later he left Hopkins and accepted a faculty position at Harvard. He told her good-bye on the phone. That hurt like hell. It took her a long time to get over him.

And forgetting him was even harder because his name kept cropping up. Within two years of leaving Hopkins, Mark was offered the chance to return as director of infectious diseases. He declined and opted to leave academic medicine altogether. The writing on the wall was clear to Mark Alexander: the academic centers in America were no longer producing great research. The most important discoveries were coming from laboratories in the private industrial sector. This was evident in the fields of telecommunications, computers, bioengineering, and now medicine.

When Mark left Harvard he joined Meecham Laboratories, a pharmaceutical giant, to become director of research. Shortly thereafter, Meecham decided to spin off its antibiotics section because it was not very profitable. Mark became part of an investment group that bought the antibiotics division and renamed it BioMega. Within a few years they came up with a new cephalosporin-type antibiotic that now had annual sales of more than two hundred million dollars. And sales were expected to go higher.

Mark was still talking with Kagen, but now he was again smiling at Joanna. She felt herself blush and brought up her coffee cup to cover it. Damn him, she thought, for being such a perfect man. He even knew how to lose gracefully. She recalled the night they were in bed and he told her the story of the microorganism that causes Legionnaires' disease. Before starting medical school, Mark had obtained a master's degree in bacteriology at a university near Philadelphia. While there, he worked on uncovering the agent responsible for causing the strange disease. It was his ideas that were instrumental in eventually identifying the offending agent, *Legionella pneumophila.* All of the credit for the discovery went to the senior investigator. Mark was given none.

"That taught me a valuable lesson," he had told her.

"To never trust anyone in research?" Joanna had guessed.

Mark had shaken his head. "It taught me that even then I was smarter than the rest of them put together."

Kagen and Mark came back to the table. Mark handed Joanna a fresh cup of coffee. Cream, no sugar. He even remembered that, Joanna thought as she nodded to him. "Thanks."

Mark sat next to her and leaned forward, his elbows on the table. "So we have a nasty toxin that consists of two polypeptides and seems to target lung cells. And the polypeptides may or may not work in concert."

Neiderman exhaled wearily. "We've already been through this."

"And we're going to go through it again, and again if necessary," Mark said evenly. "If you want to solve the problem, you've got to ask the right question. And that's what I'm doing now—searching for the right question to ask."

"Ask away," Neiderman said indifferently.

"You've worked with bacterial toxins before?" Mark asked.

"Plenty of times."

"And you're confident this toxin is of bacterial origin?"

"Most likely," Neiderman said. "But keep in mind we're talking about an origin of sixty-five million years ago. Bacteria back then might not be the same as they are today."

Mark shrugged. "Sixty-five million years is not very distant to bacteria. They've been around for billions of years, and I can assure you they were producing toxins back then in much the same way they do today."

Kagen asked, "But if it's a bacterium, why can't we grow it?"

Mark raised an index finger. "And that is our first important question. Why can't we grow it?"

"Maybe it has peculiar nutritional requirements," Kagen suggested.

"Maybe," Mark said, agreeing. "I recall when we were working on the *Legionella* organism. We couldn't grow it until someone came up with the idea of adding L-cysteine to the culture." Mark's face hardened for a moment, then he waved away his private thought. "But let's see if there is a simple answer. Let's start at the beginning. It's the ice from the iceberg that you've been testing, right?"

"Right."

"Tell me how the ice is handled," Mark said.

Kagen hesitated a moment, thinking. "It's removed from the iceberg by a mechanical device, then placed in a container and melted down."

Mark's brow went up. "How is it melted?"

"Over a flame on a hot plate, I guess."

"Find out for sure," Mark urged. "It's critically important. If the specimen is heated and the temperature goes high enough, it can kill the bacteria. You won't grow anything from the melted-down sample."

Kagen quickly jotted notes on his legal pad.

"Do you know what culture media were used?" Mark asked.

Kagen shrugged. "I'm not certain. I can ask our technicians."

Joanna said, "I checked with them this morning before I sent them specimens from the autopsy on the coast-guardsman. They told me they used blood agar and chocolate agar plates for bacteria, and Sabourand agar for fungal cultures."

"What about thioglycolate and MacConkey's media?"

"They didn't say."

Mark turned to Kagen. "Where do the technicians come from?"

"The NIH. They are supposedly very well trained."

"Being very well trained may not be good enough for what we have to do here. It would have been better if they came from the CDC or USAMRIID."

Mark pushed his chair back and went to refill his coffee cup.

Joanna, like the others, couldn't help but be impressed with Mark Alexander. He wasted no time, he got right to the core of things. And the technicians were going to be a problem, Joanna was convinced of that. The NIH were good when it came to dealing with strange microbes, but the Centers for Disease Control in Atlanta and the United States Army Medical Research Institute of Infectious Diseases at Fort Detrick, Maryland, were the very best in the world.

Mark came back to his seat. "I want you to arrange to have my two senior technicians at BioMega flown in. They're outstanding microbiologists. I can assure you they won't miss a thing."

"All right," Kagen said hesitantly. "But they'll have to go through security clearance."

A faint smile came to Mark's face, then disappeared. "That should prove interesting."

"Will there be a security problem?" Kagen asked, concerned.

"No. It's just that their lifestyles are a little different."

"How so?"

"Let's say they have a certain zest for life."

"I'm going to need some assistants too," Neiderman chimed in.

Kagen hesitated. Did Neiderman really need help? Or was he just pumping his ego up in front of the others? After a few seconds Kagen said, "You can have one assistant."

Neiderman nodded unhappily. "I'll make up a list of candidates that you can have checked."

"That won't be necessary," Kagen said. "I'll bring in a toxicologist whose credentials are impeccable. And she's already received security clearance."

Neiderman raised his brow. "She?"

"Barbara Van Buren."

Neiderman's face colored. He hated the woman. They had once collaborated on a study of heavy metal poisoning. Their findings were new and generated a lot of interest in the scientific community. Although both of their names appeared on the article that was published, Barbara flew around the country giving talks and lectures and stealing all the glory. Everyone thought that the work was really hers and that Neiderman and the others were minor contributors. The study had propelled her up the academic ladder. She was currently an associate professor of toxicology at the University of Washington. "We don't get along very well," Neiderman said at last.

"Take it or leave it," Kagen said curtly.

"All right," Neiderman agreed reluctantly, knowing he couldn't do all the work by himself. "But I'm still in charge, right?"

"Right." Kagen jotted another note on his legal pad,

glad he had been given the opportunity to bring Barbara Van Buren aboard. She had her security clearance because Kagen had chosen her to take Neiderman's place on the ETOX team. Neiderman's term would be up in six months, and Kagen had the power to have him replaced. Neiderman would be informed once the current project was completed. "So that'll be three more scientists to come aboard," Kagen said and looked over at Mark. "Are you sure you'll need both technicians? Would one suffice?"

"I need both," Mark said and turned to Joanna. "Let's get back to the autopsy you did. I take it you cultured every tissue and fluid in the coastguardsman."

"Of course."

"Including the mouth and pharynx, I hope."

"Hey! What do you take me for?" Joanna asked indignantly.

"Just checking all the bases," Mark said. "No offense meant."

"None taken."

"Why is culturing the mouth so important here?" Kagen asked.

"Because we're dealing with ice," Joanna said at once. "There was ice on the deck and in the cabin of the fishing vessel. Maybe the coastguardsman touched it and brought his hand to his mouth, or maybe he tasted it."

"And the mouth is a wonderful place for bacteria to grow," Mark added, then asked Joanna, "Did you give the lab special instructions on how to culture the specimens?"

"I told them to look for both aerobic and anaerobic organisms."

"Good," Mark said and furrowed his brow, concentrating. "Did you specify what temperature and humidity they were to use in the cultures?"

Joanna shrugged. "Who knows what the environment for bacteria was like sixty-five million years ago?"

"That was the Cretaceous period," Kagen told them. "I can find out from my colleagues exactly what the environment was like then, if you wish."

"Please," Mark said.

Kagen hurried to the wall phone and began punching in numbers.

Mark leaned over to Joanna and said softly, "You look wonderful. You haven't changed a bit."

"Just a decade older," she said candidly.

"It doesn't show." Mark grinned.

Joanna felt her face flush. "You haven't changed very much either."

"Are you married?"

"No," Joanna said, her voice very low. "Are you?"

"Nope."

"You'll never marry."

"I didn't say that."

"You didn't have to."

Kagen walked quickly back to the conference table. "The climate was warmer and much more humid during the late Cretaceous period. The average temperature was thirty-seven degrees Celsius and the relative humidity was a hundred percent. It's believed that the oxygen content in the air was thirty-three percent."

"That's easy to reproduce in a lab," Mark said. "Maybe our bacteria will grow under Cretaceous conditions."

"Let's hope so," Kagen said. "I also talked with Colonel Hawksworth about your request. He's on his way down to get information on the two technicians you want flown in."

Joanna pushed her chair back. "I'm going for a walk topside and see if I can get my body clock back on schedule."

"You'd better wear your parka," Mark called after her. "It's cold up there."

Joanna walked to the door, feeling Mark's eyes on her. She knew he expected her to turn and smile. Don't turn, she told herself, and she didn't. She wasn't going to give him that.

Six

A Coast Guard vessel came alongside the *Global Explorer II* and offloaded two marines and an insulated plastic crate. The marines climbed up the Jacob's ladder and onto the deck where Hawksworth was waiting. The wind suddenly gusted and the men had to brace themselves against it.

"How many icebergs were sampled?" Hawksworth asked.

"An even dozen, sir," the marine corporal said.

"And radio signaling devices were implanted in each iceberg?"

"Yes, sir. We also flagged them to warn any passing ships."

Hawksworth looked out across the bay as the crate was slowly winched up. The seas were rough, with heavy swells and strong currents that could push the icebergs miles and miles from their original locales. If any of the icebergs harbored the toxin, they would have to be tracked down and contained. The radio transmitters—each set to a different frequency—allowed the *Global Explorer II* to plot the course and whereabouts of each individual iceberg. Samples had also been taken from various glaciers in an effort to pinpoint which glacier was spawning the toxic icebergs. That was like looking for a needle in a haystack, but it had to be done.

Hawksworth turned away as the wind picked up again,

now bringing cold rain with it. "Grab the crate and let's get below."

Hawksworth led the way into the superstructure and unlocked an elevator. As the car slowly descended, he ticked off in his mind the questions he had to answer. There were so many of them, all difficult and all interrelated. What was the toxin and what was its source? Was there only one iceberg filled with the toxin or were there many? And was the ecologic disaster that took place the year before caused by the same toxin?

He clearly remembered the incredible variety of sea life floating dead in the water. Whales, sharks, seals, salmon, dolphins. Nothing was spared. But despite extensive studies, no cause for the disaster was ever uncovered. It probably was the same damn toxin, Hawksworth thought miserably. Which meant the toxin was widespread. And this raised the most terrifying question of all. Was the toxin once again in the food chain, poised to affect every living creature from plankton to man?

Hawksworth's gaze went to the marine corporal's hand that was holding up the crate. On the second knuckle was a gouged-out, bleeding wound. "What happened to your hand, Corporal?"

"Injured it on the mission, sir."

Hawksworth's eyes narrowed. "On a piece of ice?"

"Yes, sir. It happened while transporting the ice from the iceberg to the container."

"Have it looked at by the medic," Hawksworth said, and made a mental note to inform the scientific group of the incident.

The elevator jerked to a stop and the door opened.

They were now in the lowermost part of the hull. All the laboratories were located in this section. In case of a toxic spill or leak, the bottom level could be sealed and locked off from the rest of the vessel. Those trapped below would die. Those above would live. It was known in

the military intelligence community as containment—
sacrificing a few to save a lot.

As he entered the toxicology lab, Hawksworth felt a
vacuum effect. The marines sensed it as well and looked
at each other nervously.

"There's negative pressure in this room," Hawksworth
explained. "That way, if there's a leak, all the air is
sucked in. No air gets out."

The marines nodded, now straining under the load of
the heavy crate.

Hawksworth gestured for them to place the crate on
the floor and gave the order to rest.

The marines snapped their hands behind their backs
and assumed the military posture of parade rest.

Hawksworth looked to the far end of the laboratory.
Joanna, Mark, Kagen, and Neiderman were sitting on
high stools, peering through a large Plexiglas window.
Their backs were to him.

"Anything interesting?" Hawksworth asked, walking over.

"We've separated the toxin into its two polypeptide
components," Kagen told him. "Now we're going to determine whether they can kill individually or whether
they have to work together to produce a lethal effect."

Behind the window Hawksworth saw a table with
three large narrow-mouthed flasks atop it. In each flask
was a clear liquid being heated by a low flame. The
flasks were connected by tubes to plastic cages, each
containing two mice.

"What does the lettering on the flasks mean?" Hawksworth asked.

"Flask A contains the larger of the isolated polypeptides," Kagen explained. "Flask B holds the other
isolated polypeptide. And the one labeled C has both
components of the toxin."

The liquid in the flasks was starting to bubble. A steamlike vapor filled the flasks and made its way through the

tubing and into the cages. The mice stood on their hind legs, nibbling on something in their paws. They glanced up at the steam coming into their cages. It didn't seem to bother them.

Kagen studied his watch, counting the seconds as they ticked off. Some of the animals were moving around inside their cages, others rubbed at their noses. None appeared ill.

A minute passed. Kagen turned to Neiderman. "How long did it take the toxin to kill mice in your lab at the NIH?"

"About thirty seconds," Neiderman said. "But keep in mind, that was the whole toxin in its native state we used."

"Do you think the electrophoretic process you employed to separate the components may have degraded the toxin?" Kagen asked, now watching the rodents run and jump around.

"That's a possibility," Neiderman said, pulling at the collar of his shirt. It was warm in the room and he had on a sweater beneath his white laboratory coat. "A distinct possibility."

"But not very likely," Joanna said. "We separate out enzymes and antibodies by electrophoresis all the time and, weight for weight, they lose very little activity."

"But this isn't an enzyme or antibody," Neiderman countered quickly. "It's something new to us, and it just might not behave the way we expect it to."

Joanna thought for a moment and nodded. "Good point."

Damn right it was, Neiderman thought, because when it came to toxins he was a thousand times smarter than she was. Toxicology was his field of expertise, not hers. He wanted to tell her to shut up and listen. She might end up learning something.

"But still, to lose all toxic activity just because an electric current passed through the toxin . . ." Joanna's voice trailed off as she tried to think it through. It didn't make sense. The minimal amount of electricity used in electrophoresis shouldn't damage a protein like that. "Maybe there's some essential cofactor that's missing. Perhaps when you separated out the polypeptides you left behind some factor necessary to initiate the toxic effect."

"Like what?" Neiderman asked.

"Like small amounts of some mineral such as calcium or magnesium," Joanna said. "What solution was used to redissolve the isolated polypeptides?"

"Saline," Neiderman replied.

"Which doesn't contain calcium or magnesium or anything else other than sodium chloride."

Joanna tapped her fingers on the countertop, now thinking of other possibilities. "It might be wise to take the whole toxin from the ice and identify every component, no matter how small or seemingly insignificant. I'd search for that cofactor."

"Look!" Kagen pointed to the cages. "The animals in C are dropping!"

Everybody leaned forward, staring at the cages. The mice in cages A and B were running around or nibbling at their paws, unconcerned with what was happening in cage C. There the two mice were down, gasping and struggling for air. Little bubbles frothed out of their mouths. Their agony was short-lived. They died quickly.

"So much for your cofactor," Neiderman said, grinning at Joanna. "I don't think I have to bother looking for all those mysterious components now. Do you?"

"You still have to look for cofactors," Joanna said, holding her temper.

Neiderman glowered at her. "You were on the wrong track and now you're being obstinate. Why not just admit you were wrong and stop wasting our time?"

Joanna pushed her chair back and stared at Neiderman. "I've only known you a short while, but I'm already getting very tired of you."

"Now, now," Kagen quickly interceded. "There's no need—"

Joanna held her hand up to Kagen. "I'm not finished yet. Let me have my say, then you can have yours."

She turned back to Neiderman. "This is not some scientific game to see who's the smartest or cleverest. We've got a real problem here, and it may very well be a life-and-death problem of worldwide proportions."

Neiderman shrugged. "Three people are dead. That's not exactly a global disaster."

Joanna couldn't believe he was so simple-minded. She pointed through the window at the dead mice. "The two polypeptides acted in concert to produce this lethal effect. That means we're almost certainly dealing with an unknown microbe that came from God knows where. And that bug might be sitting out there, just waiting to make its grand entrance into some densely populated area."

Neiderman swallowed audibly and remained silent.

"And the presence of a cofactor might be very important here," Joanna went on. "Because if it exists, it could be the toxin's weak point. And if we knew how to inactivate the cofactor, the people exposed to the toxin might not die immediately. It might take ten or fifteen minutes or maybe even longer. Maybe long enough to give people time to get treatment and maybe even receive an antidote. Do you see what I'm driving at?"

"Yes," Neiderman conceded quietly.

Kagen nodded slowly. Something had delayed the action of the toxin in the mice. Maybe there was a missing cofactor in the isolated preparations. "I think Joanna has a valid point."

Hawksworth hadn't thought about detoxifying the toxin. That could solve a lot of problems. He moved in closer to Joanna. "Are those cofactors you're talking about real or hypothetical?"

"They're real," Joanna assured him. "For example,

there is an enzyme called hyaluronidase present in snake venoms. It breaks down cellular barriers and allows the venom to be rapidly absorbed into the victim. Without the enzyme the venom's effect is delayed and diminished."

"Are there others?"

"Some venomous reactions are catalyzed by calcium, others by magnesium," Joanna told him. "And those metals can be inactivated, of course."

"Good," Hawksworth said, nodding to himself before looking over at Neiderman. "Concentrate on those cofactors."

Neiderman simmered with anger. He felt like he was a schoolboy who was being told what to do and when to do it. *I'm the goddamn toxicologist here,* he wanted to shout, *and if you stay the hell off my back I'll solve your problem.* But he held his tongue. He nodded back to Hawksworth, hating the man and the power he held. With one phone call, Hawksworth could stop all the funding Neiderman's lab received.

Mark turned his stool toward Joanna. "How did you become such an expert on toxins and cofactors?"

"From Peter Allen Weir," Joanna said. "We wrote a textbook on poisons and toxins in forensic medicine." And from the last case she solved at Johns Hopkins before leaving for Los Angeles. An Indian podiatrist murdered his wife by injecting her with cobra venom. It had taken Joanna three months and a lot of reading and laboratory work to come up with the answer. And in the process she learned a great deal about toxins and the cofactors they depended on.

Mark watched her eyes twinkling. He remembered the look from the year they went together in Baltimore. It meant she was talking about one thing but thinking about another.

His gaze drifted down to her thighs. She was sitting on a high stool with her legs crossed, the hem of her skirt a few inches above her knee. He had to pry his eyes away.

Kagen was pacing the floor, head down, hands behind his back. "So we've got a complex toxin that we believe comes from a single microorganism, probably a bacterium. Right?"

The group nodded in unison.

"Then why can't we grow it?" Kagen asked.

"Maybe we can." Mark reached into his coat pocket for a stack of color photos. They showed petri dishes containing blood agar. On its red surfaces were clusters of white and cream-colored spots. He passed the photographs around. "These were given to me by one of your technicians."

"Is that it?" Kagen asked excitedly. "Is that the microbe?"

"No," Mark said. "Those are contaminants that are growing out. There are some beta-hemolytic streptococci, some staph, and a little mold here and there."

"What does that mean?"

"It means your culturing techniques are sloppy. These bacteria are almost certainly coming from the technicians or from the air in the laboratory."

"How can you be so sure?" Kagen asked.

"See these white dots surrounded by a clear zone in the blood agar?" Mark used a pencil to point. "That's a colony of beta-hemolytic streptococcus and it came from somebody's throat. My guess is that somebody coughed near the plate."

Mark handed Joanna another photo. Their arms touched, causing an unmistakable surge of electricity between them. Her hair was close to his face, and its fresh aroma made his mind flash back to their first weekend together at a ski lodge in Vermont. "Those yellow clumps at two o'clock are probably fungi," he said, forcing himself to concentrate.

Joanna handed the photo back. "A moment ago you said that maybe we could grow out the toxin-producing microbe. All I see here is a contaminated mess. How does one go about sorting out all this?"

"With damn good technicians," Mark said, and turned to Hawksworth. "When can I expect my people to arrive?"

Hawksworth groaned to himself. His men had located the two women in a male stripper bar the night before. They were drinking shots of tequila and tucking money in a stripper's loincloth. "They should be here by late tomorrow."

Mark could tell from Hawksworth's face that he already knew about his technicians' lifestyle. "They're a bit unusual, aren't they?"

"A bit," Hawksworth said, and walked over to the plastic crate on the floor. The two marines stepped back. "We have samples from all the large icebergs in the immediate area—a dozen of them. Where do you want them stored for testing?"

Neiderman gestured to a narrow door in the side wall marked COLD ROOM. "In there. Just set the thing on the floor. I'll get them stowed right away."

Hawksworth held the door open while the marines hefted the crate. As they maneuvered it through, the corporal's lacerated knuckle collided with the door jamb. Stifling a yelp, he let go his end of the crate. It hit the floor with a loud thud, startling the ETOX team.

The crate popped open. Chips of dry ice peppered the floor, as a plastic sample collection box flew through the room toward the Plexiglas window. The box slammed into the countertop between the recoiling observers, then split apart and disgorged a grapefruit-sized chunk of ice that struck the floor with a resounding crack and broke into three pieces.

"Nobody move," Hawksworth barked, and everyone froze.

Hawksworth strode to a large red button on the wall next to the entryway and hit it hard. He hurried back to

the gaping crate and carefully studied its remaining contents before he shut the lid and secured it. Then he folded
his arms, looked up at the wall clock, and impassively
counted off the seconds.

"Do—do you believe that piece of ice also contains
the toxin?" Kagen asked nervously.

"Until proven otherwise," Hawksworth said, still
watching the clock. Thirty seconds had passed.

"So you think there's more than one toxic iceberg out
there?" Mark asked.

"That's the most likely possibility. According to our
experts, once an iceberg has broken off from a glacier, it
often sheds smaller pieces. Calving, it's called."

Hawksworth had also learned that icebergs might have
a lifespan of more than two years. Eventually they were
worn down by winds and tides and warmer waters. From
a timing standpoint, the iceberg that killed the people on
the fishing boat could also have caused the ecologic disaster a year earlier. His gaze stayed on the clock. A
minute had passed since he pressed the button.

The others were staring at the chunks of ice on the
floor, now melting and making small puddles. In the
largest piece they could see blue streaks that seemed to
glisten in the bright light. The urge to bolt out of the lab
was detectable on every face.

The door opened briefly to admit two figures wearing
space suits and carrying a caddy of supplies between
them. Their hoods were up, their plastic visors very dark.

Hawksworth pointed to the floor. "That ice may be
contaminated with the toxin. Return it to its plastic container and replace it in the crate."

One figure held the container while the other picked
up the fragments of ice with tongs and placed them within. The top was secured and the container was bagged
and returned to the crate packed with dry ice.

The contamination team went back to the puddle on
the floor made by the melting ice. It was six inches

across and so shallow it was already beginning to dry. They quickly sprayed it with a thick white foam and stepped back.

Hawksworth went to the crate and checked the number on the bagged sample box, then turned to the marines. "That ice came from iceberg twelve. I want it located right now and I want it tracked minutely until you hear otherwise. Understood?"

"Yes, sir!" the marines shouted and exited the laboratory.

Hawksworth walked over to Neiderman. "I want all the ice tested for the presence of the toxin, starting with sample twelve. And you'll call the results to me as soon as you have them."

Hawksworth gestured to the door. "The rest of you can leave now. There's no need for you to worry. The white spray we used contains Eviron Chem and a mixture of very potent disinfectants. It kills every known virus and bacterium instantly."

Mark raised his brow skeptically. "Every *known* bacterium and virus, huh?"

"Across the board," Hawksworth assured him.

"And what about unknown?" Mark asked. "Does it kill those too?"

"It should kill those as well," Hawksworth said, then gave Mark a long look. "Can you think of a reason why it shouldn't?"

Mark didn't answer, but when he walked out, he gave the foam-covered puddle a very wide berth.

So did Joanna and Ben Kagen.

Seven

Malcolm Neiderman twisted and turned in his sleep. He was on a brightly lit stage and two men were attacking him with clawlike weapons. They swung at him, ripping off his clothes and tearing into his skin. Desperately he tried to crawl away, but a snarling Doberman pinscher blocked the exit. The men came at him again and the audience roared its approval. In the front row Neiderman saw his ex-wife and her lover. They were applauding and laughing, enjoying every minute. Now the man above him swung his clawed weapon again. Neiderman felt a terrible pain. Then he saw his testicles flying through the air.

Neiderman awoke with a start in the darkness. He was groping for his testicles and scrotum, trying to protect them. It took him a moment to realize he was having a nightmare. The same nightmare he'd been having over and over again. He lay back in the bunk bed, his heart pounding, the perspiration soaking through his pajama top. *Holy shit! When will these damn things stop? When?*

The psychiatrist in Washington had told him the nightmares would come less frequently and then fade away altogether, but they hadn't. The dream was a manifestation of the emotional turmoil in Neiderman's life, the shrink had told him. And that was another way of saying his ex-wife was the reason for his nightmares.

Neiderman switched on the small bedside lamp and sat

on the edge of the bed. He reached for a cigarette and lit it, thinking about how the psychiatrist had explained every aspect of his recurring dream. His wife of twenty years had left him for a new lover, a younger man who she said made her life exciting. Just like that she was gone, taking with her half of everything. She got the house. He kept the stocks, which started dropping in value the day after the divorce. He sold at the bottom and got just enough for a cramped condominium in Maryland. And her damn alimony continued to take a third of his paycheck.

So, the psychiatrist had explained, the man with the clawed weapon in his dream was his ex-wife's lawyer who stripped him of everything, material and otherwise. The Doberman represented the law that enforced the judge's decision on the division of assets. And his wife leaving him for a younger man was emasculating, as depicted by his balls being torn off.

"But why on a stage in front of an audience?" Neiderman had asked.

"Because everything that happened to you was laid out before your friends and the public. It was very humiliating, wasn't it?"

You're fucking right it was! Neiderman thought angrily, hoping his ex-wife aged rapidly and turned into a wrinkled-up old woman. Maybe then her young lover would leave her for somebody else and then she'd know what it felt like to be discarded like a worn-out pair of shoes. Fuck her!

Neiderman puffed hard on his cigarette, wondering what his ex-wife was doing at that very moment. She was probably screwing her boyfriend on the goatskin rug in front of the fireplace in his old house, the house he had found and remodeled and paid for. And while she was living in that wonderful home, where the hell was he? He was living in a tiny condo with leaky plumbing, driving a six-year-old Toyota, and watching his dreary life slip by.

If only he had money, real money. Not the three thousand a month he managed to scrape by on, but a million or two a year. Then he could have the life he wanted. Travel, luxury cars, a big house, women. Particularly the women. They all loved money. They worshiped it and the men who had it.

But where would he get that kind of money? Neiderman had no rich relatives he might inherit from, no luck at gambling on the lottery. And he certainly wasn't going to make some discovery in his laboratory worth zillions. Even if he did, all of the patent rights would belong to the federal government.

The ship rocked slightly. The ashtray next to him slid to the edge of the nightstand. Quickly Neiderman reached for it, thinking the weather must be very rough. Usually the gigantic ship was still, with virtually no sense of motion. He stared at the bedside lamp and wondered if there was any money to be made from the experiments now going on aboard the *Global Explorer II*. Maybe he could sell the story to one of the tabloids. But they'd never give him a million for that. He'd be lucky to get fifty thousand dollars. And the news leak would cost him his job.

Neiderman's eyes narrowed as another idea came to him. Suppose the terrible toxin they were dealing with was indeed produced by bacteria. Just suppose. There were a lot of countries and organizations that would pay big money for such a lethal toxin. Even Hawksworth had mentioned it would be perfect for biologic warfare.

The cigarette Neiderman was smoking burnt at his fingers. He quickly put it out and lit another, making sure he kept his trend of thought. If the organism producing the toxin was isolated, it would be easy to carry off the ship. All he would need was a thimble-sized container with the right growth media and a few colonies of the microbe. And Neiderman would have no trouble gaining access.

He could devise any number of experiments that required the use of live bacteria. Of course, he would do the work in collaboration with the others. That way it wouldn't raise any suspicions.

It was going to be a bacterium that produced the toxin, Neiderman told himself. It had to be. And that baby would be worth a ton of money to the right customer. Neiderman listed the countries that would happily ante up millions for the microbe. The Chinese, the North Koreans, some of the new Central Asian republics, the Libyans, and a half dozen other countries in the Middle East . . . The list was endless. And Neiderman had contacts in some of those countries, particularly scientists he had worked with in his laboratory and abroad. He remembered a Chinese scientist who continually asked questions about a new nerve gas that was being studied in Neiderman's lab. It resembled sarin but was even more deadly. The scientist had given Neiderman an open invitation to lecture in Beijing anytime he wanted.

Neiderman glanced at his watch. It was only 7:30 P.M. He had slept just an hour before the awful dream awakened him. He peeled off his damp pajamas and thought about what his ex-wife would do if he ended up a multimillionaire. She'd probably crawl back on her hands and knees and beg to be forgiven. Fuck her! With all that money he could have his pick of beautiful women.

Neiderman switched off the lamp and lay back in the darkness, thinking of microbes and millions of dollars. Gradually he drifted off into a sound sleep.

The nightmare did not return.

Ann Cormier removed the clasp from her ponytail and shook her hair loose, letting it fall over her shoulders. She quickly wetted her lips with her tongue and entered the recreation room. In the far corner with his back to her there was a lone man playing pool. He turned and waved. She waved back reluctantly. It was Bobby Shea.

"You want to play some pool?" he asked.

"I don't know how," Ann answered.

"I'll be glad to show you."

"Some other time maybe," Ann said, and walked over to a rack of magazines. She flipped through an old issue of *People*, wondering how long Shea was going to stay and trying to think of a way to make him leave. He was a real talker. He'd talk about anything to anybody who would listen. Maybe if she ignored him he'd get the message that she wanted to be alone. Out of the corner of her eye she watched as he expertly made shot after shot until the table was cleared. Then he emptied the pockets and racked the balls for another game. Christ, she growled to herself. He could be here all night.

Shea looked over at the blue football jersey Ann was wearing. "Does the UA stand for the University of Arizona?"

"Yeah," she said in a monotone. Remembering she'd left her bra off, she raised the magazine higher.

"It's really pretty there, huh?"

"Yeah," she said again, but the closest she'd gotten to the University of Arizona was a sleazy bar in downtown Tucson. It was a strip joint where drunks threw money on the stage and tried to reach up and grab the dancers. It was a part of her life she wanted to forget and make believe never happened.

Ann pretended to study a picture in the magazine as her mind drifted back to the small town in southern Nevada where she'd grown up. It was the kind of place where after graduating from high school the girls either got married or waited on tables or did both. Ann had decided to try her luck in Tucson, but the only job she could find was working for minimum wages in a fast food restaurant. It wasn't nearly enough to live on, and out of desperation she became a stripper, hating it and the people she had to deal with. But the pay was good. A hundred a night, a lot more most weekends. Then the bar owner began to pressure the strippers to become call girls, to put out for selected customers. The money was so enticing that most of the girls did it. But Ann knew that was a one-way street with a dead end. She thought about returning to her hometown, but there was nothing to go back to. Her father was an alcoholic who disappeared for long stretches, her mother was remarried and not interested in seeing her daughter. Ann had nowhere to turn, so she joined the navy.

It was the best move she'd ever made. The pay was reasonable, the training excellent. She became a first-class pathology assistant. The navy had given her a profession she could take with her wherever she went. And the fringe benefits in the military were incredible, particularly the men. There were so many of them, and so many were young and good-looking. But after five years she decided to leave the service. It was too restricting. She didn't like all the rules and regulations. So she left the navy and applied for a pathology position at Bethesda. They accepted her on the spot. And her work turned out to be so good, they selected her to become part of the ETOX team. It was the proudest moment of her life.

Her gaze went back to Bobby Shea, who was intently studying his next pool shot. He too was a civilian employee at Bethesda, but Ann hadn't met him until she sat next to him on the flight from Andrews Air Force Base to Juneau. He talked the whole trip, never shutting up even when she tried to read her book. And he picked at the pimples on his face continually as he talked. She would have moved to another seat but the plane was full.

Bobby was still deliberating over his next shot, now scratching involuntarily at the bumps on his forehead. In the fluorescent lighting his facial acne had a purplish discoloration and seemed even more pronounced.

"Bobby, quit picking at your face," Ann said disgustedly.

"It itches."

"You're only making it worse."

Bobby thought for a moment. "It can't get much worse."

"They have medicines that can really help it."

Bobby shrugged. "I've tried all that stuff. You know, ointments and soaps. It just made my skin dry and itch more."

"Not ointments," she said, exasperated. "They have pills now that clear up acne."

Bobby shrugged again. He had had acne since he was a teenager and nothing had ever helped. He leaned over the pool table and carefully lined up his next shot. He struck the cue ball. It bounced off three cushions, then hit the eight ball and knocked it into a side pocket.

"You play very well," Ann said.

"I practiced a lot," Bobby said, remembering the pool parlor where he had spent all of his free time as a teenager. He had no close friends and never dated. In poolrooms nobody cared what your skin looked like. They only cared how well you stroked a cue.

Bobby put his stick down and looked over at Ann. "Do those pills really help?"

"I have a girlfriend they worked wonders on."

"Can you get the name of them for me?"

"Sure." Ann glanced at the wall clock. It was almost 7:30 P.M. She thought about asking Bobby to leave, but she'd have to tell him why. And telling Bobby a secret was like announcing it over the PA system. Damn it! Why did he have to pick tonight to play pool?

Bobby racked the balls again and reached for his pool stick. Then he noticed Ann staring up at the wall and followed her line of vision to the clock. "Uh-uh! It's nearly seven-thirty."

"So?"

"Got to go," Bobby said urgently. "They're showing an old John Wayne movie in a few minutes. Want to come along?"

"I'll pass," Ann said. "But thanks for asking."

Ann watched him hurry out of the recreation room, then rechecked the time. She wondered if Eddie Walsh was going to show up. Maybe he'd gotten cold feet because of the risk involved. Strict orders were in place to keep civilian scientists and military personnel aboard ship from socializing. They were afforded as little contact as possible. And this was particularly true for the civilian females. Fraternization between the sexes was prohibited, and if it did occur, those involved faced severe punishment. They could even be dismissed. Ann knew it was very dangerous for her and Eddie to meet. But the risks and dangers were exciting, and Ann liked that.

She flicked off the overhead lights, then went to a vending machine, inserted a quarter, and took out an orange soda. As she sipped, she felt it sting her lower lip. Damn! Maybe a fever blister was about to come out after all. While putting on makeup she had examined the inner surface of her lower lip. There was a small red sore the size of a match head, but it didn't look like a blister. She wondered if she had bitten the area accidentally, maybe in her sleep. Yeah, she nodded to herself, that would explain it.

The door opened and Eddie Walsh cautiously looked around the room before walking in. He saw Ann and hurried over.

"I can only stay a little while," he said nervously.

Ann grinned mischievously. "This won't take very long, will it?"

"I guess not," Eddie said, and kicked an imaginary object. "You—ah—you want to do some pushups?"

"Sure." Ann went over to the couch and grabbed three large cushions. She placed them on the floor, then arranged them together in a straight line. "I like something soft beneath me."

"You do pushups on cushions?"

Ann stared at him, now wondering if he was joking around. But he wasn't smiling. Maybe he was just young and inexperienced, she thought. But that was okay too. That could be fun.

She reached toward him and took his hand, pulling him with her as she sank onto the cushions. "Why don't you show me how to do pushups the right way?"

Eddie started doing pushups, his muscles swelling beneath his T-shirt. "You've got to—keep your—back straight," he huffed.

"Let me see." Ann pulled up the back of Eddie's T-shirt and put her hands around his waist. She felt the front of his abdomen and pressed into his muscles, moving up and down with him. Now she had a finger in his navel. "You like that?"

Eddie made a guttural sound. The rate at which he was doing pushups slowed noticeably.

Ann unzipped his pants and felt a large bulge beneath his jockey shorts. Quickly she wriggled out of her jeans. She pushed up against him as she felt his hand go between her legs. "Do you have some protection?"

Eddie began humping her thigh. "You don't have to worry. I haven't been with any—"

"I do worry," Ann said, nibbling at his ear. "There's something out there called AIDS. You should have brought a condom."

"I can't stop now," Eddie moaned. "Jesus! I'm going to *explode*."

"Don't do that!"

Ann rolled on top of him and guided him into her. She moved up and down, slowly at first, then faster and faster as she sensed him getting bigger. "You feel nice," she whispered.

"I can't hold it!"

"Not yet!" She slowed her rocking motion. He reached up for her and she leaned back, letting him grope for her breasts. Then she started again, riding him and feeling him move with her. In the dim light she could see the sweat on his face, and that turned her on even more. She rode him still harder and felt herself coming. "Now!" she cried out. "Now!"

Their climaxes were almost simultaneous and seemed to go on and on. Then they lay still in the quiet room, catching their breaths as the ship gently swayed in the rough seas.

"Jesus," Eddie said, holding her against him and kissing her cheek.

Ann kissed him back, her tongue running over his lips. Then she pecked at his cheek and pushed herself away. "I've got to go to the little girls' room." She stood and reached for her purse with its vial of spermicidal vaginal spray. "I'll be right back."

Eddie lay back, feeling wonderful. He'd never been with a woman like Ann before—one who really liked him. Of course, he'd only been with two other women in his whole life. There was a high school cheerleader he'd screwed after a football game. But everybody was screwing her. And then there was the whore outside the marine base at Parris Island, South Carolina. Those two meant nothing to him. But with Ann it was different. It was like love at first sight. Eddie suddenly realized he had never been in love before, not until now. Without a doubt, Ann was his type of girl. She was a little older than he was, but she was fresh and pretty and nice. He could envision himself taking her back to Wisconsin to meet his parents.

Ann came back into the room and blew him a kiss. She

picked up the opened can of orange soda and took a sip. Her lower lip began to sting again. Shit! She wished she could be sure it wasn't an early fever blister. She didn't want to pass the damn thing on to Eddie. She'd feel awful if that happened.

Eight

An armed coastguardsman escorted Joanna and Mark to the end of the dock. Another coastguardsman lifted the crime-scene tape to allow the doctors to duck under it. Then he made certain the plank leading from the dock to the fishing vessel was secure.

"If you need anything, just holler," he said in a Southern accent.

Joanna and Mark carefully walked across the plank and onto the deck of the *Donnie*. The sky was dark and overcast, and a stiff wind was blowing in from the north. A few raindrops were falling.

Mark huddled up in his parka. "Let's go below."

"Hang on for just a moment."

"Hell, there's nothing up here."

"We'll see." Joanna scanned the deck, itemizing the equipment she saw and reconstructing what had happened to Mary and Jack Kincaid. They had seen the brilliantly colored iceberg, and greed had taken over. Risking life and limb, they went to it and secured their boat to the iceberg with grappling hooks. The lines and hooks were neatly coiled on the deck, which told Joanna that the Coast Guard had tidied things up. That was going to make her investigation more difficult.

Off to her right were the pickaxes the Kincaids had used to chop away at the iceberg. Then they had piled the ice up on the deck. The Kincaids thought they were surrounded by riches, not by some deadly toxin. And their

lives were spared temporarily because the weather was
cold and the toxin was locked in the frozen ice.

Joanna could envision the Kincaids tearing into the
iceberg, filling the boat with ice as quickly as possible.
They were rushing. It reminded Joanna of the little story
John O'Hara quoted at the beginning of his novel *Appointment in Samarra*. A man was hurrying to escape
Death by rushing to Samarra. He didn't know that Samarra was where he had an appointment with Death.

"Jesus, it's cold up here," Mark said, shivering noticeably. "Have you seen enough?"

"I guess," Joanna said, wondering what else the Coast
Guard might have moved around or taken off the ship
altogether.

They entered the cabin below and unzipped their
parkas. The air was much warmer and smelled like stale
seawater. Everything seemed in disarray—pots and pans
on the floor, glasses and dishes overturned on a countertop, electrical cords dangling from appliances. But there
was nothing broken, nothing that looked like a struggle
had taken place. They didn't have time to struggle,
Joanna thought. The toxin acted too quickly. The Coast
Guard hadn't bothered to tidy up this part of the ship.
And for good reason.

Joanna heard the door starting to close. Quickly she
grabbed it and latched it open. She and Mark nodded
knowingly at each other. Who knew what the hell was
still down here? The ice was gone, but maybe a little of
the toxin was still around. And they didn't want to be in
an enclosed space with *that*.

Joanna noticed the highchair that was bolted to the
wall. She stepped off the distance between the highchair
and the small stove. "There was approximately ten feet
between the child and the ice melting on the stove."

"That's a relatively short distance for the toxin to
travel," Mark said. "Remember, the toxin was airborne
in a vapor and in a closed-off space."

"Maybe something siphoned the toxin out." Joanna went back to the highchair and looked up at the ceiling, searching for a vent or an outlet. There wasn't any. She took off her fur-lined gloves and held her hands up, feeling for a draft. Nothing. "There's no ventilation here."

"Well, something saved the kid from death, and it wasn't ten feet of space," Mark said.

"How's your knowledge of pediatrics?" Joanna asked.

Mark shrugged. "Fair in infectious diseases. Not so good in other aspects."

"Can you think of any special defense mechanisms a four-year-old might have that could protect him from a toxin that kills adults?"

"I've never heard of anything like that in man or animal. Have you?"

Joanna shook her head. "But somehow that little boy survived." She wrinkled her brow. "Could the child have unique antibodies that inactivate the toxin?"

"You mean like snake handlers?"

"Exactly."

Mark considered the idea for a moment. Snake handlers, who had been repeatedly bitten, built up antibodies against the poisonous venom. These antibodies could inactivate the snake toxin and protect the handler in case of future bites. "It's possible the kid had antibodies, but highly unlikely. In order to make antibodies against a toxin, an individual has to have been exposed to that toxin in the past. If our toxin really hasn't seen the light of day for sixty-five million years, the chances are very remote that our kid has antibodies against it."

"Maybe," Joanna said. "But we should still get a blood sample from the child and check—"

A wave suddenly pounded the side of the boat. Joanna tried to keep her footing, but couldn't. Stumbling, she grabbed on to Mark and they both fell against the wall. Mark held her tightly until the vessel settled.

"I hate small boats," Joanna said, trying not to remember a near-drowning experience when she fell from a sailboat as a child.

Mark looked down at her, loosening his hug. She was so striking with her face and neck outlined by the fur collar of her parka. He reached up and moved aside a lock of hair that had fallen across her forehead. "How did you manage to stay so young?"

"By not letting men aggravate me," Joanna told him.

"Is that meant to be a subtle message?"

"Just a statement of fact." Joanna put her hand on his chest, keeping it there for a moment, then pushed herself away. "Let's go back to why the child lived while his parents died."

"Why is that so important here?"

"Because I've learned from hard experience that the questions you can't answer are always the ones that tell you the most."

"You may be right," Mark said. "But from an infectious disease standpoint, the most important thing is not the toxin. It's the organism that generates it. If we can find the microbe, everything else will fall into place."

Joanna's eyes narrowed. "There's not much chance the bacteria are down here, is there?"

"Why not? It's above freezing and wet and there are plenty of little nooks and crannies." Mark glanced over at the pan atop the stove. "That piece of ice the Kincaids melted couldn't have been very big. Yet it was loaded with enough toxin to kill three adults almost instantly. Maybe it was loaded with bacteria too. And remember, bacteria travel on vapors as well. As a matter of fact, they do it much better than toxins."

Joanna glanced over at the door, glad it was wide open. Mark was right, of course. She had been concentrating on the toxin, not the microbe. And the damn bug could be down here, lurking in some unnoticed spot. She moved a little closer to the door, now feeling a draft.

Mark was checking all the portholes. They were intact and couldn't be opened. He snapped on a pair of latex gloves and examined all the dishes and pans, and found nothing remarkable. He glanced up at the ceiling and searched for fans or some type of ventilation system. There were none. His gaze went to the area above the radio and he saw an old air conditioner mounted high on the wall. "Ho-ho!"

"What?"

"An air conditioner," Mark said, walking over to it. "Bugs love to grow in these damn things. Remember the bacteria that caused Legionnaires' disease?"

Joanna nodded. Even if Mark hadn't helped to break the case, she'd have remembered; any pathologist would. In 1976 an outbreak of pneumonia had occurred at a hotel during an American Legion convention in Philadelphia. Two hundred twenty-one people contracted pneumonia, and thirty-four died. The microorganism responsible was isolated from lung tissue at autopsy and subsequently found to be present in the cooling tower of the hotel where the Legionnaires were staying. It was believed that the bacteria moved from the cooling tower into the airstream that was then pumped into the individual rooms.

"They had an outbreak of Legionnaires' disease in Shanghai last month," Mark went on, now standing on a stool to get a better look at the air conditioner. The machine was old and rusty, its back held on by duct tape. "Forty people came down with it before we could track the source of the bacteria. It was in a water pump at one of the factories."

"Do you do a lot of work in China?"

"It depends," Mark said vaguely. "We have a large pharmaceutical plant outside Shanghai that we co-own with the Chinese."

"I thought you didn't like partners," Joanna said,

recalling the long talks they had when they were together at Hopkins.

"I don't. But the chance to get into China was irresistible."

"Because of the market size?"

"Over a billion potential customers," Mark said, nodding. "But there were even better reasons. You see, China has an incredible variety of plant life, and their knowledge of herbal medicine is the best in the world. They've been treating people with herbs for over three thousand years."

Joanna looked at him, puzzled. "You're interested in herbal medicine?"

"You bet I am." Mark stood on his tiptoes and examined the rear of the air conditioner. "Well, well! There's a nice little puddle of water on top of this machine. Bacteria love to grow in puddles that no one disturbs."

He reached for a small case and took out a miniature pipette and a test tube. Carefully he sucked up a sample from the puddle and placed it in the sterile tube.

"You're going to sell herbal medicine?" Joanna asked, wondering if Mark was now interested only in the money.

"That's right."

"Like in health food stores?"

"Like in pharmacies and drugstores," Mark said firmly.

He sighed to himself. Joanna's perception of herbal medicines was the one most commonly held, not only by the general population but even more by physicians. They thought of it as witchcraft or snake oil being sold from the back of a wagon.

"So you're interested in all sorts of new drugs?"

Mark nodded as he pried off the back of the air conditioner and peered inside. "But mainly antibiotics."

"Why so much emphasis on antibiotics?" Joanna asked. "I thought they were awfully expensive to develop."

"Tell me about it."

Mark reached inside the air conditioner and took another water specimen with his pipette. "In America it costs a hundred million dollars to discover and fully develop an antibiotic and then put it through the clinical tests that the FDA requires. That's *before* it ever gets to the marketplace and goes up against its competition."

"Risky," Joanna said, now realizing what a high-stakes gamble Mark was involved in. "And then you have to hope the bacteria don't become resistant to your new antibiotic."

Mark shivered to himself. "If that happens, you go belly up."

"Unless some bright member of the firm comes up with another wonderful antibiotic," Joanna said, then smiled. "Maybe one that's extracted from some Chinese herb."

"You never know," Mark said and smiled back. He climbed down from the stool. "Is there anything else you want to check?"

Joanna glanced around the cabin twice before she noticed the first-aid kit. She opened it and studied the contents. Bandages, tape, gauze, an antibacterial ointment, medicines. Aspirin. An outdated vial of tetracycline pills. And a small bottle of a red, syrupy medicine. Its label was almost worn off, but Joanna could see the word Elixophyllin. "Somebody is an asthmatic."

Mark leaned over her shoulder, his cheek almost touching hers. "Can you tell if the instructions on the label are for a child?"

Joanna shook her head and knew her hair brushed against Mark. She told herself to move away, but she didn't. Taking a deep breath, she prepared to turn and tell him that nothing was going to happen between them again, that there was no way—

"I've got to run over to the coroner's laboratory," Mark said, breaking into her thoughts. He stepped back and stripped off his latex gloves. "They're growing some bacteria from Jack Kincaid's blood that was taken at autopsy. They've having difficulty identifying one of the bugs."

"Do you think they've found the culprit?"

"I doubt it. From their description it sounds like a contaminant. But we'll see. Do you want to come along?"

"No, thanks. I think I'll go over the cabin again."

Joanna watched Mark leave, thinking that he still had his touch and style. And timing. He knew exactly when to come in and exactly when to leave. It was almost as if he could read your mind. So smooth and charming. And so easy to be with, she had to admit. But that didn't change anything. What had happened twelve years ago between them was ancient history. Time passed, people and things changed. There was no going back.

Joanna walked slowly around the cabin, head down. The floor was littered with pots and pans, an overturned dish here and there. At the highchair she stopped and again searched in vain for ducts or vents. Above was the ceiling, behind the chair a paneled wall. Could the child have been asleep, Joanna asked herself, its face down and covered? Then she waved off the question. That wouldn't have mattered. There was enough toxin in the air to kill a coastguardsman in less than two minutes. The toxin would have gotten to the child, regardless of how his head was positioned.

Another wave hit the side of the boat and rocked it. Joanna held on to the highchair which was bolted in place and waited for the motion to stop. She heard a soft rumbling sound and looked down. Two small plastic objects slid out from beneath the chair. She reached down and picked them up. One was colored blue, the other yellow. They were vials of medication fitted into inhaler devices used by asthmatics. The yellow vial was labeled Proventil, the blue one cromolyn.

The answer can't be this simple, Joanna thought. It just

can't. She quickly placed the inhalers in her purse and hurried out of the cabin.

Joanna tiptoed into Donnie Kincaid's room at Juneau General Hospital. Its walls were brightly decorated with big Disney characters. Mickey Mouse, Donald Duck, Snow White, Jiminy Cricket. All smiling, all happy.

"Something I can do for you?" a gruff voice asked.

Joanna turned as a big man stood up at the bedside. "I'm here to see Donnie."

"Who are you?"

"I'm Dr. Joanna Blalock from the coroner's office."

The man looked at her skeptically. "You got papers?"

"Not with me."

"Then come back when you do."

"If I have to come back again I'll bring a United States marshal with me."

The big man smiled thinly. "That doesn't scare me."

"The idea is not to scare you," Joanna said evenly. "The idea is to get your cooperation."

He glared down at Joanna. "I want to know what killed my brother and his wife."

"So do we." Joanna looked away, intimidated by the man's physical appearance. A. J. Kincaid was very big—at least six feet three—with a large head and a scraggly beard that covered most of his face.

"You're holding something back, aren't you?" Kincaid asked, watching her body language. "It was the goddamn government, wasn't it? What was it? A toxic dump? Some new type of goddamn weapon they were testing?"

"I don't know," Joanna said.

"Well, we'll find out in court. I'm going to sue the hell out of the Coast Guard and the federal government and find out how my brother died. And if the government is at fault, then little Donnie is going to end up with a lot of money."

"If you wish to sue, that's your business," Joanna said calmly. "My business is finding out why your brother and his wife died. And the little boy may help with that."

"How?"

"He was the only witness," Joanna explained. "I need to ask him some questions. Maybe he'll remember something."

Kincaid hesitated, not trusting the visitor.

"Is the little boy an asthmatic?" Joanna asked.

Kincaid nodded. "Bad."

"Did his parents have asthma?"

"No."

Donnie sat up in bed and began coughing and wheezing. He quickly reached for an inhaler and took a deep puff. The cough eased.

Kincaid lowered his voice. "He thinks his parents are visiting up in heaven. He doesn't need to know more now. Understood?"

"Understood."

"And if you ask a question I don't like, I'll throw your ass out."

Joanna looked up at the big man, still intimidated but not showing it. "Why don't you have a seat and let me do my work?"

Kincaid hesitated, then grudgingly stepped aside.

Donnie was sitting on the edge of the bed, his feet dangling down. He was an adorable little boy with golden hair and wide brown eyes.

"Hi," Joanna said. "My name is Joanna. What's yours?"

"Donnie."

Joanna pointed to the wall. "I like Jiminy Cricket. He's my favorite."

Donnie smiled. "My mom likes him too."

"Do you remember what happened to your mom on the boat?" Joanna asked softly. "Did she get sick?"

"She was cooking something and she laid down."

"Do you know what they were cooking?"

"Ice," Donnie said quietly.

Kincaid's ears perked up. "What did he say they were cooking?"

"Rice," Joanna said and reached in her purse for the two inhalers she'd found on the boat. She showed them to Donnie. "Do you use these?"

Donnie nodded.

"Every day?"

Donnie pointed to the vial of cromolyn. "I use that one three times a day."

"And this other one?"

"Only if it's real hard to breathe."

"Like just now, you mean?"

The boy nodded.

"Tell me, Donnie, the last time you were on the boat, did you use the yellow one there?"

"N-no. I was fine then."

"Thanks for talking with me," Joanna said, and ruffled the boy's hair. "I'll see you later."

Donnie smiled at her. "Bye."

Joanna nodded to A. J. Kincaid as she hurried from the room.

He called after her. "Did you find out anything important? Something I should know about?"

Joanna walked down the corridor with a bounce to her step. Now she knew why Donnie Kincaid had survived the toxin that killed his parents.

Nine

Colonel Guy Hawksworth was livid.

"What the hell do you mean, you can't locate that iceberg?" he roared.

The seaman first class was standing at attention. Above him on the wall of the control room was a giant video screen with a blue background and blinking white dots. "It just disappeared, sir," the young seaman said.

"You mean you lost it?"

"Yes, sir."

Hawksworth reached over to the console and pressed a button. A white outline of Icy Strait and Glacier Bay appeared on the screen. It was superimposed over the dots. He pushed another button and the dots were replaced by blinking numbers. "So twelve icebergs were tagged with electronic devices and now we can only see eleven on the screen. Why is that?"

"Two possibilities, sir," the seaman said briskly. "Either the tracking device failed and is not giving out a signal, or the iceberg came apart."

"If the iceberg came apart, the device would still be sending signals, wouldn't it?"

"Not if it came apart so as to crush the transmitter, sir."

Hawksworth nodded at the seaman's reasoning, but it didn't help solve the problem. "Keep looking for the damn thing."

"Yes, sir."

Hawksworth looked up at the video screen with its

blinking numbers. Eleven of twelve icebergs were accounted for, but it was the missing one that was the most important. Studies done on the samples taken from the tagged icebergs had clearly shown that it too contained the deadly toxin. "Son of a bitch," Hawksworth grumbled to himself, wondering how many more toxic icebergs were floating around out there and how many more people and animals they would kill before everything was said and done. Hawksworth counted the blinking numbers again. Iceberg eight was indisputably missing.

"We've got some numbers for you, Colonel," Ben Kagen called out from across the room.

Hawksworth walked over to a table where Kagen and Neiderman were busily punching data into two desktop computers. "Is the news good or bad?"

"Some of both," Kagen said, leaning back in a swivel chair that was bolted to the floor. "The good news is that the missing iceberg is not as large as we feared. Its top rose twelve feet above the surface. We know the shape of the iceberg from the photographs your men were wise enough to take, and from that our computer calculated the iceberg's visible mass. Since eight-ninths of an iceberg's mass is submerged, we calculate the iceberg to be, in broad terms, about three-quarters the size of the one we have aboard the *Global Explorer II*."

"That's not a lot of difference," Hawksworth said disappointedly. "What's the bad news?"

Neiderman cleared his throat. "The missing iceberg is even more toxic than the one we already have. Of course, we have to be careful when we base our findings on one small sample, but the toxin level in the piece of ice was quite high. On a per-weight basis, iceberg eight is twice as dangerous as the one we have."

"We've got to find that damn thing," Hawksworth growled, staring up at the video screen.

"So it seems we have two new problems," Kagen said thoughtfully. "One is to find the missing iceberg. And the second is what to do with it once we find it. You can't just blow it up. All that would accomplish would be to convert one large deadly iceberg into a thousand smaller ones."

"We'll cross that bridge when we get to it," Hawksworth said, but he already knew exactly what he'd do when the missing iceberg was found. He would give the order to melt down the iceberg now on board. All of its toxic contents would be removed and concentrated, and the leftover water discarded. That would make room for the new iceberg. But what if they pinpointed the glacier that was spawning the toxic icebergs? That would be a monumental problem.

"You know, Colonel," Kagen said, breaking into Hawksworth's thoughts, "the higher toxin level in that iceberg could work to our advantage."

"How so?"

"It means there's more of whatever produced it in there as well. We all believe that bacteria are the causative agent, so a lot more toxin means a lot more bacteria. And hopefully the greater amount of bacteria will allow us to grow it out."

"Good point," Hawksworth said, nodding. "By the way, I heard from Mark Alexander half an hour ago. He visited the coroner's laboratory in Juneau this afternoon. It seems there was some kind of microbe in Jack Kincaid's blood. But they are having trouble getting it to grow. It seems to replicate briefly, then dies."

Kagen leaned forward. "Can he obtain a sample of that blood?"

"He can, and he'll bring it aboard when he returns tomorrow."

"Why wait until tomorrow?" Kagen asked, and glanced at the wall clock. It was 4 P.M.

"There's a storm brewing outside," Hawksworth told him. "The crosswinds are too strong for a helicopter to land."

Neiderman asked, "Do we know what type of bacteria it is?"

"He didn't say," Hawksworth said curtly. "We'll know more tomorrow."

"Colonel!" the seaman at the console called out. "I just got a momentary signal from iceberg eight. It gave out two blips and disappeared again."

Hawksworth and Kagen hurried over and stared up at the screen. There were only eleven blinking dots.

"Could you get a fix on the blip?" Hawksworth asked.

"No, sir," the seaman replied. "It happened too fast. But it was in the northwest section."

"Christ," Hawksworth muttered to himself. In the northwest section was a wide channel that led from the bay to the open sea. "Do we have a film record of what just showed up on the video screen?"

"No, sir," the seaman said. "We have a recording device, but it wasn't activated."

"Then *activate* it."

Neiderman was looking up at the screen with the others, but his mind was elsewhere. He was thinking about the bacteria growing out in the coroner's laboratory. That was the causative agent. It had to be. Why else would it be present in the dead man's blood? Oh, yes, it had to be. And it was going to bring Neiderman millions and millions of dollars.

Let's see now, he thought excitedly, Mark would bring the microbe back to the ship and get the damn thing to grow. Then it would produce the toxin that Neiderman himself would test in the toxicology lab. That would be his best chance to obtain a sample of the microorganism. And by then they'd know the culture media the bacteria required to grow and replicate.

But then he would face his most difficult problems. Where does one hide bacteria that can kill an adult with a single whiff? And how could he get the specimen off the ship without anybody knowing it?

Neiderman reached for a candy bar and involuntarily unwrapped it, his mind concentrating.

"Is that it?" Hawksworth asked, pointing to the video screen.

"Yes, sir," the seaman said as a blip quickly disappeared from the screen. "Its position looks a little more northerly now."

"But it's unlikely to stay there," Kagen said. "That storm can push it anywhere. And that includes directly toward us."

"I don't give a damn about that," Hawksworth said hoarsely. "I just want the transmitter to work so we'll know precisely where the iceberg is."

"That's also unlikely," Kagen told him. "Those weak, erratic signals indicate that your transmitter is about to die out. The same thing happens to the transmitters aboard our satellites in space. They sputter and die."

Good, Neiderman was thinking. It would work to his advantage if the lost iceberg were never found. That way there would be a second, unaccounted-for source for the bacteria. So when the bacteria and toxin showed up in some foreign country, the federal authorities couldn't just point the finger of suspicion at those aboard the *Global Explorer II*. They'd have to consider that somehow someone got their hands on another toxic iceberg. Good. Things were falling into place.

Neiderman turned to his desktop computer and punched at the keys. A list of the twelve icebergs tested for the toxin appeared on the screen. Eleven were benign, one very toxic. The toxic iceberg was so loaded with toxin that five pounds of its melted ice could kill a quarter of a million mice. It was scary stuff, even for scientists accustomed to working with toxic materials.

Neiderman could still remember the outright fear everybody felt when the stupid marine dropped the ice specimen on the floor of the laboratory. Everything on the ship came to a standstill until Neiderman's tests showed that the ice was free of any toxin. Man, oh man, were they scared! Neiderman thought again about its value on the open market. Maybe two million was too low. Maybe he should ask for more.

There was a sharp knock on the door and a marine guard entered. He gave Hawksworth a smart salute. "Sir, the medic is here and would like a word with you."

"Send him in."

The marine signaled the medic into the control room. He was tall and lanky, in his late thirties, with fair skin and auburn hair. Above the breast pocket of his scrub top was stenciled the name HENDERSON.

"What is it, Henderson?" Hawksworth asked.

"Sir, one of the civilians came into the sickbay really ill."

"Who is it?"

"Mr. Bobby Shea, sir."

"Do you know what's wrong?"

"No, sir. He's got a high fever and he's having trouble breathing." Henderson paused, seeming to pick his next words carefully. "It could be some type of pneumonia."

"How did he get that?"

Henderson shrugged. "Maybe from going in and out of the refrigerated area where bodies are kept."

Kagen's eyes narrowed. "What does this man do?"

"He handles the bodies down in Pathology."

"Was he involved with the autopsy on the coast-guardsman?" Kagen asked at once.

"I guess," Henderson replied.

"Oh, God!" Kagen ran a hand nervously through his hair. "Do we have a doctor on board?"

Hawksworth shook his head. "Only Blalock and Alexander, and they're stuck in Juneau until the weather clears." He furrowed his brow in thought, trying to decide how to handle the situation until the doctors returned. Turning to the marine, Hawksworth said, "I want the sickbay quarantined and a guard posted outside the door. No one goes in or out except for medical personnel."

He took a deep breath and looked over at the medic. "Wear a mask and whatever else you need to protect yourself."

"Yes, sir."

As the marine and the medic left, Hawksworth took Kagen aside and asked, "Do you know anything about medicine, Professor Kagen?"

The astronomer slowly shook his head. "Nothing. Not even a little."

Ten

Joanna swirled the snifter of brandy and stared at the fireplace through it. It felt like déjà vu to her, everything happening again just as it had happened twelve years ago. She and Mark were sitting in front of a fire in a bar at a lovely lodge. Outside the weather was dreadful, the wind howling in the night.

"How did you find this place?" Joanna asked.

"I called our travel lady at my corporate headquarters in Boston," Mark said. "She's very good at finding places like this."

"She knows your tastes."

"That she does." Mark grinned. "It's one of the perks a CEO gets."

"I never figured you for the corporate type," Joanna said as rain splattered noisily against a big bay window. "I would think it too confining for you."

"To the contrary. I have more freedom now than I ever had in academia. It's academic medicine that has become so restricted and bogged down with rules and regulations. Its lost most of its luster and all of its fun."

Mark sipped his brandy. "Just to do research in academia has become a giant pain in the butt. The consent forms, the oversight committees, the interdepartmental bickering, the never-ending grant proposals. All of my time was being taken up by this nonsense, and I knew it was only going to get worse. So when the opportunity came to join a new pharmaceutical firm that I would control, I jumped at it. They made me CEO, gave me a huge chunk of stock, and turned me loose in the laboratory. Research suddenly became fun again. But, of course, the pressure to produce is always there. I have a board of directors and thousands of stockholders who demand higher and higher profits."

Joanna smiled to herself. She had a thousand shares of BioMega in her pension fund and the last time she looked it was trading at 28 ¹/₂. "You've done pretty well with Megamycin."

"It's been our biggest moneymaker." Mark signaled to the bartender for fresh drinks, thinking about the luck involved in the discovery of Megamycin. They were trying to synthesize a new antibiotic to destroy a drug-resistant strain of staphylococcus. The technician inadvertently overheated the flask during the final phase of the experiment. Instead of the temperature being thirty-two degrees Celsius, it was forty-two. The increased heat activated an enzyme system and the end result was Megamycin.

Mark turned back to Joanna. "But you can't rest on your laurels in this business. The field of antibiotics is fiercely competitive, and every drug you make has a limited time in the marketplace."

"Are you referring to patent rights?"

Mark nodded. Pharmaceutical houses were given seventeen-year patents on all new drugs they discovered. During that time no one else in the world could manufacture or distribute the drug.

"But even before the patent rights expire, one has problems," he said, his voice now more deliberate and businesslike. "Antibiotics similar to yours are introduced by other companies, and your market share begins to shrivel. Then you have to push more and more money into advertising to keep your sales from dropping further, and this eats into your profits. Believe me when I tell you that no company can depend on just one drug. The only way to stay alive in this business is to continue to come up with new and better products."

Joanna watched Mark's face as the waitress set their fresh drinks down. His expression was serious and focused, and she had the feeling he had something else to say.

Outside the storm raged. A sudden blast of wind and rain rattled the big window. The lights in the bar dimmed for a moment, then came back. It really was déjà vu, Joanna thought. The same thing had happened to them at the ski lodge in Vermont twelve years earlier. Except the lights stayed out and they had to use candles to find their way. "Maybe we should check and see if they have any candles."

"Remember that?" Mark smiled broadly, his mood suddenly lighter. "I went back there a few years ago. It's been modernized and has lost a lot of its charm. Its romance is long gone."

"Time changes everything," Joanna said quietly.

"Not everything," Mark said, looking into her eyes. "You're still the brightest woman I ever knew."

Joanna felt her face glowing. "You must have a limited number of female acquaintances."

Mark shook his head. "I know a lot of women, but they don't measure up to you. None of them even come close." He sipped his brandy, smiling again. "I couldn't help but chuckle when I read the newspaper accounts of how you caught that HMO doctor who was killing off his patients with ricin. What was his name?"

"Robert Mariner."

"I thought to myself, the poor bastard must have underestimated Joanna."

Joanna grinned. "Are you trying to charm me?"

"If you can't handle the truth, you just tell me and I'll stop."

The wind gusted again, blowing rain against the window. Mark waited for the noise to die down. "But the most impressive thing you did was to coauthor the book on forensic poisoning with Peter Allen Weir. It was a masterpiece."

"Have you read it?"

"Of course! I'll send you my copy so you can autograph it. Okay?"

Joanna tapped him on the arm. "Will you stop it?"

"No."

It was always the same way with Mark, Joanna thought. Warm and easy, yet still exciting. And what a brain he had! Nothing was too small to escape his attention; everything he read went into his steel-trap mind and stayed there. And he seemed to excel at everything. He had once told her that the reason he did things so well was that he carefully picked what he did. If he didn't do it well, he didn't do it at all.

"So you never married, huh?" Mark broke into her thoughts.

"No," Joanna said.

Mark touched her hand with a finger. "Someone as special as you must have had a dozen proposals."

"It just hasn't worked out for me," Joanna said softly, now thinking that she had great taste in men and terrible taste in potential marriage partners. She sighed to herself. "What about you?"

"I'm afraid you spoiled me," Mark said quietly. "I keep looking for someone like you."

"Come on," she said, not certain he was being serious. Then she studied his face and knew he was.

"No, really. You've got brains and beauty, and that's a hard combination to find."

"You're twelve years too late, Mark."

"Time hasn't changed us that much," he persisted gently. "And things between us haven't changed at all, have they?"

Joanna stared out into space, half wanting to say yes and half wanting to say no. "I keep remembering how you said goodbye to me. On the damn phone." She shivered to herself. "That was cold. So cold."

"And stupid too. It was the dumbest thing I ever did," Mark admitted. "But I never stopped thinking about you. I must have reached for the phone a hundred times."

"But you never called," Joanna said tonelessly. "Why was that so difficult to do?"

Mark shifted around in his chair. "I was out to conquer the world and I believed I could do it best alone. To be honest, I kept trying to push you out of my thoughts."

"Well, you did a pretty good job of it."

"Not really. You were always in my mind . . . and still are." Mark took her hands in his. "We were so damn good together. It was like magic at times."

Joanna looked over at the fireplace, its logs blazing and glowing bright red. They did have magic, particularly at first. It was hot and passionate and they couldn't get enough of each other. But the way he had left hurt so much. Jesus! She could still remember the pain.

"This is our chance, Joanna," Mark said, bringing her hands up to his lips. "The gods rarely give out second chances, but they're giving us one now."

Joanna felt herself being drawn closer and closer to Mark. Her knees were touching his under the table. Her brain told her legs to move away, but they stayed exactly where they were. "I don't think we can go back to the way we were."

"Why not?" Mark asked, his voice low and throaty.

"I just can't."

"Sure you can. Just turn off your brain and let your emotions fly on autopilot."

"The last time I did that I ended up paying a terrible price," Joanna said softly. "I'm not going to let that happen again."

"This time will be different," Mark promised her. "We'll never let go of each other."

Joanna stiffened in her chair for a moment. It really

was déjà vu. Mark had said the exact same thing twelve years ago in front of a blazing fire. *We'll never let go of each other.* And six months later he was gone and she was crying herself to sleep. "I've heard that before."

Mark leaned over and brushed his lips against hers. "We're perfect for each other. You know we are."

Joanna felt her breath coming faster, her heart pounding in her chest. Now he had his hands on her waist. "Mark, I—"

"And I want you more at this moment than I've ever wanted anyone."

"You're going too fast," she said, and gently pushed him away.

"It's the only speed I know," Mark said, his voice husky. "Let's get a bottle of Dom Pérignon and go upstairs."

Joanna was tempted, very tempted. But she just wasn't buying it. Not yet. Twelve years without a call or a letter. Nothing. And then suddenly this.

"I'm not going to rush in again, Mark," she said and stood.

Mark looked up at her. "What does that mean?"

"That means I'll see you tomorrow morning at breakfast."

Eleven

Hawksworth was waiting for the helicopter when it touched down on the *Global Explorer II*. As the noise from the rotors faded, he threw open the door and helped Joanna and Mark out. "We have to move quickly. I'm afraid he's dying."

They hurried across the deck to the bridge. The air was cold and damp, a brisk breeze blowing in from the north. Hawksworth looked back at the choppy sea and saw a Coast Guard vessel heading for a group of icebergs in the distance. The toxic iceberg still hadn't been located. Its transmitter had stopped sending signals altogether in the storm.

Inside, Hawksworth led the way past a marine guard and into a warm elevator. As the car slowly descended, Joanna unzipped her parka. "So the technician worked down in Pathology?"

"Correct," Hawksworth said. "But he always wore a mask and gloves when he handled tissue specimens."

"Of course," Joanna said, but she was thinking that all it took for bacteria to gain entrance into the body was a small cut or abrasion on any exposed area of skin.

Hawksworth turned to Mark. "We started the antibiotic you suggested on the phone, but unfortunately none was on board. We had to wait until the storm let up to fly it in."

Joanna glanced at Mark, then stared down at the floor.

She had learned of the technician's illness only on the helicopter flight from Juneau back to the ship. And she thought Mark had too. He hadn't mentioned the phone call he received from Hawksworth during the night. But then again, he hadn't said much of anything since Joanna rejected his advances. Too bad.

"He's receiving cefazolin, right?" Mark was asking Hawksworth.

"I think the antibiotic is called Ancef."

Mark nodded. "That's a trade name for cefazolin."

"It doesn't seem to be working."

Mark wondered why the technician's condition had deteriorated so rapidly. He'd sounded ill, but not desperately so, from the initial description Hawksworth had given him on the phone. The diagnosis of pneumonia seemed clear, and treating it should have been easy. But the only antibiotics they had aboard were penicillin, which wasn't working, and tetracycline, which was worthless against bacterial pneumonia. They had to wait four hours before they could fly in the Ancef. Maybe the delay in starting the appropriate antibiotic had allowed the infection to become more entrenched. Maybe that was why the patient was deteriorating.

The elevator jerked to a stop and the door opened. They walked down a long corridor and through an electronically controlled door that closed after them with a hissing sound. At the entrance to the sickbay they took off their parkas and fur-lined gloves. There was a sign taped to the wall.

QUARANTINE AREA
NO ADMITTANCE

They heard a gagging sound, like someone trying to cough or throw up. Quickly they put on masks and gloves and entered.

Joanna could tell at once that Bobby Shea was desperately ill. The young man's lips and fingertips were blue, and he was shaking uncontrollably under woolen blankets. An IV was running into his arm.

"He's really toxic," Joanna said. "How long has he been like this?"

"He was doing okay up until an hour ago," the medic Henderson said. "You know, talking and complaining about pain. Then he suddenly went bad."

Joanna glanced above the head of the bed, looking for a monitor. There wasn't any. "What's his blood pressure?"

"Sixty over forty," Henderson said, his eyes red from lack of sleep. "I tried to get it up by increasing the saline flow from his IV, but it didn't help."

"Bacteremic shock," Joanna said, feeling the patient's thready pulse. "Maybe he's infected with a gram-negative organism. Those are the bacteria most likely to cause shock, right?"

"Usually," Mark agreed. "But any type of overwhelming sepsis can do it."

He pulled the covers back and carefully examined the patient. He listened to the young man's chest and heard generalized wheezes and rhonchi, indicating the presence of a widespread pneumonia. Then he looked at Bobby Shea's face and noticed the severe acne. On his forehead was a draining, pus-filled carbuncle. Mark pointed to the infected area and glanced over at Joanna. "What do you think?"

Joanna studied the patient's face, quickly putting all the clinical clues together. "He probably touched an open pimple and got it infected. And now he's got a carbuncle that's loaded with bacterial organisms which have spread to his lungs."

Mark nodded as he envisioned abscesses forming throughout the patient's lungs. "And that bacterial organism is almost certainly a staphylococcus."

The patient stopped shaking for a moment, then started again. His chills were so hard his teeth were chattering.

Joanna said, "Maybe it's not staph. Maybe it's something else."

"Like what?" Mark asked.

Joanna shrugged. "Like any of a hundred bugs that might be lurking around this ship."

"Particularly down in Pathology," Henderson chimed in. "And the men who work there know it, too. Guys like Shea, who work around dead bodies, are really antsy. They run to the sickbay every time they sneeze."

Joanna jerked her head around. "This patient handled the body of the dead coastguardsman?"

Hawksworth nodded. "But he apparently wore protective garb, according to his colleagues."

"Jesus," Joanna groaned. "He could be infected with the microbe that produces the deadly toxin. And it could have gotten into his system through the acne on his forehead. That area wouldn't be covered by his cap or mask."

"That's possible," Mark agreed. "But chances are it's a staphylococcal bug that's doing the damage here. Almost all carbuncles are caused by staph."

"He could even be infected with both," Joanna said, thinking aloud. "Maybe the initial infection was caused by the staph, and that opened the way for the toxin-producing microbe."

A chill swept through the patient. He shook so violently that the bed shook with him.

As Mark was about to pull the covers back up, Joanna pointed to the patient's legs. They were covered with round, dime-sized hemorrhagic spots. Joanna pressed on the biggest spot and the patient moaned, quickly withdrawing his leg.

"His blood vessels are breaking down and he's bleeding into his skin. He's got septicemia," Mark said.

Joanna nodded. "We've got to get him to a hospital in Juneau as fast as possible."

"Can't he be treated here?" Hawksworth asked at once.

"Not a chance. He needs to be in an intensive care unit. You'd better get the helicopter ready."

Hawksworth hesitated. "Our helicopter is now on its way to Juneau for supplies."

"Then get it back here."

Hawksworth left the room, went to a wall phone, and slowly picked up the receiver. If the patient were admitted to a civilian hospital, he knew, questions would be asked and would have to be answered. It would be impossible to keep things under wraps. He thought about the military bases in Alaska that might have a hospital attached to them. There were none near Juneau. He brought the receiver to his ear and made the call.

Hawksworth returned to the sickroom, pulling his mask up over his nose. "They'll be back on the helipad in fifteen minutes."

Mark nodded as he again examined the patient, now feeling for cervical lymph nodes. "I'm almost certain this is a staph infection, and if that's the case Ancef should cover it."

"And what if he's infected with the toxin-producing microbe?" Joanna asked.

"Then all bets are off," Mark said somberly. "I'd have no idea what antibiotic to use."

Hawksworth seemed puzzled. "I'm not sure I follow you. If this man is infected with our strange bacteria, wouldn't its toxin have killed him by now?"

"Not necessarily," Joanna told him. "Bacteria may behave differently when injected into the body as compared to what they do in a test tube."

Hawksworth was still confused. "But shouldn't it still be producing its toxin?"

"Maybe it is," Mark said, reaching for a stethoscope and listening to the patient's lungs again.

Hawksworth scratched his head. "This is all beyond me."

Joanna explained, "Perhaps the toxin only causes a pneumonia when it reaches the lungs via the bloodstream rather than through an aerosol."

"Or maybe it's partially inactivated in the blood so that its effect is less toxic and, rather than kill outright, it causes inflammation." Mark looked over to the medic. "Have you taken a chest film?"

"Yes, sir."

Hawksworth waited for the medic to leave the sick-room, then asked Mark, "Were you able to identify the bacteria that the coroner found in Jack Kincaid's blood?"

Mark shook his head. "They could only grow out a few colonies, and those seemed to disappear in an hour or less. It's a very fastidious bug, and it doesn't grow in our routine culture media."

"Did you bring any back with you?"

"There wasn't anything to bring back. But I did get a sample of Jack Kincaid's blood."

The patient began babbling incoherently and groaning. Mark patted his shoulder and he quieted. "When are my technicians arriving?"

"This evening at the latest."

"Good. Let me tell you what we'll need." Mark held up his gloved hand and counted off the instructions on his fingers. "First, I want your personnel in the bacteriology lab out by early morning. They're moderately competent, but definitely not innovative. And that's what it's going to take to make this microbe grow."

"They will be reassigned elsewhere," Hawksworth said agreeably.

"Second, the entire lab will have to be scrubbed down and sanitized. My technicians will tell your men what to do and how to do it."

"Their orders will be followed to the letter."

"Finally, they'll be bringing a lot of boxes and crates on board."

Hawksworth's brow went up. "Containing what?"

"Plastic dishware, culture media, reagents, antisera, and a bunch of other things necessary to grow out and identify this microbe. They'll bring only the things I told them to bring."

"You told them? How did you manage that?"

"I phoned them from Juneau yesterday," Mark said matter-of-factly.

Hawksworth's face hardened. "All communications to the outside will go through this ship and only through this ship. Understood?"

"Right," Mark said, ignoring the reprimand. "Make sure your men don't go rummaging through the boxes and crates and contaminating everything."

Henderson returned with the chest X-ray: an anterior-posterior view of the thoracic cavity. He handed it to Mark. Holding it up to the light, Mark studied the film carefully. "He's got pneumonia everywhere."

Joanna looked up at it. "He's developing a whiteout too."

Mark nodded. A whiteout referred to a pneumonic process that was so thick and extensive that all areas of aeration disappeared from the X-ray. Everything inside the man's chest looked white, like a dense snowstorm. "His lungs are probably filled up with pus."

"Or blood," Joanna suggested. "He's bleeding into his skin. He may be bleeding into his lungs as well."

"A nightmare," Mark said, wondering if Joanna was right. If so, the patient was drowning in his own blood.

"Maybe cromolyn will help," Joanna suggested.

"Cromolyn?" Mark asked quizzically. "The stuff used for asthma?"

"Yes," Joanna told him, watching the patient gasp for air. "I think I found out why the little Kincaid boy survived the toxin. He's an asthmatic and uses a cromolyn inhaler three times a day. As you probably know, cromolyn acts by blocking the release of toxic mediators from mast cells present throughout the lung. At least, that's how it acts in asthma. So maybe, just maybe, the bacterial toxin from the melting ice did its killing by causing a massive release of noxious mediators from the pulmonary mast cells. If that's the case, then cromolyn saved the boy's life. And if those bacteria are now in our patient's lungs making their toxin, cromolyn could help and maybe buy us some time."

Bobby Shea suddenly gasped and coughed up a stream of red blood. He coughed weakly again. Then his head went back and he lay very still. His chest no longer moved.

Henderson reached down and felt for a carotid pulse. He tried again to find it, but couldn't. Reflexively, Henderson bent over to start mouth-to-mouth resuscitation, but Joanna grabbed his shoulder and pulled him away. "Don't!" she said.

"But he's—"

"Infectious," Joanna completed his sentence. "And that microbe can kill you just as fast as it killed him."

Henderson backed away from the bed and stepped around a small splatter of blood on the floor. He glanced around at the others, now noticing the gloves and masks they were wearing. Shit! He had forgotten to pull his mask up when he came back with the chest X-ray. He looked down at his gloveless hands and saw a few flecks of blood. "Should I—ah—take some antibiotics prophylactically?"

"Not unless you develop symptoms," Joanna advised.

Henderson nodded, but he wasn't going to wait for symptoms to show. Fuck that! He had a big stash of penicillin and tetracycline pills in the pharmacy. He'd take both of them. In large doses.

Twelve

"We got us a problem here," Reetha Sims said.
"Big-time," Doreen Sims agreed.

The Sims sisters were on the scaffolding, looking through the Plexiglas at the giant iceberg. They watched a robot arm move out to the iceberg and bite off a piece. Slowly the arm retracted and placed the sample of ice in a large plastic container. The floor opened and the container disappeared.

"There's a trapdoor apparatus next to the iceberg," Hawksworth explained. "Of course, it's remotely controlled."

"And probably crawling with bacteria," Reetha said.

"And what about the glove on that robot arm?" Doreen asked. "It's about as sterile as warm spit."

"You realize that the temperature within the cylinder is twenty degrees Fahrenheit," Hawksworth said.

Reetha shrugged. "So? Bacteria won't grow at twenty degrees, but that temperature sure as hell won't kill them."

"Yeah," Doreen said, now nibbling intently on a hangnail. "Those little bacteria just sit out there in the cold waiting for some sloppy technician to warm things up for them."

"We don't have sloppy technicians aboard the *Global Two*," Hawksworth said, an edge to his voice.

"Sure you do," Reetha said promptly. "If you didn't, we wouldn't be here. And to make matters worse they've been handling this bug like it's an ordinary strep or staph which it's not. I'm surprised they haven't gotten themselves injected. From here on, all cultures will be done by personnel wearing protective gear."

"And all culture plates will be sealed," Doreen added. "So that little bug won't go anywhere we don't want it to."

The Sims sisters were identical twins. They looked alike, talked alike, and even thought alike. At forty-five, the sisters were buxom and attractive with dark eyes, full lips, and flawless skin. But they had their differences. Reetha's hair was long and brunette, Doreen's short and streaked with blond. And Reetha was more open and extroverted, particularly around men. They both had master's degrees in microbiology and had worked at the CDC in Atlanta before joining Mark Alexander at BioMega.

Reetha leaned forward and stared down at the base of the cylinder, trying to locate the area where the container had been. "Tell me about the trapdoor. Where does it lead?"

"To a tunnel where there's a monorail that takes the specimen to a sealed room," Hawksworth said. "There the ice is melted down and tested."

"Do all the specimens come from the surface of the iceberg?"

"Some do. Others come from borings that go a foot or so into the iceberg."

Reetha's eyes narrowed. "Nothing deeper than that?"

"Not to my knowledge."

Reetha turned to Doreen. "What do you think?"

"I think the borings may hold the key."

"Yes, indeedy."

Hawksworth led the way down the steps, increasingly unhappy about bringing the Sims sisters aboard. They had the expertise he needed, but they were going to be trouble. Hawksworth felt that deep down in his bones. The security report on the sisters stated that they were bright and highly competent, but that they spent most of their after-work hours in bars and dance clubs drinking tequila shooters. And Hawksworth knew that drinkers talked too much to anyone who would listen. The sisters would have to be kept aboard ship until the ETOX mission was completed. There would be no shore leave for them, and all their phone calls would be screened.

At the bottom of the cylinder the scientific group was waiting. Hawksworth ushered the sisters forward. "I think you've met everyone except for Professor Kagen."

Ben Kagen bowed his head in courtly fashion as the introductions were made. "Ladies, it's a pleasure. Thank you for joining our team."

The sisters, charmed by Kagen's old-world manners, said in unison, "It's our pleasure."

"Doctor Alexander tells us you're the very best at finding and identifying strange bacteria."

"Well, let's hope we can live up to our billing," Doreen said.

"I'm sure you will."

Doreen ran a hand through her short blond hair, mussing it. Then she stroked it back into place.

Reetha smiled to herself. Doreen always did that when she was interested in some guy. It had to be Benjamin Kagen. Her sister liked the cerebral type. And this one was famous, too. They had watched Kagen on television a dozen times.

"Well, now," Reetha said, "let's begin with the borings taken from this iceberg. Do we know if the level of toxin increases as you go deeper into the iceberg?"

"I'm not sure," Kagen said, turning to Neiderman. "That would be Dr. Neiderman's area."

"Have those tests been done?" Reetha asked.

"No," Neiderman said. "But it shouldn't be any problem." His eyes fixed on the technician's bust. He was drawn to big women, particularly those with pretty faces. He gave her a half smile. "I'll run the tests tonight."

Reetha thought she saw Neiderman give her a quick wink along with his smile. She shivered to herself, hoping the guy with the double chin wasn't going to try to hit on her. Not in your wildest dreams, she wanted to tell him.

She refocused her mind and looked at Mark. "So, we've seen bacterial growth in the cultures from the dead coastguardsman and from Jack Kincaid's blood."

"Correct," Mark said, "but not our elusive bug."

Doreen asked, "What culture media did they use?"

Mark reached into his pocket for an index card. "Blood agar, MacConkey's, chocolate agar, and a thioglycolate broth."

Doreen sighed wearily. Most bacteria would have grown out on at least one of those media.

"That's a problem," Reetha said.

"Can it be solved?" Kagen asked, his concern showing.

"It's going to take a lot of work," Doreen said.

"And some luck," Reetha added. "It can be a real bitch finding the right culture medium."

"And an even bigger bitch if the right medium doesn't exist and we have to make up our own formula," Doreen said.

"Please keep in mind that you'll only be able to do a limited number of experiments," Mark warned them. "Jack Kincaid's blood may be the only source of this microorganism, and we have just five milliliters remaining. That's all that is left on the face of this earth."

Kagen asked, "What about the body of Bobby Shea? Shouldn't that be flooded with the offending organism?"

"It may be, but we'd have a lot of trouble growing it out," Joanna told him. "Remember, no cultures were taken before he was given large doses of a powerful antibiotic. That antibiotic is now in all of his bodily fluids and tissues. It's unlikely any microbe will grow out."

"Which antibiotic was used?" Reetha asked.

"Ancef," Joanna said. "And some penicillin before."

"Shit," Reetha grumbled, wondering what other obstacles awaited them.

"I'm afraid the tide is going against us," Kagen said dispiritedly. "We're going to need another source of the microorganism, and I'm not at all sure we can depend on the iceberg for it."

"Oh, it's in there," Mark assured him.

"I know that," Kagen said. "But if we can't grow it out from the ice, then for all intents and purposes it doesn't exist, does it?"

Kagen glanced around the group, seeking advice and suggestions. There was only silence. "Would an autopsy on Bobby Shea help?"

"Probably not," Joanna said at once. "But it will have to be done."

Mark looked at her in disbelief. "You'd be crazy to do an autopsy. One mistake and you could be dead."

"I'd be very careful," Joanna said, thinking about all the precautions that would be necessary. "The autopsy would have to be done in a sealed room. And I'd need a space suit." She turned to Hawksworth. "Do you have one aboard?"

"We do," Hawksworth said. "It's a self-contained unit with an oxygen pack attached at the back, identical to the ones used on space walks. Your air supply will last for one hour."

"That's enough time," Joanna said, though she knew it wasn't. The space suit would slow her down and make all movements cumbersome. She might have to limit the autopsy to the chest and abdomen.

"And what happens if there's a tear or leak in your space suit? What if you stick yourself?" Mark asked, his worry obvious. "There's too much risk here. Hell, we're not even sure it was the toxin-producing microbe that killed him."

"Chances are it was," Joanna said, touched by Mark's concern. "That's why the autopsy has to be done."

Kagen edged between them. "I think Mark is right, Joanna. It would be a terrible risk for you. I'm sorry I brought up the question of an autopsy. I can't expose you to that danger."

"Do you want to get to the bottom of this?" Joanna asked.

"Of course, but—"

"No buts," Joanna cut him off. "If you overlook evidence, you doom yourself to failure. For some strange reason, the thing you choose to overlook is the thing that matters the most. Let me give you a possible example. Within Bobby Shea's lung there may be a pocket of loculated fluid or pus containing the bacteria. And the antibiotic can't penetrate through the pus and fluid to kill it. One specimen from that walled-off pocket and we've got our bug." She turned to Mark. "Am I right or not?"

Mark nodded reluctantly. "She's right, of course. But I'm still against it."

Kagen walked over to the cylinder and stared in, trying to find an answer to his dilemma. He didn't want to risk Joanna's life. But this was not just some academic exercise. They might well be dealing with a microbe that had the potential and the power to cause an ecologic disaster of immense proportions.

Kagen took a deep breath and slowly turned to the group. "We will search for the organism in Jack Kincaid's blood and in the iceberg. If we fail to find the microbe in two days, I'll allow the autopsy to be done."

"I'm against it," Mark protested. "And I'm certain the others are too. I'll bet if we voted it would—"

Kagen held up his hand. "This isn't a democracy, Mark. I make all the scientific decisions based on my best judgment. They've given me that power for better or worse. And you're going to have to accept it."

Mark gestured lamely.

Doreen smiled to herself, watching Kagen take control. He was a small man, but he had a quiet force about him, something that told you not to push further. She liked that quality in a man. Without thinking, she began to muss her short blond hair.

"We should step up the iceberg studies, since we've got plenty of ice to fool around with," Doreen said. "How deep can we bore into the iceberg?"

Kagen deferred to Hawksworth, who said, "Six feet."

"Good," Doreen said approvingly. "I'd like to start with two core samples. One from the near side, one from the far side. Both six feet long, of course."

Hawksworth went to the phone on the console and called the instructions to the control room. He now realized that he had underestimated the Sims sisters, expecting them to be servile technicians who would only do what they were told. But they were clearly the creative, take-charge type.

Hawksworth rejoined the group and watched as a thick metal tube was guided by the robot arm to the surface of the iceberg. The tube began to rotate and slowly bore into the ice. It made a low grinding noise.

Mark moved close to Joanna and whispered, "If you get yourself killed, I'll never forgive you."

Damn him and his charm, Joanna thought. But she found herself smiling.

"We've never gone in this far before," Hawksworth said. "So we'll go slowly."

The tube penetrated deeper, now almost a third of the way in. Ice chips began to flake off and fall to the floor within the cylinder. A steamlike vapor came from the boring site.

"That's from heat generated by the friction of the metal tube against the ice," Hawksworth explained.

The boring stopped for a moment, then started again. Now the metal tube was rotating faster and faster. The steam vapor intensified and clouded the view of the iceberg.

Suddenly there was a loud cracking sound from within the cylinder. The drilling stopped once more, and the vapor slowly cleared.

"What was that?" Kagen asked nervously.

"I don't know," Hawksworth said, his gaze riveted on the metal tube penetrating the iceberg. "Perhaps the drill hit a weak—"

The cracking sound came again, louder this time. Then the iceberg seemed to groan as its front section began to move.

The scientists quickly backed away from the cylinder. Red lights above them started to blink. An ear-splitting siren went off.

The iceberg groaned again, and its front section abruptly broke away. It hit the floor with a loud thud and slid toward the Plexiglas cylinder.

Everyone froze for an instant, then dove under tables and consoles, covering their heads with their hands. There was another thud as the split-off section of the iceberg hit the Plexiglas. Then there was silence. Even the siren stopped.

The scientists got to their feet slowly. Then they looked at the cylinder. It had held. It was intact. Collectively they breathed a sigh of relief. The piece of ice that had split off was relatively small, no more than eight by eight feet. Anything bigger and they all knew it would have crashed through the Plexiglas and killed them.

Hawksworth moved in to inspect the cylinder more closely for cracks or leaks. His eyes suddenly narrowed. "What the hell is that?"

Everyone looked into the cylinder. Between the two sections of the iceberg was a foreign object. It was four feet tall, with a span of nearly two feet. It had a pale green color with blotches of brown here and there. On closer inspection they could now see it consisted of delicate green leaves coming off branches.

"It's a plant of some sort," Kagen said quietly. Then he asked the question they were all thinking. "Could it be sixty-five million years old?"

Thirteen

Ann Cormier had on her warm-up outfit, but she didn't feel like jogging around the deck of the *Global Explorer II*. The cold sore was bothering her more, and it seemed a little bigger than before. But at least the lesion was solitary and hadn't broken out in a crop the way her fever blisters usually did.

The day was chilly and heavily overcast, with a cold wind coming in from the north. Ann pulled the hood of her jacket up and began to walk. One turn around the ship, she told herself. Just to start the blood pumping and maybe get some of the loginess out of her legs.

Up ahead she saw Eddie Walsh and the medic Henderson leaning against a lifeboat that protected them from the wind. They waved to her and she walked over.

"It looks like we've got some weather coming in," Ann said cordially.

"Yeah, but it's supposed to be a quickie," Eddie said, then grinned. "You know, in and out."

Ann grinned back. "My favorite kind."

Henderson saw the two exchanging smiles but didn't make anything of it. He busied himself trying to light an unfiltered cigarette in the wind. On the third try he got it going. He inhaled deeply and looked over at Ann. "Any news on Bobby Shea?"

Ann shook her head. "Nothing so far. But they're planning to do an autopsy on him. Maybe that'll tell us why he died."

"Yeah, maybe." Henderson's mind flashed back to Bobby Shea's deathbed. He could still see the stream of blood spewing out of the boy's mouth.

Eddie looked at the others, puzzled. "I thought he died of blood poisoning."

"Well, let me tell you what the docs are really thinking," Henderson said and lowered his voice. "They think he caught something from that dead coastguardsman."

"Shi-i-t!" Eddie muttered under his breath, glad he didn't work in the morgue and gladder that he had no contact whatsoever with Bobby Shea. "What the hell could he have caught from the dead body?"

Henderson shrugged. "Whatever it is, it's in that damn iceberg below."

"Whoa!" Ann said, holding up a hand. "There's no evidence there's anything contagious in that iceberg."

"Oh yeah?" Henderson asked skeptically. "Then why is it kept in a sealed-off container? And why does anybody who goes near it have to wear a space suit?"

"It could just be a poison of some sort," Ann countered.

"Yeah," Eddie agreed. "A real nasty poison. That would explain it."

"Bullshit," Henderson scoffed. "The government doesn't spend millions and millions of dollars and bring out a big team of famous scientists for some damn poison. There's something contagious in that iceberg."

"You're guessing," Ann said.

"Am I?" Henderson smiled thinly. "Then tell me why they just brought two more bacteriologists on board."

"Jesus," Ann whispered softly. "When did they arrive?"

"Last night."

The wind suddenly gusted and swirled, now very cold. They turned their backs and huddled against the lifeboat, waiting for the wind to subside. Eddie felt Ann's shoulder against his, and he pressed closer to her, thinking about their rendezvous in the rec room. He wished he was with her again, just them, away from everybody.

God, she was beautiful! He still had trouble believing that she had picked him out from all the guys.

The wind died down, but the air was frigid.

Ann moved away from the lifeboat and said thoughtfully, "If they're bringing in more bacteriologists, they must know they're on the right track. Maybe they're getting close to solving the problem."

"Don't bet on it," Henderson said, taking a final drag on his cigarette before crushing it out on the deck. "I've been in this man's navy for seventeen years, and it's been my experience that when the big brass don't know what to do, they bring in more people to do it."

Eddie nodded at Henderson's assessment of the situation. He liked the medic. He admired the older man's wisdom and good common sense. "How long have you been out here?"

"This is my second tour."

Eddie asked, "When was the first?"

"Last year." Henderson told them about the dead whales and dolphins and seals. "But this time it's different. This time people are dying."

The wind gusted again and the others turned away, but Henderson stared straight ahead, thinking about his career in the navy. Seventeen years in, three to go. And this would be his last tour with ETOX. He didn't want to take any more unnecessary chances, and he sure as hell didn't want to get killed by some goddamn iceberg. All he wanted to do was put in his twenty years and retire to his small house in Norfolk, Virginia. He wondered if his ex-wife still lived in the area and what would happen if they accidentally ran into each other. Probably nothing. They hadn't spoken in years.

The wind quieted, but the temperature continued to drop and a light rain began to fall.

Ann glanced up at the darkening sky. "I think we're in for a hell of a storm."

"And I've got duty topside tonight," Eddie said unhappily.

"You be real careful up here," Ann told him.

Eddie smiled, liking the sound of her voice and touched by her concern. "I'll be fine," he said, and checked his watch. "Geez, I've got a squad meeting in five minutes. I've got to run."

"Yeah," Henderson said. "I got to go below too."

Ann watched them hurry away, then debated whether to continue on her walk. The air was so cold and the rain was coming down harder. It was only a matter of time before ice began to form, making the deck slippery and treacherous.

She was about to turn and go below when she heard the sound of an approaching helicopter. She looked up and searched the sky for the aircraft. Then she saw it hovering in the mist above the helipad. The wind began to swirl unpredictably, first one way, then another. There was no way they were going to land in this weather, Ann thought. It was way too dangerous. They'd have to fly back to shore. Abruptly the wind eased, now little more than a breeze. The helicopter rapidly descended and touched down, bouncing twice before settling on the deck. The sound of the rotors faded and died.

Ann watched as a marine guard ran up to the helicopter and threw open the door. A small woman, no more than five feet tall, was helped out and escorted across the deck.

The pilot climbed out of the helicopter and stretched his back while his crew brought out cables to anchor the aircraft. Ann studied Mike Mallory's face, thinking he had to be the most gorgeous man she'd ever seen. Damn! He probably knew it too. She waved to him and strolled over to the helipad. "That was an amazing landing."

"We got lucky," Mallory said matter-of-factly. "The wind calmed down just at the right time."

"And what if it had picked up again while you were descending?"

"That would have made it kind of interesting." Mallory smiled widely.

Ann stared at his even, pearl white teeth, wondering if he had any flaws anywhere. "You've got to take me up in this thing sometime."

Mallory took his gloves off and unconsciously played with his wedding band, twirling it around his finger. "You really want to go up, huh?"

"I sure do."

"We should probably start with me showing you the instrument panel."

"When?" Ann asked with a slow grin.

"Oh, some night when everything is nice and dark," Mallory said huskily. "Some night when the only light comes from the stars and moon above."

Ann wetted her lips. "You'll let me know when?"

"I'll let you know when."

Fourteen

"Olive or lemon peel?" the steward asked.

"Olives," Mark said. "Two."

He was standing at the bar in the civilian dining area. It was by far the plushest room aboard the *Global Explorer II*. The walls and bar were paneled in oak and the steel deck was covered with deep-pile wool carpeting. In the center of the room was a long polished dining table that could comfortably seat twelve.

"Two vodka martinis," the steward said and pushed the glasses forward. "Dry. Two olives."

"Thanks."

Mark went over to a couch against the wall and sat next to Joanna.

She looked at the size of the drink he handed her. "Wow! This is a monster."

Mark nodded. "The steward knows we're the only two doctors aboard this ship, and if someone becomes really ill we're the only ones who can look after them."

"Well, we didn't do such a great job with Bobby Shea."

"I doubt if anybody anywhere could have saved him." Mark sipped his martini, savoring its taste before swallowing. "I wish you'd think again about doing an autopsy on him."

"It's got to be done," Joanna said simply.

"It's dangerous as hell," Mark warned, "even with a space suit on." He turned to face Joanna. "A good friend

of mine at USAMRIID—a highly trained microbiologist—
was studying the Marberg virus. Now, this bug is every
bit as vicious as ebola. All work done on it is performed at
Level Four, which means extreme biohazard. It's like a
hot zone. Everybody down there wears a space suit. My
friend did, and he still got infected with the virus. To this
day they don't know how that virus got past all their barriers and killed my friend. So what I'm telling you is, we
don't know everything, and to believe we can protect you
with any degree of certainty is nonsense. You could be
taking a tremendous risk. You could be walking into a
hot zone."

"You might have told me that story at the time I volunteered," Joanna said quietly.

"Would it have mattered?"

Joanna thought for a moment. "Probably not."

"That's what I figured," Mark said. "You're bright and
you're brave, but you're also foolhardy."

Joanna smiled. "I like the bright and brave part better."

"You think that fits you, huh?"

"Oh, yeah," she said playfully.

Mark smiled back at her and had to resist the urge to
reach over and touch her. For a moment his mind went
back to Vermont and the feather bed they first made
love on.

He glanced at the door, hoping the others would be
late. Carefully he tried to choose the right words. "You
know, I meant every word I said to you the other night. I
really have missed you. The dumbest thing I ever did was
to leave you."

Joanna's face became serious. "Mark, you want me to
go back twelve years, and I can't do that. I'm not the
same person now I was then."

"Nor am I," Mark said earnestly. "But you're still
smart and sexy and wonderful. And we click when we're
together, and you know it."

Joanna looked away as she sipped her martini. Mark

was right: she did know it. Damn it! When they were together they were drawn to each other like the proverbial moths to a flame.

"Maybe I moved too fast when we were in Juneau," Mark went on. "But I wasn't just trying to hit on you. You matter a great deal to me, and I want us to be close again. We'd be stupid not to give it another try."

"You can't expect—"

Mark put a finger on her lips. "Don't answer now. Just think about it, and think about where you are in your life at this moment and what you want to do with the rest of it."

The door to the dining room opened. The Sims sisters walked in, followed by Kagen and Hawksworth. The steward behind the bar came to attention. Hawksworth waved him back at ease.

"Well, well," Kagen said happily, seeing Mark and Joanna with their drinks. "I see you've got a head start on us. But don't worry about it. We'll catch up." He turned to the Sims sisters. "Can I interest you ladies in a martini?"

"I guess I'll try one," Doreen said demurely.

"I'll have a double," Reetha said at once.

The steward looked at Hawksworth, who shook his head ever so slightly, declining a drink. Hawksworth didn't approve of alcohol aboard ship, and he particularly disliked it when the civilian scientists could drink and his men couldn't. But Kagen had strongly insisted and had even threatened to call a friend at the White House to get the matter squared away. Reluctantly Hawksworth had agreed, but with the proviso that drinks would be allowed only between six and eleven p.m.

As the martinis were being served, Neiderman entered the dining room and approached the group. "Sorry I'm late. I wanted to finish the experiments on the ice borings."

"What did you find?" Reetha asked.

"You were right. The deeper you go into the iceberg, the higher the concentration of toxin."

"That fits," Reetha said. "The closer you get to the vegetation, the more toxic the iceberg should be. It must be the microbe's food source."

Kagen swallowed his martini in a gulp. He sat back and grinned. "This is the best kind of science. A puzzle that consists of a circle within a circle. We're just going to have to continue peeling back the layers, aren't we?"

Hawksworth cleared his throat loudly. "Folks, let's keep our eyes on our mission here. There are only two questions we need to answer. What is the microorganism producing the toxin, and which antibiotics work best against it?"

"Assuming there is such an antibiotic," Mark said.

"Why wouldn't there be? There weren't any antibiotics back then for them to become resistant to," Hawksworth argued.

"Sure there were," Mark told him. "The first antibiotics were produced by fungi, not by some laboratory. Penicillin was discovered by Fleming when a mold accidentally fell into a culture plate of bacteria. The fungi grew and produced a substance that killed off the bacteria. Fleming isolated that substance and called it penicillin. No one knows why the penicillium fungi produce their antibiotic, although most believe it acts as a defense mechanism for them. In any event, I can assure you that fungi have existed for millions and millions of years and so has penicillin. So there's been plenty of time for bacteria to acquire resistance."

"But what about the newer antibiotics?" Hawksworth asked. "Certainly the bacteria can't be resistant to them."

"Oh no? What about Bobby Shea? We gave him large doses of cefazolin, which is one of the newer cephalosporins. It had absolutely no effect."

"Perhaps if we had started treatment earlier—"

"It might not have mattered a damn."

There was a long silence. Everyone was contemplating the nightmare of a pandemic caused by a microbe that was resistant to all antibiotics.

"That's very encouraging, Mark," Kagen said drolly, trying to lighten the mood. "Perhaps you'll share more of your optimism with us after dinner."

The group laughed nervously.

The door opened and a small woman entered the dining room. She was in her mid-forties, slender, with short brown hair that was softly swept back. Her eyes were dark and catlike. "I hope I'm not late."

"Not at all," Hawksworth said. "You're right on time, Dr. Van Buren."

Hawksworth introduced her to the group. She shook hands with each of them, repeating their names, asking them briefly about their specialties and where they were from. She spoke in an easy, informal manner, seeming disposed to like everyone she met. Until she got to Neiderman.

"How have you been, Malcolm?" Barbara Van Buren said, all warmth gone from her voice. She extended her hand and gave him the briefest of handshakes. "I understand we'll be working together."

"Yeah," Neiderman said unenthusiastically. This was the woman who had taken work that had been done collaboratively—some of it his—and claimed it for her own. And she had gotten away with it. "I can always use another set of hands."

Barbara Van Buren's face colored at the insult. He was going to treat her like a technician and he wanted everyone to know it. "Well, these hands come with a brain," she said tersely.

"How reassuring," Neiderman said, pleased that he had embarrassed her.

There was an awkward silence, everyone now aware of the tension between the two scientists. Neiderman and Van Buren stared at each other, neither backing down.

Hawksworth cleared his throat again and asked Van Buren, "May I offer you a drink?"

"A Manhattan, if you please, Colonel," she said, her voice softer as she looked away from Neiderman.

The steward mixed the drink quickly and brought it over on a tray. He waited for Van Buren to sample it.

"Wonderful," she pronounced, and grinned at the steward. "Don't stay too far away. I'm on empty and I may need a refill shortly."

Everyone smiled, the tension broken. Even Neiderman managed a crooked grin.

Van Buren moved over to Joanna. "Are you the Dr. Blalock who coauthored the textbook on poisons with Peter Allen Weir?"

Joanna nodded. "It's my only claim to fame."

"It's an important book," Van Buren said admiringly. "We all use it as a reference."

"You're too kind," Joanna said.

Van Buren turned to Hawksworth. "You seem to have a very impressive scientific team in place. I'm not sure how much I can add."

"A lot, we hope," Hawksworth said. "I think we shouldn't delay filling you in on the project. Professor Kagen will give you a broad outline. The others can supply the details."

Kagen signaled to the steward for another drink, then told about the Kincaids and the coastguardsman and Bobby Shea and how the toxic iceberg was related to their deaths. He described all the tests that had been done on the iceberg, and their failure thus far to determine the source of the toxin. "Everything indicated that the toxin is produced by a microbe. We just can't prove it."

Van Buren let the information sink in as she organized her thoughts. The toxin did sound bacterial in origin. But then, who knew what kinds of poisons were lurking around sixty-five million years ago?

"Has this toxin gotten into the food chain?" she asked.

"Maybe, maybe not." Kagen told of the marine-life disaster that had taken place a year earlier.

"And nothing was found to suggest there was a microbe at the bottom of it all?"

"Nothing," Kagen said, and looked at Mark. "Dr. Alexander headed up the bacteriology team on that mission. He can answer your question better than I."

Mark gestured with his hands. "There's not much to add. We studied whales, seals, sharks, dolphins, and everything else that died in those waters, and we never came up with a causative agent. All of the bacterial cultures were negative. We even looked for microbes with an electron microscope and couldn't find any."

"Are animals still dying out there?" Van Buren asked.

Mark shook his head. "The episode ended as mysteriously as it started."

Van Buren glanced at Kagen. "Sounds like a very big problem here."

"No one will argue with that," Kagen said as his martini arrived. "Can I get you another drink?"

"I'll coast until dinner," Van Buren said.

Hawksworth gestured to the steward, who headed for the galley and proceeded to ferry trays of salads and shrimp cocktails to the table.

The scientific team sorted itself into two groups. On one side of the table Joanna and Barbara Van Buren were seated between Mark and Hawksworth. On the other side Kagen was between Doreen and Reetha. Neiderman pulled up his chair and moved closer to Reetha.

The steward served a chardonnay as the group started their appetizers. They steered the conversation away from toxins and bacteria and antibiotics. Hawksworth now had their attention, describing an ETOX mission in which a suspected meteorite turned out to be a piece of a Russian satellite that had fallen from outer space.

Kagen tilted back in his chair, uninterested. He had been on that mission. It was a big dud. A nothing, hardly worth talking about. He leaned over to Doreen and spoke in a low voice. "Are you getting settled in all right?"

"Just fine," Doreen said. "I'm so excited to be here."

"We're delighted to have you with us."

Kagen picked up the scent of her perfume. Arpège. It had been his wife's favorite. His wife—alive and well one moment, dead the next from a cerebral hemorrhage. Ten years. It seemed longer than that.

"Your curriculum vitae is very impressive."

"Oh, it's not that great," she said, her face flushing.

"To the contrary. I particularly like the study in Guatemala where you had to track down the source of the dengue fever."

"Well, everyone knew it was transmitted by a mosquito," she said modestly. "But the important question was, where did the mosquito get the virus? We looked for the source and were lucky enough to trap a monkey that was carrying the dengue virus."

"So monkeys were the reservoir?"

"That's what we believed, but we could never really prove it."

Doreen nibbled on a shrimp and looked down at Kagen's ring finger. There was no ring or any sign that one had been worn recently.

"I don't understand how you could leave an exciting research position like you had at the CDC for a pharmaceutical laboratory."

Doreen gave the question some thought as she licked cocktail sauce from her thumb. "I guess I thought it was time to reinvent myself. I didn't want to keep doing the same thing over and over again for the rest of my life."

Kagen smiled. " 'Reinvent yourself,' huh? I like that."

The door to the galley swung open and the steward wheeled out a cart bearing plates of prime rib, baked potatoes, and asparagus with hollandaise sauce.

Reetha leaned back as a plate was set before her and removed her wine glass to be replaced by one containing a robust red. Her arm touched Neiderman's hand. He smiled at her and she smiled back lamely, seeing the red stain on his tie. Just my luck, she thought, to get stuck with the guy who drips cocktail sauce all over himself.

Out of the corner of her eye she watched Doreen and Kagen, still engaged in conversation, their chairs even closer together. For a moment Reetha felt a pang of jealousy, wishing she were close to someone she liked. But she quickly pushed her envy aside. *Good for you, sis! Go for it!* It was about time Doreen latched on to a good man. Reetha cut into her prime rib, thinking how strange it was that identical twins had such different tastes in men. Doreen went for the brainy type. Reetha preferred the rugged, outdoorsy kind. And if there were any of those at the table, Neiderman, still smiling at her, wasn't one of them.

Reetha looked across the table at Barbara Van Buren, who was now motioning to the steward for more wine. Reetha liked the woman, and she particularly liked the way Van Buren had stood up to Neiderman when he tried to bully her. "Dr. Van Buren, what's—"

"Barbara, please," she said pleasantly.

"Barbara," Reetha began again, "what's your major research interest?"

"Heavy metal poisoning," Barbara said, and watched Malcolm Neiderman stiffen. Such a horse's ass, she thought, always blaming others for his failures. They had once been collaborators on a study in which she did ninety percent of the work. And he resented the hell out of her taking ninety percent of the credit. Screw him!

"More recently I've been working on snake venom neurotoxins."

"I'm afraid that's not going to help us very much," Reetha said, decapitating another asparagus. "We've got a nasty little bug here and we just can't seem to grow it out."

"Maybe we could go after the microbe immunologically," Barbara suggested.

The table suddenly quieted, everybody's attention going to Barbara Van Buren.

Barbara organized her thoughts quickly, then said, "Let's say we take samples from the iceberg and inject them into experimental animals. If there are bacteria present, the animals will make antibodies against them. You can then take the antisera and test them against a broad range of different bacteria and see if the antibodies react with any of them. Maybe your bug is related to one of the known bacteria."

"It's a long shot," Reetha said slowly. "But it's worth a try. How do we do this immunization?"

"It has to be done by an expert—which I'm not," Barbara said. "But my husband is. He's an immunobacteriologist."

Kagen asked, "Is he at the University of Washington too?"

"He is, but he's not there now," Barbara told him. "He's in China tracking down the origin of the outbreak that's currently spreading across the western part of America."

"What outbreak?" Mark asked at once.

"There've been about a dozen cases of a very virulent infection that seems to have originated in China," Barbara said. "It looks like cholera but it's not. It's lethal as hell and doesn't respond to antibiotics."

"So it's a limited outbreak thus far," Mark said.

"Yes, but it's spreading," Barbara told him. "The initial cases were in Los Angeles, San Francisco, and Seattle. Now it's reached Salt Lake City."

Joanna remembered the beautiful Chinese baby she'd done an autopsy on just last week. The child had died from a choleralike illness despite being treated intensively. "Do you know anything about the cases in Los Angeles?"

"No," Barbara said. "But my husband would. As I told you, he's part of the team that's tracking the outbreak. He provided the antisera which they're using to detect the bacteria and its carriers."

Kagen rubbed his hands together, delighted he had invited Barbara Van Buren to join the team. She was going to be worth ten Malcolm Neidermans. "When is your husband expected to return?"

"Within a week."

"When he returns, I'd like you to contact him on our behalf," Kagen went on. "I hope he'll be kind enough to show us how to do the immunization."

"Oh, I'm sure he will," Barbara said. "And he'll be glad to send us a broad range of bacteria to test the antisera against. I'll ask him to include the strange choleralike organism as well."

"Excellent," Kagen said cheerfully. "Take as much space in the toxicology lab as you need. If additional equipment is required, let me know."

Neiderman was fuming, barely able to contain himself. Barbara Van Buren had just arrived and she was already taking over and pushing him aside. Next thing he knew, she'd have the whole goddamned lab and he'd be working for her. He wasn't going to allow that. No way! She wasn't going to fuck him over again—not with so much at stake. He had to keep control of the toxicology lab so he could have easy access to the toxin-producing microbe when it was finally isolated. And he wasn't going to let Barbara Van Buren or anybody else get in his way.

"Let's have more wine," Kagen called over to the steward.

"We have one more piece of business to talk about," Hawksworth said, reaching for the horseradish. "That's the matter of the vegetation we found in the iceberg. Have you decided what it is and how it might be related to the microbe?"

"We're not sure," Kagen told him. "It could represent the food source for the bacteria. It could conceivably contain something that is essential for the bacteria's growth."

"It could just be a red herring," Mark said. "The leaves of that damn thing are still green. That's not something you'd expect to find in a plant that's sixty-five million years old."

Hawksworth looked over at Kagen expectantly.

Kagen thought for a moment. "We need a paleontologist," he said, nodding to himself. "I think that would be our best bet."

Hawksworth raised his brow quizzically. "Any suggestions?"

"There is a marvelous paleontologist at Montana State," Kagen told him. "His name is Joe Wells and he knows plants. He'd be our man."

"I'll have him checked out," Hawksworth said and reached into his pocket for a pen.

"Once he's cleared, my advice would be to take multiple photographs of the plant and have them hand-delivered to Professor Wells."

"And who would you have deliver the photographs?" Hawksworth asked suspiciously.

"The man you trust the most," Kagen said simply.

"And who would that be?"

"Yourself."

There was a loud knock on the door. A marine guard entered.

"Yes?" Hawksworth snapped at the interruption.

"Sir, another piece of the iceberg has split off."

Hawksworth flinched, hoping the integrity of the Plexiglas cylinder hadn't been compromised. "And?"

"And, sir," the marine went on, "there's something else stuck in that iceberg and it's bigger than hell."

Fifteen

Everybody gathered to watch the autopsy from Neiderman's laboratory.

The body of Bobby Shea lay on a dissecting table in a sealed room visible through a picture window. In its own transparent compartment stood the giant plant, now nearly thawed out. It had been transported on the monorail from the iceberg's cylinder. Around the plant were puddles of water and cages containing mice and guinea pigs.

Mark had his nose practically against the Plexiglas window, staring at the corpse. Joanna was standing next to him. "I don't like this," he said, then wheeled around to Kagen. "Ben, will you talk some sense into this woman?"

Kagen remained quiet. They'd already had this discussion a dozen times.

Joanna was concerned but not showing it. "Pathologists deal with this problem every time they do an autopsy. One slip, one puncture, and you've got AIDS or some other infection that's a death sentence. So we learn to live with that danger and be very, very careful."

Doreen and Reetha watched Joanna leave, then exchanged glances, glad it wasn't them going into that sealed room. The sisters had seen too many people filled with bravado go into dangerous contagious areas and later wished to Christ they hadn't. Even experienced, careful people got killed. A year earlier the sisters had attended the funeral of a longtime friend who worked at the Pasteur Institute in Paris. The woman had died of Lassa fever despite taking every precaution. They still didn't know how she got infected with the lethal virus.

Doreen looked over at Ben Kagen. "Do they have a decontamination procedure if an accident occurs?"

"Some sort of spray," Kagen said absently.

The space suit was more cumbersome and heavier than Joanna had expected. She was bothered most by the oxygen pack on her back, which weighed at least twenty pounds. Inside the suit the temperature was a comfortable seventy-four degrees Fahrenheit, but it seemed warmer. Perspiration was forming on the back of her neck and dripping down her spine. She could hear herself breathing and feel her heart pounding away. *Handle the body like it has AIDS. Take your time, be careful, and get the hell out.*

Joanna raised her hands and signaled by making a circle in the air.

The door opened and Joanna entered the sealed room, feeling a strong pull from the negative pressure within. As the door closed, the light above it turned from red to green.

Joanna opened a drawer in the wall next to the table and removed two trays. The first contained instruments—forceps, hemostats, probes, a magnifying glass. The other was loaded with materials for bacterial culture. She placed the trays on a table, then moved to the body of Bobby Shea and quickly studied its external features. There was a venipuncture mark where he'd received his IV fluids, and crusted blood around his mouth and nostrils. From the knees down, his legs were covered with hemorrhagic spots. But the most striking feature was the young man's severe acne. It had cost him his life.

Joanna glanced at the wall clock. Four minutes gone. She'd better go straight into the chest. That's where the important findings would be, and that's where the bacteria would most likely be growing.

She reached for an electric saw that had a specially designed safeguard which protected her hands from the blade. Cautiously she sawed through the bony sternum and pulled the edges apart, exposing the contents of the thoracic cavity. There was dark unclotted blood everywhere. At least five hundred milliliters, Joanna estimated. Using a suction tube, she removed the blood and cleared her field of vision.

"What do you see, Joanna?" Mark asked over the intercom.

"There's a lot of hemorrhaging, much more than you'd expect in a case of pneumonia."

"What about inflammation?"

"Some," she said, separating the lungs with a dull probe. "I see some small abscesses near the mediastinum, but there's not much pus."

"There should be," Mark said. "His lungs should be filled with it."

"Well, they're not."

"Christ," he said sourly. "No answers and more riddles."

Joanna repositioned herself so that the bright overhead lights shone down directly into the chest cavity. The visor in the space suit was made of black-colored plastic, but her vision was excellent through it and there was absolutely no glare. "There's a great deal of hemorrhaging into the lung tissue itself," she said. "More on the left than the right."

Joanna reached in deeper and pushed the heart aside. She felt something snagging at the sleeve of her space suit and was about to pull her arm away. Then she abruptly froze. The sleeve was hung up on a jagged projection of bone near the top of the sternum. Carefully she moved her arm back and it came free. She studied the sleeve, looking for a break or tear in the material.

"What's wrong?" Kagen asked, concerned.

"Nothing," Joanna said calmly, but her heart was pounding away.

She went back to the lungs, avoiding the sharp edges of the split-open sternum. At the periphery of the lower lobes she saw small blisters on the surface of the lung. "I think our bug is a gas former," Joanna said. "I see some bulbous lesions on the left lower lobe."

"Let's culture those," Mark said at once. "That's where the bacteria will be."

Joanna punctured a bulb and scooped out the necrotic material, placing it in small vials. She took multiple cultures from the area, then reexamined the lungs. On the outer surface of the lower lobe was a very large blisterlike lesion. It was so puffed out that the tissue over it seemed almost transparent. Using a probe, Joanna burst the blister. She held an opened vial over it to catch the blister's vaporous discharge, then quickly capped the vial.

"I've got some of the gas in this vial," Joanna said, and held it up for the others to see.

Everyone leaned forward, wondering if the vial contained the deadly toxin.

"Good work," Kagen said. "But once we get it out of the sealed room, won't it be even trickier to handle than the cultures you've taken?"

"I had something else in mind," Joanna said, and gestured toward the cages that contained the experimental animals. Crossing the sealed room to the compartment that held the thawing plant, she detached a cage containing a guinea pig and carried it back to the autopsy table. There she scooped up the furry creature with one hand, positioned the vial of gaseous discharge in front of its nose, and worked the cap loose. The animal rubbed at its nose with its paws, obviously bothered by the fumes.

Then it began to suck for air. It took less than twenty seconds for the guinea pig to die.

Joanna held the dead animal up. "Now we know for sure that Bobby Shea was infected with the toxin-producing microbe."

Sixteen

"What branch of the service are you in, Colonel?" Joe Wells asked.

"The marines," Hawksworth said.

"Semper fi," Wells said, identifying himself as a former marine. *Semper fidelis* was the motto of the United States Marine Corps.

"Where did you serve?"

"Nam," Wells said tonelessly. "I got half my ass shot off over there."

"Oh?"

"I was running away. Thought I could make it."

Hawksworth gave Wells a long look. The paleontologist didn't look the type of man who ran away from anything. Wells was six-three and barrel-chested with broad shoulders. His face was tanned and lined from too much sun. "You were running away from the enemy?"

"Hell, yes," Wells said easily. "They had us outnumbered four to one. I was trying to get to high ground."

"Did you?"

"Yeah. And somehow we fought our way out of there." Wells's mind drifted back to the firefight. All hell had broken loose and his platoon was caught in an exposed position. Six of his men were killed. All boys. All so young. And the dead Viet Cong were even younger. No one won that battle, he thought sadly, and no one won that war, either.

He waved the memory away. "Well, you didn't come here to talk about Vietnam, did you, Colonel?"

"No. I need your expertise as a paleontologist."

"Then let's get to it." Wells pointed to a well-worn leather armchair. "Have a seat."

Hawksworth picked up a wooden model of a strange-looking creature that was on the chair. It appeared to be a toy.

"I'll take that," Wells said, reaching over.

As Hawksworth sat down, he glanced around Wells's office. It was small and cluttered with books and journals and papers. On the wall were pictures of prehistoric animals and fossils and one very large photo of a group standing around a huge skull that Hawksworth couldn't identify.

Wells sat back and studied the wooden model for a moment. Then he glanced over at a bay window that overlooked the rolling landscape at Montana State University. "Do you know anything about birds?"

"Not much." Hawksworth stole a quick peek at the wall clock. It was already 11 A.M. He'd have to hurry if he expected to touch down in Juneau before dark.

"The one you almost sat on is supposedly one hundred and fifty million years old."

"Around the time of the dinosaurs, right?"

"Yeah," Wells said, surprised that a marine colonel would know anything about prehistoric creatures. "It lived during the mid-Jurassic period. Most people believe it's the oldest bird ever found." Wells held the model up to the light and turned it so Hawksworth could get a good view. "It's a bizarre-looking thing, isn't it?"

"It's unlike any bird I've ever seen."

"That's because it's half bird and half reptile," Wells explained. "As you can see, it's about the size of a crow, and it's got wings and feathers. But it also had a reptile-type tail, claws on its wings, and teeth. Hell of a mixture, huh?"

"Indeed," Hawksworth said, now interested despite himself. "And you know all of these things just from fossils?"

"And some guesswork."

"Some very plausible guesswork," Hawksworth said admiringly. "That bird looks very real."

"Doesn't it, though?" Wells moved the wooden bird through the air like a boy playing with a model airplane. "From the shape of its wings, I'd say it couldn't fly very well. But I suspect it was a damn good glider."

"Why the claws on the wings?"

"To climb trees, probably." Wells pointed with his thumb to a large picture on the wall behind him. It showed the birdlike creature flying over a forest with tall palm trees and dense vegetation. "That's a pretty good depiction of what archaeopteryx looked like in its natural habitat."

Hawksworth studied the picture, paying particular attention to the trees and dense foliage. "It lived in a jungle?"

Wells nodded. "Swamps and deltas lined the seacoasts back then. Most of Europe was very similar to the present-day wetlands of Louisiana. So was most of North America for that matter."

"The trees and plants grew that abundantly?"

"Better then than now," Wells said. "But of course most of the plant life in that picture became extinct after the big boom."

"What big boom?"

"About sixty-five million years ago a giant asteroid slammed into the earth and killed just about every living thing."

"Plants as well as animals?"

"Oh, yeah."

Hawksworth picked up his briefcase and opened it. "I understand you're an expert in prehistoric plants. Is that correct?"

Wells shrugged. "I was a botanist before I became a paleontologist. I guess that gives me a little more insight than most."

Hawksworth took out a large manila envelope. "Professor Wells, I'm going to show you a set of photographs. We took multiple views of a very unusual plant. I would like your thoughts on it."

Hawksworth handed Wells the color photographs of the fern.

Wells studied the photographs carefully. Then he went over them with a magnifying glass, noting in particular the small, delicate leaves and drooping branches. "Nice," he said, unimpressed.

"What do the photographs tell you?"

"That you've recently been to the wetlands of Brazil or Colombia," Wells said and put the photos down on his desk. "That's the only place you find this kind of fern. It's called *Serenna veriformans*."

"I have not been to Brazil or Colombia," Hawksworth told him. "This plant comes from Alaska."

"Impossible," Wells said at once. "Unless you go back a hundred million years ago when the weather in Alaska was moist and mild. Back then the ground was literally covered with this type of fern."

"Suppose I told you we found this plant frozen away in an iceberg off Alaska?"

Wells leaned forward, his ears pricked. "Any chance this could be a hoax?"

"None," Hawksworth assured him. "The fern was frozen in the middle of an iceberg that happened to split apart."

Wells licked at his lips, his eyes never leaving Hawksworth. "Is there any way to date this ice?"

Hawksworth nodded. "It's loaded with iridium. Our scientists believe it to be sixty-five million years old."

"Oh my God!" Wells snatched the photos up and studied them again, then again. "No question about it. It's *Serenna veriformans*."

He put the photographs down and stared across at Hawksworth. "What else is inside that iceberg?"

"Something big and gray and indistinct."

"Do you have any idea what it is?"

"That's what we're in the process of finding out. Unfortunately, we don't have a paleontologist on our team." Hawksworth paused and watched the glow in Joe Wells's eyes. He smiled thinly. "Would you be interested in assisting us?"

Wells reached for the phone. "I can be packed in ten minutes."

Seventeen

Barbara Van Buren detested Malcolm Neiderman more with each passing moment. All afternoon he had been giving her the silent treatment, ignoring her questions altogether or answering them with unintelligible grunts. He was going out of his way to make things difficult for her.

She opened a giant freezer and looked inside. "Are all specimens kept in here?"

"Shut that door," Neiderman blurted out. "Open it only when you have to take something out."

"How do I know what's in there?"

"Try looking at the logbook on top of the freezer," Neiderman muttered under his breath and went back to adjusting the setting on the ultracentrifuge machine.

At four feet eleven, she had to stand on her tiptoes to reach the logbook. In it were listed all the contents of the freezer. The handwriting was messy, some of the pages stained and soiled. Just like Neiderman, she thought. Sloppy, deep-down sloppy.

By nature, Barbara Van Buren was neat and couldn't stand for things to be out of order. To her, Neiderman's lab was a disaster. Drawers and cabinets weren't labeled. Glassware and equipment was strewn about the countertops in a random and disorganized fashion. Even the furniture was in disarray. A metal stool stood atop the desk, the desk chair nowhere to be found.

"I can't work in this mess," Barbara said, exasperated.

"Too bad," Neiderman said, not bothering to look up.

Barbara quickly estimated the dimensions of the laboratory. It was large, at least forty by twenty feet. "Let's divide the lab in two. You'll have your section and I'll have mine."

"Get lost!" Neiderman snapped. "This is my lab and you'll take what I give you."

She clenched her fists tightly, trying to control her temper. "Well, I'll have a little chat with Colonel Hawksworth and see if he can change your mind."

"You do that," Neiderman said, unmoved. "Maybe he'll give you your own lab."

"Maybe he will."

But Barbara really didn't want that. If she were given a new lab, it would take at least a week to get it equipped properly. And during that time she'd have to beg Neiderman to let her use the sophisticated equipment in his lab. "Or maybe he'll just give me a big chunk of your laboratory space."

Neiderman stiffened, hating the small woman as much as one person can hate another. "You do what you have to do. But don't think I'm going to let you take over my lab or any part of it."

"I don't think you'll have much say in the matter," Barbara said evenly. "We're going after the bacteria using my husband's immunologic methods. I feel confident that Hawksworth will give me as much space as I need."

"Fuck you," Neiderman mumbled under his breath, glaring at her and knowing she was right.

"Not in your wildest dreams."

Barbara glanced through the window into the sealed room. The body of Bobby Shea was gone, but the giant fern was still there in its puddle of water. Lord! How lucky she was to be part of this project. A prehistoric microbe that was killing people sixty-five million years later. It was like the best science fiction. Barbara would have done anything to be involved in the project, including putting up with a rude pain-in-the-butt like Malcolm Neiderman. She was even willing to be away from her husband for weeks and weeks, and that was the most difficult thing of all.

Barbara leaned against the countertop and thought about her husband. Jonathan Moore was a lithe, handsome man with short gray hair and a quick wit. She had met him at a faculty dinner last year and had fallen madly in love with him. Just like that. And within two months, Barbara Van Buren, who at forty-five was certain she'd spend the rest of her life alone, got married to the perfect man. He was kind and sexy and bright, and her intelligence didn't threaten him, not even a little. While she was traveling around the country giving lectures and being feted at scientific meetings, he was delighted she was in the spotlight. He was happy for her and wanted to hear the details of her travels. But now his time had come. Now he was on the road, excited to be part of a team that was tracking down the origin of an epidemic brewing in China. Good for him, she thought, wondering if he missed her as much as she was missing him.

There was a brief knock on the door. Barbara looked up as Joanna and Mark entered and hurried over to Neiderman.

"When I first got here I gave you some specimens to study," Joanna said to Neiderman. "One of them was labeled Tg-Bx. Do you still have it?"

"Yeah, I guess," Neiderman said. "What does Tg-Bx stand for?"

"Biopsy of the tongue," Joanna told him. "It came from the coastguardsman I did the autopsy on. We think it contains the bacteria we've been searching for."

Neiderman's eyes widened. "You've found the bug?"

"Maybe, maybe not," Mark said. "The organism we're growing only stays alive for an hour or so, then it dies."

"What type of bacteria is it?" Neiderman asked.

Mark shrugged. "It looks like a gram-negative bacillus, but we can't be sure. It dies off too quickly."

"But you think it's the bug, right?" Neiderman rubbed his hands together, thinking that for once luck was going his way.

"It could well be," Joanna said. "But we need more of the tongue biopsy to do further studies."

Neiderman smiled to himself. Things were getting better and better by the minute. "Let me check my logbook."

Neiderman opened the book and began to scan the pages. He knew exactly where the tongue biopsy was listed, but he decided to let the others wait while he formulated his plans. Neiderman had the habit of dividing all specimens he received into two and freezing the portions away in separate containers. And he distinctly remembered doing this with all the autopsy specimens.

Perfect, he thought, trying to keep his expression even. He would give one sample to them and hold the other for himself. Then he'd wait while the others learned about the factors and conditions the bacteria required to stay alive. This information would be vital in helping him carry the bacteria off the ship once the ETOX mission was over.

Out of the corner of his eye he saw Barbara Van Buren walking over to Joanna. To hell with her, he grumbled to himself, and went back to turning pages in the logbook.

"I thought the coastguardsman was killed by the toxin," Barbara said. "I didn't know he was infected with the bacteria."

"I didn't either." Joanna shivered to herself as she recalled doing the autopsy on the coastguardsman while wearing only gloves and a mask. One small slip and she could have gotten infected with a lethal organism. "But the bacteria appear to be growing out of his tongue."

"And not from any of his other tissues?"

"Not so far."

Barbara scratched at the back of her neck. "What's so special about a tongue? Why would bacteria prefer to grow there?"

"I don't know, but it's a damn good question." Joanna looked at Mark. "Have you got any ideas?"

"None," Mark said, and began to pace around the room. "But there's got to be a reason for it."

Joanna closed her eyes and tried to think. "Maybe the coastguardsman tasted the ice in the cabin."

Mark stopped pacing. "Why would he do that?"

"To determine what the multicolored ice really was." Joanna imagined the coastguardsman tasting the ice, his head close to the stove where the concentration of toxic vapor was the highest. Then he'd begin to choke and gasp for air. He'd run up to the deck and die.

Joanna's eyes opened. "I think that's how it happened."

"It fits," Mark agreed. "Particularly if he had a little cut or abrasion on his tongue to begin with."

Joanna said, "We were so stupid to believe that only the toxin and not the bacteria were in the outer layers of that iceberg. Of course the microbe was there. We just didn't know how to get it out. And still don't."

"But we're getting closer," Mark added.

"And keep in mind we won't need many of the bacteria to immunize animals using my husband's technique," Barbara told them. "Once we raise an antiserum to this microbe, it'll be easier to characterize it."

Joanna nodded. "By the time your husband returns from China, maybe we'll have enough bacteria to work with."

"Here it is!" Neiderman called out, trying to sound excited. "It's specimen number eighty-four."

"Can you get it for us?" Joanna asked.

"It'll take a while to dig it out," Neiderman said.

"How long?"

"A half hour or so."

"As soon as you find it, give us a buzz," Joanna said. "We'll be in Mark's lab."

Neiderman watched them leave, then opened the giant freezer and began rummaging. He knew exactly where it was located, but he would take his time finding it.

"I can give you a hand," Barbara offered.

"You'd only be in the way," Neiderman said curtly. "And don't touch anything I pull out."

Barbara took a deep breath, trying to ignore his rudeness. She now realized there was no way she could work with Malcolm Neiderman. Either she would have her own fully equipped lab or she would leave. Hawksworth could make the choice.

She moved over to the countertop where Neiderman had left the logbook open. His handwriting was a scribble, but she could read most of it. "Why is the tongue biopsy listed as A and B? Are there two biopsies?"

Goddamn her nosy ass! Neiderman seethed as he tried to think of a quick answer. "There were probably two pieces of tissue. But they were frozen together in a single container."

"I see," Barbara said. But she really didn't. Most scientists would have frozen the two pieces in separate containers. That would be the smart move, just in case one of the specimens got lost or became contaminated. That's how most scientists would think. But then again, she reminded herself, she was dealing with Malcolm Neiderman.

Neiderman could see the suspicion in her eyes. She wasn't buying his answer, he thought. And she was the type who liked to stick her nose in places it didn't belong. She might even decide to go through the freezer. He would have to relabel the second Tg-Bx specimen when no one was around.

"Well, I've got better things to do than watch you rummage through a disorganized freezer," Barbara said.

"Then go do them," Neiderman growled. "And stay the hell out of my way."

Barbara stared at him, stung again by his rudeness. She hurried from the room before saying something she'd regret.

It was early evening when Barbara returned to the toxicology laboratory. She had decided to have it out with Neiderman once and for all. She would take over one half of the lab and do her studies separately and away from him. The colonel had offered her as much space as she needed. She would now take him up on his offer.

The lab was even more of a mess than before. He was such a pig, she thought, wondering if she should try to tidy things up. To hell with it! She'd clean up her half of the lab. Neiderman could work in his own sty if he wished.

She began stepping off the length of the room. It was just over forty feet long, with the freezer marking the halfway point. She decided to take the portion of the lab nearest the sealed room.

Barbara cleared the countertops of soiled glassware and used test tubes, dumping everything into a large sink. Then she poured in a strong detergent and let the water run. Next she went to the drawers and emptied them before rearranging their contents.

Neiderman was going to blow his top, she thought mischievously, when he found half of his lab gone. He would rant and rave, knowing there wasn't a damn thing he could do about it. And of course she would outperform him and that would make him even madder. She grinned, now eyeing the cabinets that were attached high up on the walls. They were at least six feet off the floor. There was no way she could reach them.

Barbara saw a small metal stepladder in the far corner and dragged it over to her side of the laboratory. Placing it against the wall, she kicked off her shoes and climbed up.

Behind her she heard the door open. It must be Neiderman. Screw him! Let him scream and holler. It wouldn't change a damn thing. She opened the cabinet and looked in. It was filled with brand-new beakers and flasks and test tubes. She removed a rack of test tubes and started down the ladder.

Suddenly she was falling backwards, pulled by a force she couldn't see. Her body slammed into the rock-hard floor. It knocked the breath from her lungs and she heard herself gasping. For a brief moment she saw a man's arm reaching down for her. He grabbed her hair and began banging her head against the steel floor again and again. The pain was excruciating, and she tried to scream but couldn't get any air.

Then she heard a loud crunching sound and felt nothing.

Eighteen

Hawksworth glanced around the large conference table. One chair was empty. "Has anyone seen Barbara Van Buren?"

"She left the dining room about an hour ago," Joanna said.

"Has anyone seen her since then?" Hawksworth asked, and got no response.

He picked up the phone and instructed a marine guard to find Barbara Van Buren and escort her to the meeting. Stifling a yawn, he decided not to wait for her. It was late and he and the others were tired. If Van Buren missed anything important, she'd have to learn about it another time.

He looked over at Joe Wells. "Dr. Wells, you can start whenever you like."

Wells was at the head of the conference table, adjusting the lens on a projector. "Give me a moment, folks, and we'll begin."

At the other end of the table Reetha leaned over to Doreen and whispered softly, "He's not bad, huh?"

"Yeah," Doreen whispered back. "But he's not your type."

"Why not?"

"Because I think he's got a brain."

Reetha gave her sister a gentle elbow in the side and chuckled, her eyes still on Joe Wells. She tried to see if he was wearing a wedding band, but he was too far away.

"All set," Wells said, sipping coffee from a styrofoam cup. "Folks, I'm going to take you on an incredible journey. It's going to be the damnedest trip you ever took. Now this isn't a lecture. It's what I like to call an informational conversation. So feel free to break in and ask questions whenever you want."

The lights in the room dimmed and the first slide was projected onto a big screen. It showed the sky, blue with occasional puffs of white cloud.

"Sixty-five million years ago, in the Cretaceous period, the sky appeared pretty much as it does today. Nice and blue, with clouds here and there. Then something terrible happened. An asteroid eight miles in diameter slammed into the earth at an incredible speed. It hit with so much force that it created more destructive energy than a billion tons of TNT. That's a destructive force greater than that which would be produced if we exploded all the nuclear bombs now in existence at the exact same moment. The effect of this collision was global and catastrophic. In an instant, day turned to night. Huge amounts of dirt and debris flew up into the atmosphere. The sulfur-rich dust actually caught on fire."

Another slide came onto the screen. It showed a sky filled with black smoke and flames. "The sun was totally blocked out. The temperature began dropping, and it went on dropping for months and months, if not years. This event was far and away the single greatest calamity ever in the history of the earth. And it changed everything forever."

"Is there any proof this actually happened?" Neiderman asked, a hint of derision in his voice. "Any real proof?"

"You're a scientist," Wells said affably. "Tell me what proof you'd need to believe this event occurred."

"Well, a videotape would be nice," Neiderman said, and laughed.

No one laughed with him.

Wells stared down at Neiderman. "You're a toxicologist, right?"

Neiderman nodded.

"Can you tell me what a toxin looks like? Can you show me a videotape of a toxin?"

"No. But I can show you what effect it has."

"And I can show you what effect that asteroid had when it crashed into the earth." Wells pushed a button on the projector. An aerial view of a large green peninsula appeared on the screen. "On the Yucatán Peninsula in Mexico there is a crater more than one hundred miles across. From our calculations, this would have been made by an asteroid eight miles in diameter."

Mark asked, "And there's no question about this occurring sixty-five million years ago?"

"None at all," Wells said. "We tested some of the mica from the crater by a potassium–argon dating method, which can date materials back a billion years."

Wells sipped his coffee, his eyes now on the screen that showed the sky on fire. He always had the same thought when he saw it. How terrified the animals must have been. "So," he continued, "we know this huge asteroid slammed into the Yucatán Peninsula with a force that's beyond our imagination. In a matter of seconds it emptied out the Gulf of Mexico."

"Holy Christ," Mark muttered under his breath. "What happened to all that water?"

"Some went on land, some flooded back into the Gulf. And a fair amount of water probably evaporated. Keep in mind that when that asteroid hit, it created a temperature at the point of impact twice as hot as the sun. All this happened in an instant."

"Then what happened?"

"Then the sky turned into smoke and fire and the darkness came," Wells went on. "Remember the pictures on television during the Gulf War when the Iraqis set the Kuwaiti oil fields on fire? Remember the dark, gloomy air? Well, multiply that a hundred times and you'll have a sense of what happened here on earth sixty-five million years ago."

Hawksworth nodded to himself. He had been aboard an NSC plane that visited Kuwait shortly after the war. The oil fields were still ablaze. From the air it resembled an inferno. "It's amazing anything survived."

"Not much did. It's estimated that seventy percent of the earth's species were wiped out. First, of course, the plant life died off because of lack of sunlight. Which brings us to the plant you found in the iceberg. You guessed it was prehistoric, and you were right."

Wells pressed a button and another slide came up. It showed a field filled with lush vegetation. Giant ferns were everywhere. "The plant you discovered is called *Serrena veriformans*. In the Cretaceous period it flourished in abundance in every swamp and delta and along every seacoast. Today the plant no longer exists except in a few isolated areas in South America."

Reetha asked, "So it was an important food source?"

"No way," Wells said quickly. "This plant is poisonous to virtually every animal, then and now."

Everybody leaned forward, all wondering if the toxicity of the iceberg was in some way due to the plant.

"How poisonous is it?" Joanna asked.

"Its spores contain a deadly alkaloid," Wells told her. "And just touching its green fronds can make you sick. If a child ate a mouthful, he would die."

"Could it kill an adult?"

Wells considered the question, then nodded. "But he'd have to eat a lot of it."

Joanna asked, "Could this alkaloid be heated and turned into a poisonous vapor?"

"No," Neiderman answered at once. "Alkaloids are inactivated by heat."

Kagen brought his fingers together in a steeple and looked over them at Wells. "Even though it's poisonous to animals, could this fern still serve as a food source for our bacteria?"

"Oh, sure," Wells said easily. "Some bacteria grow in the roots of plants in a symbiotic relationship. The plants provide the bacteria with food and the bacteria produce nitrogen compounds which the plant needs to grow."

"So the roots might contain the bacteria we're looking for?"

"They might."

And might not, Kagen thought. So far, cultures of the fern had turned up nothing. His mind went back to the iceberg. "Do you have any idea what the big gray mass deep in the iceberg is?"

"It could be a lot of things," Wells said. "It could be chunks of earth or a dead tree or God knows what. We're going to have to dig farther in to find out what it really is."

Hawksworth didn't like the idea. Digging into the iceberg could cause more big chunks to break off and threaten the integrity of the Plexiglas shield. "I think we already have enough specimens to study."

"But you still don't have your bug," Wells argued. "Deep within that iceberg there may be a very high concentration of organic matter. And if there is, that's the most likely place to find your bacteria."

There was a sharp knock on the door. A marine guard hurried in and paused to catch his breath.

"Well?" Hawksworth asked.

"Sir, there's been an accident," the marine said between breaths. "A real bad accident."

Nineteen

The ETOX team stared down at the body of Barbara Van Buren, stunned. She appeared to be staring back at them through unblinking eyes.

"Dreadful," Hawksworth muttered under his breath. "Absolutely dreadful."

"A stupid damn accident," Mark said. He walked over to the stepladder and pointed to the high-heeled shoe stuck in the corner of the middle step. "Her shoe gets caught in the ladder and she falls back and hits her head on the steel floor. What a rotten, stupid waste."

Kagen shook his head sadly. He'd liked Barbara Van Buren, admiring her spunk and drive and brains. And now she was dead.

He sighed to himself, knowing he would be the one to break the news to Barbara's husband. He'd met Jonathan Moore briefly. A nice fellow, a good scientist currently doing exciting research in China. He would return to the worst of all possible grief. Kagen knew all about that pain. It was ten years since he had lost his wife, and it still hurt.

"You'll make the arrangements for the body," he said to Hawksworth.

"Of course."

"Shouldn't we cover her with something?" Reetha asked softly.

Hawksworth gestured to the marine guard. "Get a sheet and a gurney and another marine to assist you."

"I'll help," Wells offered.

"Please leave everything the way it is," Joanna said.

Her gaze went back and forth between the shoe on the ladder and Barbara Van Buren's body. She studied the shoe with its two-inch heel, thinking that most women wouldn't climb a ladder wearing heels. Her eyes went back to the space between the body and the base of the ladder. She studied it at length, then turned to the marine guard.

"Did you move anything before we got here?"

"No, ma'am," the marine said sharply.

"Did you touch anything?"

"Only her neck to feel for a pulse."

"So the body and the ladder are in the exact same position that you found them?"

"Yes, ma'am."

Joanna went over to the desk and found a ruler. Kneeling, she measured the distance between the base of the ladder and Barbara Van Buren's body. "Her head is ten feet away from the ladder."

"So?" Hawksworth asked.

"If she fell backwards, she shouldn't have ended up this far away from the ladder," Joanna explained. "She should have dropped almost directly down, her head no more than six feet away."

There was an awkward silence as Joanna measured the distance again. It was the same. She checked the stepladder, making sure it was firmly up against the wall. "Her body is too far away from the ladder."

"Maybe she pushed herself away from the ladder as she was falling," Neiderman suggested.

"She couldn't have," Joanna said, and pointed to the shoe caught in the middle of the ladder. "Her foot was stuck on that step."

"Maybe she tried to get up," Mark said thoughtfully. "Maybe she stumbled a few feet forward."

Joanna shook her head. "If that were the case, she wouldn't have ended up on her back."

"Then how do you explain it?" Hawksworth asked.

Joanna didn't answer the question. She knelt again and examined Barbara Van Buren's head. There was clotted blood in both ear canals, more on the right. The back of the head was grossly misshapen and sitting in a pool of blood.

As Joanna lifted the head, she heard Doreen make a revulsive sound. Joanna looked up. "This is going to be somewhat gruesome. So if you're unaccustomed to death and blood, now would be a good time to excuse yourself."

Reetha and Doreen nodded to one another and left the laboratory. Ben Kagen was a step behind them. The marine followed them out.

Joanna waited for the door to close, then lifted the head up again. The back of it was virtually flattened out. "So much trauma," she said, thinking aloud.

"She took a hell of a fall," Mark said. "And she landed on a steel floor."

"That shouldn't cause a bilateral skull fracture."

"How do you know it's bilateral?" Mark asked, bending over for a closer look.

"Because she's got blood coming out of both auditory canals."

Mark rubbed at his chin. "A big basilar skull fracture could do the same thing. She could have just crushed the entire back of her head."

Joanna took a magnifying mirror from her purse and carefully examined the posterior aspect of the skull. There was so much blood and matted hair, she couldn't determine if there was any exposed bone or brain tissue. Next she studied the ears to make certain there wasn't any localized trauma to account for the bleeding. As far as she could see, the auditory canals were intact. The blood was coming from within the skull. It had to be a bilateral skull fracture, she told herself. And a single blow couldn't cause that.

She moved to the front of the head and magnified the forehead and temporal areas. Then she saw it. Along the scalp line was a large area of broken-off hairs. In some places there were pinpoint hemorrhagic spots where hairs had been pulled out by their roots.

Joanna stood and brushed the dust from her knees. "I'm going to need some X-rays of her skull."

"What will that tell you?" Hawksworth asked.

"Whether or not she was murdered."

Hawksworth's jaw dropped. "What!"

"Everything points to it," Joanna said evenly. "Her body was too far away from the ladder, way too far. Somebody pulled Barbara Van Buren off that stepladder and slammed her to the floor, then beat her head against the steel floor until she was dead."

Mark gave her a strange look. "Based on what? On blood being present in both auditory canals?"

Joanna nodded. "That was the first clue. The second was the appearance of her hair along the frontal scalp line. A lot of strands were broken off. Some were even pulled out by their roots. Those are the characteristics of hair that has been grabbed and violently pulled." Joanna nodded again. "Somebody grabbed her by the hair and slammed her head against the steel floor. Probably over and over again. That's why there's so much damage to the back of her head."

"And what if she has only a single fracture of the skull?" Mark asked.

"Then I'm wrong."

The body of Barbara Van Buren was lifted onto a gurney and covered with a sheet, then quickly wheeled down a passageway to the sickbay. Marine guards were everywhere and they snapped to attention as the gurney rolled by.

Hawksworth leaned over to Joanna. "I hope you're wrong."

"So do I," Joanna said, but she knew she wasn't.

She glanced down and saw, sticking out from under the sheet, Barbara Van Buren's hand with its shiny wedding band. Joanna's mind drifted back to the conversation she'd had with Barbara at dinner. The woman was so happy, her marriage and her work going wonderfully well. Barbara had told her that she wished time would freeze and that everything would stay exactly as it was now. Joanna sighed sadly, thinking that Barbara Van Buren had gotten her wish. Time for her was now frozen forever.

Henderson was waiting for them in the sickbay. He listened carefully to Joanna as she described the X-rays she wanted taken. He had never taken X-rays on a dead person, but he didn't think it would be a problem. The X-ray facility had small sandbags to hold the head in a variety of positions.

Henderson looked down at the clotted blood about the dead woman's head. "She's not contagious or anything, is she?"

"No," Joanna assured him.

Henderson nodded, but he decided to wear gloves just to be on the safe side. He wasn't going to take any chances, not after what happened to Bobby Shea. Shit! That bug could be anywhere. In the air. On the ground. Anywhere.

Henderson started coughing and put his hand up to his mouth. It took him several seconds to clear his throat. "The flu," he explained. "The damn thing just seems to hang on."

"Maybe you shouldn't be working in sickbay," Hawksworth said.

"Oh, it's a lot better than it was, Colonel," Henderson lied. In fact the cough was in its second day and getting worse, and he felt feverish most of the time. Goddamn flu! He grabbed the foot of the gurney and motioned to the marine guard. "Want to lend a hand?"

As the gurney disappeared, Hawksworth turned to the others. "There's really no need for all of you to wait here."

Wells didn't budge. "If there's a killer on this ship, I damn well want to know about it."

"We have no real proof that's the case," Hawksworth said. "Everything up to now has been speculation."

"Well, that little lady's dead body isn't speculation," Wells said grimly. "I'll wait for the X-rays."

"Me too," Neiderman chimed in. "And if Joanna is right, I want a double lock put on the door to my sleeping quarters."

Joanna looked at him disgustedly. It was so characteristic of Neiderman. He thought only about himself and his own narrow interests, not giving a damn about the poor dead woman.

Neiderman took a candy bar from his coat pocket and peeled off the wrapper. "How long will those X-rays take?"

"Just a few minutes," Joanna told him. "They are developed almost as soon as they're taken."

Neiderman chewed on his candy bar, ignoring the looks the others were giving him.

Wells began to slowly pace the floor. "How old was that little lady?"

"Forty-six," Hawksworth said.

"Young," Wells murmured softly. "Far too young to die."

Neiderman licked at the chocolate on his fingers. "Nobody has a guarantee on years."

"Tell me about it!" Wells said, his mind flashing back to Vietnam and the boys he'd seen blown to hell and back. They were too young to die too. More than twenty years had passed since then, but he could still clearly see their faces.

Henderson hurried back in and handed a set of X-rays to Joanna. "Here you go. The lateral views are a little fuzzy, but it's the best I could do."

Joanna put the X-rays up on a view box and stepped back. The others gathered around to peer over her shoulders.

"What do you see?" Hawksworth asked.

"Depressed fractures of the posterior parietal and occipital bones," Joanna said, pointing to the involved areas.

"What does that mean?"

"It means we have a murderer aboard the *Global Two*."

Twenty

Hawksworth and Joanna were in the conference room by themselves. The door was closed, a marine guard posted outside to make certain they weren't disturbed.

"Are you sure she was murdered?" Hawksworth asked.

"Positive," Joanna said firmly.

Hawksworth paced around the table, shaking his head. "No doubts at all?"

"None."

"And you're basing everything on the fact that she had more than one skull fracture?"

"It's more than that."

"I know, I know," Hawksworth said irritably. "The broken-off hairs."

"And there was something else, too," Joanna went on. "When I examined the floor around the victim's head, I found a twelve-inch area where bits of her skull and skin had been ground into the steel. That's twice the size it should have been from a simple fall. The reason the area was so large was the killer kept slamming her head against the floor, but not always in exactly the same place."

"And then he ran the hell out of the laboratory and disappeared into the woodwork."

Not "ran," Joanna thought. The killer was in no hurry. He—assuming it was a he—even took the time to wash his hands. Joanna had found blood on a towel near the sink. The blood almost certainly belonged to Barbara Van Buren, put there by the killer after he washed her blood from his hands. It would be easy to prove. Just have the blood on the towel typed and compared to Barbara's.

Joanna sighed wearily, thinking what would have happened if the murder had been committed in Los Angeles. Everything would have been cordoned off with yellow tape, the crime scene unit called in to gather clues and look for traces of evidence the killer might have left behind. But there was no crime scene unit aboard this ship and no crime lab to send the evidence to.

Joanna glanced at the wall clock. It was almost 10 P.M. She decided to go back to the crime scene in the morning and check it out one final time before sending all the specimens to a laboratory on the mainland.

"Why?" Hawksworth broke into her thoughts. "Why kill a defenseless woman?"

"Cui bono," Joanna said tonelessly. "Who benefits?"

Hawksworth wrinkled his brow, concentrating. "No one that I can think of, except maybe Neiderman."

"Why him?"

"There was a lot of bad blood between the two," Hawksworth told her. "Apparently he believed she had stolen some of the scientific work they had done together some years ago."

"Had she?"

"She denied it," Hawksworth said. "But there's no question there was a real dislike between them."

Joanna shook her head. "Scientists steal from one another all the time. That's not a good enough reason to kill."

"There's more," Hawksworth continued. "Apparently Neiderman was going to be replaced on the ETOX team. According to Kagen, Neiderman's performance had been slipping, and his standing in the academic world was on a downward spiral. After our current mission was completed, Kagen planned to replace Neiderman with Barbara Van Buren."

Joanna's eyes narrowed. "Did Neiderman know about this?"

"No, but he might have guessed when Kagen brought her aboard," Hawksworth said. "You don't bring in someone of Barbara Van Buren's stature just to be an assistant."

"And if Neiderman lost his position on the ETOX team," Joanna reasoned, "the news would leak out and his scientific career would be finished. He'd be a dead man alone in his lab waiting for his pension to start."

"Exactly."

Joanna thought the matter through carefully before nodding. "Neiderman's name goes to the top of the list."

"So you think it's a good enough reason to kill?"

"Plenty good enough."

Joanna thought back to something Jake Sinclair had told her. Money, sex, or power was at the bottom of almost every crime. It was a simple fact, but it held true time and time again. A picture of the good looking Jake flashed into her mind. He was smiling at her. With effort she pushed it aside.

"How do we go about proving he's guilty?" Hawksworth asked, gesturing with his hands and clearly out of his depth. "Do we see if he has an alibi?"

"That would be a start," Joanna said carefully. "But we shouldn't concentrate only on Neiderman. We'll have to question everyone and find out where they were and what they were doing between seven and eight this evening. And don't be surprised if most of them can't come up with an alibi. Remember, it was right after dinner. I'll bet a lot of them spent some time alone in their quarters before coming to the meeting. I know I did."

Hawksworth squinted an eye. "Are you saying you're a suspect?"

"I'm saying I can't prove that I wasn't in Barbara Van

Buren's lab between seven and eight. And any good detective will tell you that makes me a suspect."

Hawksworth began pacing again. "Let's assume it's not you or me. And I can vouch for Wells, since he was with me all the time from dinner on."

"Did he excuse himself to use the bathroom?"

Hawksworth thought for a moment. "Yes, but only briefly."

"How long?"

"Five minutes or so."

"And you were in this conference room?"

"That's right."

"Then he had enough time to get to Barbara Van Buren's lab, kill her, and get back."

Hawksworth groaned. "This isn't going to be easy, is it?"

"Murder cases rarely are."

Hawksworth continued to pace, with his hands clasped together behind him. "I think we can safely say it wasn't you or me who committed this crime. And you would agree that Wells is a very weak suspect. That narrows the list down to Neiderman, Kagen, Mark Alexander, and the Sims sisters."

"Colonel, you've got an entire *shipload* of suspects."

Hawksworth stopped in his tracks. "What are you talking about?"

"I'm talking about a shipful of young men with sky-high testosterone levels," Joanna explained. "Barbara Van Buren was an attractive woman. Maybe she was sexually assaulted before she was killed."

"Christ," Hawksworth growled. "Is that a real possibility?"

"Of course it is, although there's no proof to back it up. At least, not yet. In my preliminary examination of the body I saw no signs of a struggle. There were no bruises on her face or arms, no skin or blood under her fingernails."

"So there's nothing to suggest a sexual attack."

"Not so far," Joanna said. "But if I find evidence of trauma to her genital area or semen stains, we'll have our answer."

"My God!" Hawksworth moaned, shaking his head. "This gets worse by the minute."

"I'm only pointing out possibilities."

Hawksworth waved away the sexual scenario. "The scientific team is separated from most of the men. The only crew in this section of the ship are the marines, and I can assure you they are very disciplined men."

"And they're trained killers, too," Joanna said evenly.

"Are you saying we could have a maniac aboard the *Global Two*?"

"It's possible, but most of the real nuts don't go to the bother of trying to cover things up. And our guy did. That's why he put the shoe in the ladder."

Joanna reminded herself to have the shoe tested for fingerprints. Maybe he left his prints on it, though she doubted it. He wasn't that stupid.

"You keep referring to the killer as a man. How do you know it wasn't a woman?"

"Because females almost always kill with a weapon and not by brute force," Joanna said promptly. "And then there's the shoe in the ladder. A female wouldn't have put it there. She would know that a woman doesn't normally climb a stepladder wearing high heels."

Hawksworth gave her an admiring look. "How are you able to make so much from so little?"

"I'm trained to do it," Joanna said and pushed her chair back. "We'll need two separate rooms to interrogate people."

"Why two?"

"So you and I can question each person separately," Joanna told him. "And make sure we tape-record everything they say. Let's see if there's a liar among this bunch."

"I'll set it up right now." Hawksworth reached for the door.

"And one more thing," Joanna said. "I want you to ask each person if they'd mind being fingerprinted."

Hawksworth spun around. "Did you find some prints at the murder scene?"

"No," Joanna said, smiling thinly. "But let's make them think I did. Let's make someone nervous."

"What do you think the killer will do when he hears about the fingerprints?"

"Something stupid, I hope."

Twenty-one

Corpsman Henderson opened a new bottle of tetracycline and quickly swallowed two tablets. Now he was up to a thousand milligrams every six hours and it was barely holding his symptoms in check. His fever never went above 101 degrees Fahrenheit, but his muscles were aching and the nagging cough seemed to be getting worse. Goddamn flu, he thought, and wondered if he shouldn't take a few aspirins too.

Leaving the pharmacy room, he returned to the clinic and sat down wearily on a small stool. He closed his eyes and leaned his head back against the cool metal wall, glad that sick call had been so light that morning. A sore throat, a cold, a bad case of jock itch. With a little luck, no one else would show up and he could get some rest. Yeah, a little rest and maybe double his dosage of penicillin too. Knock that flu bug out once and for all.

Henderson looked up as a marine corporal entered the sickbay and signed in. His name was Russell Kirby. He looked like a weight lifter with his broad shoulders and heavily muscled arms.

"Got a minute?" Kirby asked.

"Sure," Henderson said, motioning the marine to a nearby stool. "What's up?"

"My damn hand. I think I got it infected."

"How'd you do that?"

"Getting samples of ice from one of those fucking icebergs." Kirby placed his hand on a small table, palm down. "I kind of gashed it."

"When?"

"Last week sometime."

Henderson examined the hand. The wound was the size of a quarter, with a thick scab over it. But there was a lot of pus under it.

"Just some antibiotics should take care of it, huh?" Kirby asked hopefully.

"It needs to be lanced."

Kirby's eyes widened abruptly. "You're going to cut into it?"

"You won't feel anything," Henderson assured him. "I'll numb it with some spray first."

"You bullshitting me?"

"Nope." Henderson started coughing, a wet, hacking cough. He quickly covered his mouth. "Damn flu." He got to his feet and stood for a moment, gathering his energy. Then he went to the basin and scrubbed his hands.

Kirby thought the medic looked like death warmed over. Henderson's face had a pasty white color, and his cough sounded like he had a lot of phlegm rattling around in his chest. "You're kind of under the weather yourself, huh?"

"It's some damn virus," Henderson said, putting on latex gloves and unwrapping a surgical tray. "As soon as I'm done here, I'm going to crash."

"I wish I could," Kirby said, trying not to look at the instruments on the tray. "But we've got to go back out and look for that toxic iceberg. And that's going to be a big waste of time, because without its transmitter working we've got no chance to find it. None."

"Maybe the goddamn thing will just melt away and disappear."

"Yeah. And maybe Heather Locklear will come aboard tonight and entertain the troops."

Henderson began cleaning the infected area on Kirby's hand with alcohol. "After this, I'll spray it with ethyl chloride. That'll freeze it and numb it up good."

Kirby moved in closer and lowered his voice. "You heard anything new about Bobby Shea?"

"Nah."

"You were in there at the time he died, though, right?"

Henderson nodded. "He was sicker than hell with a real high fever." He snapped his fingers. "And he died. Just like that."

"It gives me the creeps having those bodies still aboard the ship."

Henderson started coughing and turned his head away for a moment. "Don't sweat it. Those bodies are in sealed refrigerator rooms. No bugs are going to get out of there."

"And what happens if they do?"

"Then we're up Shit Creek without a paddle."

Kirby glanced over his shoulder and lowered his voice even more. "Somebody told me that you saw the doc who got killed last night."

Henderson shrugged. "It wasn't that much to see. She was just lying there with a skull fracture."

"I heard that the back of her head was caved in."

"That's what it looked like on the X-rays."

"Fuck!" Kirby said hoarsely. "We got us a killer running around this ship. Maybe some bastard who likes to hit small women. Maybe some wacko."

Henderson shook his head. "They think it was one of the other docs who did the deed."

"Get out of here!" Kirby said in disbelief.

"I'm telling you," Henderson went on. "The scuttlebutt is that each member of the ETOX team was questioned twice last night. Once by the colonel, once by the good-looking forensic doc. And the questioning lasted until three in the morning. That tells me they're zeroing in on those scientists. They must figure one of them did it."

Kirby nodded in agreement. "Yeah."

"Hard to believe a doc could do that kind of thing, ain't it?"

"I guess," Kirby said, then smiled malevolently. "All the marines are sleeping with their weapons close at hand. They're all hoping the murdering son of a bitch tries something with them."

"You figure they'd kill him?"

"Faster than you can spit."

Kirby watched as Henderson pulled the surgical tray closer. A gleaming scalpel looked razor-sharp, and Kirby knew that it was going to hurt like hell. "You've got to drain it, huh?"

"Got to."

Kirby took a deep breath, readying himself. "By the way, I'd appreciate it if my visit to the sickbay didn't get to the colonel's desk."

"Why?"

"Because he saw my wound last week and told me to take care of it pronto, and I didn't."

"I'll cover for you." Henderson picked up a bottle of ethyl chloride and sprayed the top of the wound. As it frosted up, he reached for the scalpel and made a stab wound through the scab. Greenish pus drained out.

"I didn't even feel it," Kirby said, relieved.

"Good." Henderson pushed on the sides of the wound and more pus came out.

"Jesus! You hit a gusher."

Henderson started coughing again, phlegm rattling around in his throat. He turned his head away. He really should have worn a surgical mask, he realized. Not that he was going to give anything bad to Kirby. More like the other way around. He'd be careful handling that pus. The last thing he needed now was to catch any more germs.

* * *

Russell Kirby zipped up his parka and hurried onto the deck of the *Global Explorer II*. Men were scurrying about, preparing to put rigid hull inflatable boats in the water and begin another search for the toxic iceberg. The day was overcast and cold, the wind blowing in from the north.

Kirby ran over to a marine lieutenant and saluted sharply.

"You're late, Kirby," the lieutenant said.

"I was at sickbay, sir."

"You cleared for duty?"

"Yes, sir."

"Then fall in."

Kirby lined up with the patrol team. He stood next to his roommate, Eddie Walsh. The wind suddenly gusted and swirled. "Fucking wind," Kirby muttered.

"What'd they do about your hand?" Walsh asked, his voice low.

"Drained the pus out."

"Did it hurt?"

"Some." Kirby pulled the glove off his injured hand and stretched his fingers. The wound was beginning to throb again.

"Did you ask the medic about the lady who got killed?"

Kirby nodded. "They think one of the docs did it."

"No shit!"

Kirby nodded again, enjoying having the inside scoop. "They kept the docs up all night, questioning each one twice."

"The colonel will find out who did it," Walsh said with certainty. "You just wait and see."

"Meanwhile, we've still got a killer running around on the loose. A real mean son of a bitch."

The squad of marines looked across the deck and watched Ann Cormier approaching. She was wearing tight-fitting warm-ups, and with each step her long ponytail bounced up and down. As she jogged by she smiled at the squad. Every marine smiled back at her.

"Nice ass," Kirby commented.

"Nicer than you can imagine," Walsh said, his voice now husky. "With perfect thighs."

Kirby stared at his roommate. "How would you know that?"

Walsh smiled. "I'm not talking."

"I hope you ain't stupid enough to try to grab her ass," Kirby said hoarsely. "Because if you do, the colonel will bounce your butt right out of the Corps. You'll get a dis-honorable discharge surer than hell." Kirby gave Walsh a long look, waiting for a response. "Well?"

"I know how to handle myself."

"Uh-huh," Kirby said, wondering if Eddie had already screwed the woman. "Well, you keep in mind what I just told you. And also keep in mind that Miss Tightass works down there with all those dead bodies. You know, the ones that are infected with that goddamned bacteria."

Walsh's face became serious. "She knows how to pro-tect herself while she's working."

"Yeah, just like Bobby Shea knew how to protect him-self," Kirby said tersely. "And remember, they worked together on those damn bodies."

"Shit," Walsh said, now worried.

"Be smart," Kirby said under his breath. "Keep your pecker in your pants."

Walsh nodded slowly, wishing that he had used a rub-ber and hoping he was still safe.

"Prepare for inspection!" the lieutenant barked out.

The marines snapped to attention.

Twenty-two

"Are you all right?" Joanna said.

"I'm fine," Ann Cormier said, wiping perspiration from her forehead with her sleeve. "It's just a damn cold that keeps coming on."

"There's not much you can do about that."

"I know." Ann licked at the opened blister on the inside of her lip, wishing it would disappear but knowing it wouldn't until her cold had come and gone.

Using a cotton swab, Joanna took a vaginal smear from the body of Barbara Van Buren, then handed it to Ann. "Have this examined for the presence of sperm."

"You think she was raped?" Ann asked quickly.

"There's no indication she was sexually assaulted," Joanna told her. "But we have to check out the possibility."

"So the only real finding is the bashed-in skull."

"And the bruise on her spine." Joanna turned the body on its side and pointed to a large bruise over the thoracic spine. "It's rather extensive, isn't it?"

"What do you make of that?"

"It tells me that when she was slammed to the floor, her upper back took a lot of the force. After the initial hit, she was probably stunned but still conscious," Joanna said. "I think Barbara Van Buren knew someone was bashing her head in."

"Jesus," Ann murmured softly. "You think she felt it?"

"I'm sure she did."

Ann stared down at the ruined skull. "How could one scientist do this to another?"

"It might not be a scientist," Joanna said. "The murderer could be anyone aboard this ship."

Ann shook her head. "I don't buy that. There's always a marine guard posted in the passageway that leads to the scientific section. Nobody gets by him."

"Oh, really? What about the stewards and cooks and helpers that work in our dining room and living quarters? What about the sailors who maintain the Plexiglas cylinder and the monorail beneath it?"

"I hadn't thought of them."

Well, I have, Joanna said to herself, and every one of them has an alibi. "And there's always the possibility that someone managed to sneak by the guard."

"I don't think that's very likely," Ann said as she labeled the test tube. "That passageway is very well lit. You can see way down past all the laboratory doors. A guard wouldn't miss anything that went on in there."

"No, he wouldn't," Joanna said slowly, her eyes narrowing in concentration. She reached for the plastic bag containing Barbara Van Buren's panties. "Finish up here for me, will you?"

"Sure."

Joanna stripped off her gloves and mask and hurried out of the autopsy room, her mind on the guard in the passageway. She had been with Hawksworth when he questioned the guard in the early hours of the morning. The guard assured them there had been no crewmen in the passageway between 7 P.M. and 8 P.M., only civilians. Only civilians! Goddamn it, she berated herself, wondering where her mind had been when the guard made that statement.

She turned a sharp corner to the long corridor. Up ahead she saw the guard they had questioned earlier. She concentrated for a moment, trying to remember his name. Walsh. Eddie Walsh.

"Private Walsh, there are a few more questions I need to ask you."

"Yes, ma'am," Walsh said and involuntarily snapped to attention.

"Last night when we questioned you, you said there were no crewmen in the passageway between seven and eight p.m. Right?"

Walsh nodded stiffly. "Just like I told the colonel. I didn't see any military personnel."

"But you said there were civilians."

"Yes, ma'am."

"Who did you see?"

Walsh thought back. "Well, there was the colonel and the new guy who just came on board. And I saw one of the twins. The dark-haired one. I guess that's it."

"Are you certain it was between seven and eight?"

"Oh, yeah. I was here during your chow. You all were eating until after seven."

"Who else did you see?"

"I saw Ann—" Walsh caught himself, not wanting Dr. Blalock to know how familiar he was with Ann. "You know—ah—the technician."

"Ann Cormier?"

"Yeah," Walsh said nervously. "She was wearing a jogging outfit."

Joanna made a mental note to check with Ann to see if it was between 7 and 8 P.M. when she came through the passageway in her jogging warm-ups. That would clearly establish that Walsh's time frame was correct.

She looked up at Eddie Walsh. His eyes avoided hers, and she wondered if he was holding something back. "Did you see Dr. Van Buren in the passageway last night?"

Walsh hesitated, wrinkling his brow in thought. "I might have. I can't be sure."

"Think hard."

After a long pause, Walsh said, "I believe I did."

"Was she by herself?"

Walsh tried to envision the petite woman. Was she walking by him or going into a lab? His mental image was vague, but he had the feeling she was entering the laboratory. Was someone close to her or maybe right behind her? He couldn't recall. He shook his head.

Joanna groaned to herself. "You think on it. I mean, really think. That information is very important."

"Yes, ma'am."

Joanna walked away, wondering if Eddie Walsh held the key to the murder. The crime was almost certainly committed by a member of the ETOX team. There were other possibilities, but all the evidence pointed to one of the scientists. And all of them had denied seeing Barbara Van Buren between 7 and 8 P.M. But one of them was lying. One of them had seen her during that time. The murderer. And maybe, just maybe, Eddie had seen the killer and would eventually remember him. Joanna would give the marine twenty-four hours to think about it and then she'd talk with him again.

Joanna came to the bacteriology lab and knocked gently on the door before entering. Reetha was studying a slide under the microscope. She glanced up at Joanna briefly, then went back to the slide.

"This bug is a real son of a bitch," Reetha said. "We can't get it to grow. No matter what culture media we put it in, it dies within an hour."

"Have you tried growing it in an extract from the fern?"

Reetha flicked her wrist in disgust. "It doesn't work worth a damn. The bacteria still died, only quicker."

"So what do you do next?"

"We keep at it." Reetha reached for a cigarette and lit it. "Joe Wells found more plant life in the iceberg. He's got some frozen moss and giant horsetails thawing out. We'll try those next. And Doreen is mixing up some new enriched media. We'll give those a shot too."

"It sounds like you're looking for a needle in a haystack."

"Tell me about it." Reetha blew a smoke ring up at the ceiling. "I think we've got a long haul in front of us. This organism is turning out to be incredibly fastidious."

"And there are no shortcuts, huh?"

"None that I'm aware of." Reetha pointed to the plastic bag Joanna was holding. "What have you got there?"

"Barbara Van Buren's panties," Joanna told her. "Have you got an ultraviolet lamp?"

"Sure," Reetha said, and gestured with her thumb to a nearby countertop. "What do you need it for?"

"To test for semen stains. They give off a greenish-blue fluorescence when placed under an ultraviolet light."

Reetha's expression hardened. "Don't tell me she was raped."

Joanna shook her head. "Just checking all the bases."

Reetha crushed out her cigarette. "They're putting deadbolt locks on the doors to our sleeping quarters and doubling the marine guards outside. But I still think I'll sleep with one eye open."

"Everybody will until the killer is caught." Joanna turned on the ultraviolet lamp and placed the silk panties under it. "Would you get the lights?"

The room went dark except for the eerie glow from the ultraviolet lamp. There were no fluorescent stains on Barbara Van Buren's panties. Joanna turned the garment inside out, exposing its crotch to the lamp. Everything stayed dark.

The side door suddenly burst open.

The two women spun around. For a moment they froze, then they slowly backed away. Reetha reached for a thin-necked flask and raised it high, ready to defend herself.

The light came on.

It was Malcolm Neiderman.

Reetha lowered the flask and glared at Neiderman. "Goddamn it! Don't you ever bother to knock?"

"Not when I've got really important news," Neiderman said, and paused to catch his breath.

"Such as?"

"Such as the guinea pigs I injected with that tongue biopsy are getting sick as hell. One is already dead."

"So?" Reetha said, unimpressed. "That's not helping us grow out the bacteria."

"Sure it is. We know we can grow it in guinea pigs."

Dummy, Reetha wanted to say, but didn't. "I'm talking about growing it out in a culture plate so we can study it."

"Well," Neiderman said, "let's put ground-up guinea pig tissue in the culture media."

"You can't just add ground-up tissue to culture media," Reetha said, waving away the suggestion.

"You can if I solubilize it first."

Reetha's interest perked up and she moved closer to Neiderman. "Tell me about the process."

"It's easy," Neiderman said, his arm so near to hers he could feel its warmth. "You just take a guinea pig organ, like the lungs or liver, and grind it up into fine particles. Then you put it in a high-speed ultracentrifuge and spin the hell out of it. This will separate out the cellular debris and leave us with a clear supernatant, which contains all the soluble substances."

Reetha nodded slowly. "And the clear supernatant can be incorporated into our culture media without any problem?"

"It should be a snap," Neiderman said. "And if your bacteria grow out, we can analyze the supernatant and see what it contains. In other words, we can identify your so-called growth factor."

Reetha nodded again, thinking that she had underestimated Malcolm Neiderman. He could be plenty sharp when he wanted to be. There are no dummies on the

ETOX team, she reminded herself. "It sounds good to me, but let me think on it for a moment."

Neiderman leaned back against the counter, delighted with the way things were turning out. Now he would be intimately involved in growing the bacteria. He would learn exactly what factors and conditions the bacteria required to stay alive. This information would be vital in carrying out his plan. He wondered again how much the microbe and its toxin would be worth to some foreign power. Millions and millions, he decided.

Out of the corner of his eye, Neiderman observed Reetha and the outline of her breasts pushing against her white laboratory coat. His arm was now touching hers lightly and she didn't seem to mind. He smiled to himself. It wouldn't be long before he got her in bed. Then she would happily tell him everything he needed to know to carry the bacteria off the ship. Everything.

"I like it," Reetha said, breaking the silence. "It just might work."

You'll like it even more when I'm between your legs, Neiderman was thinking, his arm firmly against hers.

"I have one suggestion," Joanna said. "I wouldn't use the lungs in this experiment. They are likely to be contaminated with bacteria from the air, and the last thing we need is a contaminant to confuse us."

"Good point," Reetha agreed. "We shouldn't use the animal's intestines either, which are also filled with bacteria."

"Fine," Neiderman said. "We'll start with the liver, then go to spleen, kidney, and brain."

Reetha reached for another cigarette. "This is going to require a tremendous amount of work. It looks simple on paper, but it involves hundreds of different media and culture plates. We'll need some technical assistance."

"I can help," Neiderman volunteered. "I did some bacteriology way back when, and I can do a pretty good job of mixing media and pouring culture plates."

Reetha smiled appreciatively. "Thanks, Malcolm. That would take part of the load off of Doreen and me."

Neiderman smiled back. This was going to be so easy, he thought. He let his arm drop so the back of his hand touched her thigh, and she moved a half step away. But not too fast.

Neiderman's smile widened. So easy, he thought again.

Twenty-three

Everyone was on deck watching the aurora borealis, one of nature's grandest shows. Yellow and green streaks danced across the black sky. An intense arc of gold suddenly brightened, then faded and died, only to be replaced by another.

Joanna stared at the colors. "I feel as if I'm in some strange world."

"You are," Mark said. "Up here cosmic events are occurring so rapidly you can't keep up with them. Take the elevator down to the cylinder room and you'll find a microbe that has been frozen in place for sixty-five million years."

"It's like some bizarre science-fiction story that no one will believe."

"Would you, if you weren't here?"

"No."

They were standing at the stern of the ship near the helipad. The others were amidships, taking turns looking through a small telescope that Hawksworth had set up. A bright yellow cloud suddenly appeared and illuminated the water, giving it a fluorescent glow. Icebergs floated by and disappeared like ghosts.

"It's eerie as hell out here," Mark commented.

"Not as eerie as an iceberg that comes out of nowhere and starts killing people. And we don't even know what the lethal agent is. It could be part bacteria, part virus, part God knows what."

"Anything is possible," Mark agreed. "Until we learn how to grow that microorganism, everything we say is strictly a guess. It's like the Great Plague of the Middle Ages. Everybody knew the plague killed, but nobody knew why until they identified the organism *Pasteurella pestis*."

Joanna's eyes narrowed. "Are you saying this could turn into another Great Plague?"

Mark didn't answer at once. He waited for a flashing streak of green to fade from the sky. "I think the bacteria in all likelihood entered the food chain a year ago. I saw it with my own eyes on my first mission out here. It wiped out an incredible amount of sea life before it seemed to disappear. If it can do that to the creatures of the sea, there's no reason it can't do it to man. And if it suddenly appears in the general population, all hell is going to break loose, because we don't know what this microorganism is."

"On your first mission, did any humans get sick or die?" Joanna asked.

"Not that I'm aware of."

"I wonder why," Joanna said thoughtfully. "I mean, if it's the same bug, it should have killed people then the same way it's killing them now. Right?"

Mark pondered the question for a moment. "Maybe the damn thing has mutated to a form that's particularly lethal to man."

"Or maybe it's two different bugs."

"That's always a possibility, but I doubt it. Chances are it's the same bug."

"I guess we won't know for certain until we identify the microbe in this outbreak and see if it's present in the specimens from the first outbreak."

"That's a hell of lot easier said than done."

"Have you had any luck at all in growing the bacteria out?"

"If anything, we're going backwards. Now the bug is only living for thirty minutes in our cultures."

"Maybe Neiderman's idea will work out. You know, using guinea pig tissue in the culture media."

"You're dreaming," Mark said. "We've already tried the first batch of his preparation. Nothing grew out."

"Nothing at all?"

"Not even a single colony," Mark said sourly. "The fact of the matter is that there are no shortcuts in science. Complex problems seem to require complex solutions. I'm afraid we're going to have to go about this business in a slow, methodical fashion."

"We're going to be on this ship for a while, aren't we?"

"A long while."

The wind suddenly picked up, cold and heavy with moisture. Joanna reached for the zipper on her parka but had difficulty grasping it because of her gloves.

"Here," Mark said, taking the zipper. "Let me do that."

He pulled the zipper up, then brought the hood of her parka up over her head. He stared at her, catching her eyes and holding them. She was absolutely stunning in the light of the aurora. He brought her closer and kissed her gently. He expected her to pull away, but she didn't. For a moment he felt her kiss him back. His arms tightened around her.

"This isn't going to work, Mark," Joanna said in a whisper.

"Why not? We're both unattached. We can start anew."

"It would be the same thing all over. You're never going to change."

"Would you want me to?"

Joanna smiled. "Probably not."

Mark touched her cheek and ran his finger down it. "I never stop thinking about you. Never."

They heard people approaching and quickly disengaged. Their arms still touching, they turned and waved to Doreen and Kagen.

"Quite a show, huh?" Kagen called out.

"Glorious," Joanna said and meant it. "But I've never understood what causes the aurora borealis."

"It's actually quite simple," Kagen said, his words slightly slurred. "It's a natural display of light. It's associated with the solar wind, which is a continuous flow of charged particles from the sun. When the particles strike molecules in the atmosphere, energy is released, and some of this energy appears in the form of light. And voilà! There's your aurora."

"Fascinating," Mark said.

"Not as fascinating as a prehistoric iceberg." Kagen grinned. "And now we've found even more plant life within it. Joe has just uncovered a flowering plant that looks very much like a magnolia. Can you believe it? A sixty-five-million-year-old magnolia?"

"It makes me wonder what else is stuck in there," Joanna said.

"Doesn't it, though?" Kagen asked and smiled broadly. A huge flash of yellow went by overhead and quickly died away. "Well, if you'll excuse us, we'll continue on our stroll through the aurora."

Kagen leaned on Doreen as they walked away. He was feeling the effects of three double martinis and the wine he'd had with dinner. His mind was functioning fine, but he knew his speech was slurred. He also knew he couldn't walk a straight line if his life depended on it. "I'm afraid I overindulged this evening."

"You're doing fine," Doreen said softly.

"No, I'm not. I'm getting drunk and that's something the head of the ETOX team shouldn't do."

"Oh, I see," Doreen said, nodding. "You're not supposed to be human."

"You refuse to find fault with me, don't you?" Kagen asked, his head up against her shoulder.

"Absolutely."

"I never really drank until my wife's death," Kagen said sadly. "I guess I never learned how to handle it."

"That's not something you handle," Doreen said, her head now resting against his. "It's something you live with until enough time has passed to heal the pain."

Kagen smiled at her. "You're a lot smarter than I am, aren't you?"

The aurora was ending. As the brilliant lights faded, the wind increased and a cold sleet began to fall. Doreen and Kagen turned and headed for the bridge. Through the mist they saw Hawksworth hurrying toward them.

"Have you seen Dr. Blalock?" Hawksworth asked.

"She's by the helipad. Why?" Kagen replied.

Hawksworth didn't answer. He walked rapidly across the deck to Joanna. "An urgent message just arrived for you from Los Angeles, Dr. Blalock. You're needed back at Memorial Hospital. They have some sort of epidemic going on down there."

The crew chief waited for a drifting cloud to block the moonlight, then darted across the deck to the helicopter. He glanced over his shoulder, making sure no guards were close by, and rapped gently on the cockpit window. Nervously he looked around again before knocking on the window once more, harder this time.

"Come on, come on!" he muttered nervously to himself.

The window slid halfway open and Mike Mallory peeked out. "What?"

"We just got orders, Commander. We're taking off in two hours."

"Shit," Mallory grumbled. "Where to?"

"Juneau. We have to give one of the docs a lift."

Mallory checked his watch. "I need another half hour."

"Five minutes and no more," the crew chief told him.

"Then get the hell out. And be careful. The marine guards are everywhere."

Mallory closed the window and worked his way back to the cabin of the helicopter. It was very cold and he could see his breath frosting in the air. The only clothing he had on was a T-shirt.

"Who was that?" Ann Cormier asked.

"My crew chief." Mallory crawled under the blankets and snuggled up against her. "We've got to get out of here."

Ann draped a leg over him and began nibbling on his ear. "Now?"

"In five minutes."

She giggled. "Well, that's enough time for one more go-around."

"Hey, remember I'm an old man," he protested jokingly.

"Like hell you are."

Ann lifted his T-shirt and started down his chest with her tongue.

Joanna was packing only the essentials. Her stay in Los Angeles would be brief. She had promised Hawksworth she would be away for no more than two days.

Mark was leaning back on the bunk in her sleeping quarters, watching her neatly fold a sweater. "I don't understand why the people at Memorial need a forensic pathologist to deal with an epidemic."

"Apparently I did the autopsy on the person who brought the bug to Los Angeles."

"Were there some unusual findings?"

"Not that I recall," Joanna said, and closed the suitcase. "But the CDC has sent a team of investigators to Memorial, and they insist on talking to me about the autopsy."

"Can't one of your assistants handle that?"

"Not really," Joanna told him. "And there are also

some important forensic matters that need to be sorted out."

"And an assistant forensic pathologist couldn't do that either, huh?"

Joanna smiled at him. "Are you worried I won't come back?"

"That thought crossed my mind."

"You're the one who is so good at disappearing and not coming back."

"Are you ever going to let me forget that?"

"Of course not." Joanna grinned. "It's a wonderful card. I plan to play it over and over again."

He grabbed her by the wrist and pulled her to him. "You know you're driving me crazy."

"Good." She laughed.

"And you want me to believe you don't care, don't you?"

"You can believe anything you want," she said, her voice now lower.

Mark drew her closer, his face almost touching hers. "Up on that deck I kissed you and you kissed me back. You may not have wanted to, but you did."

"Maybe I wanted to," Joanna teased. "But just a little."

"You wanted to a lot," Mark said. He put a finger under her chin, lifting her head, and softly kissed her.

She kissed him back, running her tongue along his lips. "This is never going to work."

"Never."

Mark unbuttoned her silk blouse and gently stroked the skin between her bra and panties.

"Damn you," she purred breathlessly. "You're nothing but trouble."

"I know," Mark said and pulled her down on top of him.

Twenty-four

Mark was abruptly awakened by a loud knock on his door. He groped in the darkness for the light switch before finding it. Sitting up, he glanced at his wristwatch. It was 4:30 A.M.

"Dr. Alexander," Hawksworth called out, knocking even louder. "We have an emergency."

Quickly Mark got into a Harvard sweat suit and opened the door. "What?"

"It's Corpsman Henderson. He has a very high fever and looks terribly ill."

"Did this happen suddenly?"

Hawksworth gestured helplessly with his hand. "I have no idea."

Mark hurried down the corridor, his mind racing as all vestiges of sleep disappeared. Henderson! The medic who had spent hours with Bobby Shea before the young man died—the medic who at the end wore no gloves, no mask. Mark thought back to Bobby Shea's coughing paroxysm that had sent a bloody spray into the air. It was probably loaded with the bacteria.

As they approached the sickbay, a marine guard snapped to attention.

Mark went into the supply room and came back carrying folded gowns and boxes of masks and gloves. "If you want to come in with me, put these on," he said to Hawksworth.

They dressed in surgical garb and entered the sick-room. Henderson was lying atop the sheets, wearing only his shorts. He was moaning in agony and moving very little. There were bright red spots on his legs.

Mark leaned over the bed. "Henderson, this is Dr. Alexander. How are you feeling?"

"Awful," Henderson said, his voice very low and raspy. "I'm burning up."

"Are you having any pain?"

"Burning up," Henderson said again and coughed hard. Spittle and phlegm flew out of his mouth, some tinged with blood. He fought to catch his breath and finally did.

Mark quickly took Henderson's vital signs. The medic's pulse was 118 per minute, his blood pressure was 100/70, his axillary temperature 104 degrees Fahrenheit. He was breathing very rapidly, twenty-two times per minute. Mark could hear the mucus rattling around inside Henderson's chest.

"When did your illness start?" Mark asked.

"A couple of days ago," Henderson said weakly. "I thought it was the flu."

It wasn't the flu, Mark thought. Influenza didn't build up gradually, but had a sudden onset. And besides, cutaneous hemorrhages were never seen in cases of influenza—at least none that Mark was aware of. "Do any of your shipmates have the flu or a high fever?"

Henderson shook his head.

Mark carefully examined Henderson, beginning with his skin. It was hot and flushed, and his lower extremities were covered with tender hemorrhagic areas. The medic's lungs were filled with rhonchi and wheezes, and his dental hygiene was terrible. Mark looked farther back into the medic's oropharynx. There was obvious pyorrhea near the molar area. It was a perfect place for bacteria to grow.

Backing away from the bed, Mark said, "We'll have to

look at the sickbay log and see who was treated by Henderson over the past three days."

"Why?"

"Because I think he got infected when he was looking after Bobby Shea," Mark said, lowering his voice. "Henderson's mouth and lungs are loaded with bacteria."

"And you think he may have infected others?"

"It's a real possibility. That's why I need to look at the sickbay log."

Hawksworth hesitated, not liking the idea. "I don't want to start a panic on this ship."

"You may not be able to prevent it, once word of Henderson's illness spreads."

"Perhaps," Hawksworth said, looking for a way around his dilemma. "It might be best if I were to speak with the men individually."

"Just find out if any of them are ill."

Mark started an intravenous infusion of Ancef. He adjusted the IV drip to twenty drops per minute. "Let's hope this helps."

"Should we have him transported to a hospital in Juneau?" Hawksworth asked.

Mark frowned, glanced at the patient, and fixed Hawksworth with a level gaze. "Let's go check on the status of the helicopter."

The two men walked out into the reception area. The marine guard came to attention, heels clicking together. His uniform smelled of tobacco smoke.

Hawksworth said to the guard, "Take a cigarette break."

"Yes, sir."

"Five minutes."

Hawksworth waited for the marine to leave, then turned to Mark. "What is it you want to say?"

Mark pulled his mask down. "If Henderson is taken ashore, the consequences could be catastrophic. For now, the bacteria are limited to this ship and one floating iceberg. But if Henderson were placed in an ICU in Juneau, the bacteria would spread just as all antibiotic-resistant bacteria have done in the past. Despite the best protective measures, the bacteria would eventually spread to hospital personnel and other patients, and then to the outside world. Henderson could end up being case zero—the starting point—for a worldwide pandemic."

"You're saying we have no choice but to keep him here."

"I'm afraid so."

"And if he stays here he'll almost certainly die."

"That's the most likely prospect."

Hawksworth pondered at length before speaking again. "I know you and Dr. Blalock have tried your best to look after these patients, but the fact of the matter is that neither of you deals with sick patients in your professional lives. You're in research and she's in forensics."

"I don't think anyone could do more than we've done under the circumstances."

"Maybe, maybe not," Hawksworth said. "But there is one person in particular who might be able to help us with Henderson. She's an infectious disease specialist who is a consultant to the ETOX team. Her name is Paula Garrett. Do you know her?"

Mark shrugged. "The name is not familiar."

"Dr. Garrett is codirector of the infectious disease division at Walter Reed Hospital. And she's their expert when it comes to treating patients with esoteric infections." Hawksworth paused for a moment, thinking, then nodded to himself. "I've decided to bring her aboard to treat anyone who falls ill. That will free up you and Dr. Blalock to concentrate on identifying our mysterious bacteria."

Mark rubbed his chin as he weighed the benefits and risks of taking Henderson ashore. "Henderson's chances of survival might be better in an ICU, but not by much."

"Then, if you were in charge, you would not give the order to transport him ashore where he could start a pandemic?"

"No, I wouldn't," Mark said at once.

"Then he stays put."

Twenty-five

"I'm in way over my head," Lori McKay said dejectedly. "I feel like I'm juggling a dozen different things and dropping most of them."

"You're doing fine," Joanna reassured her.

"No, I'm not," Lori went on. "I'm not handling things worth a damn and everybody knows it."

"That's not what I heard."

"Then you're talking to the wrong people," Lori said flatly. "Just ask the homicide detectives who are jumping all over me because I can't give them the evidence they need. Or the people from the CDC, who must think I'm a real idiot. There's an epidemic raging out there and they need information on the baby we autopsied and I'm not coming up with it." Lori sighed wearily. "I guess I've let you and everybody else down, huh?"

Joanna held out her hands. "Grab my wrists as tightly as you can."

Lori looked puzzled but reached out for Joanna's wrists and squeezed them. "So?"

"Now with your third hand pick up your cup of coffee."

Lori looked at Joanna strangely, then smiled. "I don't have a third hand."

"Neither does anyone else. You just do the best you can with the two you've got. Okay?"

"Okay."

Joanna went over to the coffeemaker in her office and

refilled their styrofoam cups. Handing Lori hers, she said, "Let's start with the homicide business and get that out of the way."

Lori took out a stack of index cards and began flipping through them. "Remember the Brentwood murder case Jake Sinclair was working on?"

Joanna thought about Jake and the last time she had seen him. They had fought again and parted angry with one another. Why couldn't he be like other men and want a home and family? And why couldn't he be just a little more sensitive to her needs? She felt her shoulders sag. Even if she'd been able to push him from her mind when she was away from L.A., clearly she still wasn't over him. It wouldn't be that easy. And to complicate matters, she was now getting involved with Mark Alexander again. She had said goodbye to Jake Sinclair and within two weeks she had jumped into bed with another man. Nice going.

"Joanna?" Lori asked, seeing that faraway look on her face. "Are you all right?"

"I'm fine," Joanna said, and cleared her mind. "The Brentwood murder was the one where the sons murdered their parents for the family wealth?"

"Right," Lori said as she found the card she was searching for. "Well, the sons tried to make it look like the couple was shot during a burglary, but they weren't very bright. One of them left a knit ski mask at the scene."

"The one with the hair in it," Joanna recalled.

"It was a single strand of human hair that had been bleached to hell and back," Lori said. "We'll never be able to match this one up."

"Too bad."

"Maybe not," Lori went on. "There were two other fibers attached to the wool of the ski mask. One was a golden brown synthetic fiber from a shag carpet. You want to guess who has a golden brown shag carpet in their apartment?"

"One of the brothers."

"Exactamento! I went there this morning and got a nice sample to compare to the fiber in the mask."

Joanna tilted back in her chair, looking out into space. "Unless the rug is very, very rare—which I doubt it is—that kind of evidence isn't going to be very compelling to a jury."

"But it would strongly suggest he was at the murder scene."

"Juries don't convict people of murder on the basis of strong suggestions."

"Well, every little bit helps."

"You said there were *two* other fibers attached to the mask. What was the other one?"

Lori shrugged. "We can't be sure. It's a long brown strand, but it doesn't look like human hair."

Joanna rocked gently in her chair, still staring into space. That was not a new ski mask, she was thinking. It had too many things attached to it. The only certain fact was that the mask had been on a carpet. Maybe it had picked up the long brown strand of hair there too. "Do the suspects have any pets?"

Lori's eyes suddenly widened. "Yes! The guy had a cat."

"Long-haired and brown?"

"I didn't see it. But I could sure smell it."

"You've got to get a hair sample from that kitty and match it to the hair on the mask."

"Right," Lori said, her voice even, but inwardly she was cursing herself for not putting the clues together. Everything was in front of her—the nonhuman hair, the smell of a cat—yet she had missed the connection. She sighed to herself, wondering how long it would be before she acquired the judgment and insight of Joanna Blalock.

"And don't forget to take the cat itself as evidence,"

Joanna said. "We don't want it running away or conveniently getting lost."

Lori quickly wrote down the instructions, more furious at herself than before. She hadn't thought of that either. "I've got to learn to focus better. Sometimes I let things slip by."

"You're doing fine," Joanna assured her. "This is not an easy business to learn."

"But you're so far ahead of me."

"I had a ten-year head start," Joanna said, bringing her chair back to the floor. "Now, tell me about this epidemic that's breaking out down here."

"I thought you already talked with the people from the CDC."

"I have," Joanna said. "But they're being very close-mouthed. At this point they're only interested in our specimens and microscopic slides."

"Why all this hush-hush business?"

"Because they know that whatever they say will find its way into the newspapers," Joanna told her. "It's best not to say anything until you have the answers. That way the press can't distort and exaggerate things."

"Yeah, I guess that's the smart move," Lori agreed. "Well, from what I hear, they think everything began with the Chinese baby we did the autopsy on."

"It sure as hell looked like cholera," Joanna said, thinking aloud. "All of the infant's symptoms and signs pointed to that diagnosis. And as I recall, a gram stain done on the baby's feces showed comma-shaped, gram-negative bacilli. If you put all of that together, nine out of ten times it'll turn out to be cholera."

"Well, this is the tenth time," Lori said and went to another index card. "When they cultured the baby's feces, the bacteria they grew out didn't have the characteristics of *Vibrio cholerae*. And most important, the baby's serum didn't have antibodies against *Vibrio cholerae*."

Joanna started rocking in her chair again. "If it's not cholera, then what is it?"

"Nobody knows. But it's a scary kind of bacteria. In vitro, it's resistant to all antibiotics. And to make matters worse, we've now had four cases with this infection at Memorial."

Lori went to another index card. "The second case occurred in a baby who was in a crib next to our baby's in the pediatric ICU. And the third and fourth cases occurred in nurses who were looking after the babies."

"Are there other cases in Los Angeles outside of Memorial?"

"At least four," Lori answered. "Two in Santa Monica, two in the Valley. And there may be a fifth case in Culver City."

"Is there any connection between the cases?"

"Apparently all of them came from China or had contact with someone who did."

"It's turning out to be a real epidemic indeed," Joanna said, concerned. "I've heard there are cases popping up all over the West Coast."

"And beyond. I overheard one of the CDC people say that there were already over a hundred cases and that it's now showing up in New York and Chicago." Lori took a deep breath and slowly exhaled. "It's deadly as hell and it's spreading fast. And it doesn't take much to catch it, either."

"We're lucky," Joanna said quietly. "We're lucky we were wearing masks and gloves and gowns when we did the autopsy on the baby."

"And we're lucky the autopsy was done in the contaminated-case room," Lori added. "And that the room was scrubbed down thoroughly after the autopsy was done. Otherwise the whole pathology department could have become infected."

Lucky was an understatement, Joanna was thinking. A hospital was a perfect place to breed and disseminate an infectious agent. The patients were ill, many debilitated and immuno-compromised. It would be easy for bacteria to get past the patients' defense mechanisms and enter their bodies, where they could grow and multiply, consuming the patients while waiting for some nurse or doctor to pick up the microbe and spread it to others.

"Did the other cases die?" Joanna asked.

"The second baby and one nurse did. The other nurse is still hanging on." Lori stared at her hands and nervously picked at her nail polish. "You know, I think it's only a matter of time before some nasty, antibiotic-resistant bug jumps out of nowhere and starts a worldwide pandemic."

"I think you're right," Joanna said slowly, her mind on the toxic iceberg and the deadly microbe it contained. "It's only a matter of time."

"Let's just hope that what we're seeing now isn't it."

"And none of the antibiotics work against this bug, huh?"

"None so far."

"Bummer." Joanna picked up her purse and cellular phone. "If there are any new developments in this case, I want you to call me again. And don't let Colonel Hawksworth intimidate you."

"Aren't you going to be around tomorrow to meet with the CDC people again?"

Joanna shook her head. "You can take care of that."

Lori sighed softly. "I'm way out of my depth on this one."

"Welcome to the club," Joanna said and headed for the door.

Twenty-six

Major Paula Garrett flipped rapidly through Henderson's chart, then went over it again. She looked at Mark. "Where is his blood work?"

"There is no blood work," Mark told her. "We don't have a medical laboratory."

"I want one set up pronto," Garrett said. "We'll need machines that can do blood counts, blood gases, chemistry panels, and electrolytes. And we'll need a technician who knows how to run everything."

"That's Hawksworth's department."

"I don't care whose department it is," Garrett said sharply. "Let's just get the lab set up. Okay?"

"Right," Mark said, not liking the woman's brusque manner. "What else?"

"A nurse or medic to take Henderson's place."

"I think Hawksworth has one on the way."

Garrett next read through Bobby Shea's chart, ending with a lengthy doctor's note. It was written by a woman and signed J. B. "Who is J. B.?"

"Joanna Blalock. She's a forensic pathologist who helped out down here."

Garrett cast her eyes to the ceiling. A forensic pathologist looking after terribly ill patients. Unbelievable! "Is she any good?"

"The best."

Garrett closed the chart and set it down. "Well, I think it's time for me to examine the patient."

Mark watched Garrett as she slipped her arms into a surgical gown. Her army uniform was neatly pressed and showed no wrinkles despite the fact that she had been on an airplane for the past eight hours. Everything about her seemed military. She stood tall and erect, her face thin and expressionless with unsmiling lips, her hair short and grayish brown. If she had any warmth, Mark hadn't detected it so far. She was all business.

Garrett snapped on a pair of latex gloves. "Do we have electronic monitors for his vital signs?"

"No."

"We'll need those too." Garrett pulled her mask up and walked into the sickroom.

The facility was even worse than she had imagined. A bed, a chair, an IV stand, and a blood pressure machine that looked twenty years old. The room was poorly ventilated, the air stale and still. She quickly examined Henderson, then stepped back, aghast at his condition. He had all the signs of a dying man. His skin was cold and clammy, his breathing labored and shallow. And his responses were very slow. The medic was having difficulty answering simple questions.

"Do you have a headache?" Garrett asked loudly.

Henderson blinked for a moment and moved his head.

"A headache?" Garrett said again. "Do you have a headache?"

"No," Henderson groaned.

"Does your neck hurt?"

Henderson swallowed and slowly moved his head from side to side.

Garrett flexed the corpsman's neck gently. She was looking for the presence of muscular rigidity, a sign of meningitis. Henderson's neck was supple, but that didn't exclude the diagnosis. Meningitis or meningoencephalitis was still a possibility, Garrett thought, a very real possibility. Or Henderson could be bleeding into his brain.

She stepped back and pondered what to do next. She could increase the dose of Ancef to three grams every six hours and wait and watch. But she knew that wasn't the answer. Henderson's condition was deteriorating and he was near death. He needed to be in a proper medical center where diagnostic tests could be done and treatment with more potent antibiotics started. Even that might not help, particularly if the infection had spread to his brain. But at least it would give him a fighting chance.

Garrett reached for the phone and asked to be connected to Colonel Hawksworth.

"Colonel, our man is going downhill," she said. "We have to get him to a hospital in Juneau."

There was a long pause, then Hawksworth said, "That may not be in everyone's best interest."

"I'm only concerned with Henderson's best interest, and he's going to die unless he gets to an ICU."

"You do realize that by sending him ashore you could be spreading this deadly bacteria to the population at large," Hawksworth said evenly. "You are aware of that?"

"Colonel, that bug is going to get ashore with or without Henderson. It's only a matter of time before it does."

"But given enough time we could isolate it and—"

"Isolating bacteria doesn't mean you'll come up with a cure," Garrett interrupted. "That could be years away. In the meantime, let's see if we can learn how to treat these patients and maybe save some lives."

There was another long pause.

"All right," Hawksworth said reluctantly. "But we'll have to wait for our helicopter to return to ship."

"How long will that be?"

"Two hours."

Garrett put the phone down, wondering if Henderson was going to live that long.

Henderson moaned and coughed weakly. A string of blood-tinged spittle clung to his lips.

"We're going to take a helicopter ride in a little while," Garrett told him. "We'll put you in a hospital and get you fixed up."

Henderson stared into space. He gave no indication he had heard, let alone understood what Garrett had said.

Garrett left the room, closing the door behind her. She quickly stripped off her surgical garb and went over to the marine guard who was seated at a small table. The guard was watching the sickbed on a television monitor. He was wearing a mask and latex gloves.

"Keep a close eye on him," Garrett said.

"Yes, ma'am."

"And if Henderson gets in trouble and you have to go into the sickroom, you put on a gown and keep on the mask and gloves. Understood?"

"Yes, ma'am," the guard said. But he was thinking there was no way he was going into that goddamn room. No way! Everybody who went in there ended up dead.

Garrett hurried down the passageway, her mind listing the preparations that would be necessary to transport Henderson ashore. All personnel involved, including the pilot, would have to wear protective gear. A window would have to remain open to provide extra ventilation and hopefully dilute any bacteria that Henderson coughed into the air. The cold would not be good for Henderson, but under no circumstances was Garrett going to allow the cabin of the aircraft to be closed off. And of course the people at the Juneau hospital would have to be alerted. They'd need an infectious disease specialist, and nurses who were experienced in strict isolation techniques. Yet even with these precautions, the bacteria would still slip through and spread, Garrett thought grimly. These types of microorganisms always did.

Garrett came to the bacteriology lab and entered, closing the door quietly behind her. Reetha Sims was tilted back in her swivel chair, holding a small culture dish up to the light.

"No bacterial growth," Reetha said sourly. "Not even a single colony."

"So much for Neiderman's idea," Doreen said, and took the culture dish from her sister. She was about to discard the dish, then changed her mind. "Let's allow it to incubate for another twenty-four hours."

"It's not going to help, but be my guest."

Reetha turned in her chair to Paula Garrett. "Are you finding your way around okay?"

"So far all I've really seen is the sickbay," Garrett replied. "And it looks like something out of the nineteenth century."

"This is not a good place to get sick," Reetha agreed, nodding. "How is Henderson doing?"

"Not good," Garrett said. "As soon as the helicopter returns, we'll take him to an ICU ashore."

"That's too bad," Reetha said. "Let's hope he makes it."

Garrett watched Reetha light a cigarette and wondered for the thousandth time how people could smoke, knowing it was killing them. "When we met a little while ago, you mentioned that you had once been part of a CDC team that went into hot zones."

Reetha nodded. "Both Doreen and I did. Why?"

"Because I may need your help ashore," Garrett told her. "If the doctors and nurses in Juneau don't know good isolation technique, we'll have to show them how to do it."

"No problem."

A side door that led to the toxicology lab opened. Joe Wells and Neiderman walked in, each holding a large rack of test tubes with screw-on tops.

"Here are the extracts from the magnolia plant that

was inside our iceberg," Wells said, and put the test tubes on a countertop.

"Why are there so many specimens?" Reetha asked.

"Because we made extracts from the leaves, roots, and stems, then isolated the individual components by chromatography," Wells said. "If your damn growth factor is in that magnolia, it'll be in one of these test tubes."

Garrett furrowed her brow, not certain she had heard correctly. "Did you say there was a magnolia inside the iceberg?"

"I sure did," Wells answered, trying unsuccessfully to remember the major's name. "In the Cretaceous period there were plenty of flowering plants, and the magnolia was one of them."

Garrett studied the row of test tubes. Some contained a clear liquid, others a green or rust-colored fluid. Hawksworth had told her about the iceberg, but not about the plants it contained. "What else is in this iceberg?"

"That's what we're in the process of finding out."

"I'll tell you this," Neiderman chimed in. "The air back then was dirty as hell. That black mass in the iceberg may only be a cloud of burning sulfur. It was filled with sulfides and sulfoxides and even some sulfuric acid. The sky must have been on fire, just like Joe said."

The black material would have to be cultured too, Reetha thought as she extinguished her cigarette. Maybe the damn bug needed one of the sulfur compounds to grow. She reached for the test tubes, pushing her swivel chair back. The wheels of the chair caught in the rug on the floor and it began to topple backwards. Her hands flew up as she tried to regain her balance.

Joe Wells rushed over and grabbed the back of the chair before it could topple over. "You've got to be careful, Reetha, or you'll hurt yourself."

"Thanks," Reetha said gratefully and took a deep breath. "That's the second time that's happened this week. I told Mark I need a new rug in here."

"Why have a rug at all?" Garrett asked.

"Because the floor by my desk gets very damp and cold for some reason," Reetha said. "And it goes right through my shoes."

"I'll make sure a new rug gets put in here," Wells said. "One that your chair won't get stuck in. In the meantime, you be careful."

"I'll try," Reetha said, touched by his concern. She wondered when they'd have a chance to be alone together again, like they were on deck during the aurora borealis. She glanced up at him and felt her face flushing.

Quickly she looked over at the test tubes. "Culturing all these specimens on a dozen different media is going to take a lot of work. We'll need to get started right away."

"I can help," Neiderman volunteered once more, pleased to have a reason to be in the bacteriology lab. He wanted to be close by when the organism was finally grown out.

Reetha looked up at Garrett. "As you can see, we're having a hell of a time making that bug grow. So if you have any suggestions, don't be shy."

"I won't," Garrett said, liking Reetha and her directness. "There is one thought that crossed my mind. Maybe it's not some critical missing ingredient that's the problem. Maybe there's some inhibitor in that iceberg which prevents bacterial growth."

"Some sort of inhibitor," Reetha said, more to herself than the others. "We hadn't thought of that. But how do you look for the inhibitor of something you can't grow in the first place?"

"I'm afraid I can't help you with that."

The door burst open and Hawksworth hurried in, glancing around until he saw Garrett. "Henderson is worse. He's having trouble breathing."

Paula Garrett ran for the sickbay.

Twenty-seven

Henderson died as the helicopter touched down at the Juneau airport. He gasped one final time before his eyes rolled back with fixed and dilated pupils. Garrett tried to find a carotid pulse. There wasn't any.

The door of the helicopter opened and Garrett saw a woman running across the tarmac toward them. Behind her was a stationary ambulance, its lights blinking. The day was dark and overcast, with a light rain starting to fall.

Joanna hurried up and nodded to the doctor Hawksworth had told her about on the phone. "I'm Joanna Blalock. How is Henderson doing?"

"He just died," Garrett said. "There wasn't anything I could do."

Joanna glanced over her shoulder and saw the ambulance approaching them. "Let's get airborne right now," she said quickly.

Garrett gave her a strange look. "What the hell for?"

"Because as soon as this body leaves the helicopter, it belongs to the medical examiner in Juneau. We'll have no control over anything." Joanna glanced again at the oncoming ambulance. "And if you think he'll keep this quiet, particularly after what happened on that fishing boat, then you're crazy."

"There's going to be hell to pay for this," Garrett said.

Joanna climbed into the helicopter and called out to the pilot. "Commander, get this ship up in the air."

"Ma'am, my orders are—"

"Get this damn ship up!" Joanna snapped. "Then you can call your C.O. and see if you made the right move. You can always land again."

The rotors began to swing with a loud whine. Abruptly the approaching ambulance stopped and backed up. Now the rain was coming down harder, splattering up against the window of the helicopter. Joanna peered out at the tarmac. The blinking lights on the ambulance were a blur.

Moments later they were airborne. The wind and rain whipped at them, causing a horizontal turbulence. Everything was shifting and bouncing. Joanna and Garrett had to struggle through three tries before they got Henderson's corpse into a body bag.

"This is turning into a circus," Garrett said, leaning back in her seat. "And don't think this won't get into the newspapers. The airport authorities and the hospital are going to raise Cain and want to know what happened to our critically ill patient."

"Tell them he had a miraculous recovery," Joanna said.

"They won't buy that."

Joanna shrugged. "Then that'll be Hawksworth's problem."

Garrett sighed wearily. "Maybe it's better this way. At least we didn't bring the bacteria into Juneau."

The pilot turned his head to the cabin. "The colonel says your decision was the correct one. We are to proceed directly back to the *Global Explorer*."

The helicopter climbed out of the turbulence and leveled off. Below them the outskirts of Juneau quickly passed by.

Joanna stifled a yawn, trying to fight through her fatigue. "I feel like I could sleep for twenty-four hours straight."

"Tough trip, huh?"

"Draining," Joanna said and snuggled up in her fur-lined parka. "Why is the cabin so cold?"

"We left a window open on our way over to keep the aircraft ventilated."

The helicopter suddenly dipped and Garrett tightened her seat belt. She glanced over at Joanna. "We really haven't been introduced. I'm Paula Garrett."

Joanna nodded. "Welcome to Nightmare City."

"I knew it was going to be bad, but not this bad."

Joanna looked over at the body bag that held Henderson's corpse. "Do you have any idea how he got infected?"

"I can't be sure," Garrett said. "But most likely it entered via the oropharyngeal route. Henderson's teeth and gums were a mess."

"So you think the bacteria spread through the air?" Joanna asked anxiously. "You think Bobby Shea coughed and some of the spray got into Henderson's mouth?"

"Probably. But I'm told he wasn't wearing a mask or gloves. All it would have taken for Henderson to get infected was for him to touch the patient, then bring his fingers to his mouth."

"But aerosol transmission is still more likely."

"I'm afraid so. And if that's the case, we're going to have an awful time trying to control it."

"But you need an open wound to get infected—at least so far."

"Hell, everybody has an open wound," Garrett said unhappily. "People cut themselves shaving or nick their cuticles with manicures or fall and scrape a knee. The list is endless. Somehow bacteria always manage to find a portal of entry."

"So how do we contain it?"

"I'm not sure we can," Garrett said honestly. "At least not until we've identified the organism and its mode of transmission."

"Are we making any progress culturing it out?"

"A little," Garrett said. "But it keeps dying so rapidly. On the last run they added increasing amounts of sucrose and the bacteria lived a bit longer, though not much. Sucrose is the very first ingredient they've found that the bacteria *might* like."

"Why did they use sucrose?"

"Just on a whim," Garrett told her. "The Sims sisters think our organism is a gram-negative bacillus and so is *Vibrio cholerae*, which needs sucrose to grow. So Doreen suggested they try it."

"Are you saying that our bacteria and the cholera organism may have things in common?"

"Could be."

"But surely our patients don't have any of the clinical features of cholera."

"That's for sure," Garrett agreed. "The symptoms of cholera are so clear-cut that the diagnosis is easy. No doctor worth his salt would miss it."

"Well, a group of very fine specialists at Memorial recently did."

Joanna told her about the Chinese baby who had arrived in Los Angeles with a high fever and devastating diarrhea. "And the infant's feces was loaded with gram-negative bacilli."

"That's cholera until proven otherwise," Garrett said firmly.

"That's what I thought too. But when they cultured the feces, it grew out some strange bacteria and not *Vibrio cholerae*." Joanna paused to stretch her back. "And that baby was the first case of the epidemic that's now spreading across America."

Garrett leaned forward, ears pricked. "You're referring to the epidemic that started in China?"

"Right."

Garrett shook her head slowly. "The cases I've heard about don't have choleralike symptoms. They're sick as hell with sepsis and pneumonia, but they don't have diarrhea."

Joanna thought for a moment. "Maybe the disease behaves differently in babies."

"It just might," Garrett said. "Or maybe the symptoms depend on the bacteria's portal of entry. For example, if it enters via the gastrointestinal tract, that's where it does the most damage."

"Well, one thing is for certain," Joanna said. "Whatever way it gets into the body, it's lethal as hell."

"And it's spreading so fast," Garrett told her. "It's going like wildfire."

"I heard it has already reached New York."

"It's gone even farther. There are now two suspected cases in London."

"Nasty business," Joanna said and glanced out at the sea, its color deep gray in the twilight hours. She closed her eyes and tried to sleep, but couldn't. She kept thinking about the hot zone she had just left and the even hotter one she was returning to.

Neiderman was beginning to get on Reetha's nerves. He was asking question after question about culture media and bacteria and how to keep a culture going once it was established. And now Neiderman wanted to know about plant extracts, a topic Reetha knew little about.

"These extracts are such amazing stuff," Neiderman said.

"Sure are," Reetha said, holding a culture plate up to the light and seeing no growth. The culture medium was an extract of the magnolia.

"I have trouble understanding how an extract can make bacteria grow."

Reetha shrugged. "I guess because it contains a foodstuff."

"Like something from the prehistoric era that doesn't exist today?"

Reetha took a deep breath, trying to keep her patience. "I'm not an expert on plants, but I think Joe Wells is. Why don't you ask him?"

"Good idea." Neiderman was close to Reetha, looking over her shoulder as she studied the culture plates. He glanced down at her breasts, round and big under her sweater. He moved in a little closer. "Do you see any growth?"

"None," Reetha said and reached for another culture plate.

Neiderman leaned forward, pretending he was trying to get a better look. Now his head was next to hers, some of her hair touching his face. It smelled as if she had just shampooed it.

Reetha held the plate up and her back pressed lightly against Neiderman. She continued studying the plate, unaware of her body contact with him. "Nothing here either."

"Yeah, nothing," Neiderman agreed, and looked over at the door, wondering if he should make his move on her. Oh, how he loved women with big breasts! He began fantasizing about fucking her on the table.

Reetha turned away and placed the culture plates back in the incubator.

Neiderman tried to come up with another idea so he could spend even more time working with her. He wanted to be close by when the bacteria finally grew out. And he also wanted to screw Reetha. Maybe they could work together to sell the toxin and become fabulously wealthy and happy.

"I think we can say that this organism doesn't like dead guinea pig tissue," Reetha said, breaking into his thoughts. "It seems to require living guinea pig tissue to grow."

Neiderman's eyes lit up. "Then let's give it living tissue."

"Are you referring to cell lines?"

Neiderman nodded. "I'm talking about establishing a long-term cell line in vitro using guinea pig fibroblasts or lymphocytes."

Reetha nodded back, thinking about cell lines. Certain animal cells, like lymphocytes, could be made to grow and replicate in culture plates as long as the appropriate nutrients were provided. "Can you do that in your lab?"

"I sure can."

Reetha looked at him dubiously. "Have you done it before?"

"Dozens of times."

"Show me." Reetha took his arm and guided him to the door.

Twenty-eight

The tension in the conference room was high. Around the long table, members of the ETOX team sat stone-faced as Hawksworth laid down a new set of rules.

"We've done it your way and it hasn't worked," Hawksworth said disapprovingly. "We've made no progress in identifying the bacteria. None."

"I'm not sure that's a fair statement," Kagen argued mildly. "We know it can infect man and some experimental animals."

"And that it can kill by two mechanisms," Mark chimed in. "It can kill with its toxin or by actual infection. And for the latter it requires an open wound to gain entrance."

"And we believe it's a gram-negative bacillus that needs sucrose to grow in vitro," Reetha added.

"That's all well and good," Hawksworth said testily. "But you are all dancing around the fact that we do not have the information we need. Namely, what is this bacteria and how do we destroy it?"

"That takes time," Kagen said.

"Which we are running out of," Hawksworth told them. "In a few weeks the winter storms begin and we'll lose our missing toxic iceberg forever. Now, you may say that's my problem, but it's yours too. Because the bacteria in that iceberg—wherever the hell it is—could get into the food chain again and spread. And we don't have any idea what it is or how to treat it." Hawksworth paused and sipped water, his jaws tight. "And from a personal standpoint, that's not the worst part. The very worst part for each of us is that we're sitting on a death ship. Two of our crew have already died from this bacteria and there's sure to be more."

"That's not a certainty," Mark said. "If everyone is very careful and—"

"It *is* a certainty," Hawksworth cut him off. "With all due respect, Dr. Alexander, I have had the matter reviewed by other experts who are consultants to the ETOX project. They all agree that, until the bacteria is identified and a treatment devised, more people on this ship will become infected and will die. And they also feel it's just a matter of time before the bacteria is spread to the general population by someone from this ship who goes ashore. They are so convinced of this, they have recommended that the ship be quarantined and that no one go ashore until we have our problem solved. I plan to follow those recommendations."

"You make it sound like we're prisoners," Doreen said nervously.

"We all are," Hawksworth told her, "until we identify this lethal bacteria."

"I'm not sure you have that power," Mark challenged him.

"Oh, but I *do*," Hawksworth said tersely. "And there is a platoon of tough marines aboard who *say* I do."

Mark looked away, resenting Hawksworth's overbearing manner. But he had to admit the colonel was right. The only way to really contain the bacteria was to quarantine the ship.

He looked at Hawksworth. "You understand that we'll be condemning anyone who gets sick to death?"

"Better a few of us than a pandemic that could kill millions."

Doreen raised her hand timidly. "Colonel, I didn't come aboard to die."

"Nor did I," Hawksworth said, his voice a little softer. "And for your information I have a family—a wife and two sons—waiting for me. They expect me to return to them safe and sound, and I hope to do so. But I have my orders. And now so do you."

He picked up a clipboard and studied it. A picture of his wife flashed into his mind, still pretty with her slender figure and wonderful smile. He quickly pushed the image aside. "Now, they are not going to let us just drift unaided out here. A replacement medic will arrive shortly and bring with him a supply of new antibiotics. As we all know, Ancef did not work. We've been advised to use triple antibiotic therapy on the next patient. This will include a mixture of Rocephin, gentamicin, and vancomycin. Do you agree with this recommendation, Dr. Alexander?"

Mark nodded. "That should cover most of the bacteria we know about."

"And hopefully one we don't know about. Now, I'm certain each of you will—"

There was a sudden loud thud. The entire room vibrated. Glasses fell off the table and shattered on the floor. Everyone reached for something to grab on to. Gradually the vibrations faded.

Hawksworth hurried to the phone, punched in an extension, and spoke briefly. The others remained at the table dead still, all of their senses heightened.

A creaking noise came from overhead. It lasted only a moment. Then all was silent again. Still nobody moved.

"We were rammed by a small iceberg," Hawksworth said. "It was a glancing blow. Our hull is intact."

"And suppose it had pierced the hull?" Kagen asked, his voice trembling slightly.

"We'd still be all right," Hawksworth said. "This ship

has a double hull and compartments that isolate any damage."

"How can you be so sure that the hull hasn't been compromised?"

"Because we have sensors and alarms that would have alerted us."

Kagen stood, clearly unnerved by the incident. "I suggest we adjourn for cocktails and dinner."

Hawksworth registered the fear on everybody's face. "Let me assure all of you that this ship is absolutely safe. Nothing is going to sink her."

"That's what they said about the *Titanic*," Kagen said grimly, and led the group out of the room.

"Here, let me carry that." Mark reached for Joanna's suitcase. "How was your trip?"

"Long," Joanna said wearily.

"I'll bet."

They were walking down the passageway that led to the scientists' sleeping quarters. The brightly lit corridor was deserted except for a marine guard at the far end.

"Where is everyone?" Joanna asked.

"Happy hour started early," Mark said. "Want to join them?"

"Maybe later."

They entered Joanna's cabin and sat on the edge of her bunk. She tossed her parka aside and kicked off her shoes, then lay back on a balled-up pillow. She slowly stretched her neck, trying to loosen taut muscles. "The seats on those military aircraft are so damn uncomfortable."

"Would you like a back rub?"

"Oh, yeah." Joanna turned onto her stomach and pulled her blouse out of her jeans. "Do the midthoracic area, please."

Mark gently massaged her muscles with a side-to-side motion and felt her gradually relax. Her skin was smooth and warm and had the aroma of roses. "Is the epidemic as bad as they make it sound?" he asked.

"Worse," Joanna said, moaning as Mark touched a sore place. "It's now spread coast to coast with over a hundred documented cases. There are even two probables in London. And all they know is that it started in China and that the bug causing it is resistant to all antibiotics."

"Do they have any idea what part of China it started in?"

"Shanghai, they think."

"That's a hell of a big place," Mark said. "They'll have trouble determining who was case zero."

"Is it really that important to find out who the first case was?"

"It sure is," Mark said. "If they can determine how the *first* case got it, then they may well be able to stop the epidemic from cropping up again."

Joanna moaned again as Mark moved his hands to her waist and kneaded the lower back muscles. "That's nice."

"I've missed you," Mark said, leaning down to kiss the nape of her neck. "I couldn't wait for you to get back."

Joanna turned over and looked up at him. "We shouldn't have slept together."

"Why not?"

"Because I'm just getting out of one bad relationship and the last thing I want to do is jump into another."

"Am I a bad relationship?"

"You were the first time around."

Mark brushed his lips over her chin and cheeks. "Let the past go, Joanna. It doesn't exist anymore."

She pecked him back on the lips. "Why do I get the feeling I'm going to get hurt again?"

"Paranoia, I guess." He unbuttoned her blouse and ran his tongue down her neck to her chest. "Did I tell you you were beautiful?"

"A long time ago."

"Well, I'm telling you again. You're out-of-sight beautiful."

"Really?" Joanna said, wrapping her arms around him.

"Really," Mark said, and turned out the lights.

Twenty-nine

B eneath a brilliant sky Joanna and Mark strolled along the deck of the *Global Explorer II*. The day was crystal clear and breezy, the sea choppy with small ice floes everywhere. In the distance they could see inflatable vessels speeding toward the icebergs.

"How much longer do you think we'll stay out here with these icebergs?" Joanna asked.

"Another few weeks, according to Hawksworth," Mark said. "That's when the real winter storms are supposed to start. We'll have no choice but to move to calmer waters."

"And farther away from any port."

Mark sighed wearily. "That's what happens when you volunteer."

"Nobody volunteered for *this*," Joanna said. "Nobody wanted to come aboard a death ship, knowing that they might never leave."

They passed the helipad, now a beehive of activity. Crewmen were busily unloading boxes and crates from the helicopter which had just arrived from Juneau. A large crate with the label *cardiac monitor system* was being lowered to the deck on a hydraulic dolly.

Mark gestured with his head toward the helicopter. "They're making two round trips a day just to bring in the medical supplies that Paula Garrett ordered. Our sickbay is starting to look like a full-fledged ICU."

"We're going to need more than an ICU if we have any more cases like Henderson."

"It's only a matter of time before we do," Mark said. "Chances are this will behave like most contagious outbreaks. It'll start slow, then spread rapidly."

"And there's not a damn thing we can do about it," Joanna said grimly. "Except wait and see who goes down next." She wrinkled her brow in thought. "Maybe we should give cromolyn to the next patient."

Mark nodded. "It's worth a try."

Two more inflatable boats were lowered into the sea and zoomed away, bouncing over the choppy waters. They headed for a distant cluster of Coast Guard vessels.

Joanna shielded her eyes from the sun and watched. "Something is causing a lot of activity."

"Probably another boat getting too close to our ship."

They walked on. The huge cranes above cast giant shadows over them and the entire helipad. In the distance they heard a horn beeping intermittently. Then they saw a Coast Guard cutter moving in the direction of the patrol boats.

"Can you imagine why anyone would want to get on this ship?" Mark asked. "Particularly if they knew what was aboard?"

"A deadly microbe and a murderer," Joanna said dryly. "That's a hell of a combination, isn't it?"

"You really are convinced that Barbara Van Buren was murdered?"

"Oh, yeah," Joanna said firmly. "That was no accident."

"I don't think that most of the people on the ETOX team believe that."

Joanna shrugged. "People believe what they want to believe. But all the evidence shows that her head was bashed in by someone."

"It's hard to imagine a killer aboard this ship."

"Well, there is," Joanna said, thinking about Jake Sinclair and what he would say about an elusive killer he was having trouble tracking down: *The bastard is probably having a beer right now, laughing his ass off.* But with Jake as the lead investigator, the killer's amusement usually didn't last very long. She brought her mind back to the present. "We have a murderer roaming around this ship and we don't have the slightest idea who he is."

"What about the fingerprints you found?"

Joanna forced a laugh. "That was a ploy to see if anyone would get nervous. There were never any prints."

Mark shook his head. "It just doesn't make sense to kill someone like Barbara Van Buren."

"It did to the murderer."

They strolled on. Overhead the giant cranes were slowly being repositioned to starboard. The sailors on deck seemed unusually busy, running back and forth, manning lines and cables, responding to rapid-fire orders.

In the distance a fog was setting in and the patrol boats could barely be seen. The wind picked up again, even colder than before.

"Do you want to go below?" Mark asked.

"In a minute." Joanna took a deep breath and looked out at the sea. "Last night I had a terrible nightmare. I dreamt that we all had become infected and died on this ship. And I was the last to go. Dead bodies were everywhere, and I was just sitting here, sick as hell and waiting to die. It was really frightening."

"That's unlikely to happen here," Mark assured her.

"That's not what you told me a minute ago," Joanna said gloomily. "Your exact words were, 'It'll start slow, then spread rapidly.' "

"Not everyone dies in an epidemic," Mark said. "Even with the Black Plague most people survived."

"But they weren't stuck on a ship with some sort of deadly bacteria that kills everybody it touches."

Mark nodded. "It's a nasty bug, all right."

"And you can be sure if an outbreak spreads through this ship, Hawksworth will never let any of us leave," Joanna went on. "The government will sacrifice all of us to keep the bacteria confined to this ship. We'll just float around out here until we're all dead."

"We have to hope it doesn't come to that," Mark said somberly.

"We're depending a lot on hope, aren't we?" Joanna looked away, still haunted by her nightmare.

"Come here," Mark said, putting his arms around her and drawing her close.

Joanna nestled against his chest. "Damn! I hate to be in this kind of predicament. You feel so helpless. All you can do is sit and wait."

Mark hugged her and kissed her forehead. "I'll wait with you. How does that sound?"

"Pretty good." She reached up and touched his face. "I'm glad you're here."

"Me too."

Joanna was about to kiss his cheek when she saw, just below his sideburn, a fresh scab. She pointed to it. "You've got a cut here."

"It's from shaving," Mark said. "I try to avoid it with my razor, but every morning I seem to reopen it."

"Well, stop shaving there. Put a Band-Aid over it until it heals," Joanna told him. "Don't give the bacteria any possible mode of entrance."

Mark smiled. "Are you worried about me?"

"Some." Joanna smiled back and moved closer to him.

The PA system suddenly came on with a loud squeal. "CLEAR THE DECKS! CLEAR THE DECKS!"

Joanna and Mark hurried toward the bridge. They had to weave and dodge around sailors who were scurrying to their duty stations. A sailor tripped and fell, landing hard on the deck and skinning his elbows. He was up quickly and ran past Joanna, rejoining his mates.

Off the starboard bow a loud horn sounded. Joanna glanced over her shoulder and saw the flotilla of patrol boats returning. Behind them was a Coast Guard cutter, and behind the cutter was an iceberg in tow. The iceberg was pointed, its top resembling the steeple of a church.

Mark held the door for Joanna as they entered the superstructure. Pausing to catch their breath, they saw Hawksworth heading for the elevator.

"What's all the commotion about?" Joanna asked.

"We've found the toxic iceberg," Hawksworth said, obviously pleased.

"Well, there's some good news."

Hawksworth asked, "Would you like to see how we get the iceberg aboard?"

"Absolutely."

They took the elevator to the top level and exited onto the bridge. The view from six stories up was spectacular, the ocean deep blue and dotted with floating ice. Joanna was again awed by the immense size of the ship she was on. Its deck seemed to stretch out forever. By comparison, the Coast Guard cutter alongside seemed like a toy.

"How large is this iceberg?" Joanna asked.

"About half the size of the one already on board," Hawksworth said.

"Where will you put this one?"

"We have another compartment," Hawksworth said, the tone of his voice indicating he would give no further details. He pointed to the iceberg. "Watch."

The Coast Guard cutter disengaged and moved away from the *Global Explorer II*. Then the vessels closed in on the iceberg. Divers in neoprene suits entered the frigid water and began encircling the iceberg with thick cables.

Huge grappling hooks were lowered and disappeared beneath the surface of the sea. More wire and cable were wrapped around the iceberg, almost encasing it. Then the giant cranes swung into position.

"I don't see how those cranes can handle the incredible weight of an iceberg," Mark said.

"Oh, they can," Hawksworth assured him. "We used similar cranes to lift a Russian nuclear submarine off the ocean floor."

The divers in their neoprene suits climbed into their boats and distanced themselves from the iceberg. A portion of the deck near the bow slowly opened, its plates retracting out of sight. Joanna tried to look down into it, but all she saw was a black pit.

With a low grinding sound the cranes began to lift. The cables grew taut as the iceberg slowly came out of the water. It was huge, with a broad, irregularly shaped base. Its pointed top sparkled in the bright sunlight.

Now the iceberg was totally out of the water. Gradually it was raised above the level of the bulwarks, then brought over the deck. With care, the positioning of the iceberg over the giant hatch began. For a moment everything was absolutely still. Then the iceberg was slowly lowered.

Suddenly one of the giant cranes gave, its steel frame bending and shifting all the iceberg's weight to the other crane.

Thick cables snapped with a loud pop and whipped through the air. Two Marines were knocked flat, another beheaded by the flying cable. The man's head bounced on the deck before rolling to a stop.

Joanna gasped and looked away, horrified by the gruesome sight.

Off balance, the iceberg crashed to the deck, splitting into two jagged pieces. The larger piece slid across the deck and into the opening near the bow and disappeared. A moment later it landed with an ear-splitting bang. The

Global Explorer II tilted sharply to port, its entire hull vibrating. Then it righted itself.

"Jesus Christ!" Joanna muttered, holding on to Mark and still feeling the vibration. "Jesus H. Christ!"

Hawksworth quickly reached for the phone.

Thirty

Ann Cormier waited impatiently for Mike Mallory to arrive. It was 8:30 P.M. and he was already thirty minutes late for their rendezvous in the recreation room. With each passing minute the chances of their getting caught increased greatly. As the night wore on, the marine guards tended to check the rooms more frequently and never on a regular schedule. And now everyone was extra edgy after the ship-jarring crash that had occurred only hours earlier. If she had a date with anyone else, she would have been long gone. But Mallory was so handsome and so good in bed. And so unlike the immature and inexperienced Eddie Walsh. She could still see him fumbling with his rubber the last time they met. To hell with him! She would concentrate on Mike Mallory. She wondered if he was happily married.

The door at the far end of the room opened. Ann moved back quickly into the shadows behind the pool table.

Mike Mallory crept in silently and looked around.

"Psst!" Ann hissed loudly. "Over here."

"Sorry I'm late," Mallory said, unzipping his flight suit.

"Where the hell have you been?"

"Involved in a preflight check," he told her. "We have to fly to Juneau tonight for some special medical equipment."

"Why didn't you tell me?"

"How? Over the PA system?"

Ann giggled and put her hands inside his flight suit. She pulled down his jockey shorts and began stroking him. "I ought to make you wait like you made me wait."

"Good idea," he said, kissing her nose and biting down gently on her lip. "That should give us at least ten minutes together."

"That's not enough," she complained, and licked at his tongue. "That's barely enough to get started."

"It's all we've got," Mallory said, lifting her up on the pool table. "Now, do you want to talk or get it on?"

Ann leaned back and spread her legs. She didn't have on panties. "What do you think?"

Mallory pushed into her and she rose up to meet him. She could feel him inside her. She brought her arms around his neck and playfully put out her tongue to touch his nose.

Under the overhead fluorescent light, he smiled down at her. Suddenly his smile disappeared. "What's wrong with your lip?"

Ann looked up at him. "What are you talking about?"

Mallory disengaged and moved back. "You've got a big black spot on the inner surface of your lip. Maybe you'd better look at it."

Ann sat up and reached for the mirror in her purse. She tilted her head up so that the overhead light shone directly down on her. Then she saw it. A black spot on her lip, just like the coastguardsman had on his tongue. She tried to scrape it away with a fingernail, but it stayed in place. *Oh, shit! Oh, shit!*

Mallory tried to read her expression. "What is it?"

"Some—some type of infection, I think."

"What *kind* of infection?" Mallory asked, now worried.

"I'm not sure," she lied, thinking about the low-grade fever and cough and fatigue she had been experiencing.

"Well, you sure as hell better find out."

"Yeah, I'll have the new doc check it out. First thing in the morning."

"Goddamn it to hell," Mallory seethed. "Why didn't you *tell* me about it?"

"I didn't see it before," Ann said, now feeling the small blister inside her lip. "Maybe it's only a virus."

"It damn well better be." Mallory zipped up his flight suit, wondering if he had picked up anything from her. Goddamn it! He wouldn't know for a while. "I want to know what the doc says it is."

"I'll talk to you right after I see her." She tried to grasp his hand, but he turned away and hurried from the room, cursing under his breath.

As the door closed, Ann dropped to her knees and prayed. *Dear God, don't let me be infected. Please, dear God, not me!*

Reetha moved quickly down the passageway, hoping that she had remembered to reset the temperature gauge on the largest incubator. If she hadn't, all of the cultures that had been done that afternoon would be ruined, worthless. Everything would have to be done again. Nearly a whole day's work wasted. She passed a marine guard, his eyelids half closed with fatigue. Reetha checked her watch. It was almost 10 P.M. The guard would be changing soon, a fresh marine coming on duty.

Reetha walked on, her mind going back to the work she'd done earlier. It had taken so much time to do it, and it would be a real pain in the ass to do it again. Probably all for nothing, too. The results would be the same zilch.

Reetha entered the bacteriology lab and closed the door behind her.

Something was wrong. The largest incubator's door stood ajar. She stepped in closer and looked into the incubator and saw that the tops had been taken off all the culture dishes. She stared at them. There was a vial labeled *panamycin* sitting on a shelf, a half-filled syringe next to it. "Christ!" she whispered. Someone was sabotaging everything.

Suddenly something heavy and flat slammed against the back of Reetha's head. She dropped like a dead weight, her skull and neck hitting the steel floor with a loud thud.

The assailant went down on a knee and checked Reetha for a carotid pulse but couldn't find one. She didn't seem to be breathing. There was a small amount of blood on the floor where her head had landed. He felt again for a carotid pulse. Nothing.

He got to his feet and took several deep breaths, trying to calm himself. The nosy bitch! he was thinking. Reetha could have ruined everything. She would have eventually figured out why he was doctoring all the cultures. And when she did, his carefully laid plans would have come unraveled in plain sight for all to see. It would have cost him a fortune, and he would have ended up spending the rest of his life in jail.

He kicked at Reetha's ribs. She remained motionless. He was about to do it again, but decided not to. Joanna the Bloodhound might find the bruise mark and wonder how it got there. If Reetha's death were to look accidental, he'd have to avoid the mistakes he had made with Barbara Van Buren.

Be careful! he told himself. Don't give Joanna anything to work with. Make it foolproof.

His gaze went over to the swivel chair and the rug beneath it. Perfect, he thought. Twice in the past four days Reetha had almost fallen and broken her neck when she had tilted back and the chair had gotten caught in the rug. And others had seen her near misses.

He lifted Reetha by her shoulders and dragged her across the metal floor to the rug. Positioning her body carefully, he made sure her head was three feet away from the toppled swivel chair. Then he jammed a corner of the rug firmly into a wheel casing on the chair. Even when he pulled the rug forcefully he couldn't dislodge it from the wheel.

Again he studied the crime scene, looking for flaws. Everything was perfect, absolutely per— Then he saw two mistakes. The first was Reetha's shoes. Her loafers had come off as she was being dragged across the floor. He picked up the loafers and put them on Reetha's feet, leaving one just off her heel. The second mistake was the small pool of blood where she'd hit her head, too far from the rug. He quickly cleaned it up, using detergent and paper towels to scrub the blood away.

He was about to throw the towels into a trash can, then remembered he'd done the same thing with Barbara Van Buren, and Joanna had found the bloodied paper. He balled the towels up and stuffed them into his pockets. He looked around the area once more. Then he took the vial and syringe from the incubator. Quickly he replaced the tops on the culture dishes. Stepping back, he nodded to himself. Now everything was perfect.

He heard a sound outside the laboratory, then muffled voices. He ran for the side door that led to the toxicology lab.

Thirty-one

"She's alive," Paula Garrett said, detecting a faint carotid pulse. She placed her stethoscope on Reetha's chest and listened intently. "Her heart rate is very, very slow. No more than forty beats per minute."

"Is she going to be all right?" Doreen asked in a whisper. Her face was ashen and she was holding on tightly to Ben Kagen.

"I don't know," Garrett said. "She's got some bad head trauma, and the slow pulse is not a good sign."

Doreen moaned softly, trying not to cry.

"When I go over her completely, I'll be able to tell you more," Garrett went on. "If there's no skull fracture, she stands a better chance."

"Where the hell is that gurney?" Hawksworth asked impatiently.

"They must be looking for the special equipment," Garrett told him. "We have to immobilize Reetha's cervical spine before we can move her."

Hawksworth now regretted sending Wells and Neiderman for the gurney. They wouldn't know where things were located in the sickbay. If they didn't return soon, he would call the marine guard to assist them. He looked down at Reetha, then away. "This terrible accident should never have happened."

"I don't see how it could have been prevented," Mark said, biting down on his lip and shaking his head.

"I should never have allowed the rug to be put down," Hawksworth said quietly. "That's why military ships don't have rugs. They cause accidents."

Mark pointed to the edge of the rug caught up in the wheel of the swivel chair. "It was just bad luck."

"Most accidents are," Garrett said, glancing around. "We need a blanket to cover her with."

"I'll have the guard fetch one," Hawksworth said, and went to the door.

Joanna moved in closer. "Do you mind if I take a quick look?"

"Help yourself," Garrett said, stepping back. "But there isn't much doubt about what happened here. Reetha was pushing her swivel chair backward and one of the wheels got stuck in the rug. The chair toppled over and she hit her head on a floor that's hard as concrete."

"She was always pushing her chair back like that," Mark said, expressing anger at the misfortune. "She nearly went over a couple of times. We all warned her about that."

Joanna scanned the lab and found a magnifying glass.

Reetha's body was in the correct position for the accident that supposedly took place. Her head was approximately three feet from the back of the chair. There was a small amount of blood on the floor beneath the head, and the damage to her skull appeared to be commensurate with her fall.

Joanna scanned Reetha's arms and saw no bruises or scratches. Her fingernails were even, with no chips or breaks. There were no defensive wounds, nothing to suggest a struggle. Next Joanna went to Reetha's feet. One loafer was half off, exposing a heel with clearly abraded skin. She removed the other shoe and saw the same thing. The skin on the backs of both heels was freshly abraded. Using the magnifying glass, Joanna could see particles of dirt embedded in the abraded areas.

Joanna stood and looked over at the door of the incubator. It was ajar. "Was that door open when you arrived?" she asked Hawksworth.

"Yes," he said at once. "Why?"

"Just curious."

The gurney arrived. Reetha was carefully placed on it after her head and neck were immobilized. She was strapped on securely and wheeled out into the corridor. Garrett guided the gurney from the front, with Wells and Neiderman pushing it from the rear while Doreen and Kagen trotted alongside.

Mark hesitated, not certain whether he should follow Reetha to the sickbay or stay put. Something about Joanna's demeanor told him she knew something the others didn't. Why had she spent so much time examining Reetha's heels? What could she learn from that?

"I'll have someone clean up," Hawksworth said and turned to leave.

Joanna grabbed his arm. "Don't! At least, not yet."

"Why?"

"Because I don't think this was an accident," Joanna said evenly.

Hawksworth looked at her sharply. "Based on what?"

"A lot of things," Joanna said. "For starters, we have two women with the exact same injury. Both had substantial trauma to the back of the head and nowhere else." Joanna held up two fingers. "That's two women on the same ship with the same injury. What do you think the odds are that that would occur by chance alone?"

"But this is obviously an accident," Hawksworth argued.

"That's what you said about Barbara Van Buren," Joanna said promptly. "And that turned out to be murder."

"That's not a very compelling argument," Mark said.

"There's more," Joanna went on. "Like the incubator

door that should have been closed. A technician of Reetha's caliber would have never left the incubator door open while she sat at her desk."

Mark shrugged. "Maybe she left it open accidentally. Then she saw it from her desk and pushed her chair back to come over and close it."

Hawksworth nodded in agreement. "That would explain it nicely."

"Good," Joanna said, thinking about Mark's scenario and discarding it immediately. "Now, explain to me why the skin on Reetha's heels is abraded."

Mark quirked an eyebrow. "What could that have to do with anything?"

"Plenty." Joanna walked over to the incubator and peered in. The culture dishes were all neatly arranged in rows. She stepped back and studied the area around her. Three feet from the incubator she saw a large spot on the steel floor that looked shinier and cleaner than the area around it.

She knelt down and examined the area with her magnifying glass. The steel floor was finely corrugated for surer footing on shipboard. Small fibers of paper were caught in some of the furrows. Joanna wetted her index finger with her tongue and rubbed it over the spot. There was no dirt. None.

She jumped up and went to the toxicology lab, then came back with a small bottle. "This is guaiac reagent. It can detect blood in very minute amounts. If blood is present, the reagent turns a blue color."

Again Joanna went to her knees. She placed a sheet of white paper over the spot on the floor and saturated it with guaiac reagent. Within twenty seconds a blue color appeared. "See? It's attempted murder," Joanna said.

"Because of some blood traces on the floor?" Mark asked skeptically. "Remember, we use blood agar as a medium to grow bacteria. There are probably trace amounts of it all over this lab."

"And an open incubator door doesn't mean murder," Hawksworth said. "Nor does a pair of skinned heels."

"They do if you put them all together," Joanna said, closing her eyes and envisioning how the attempted murder happened. The attacker must have used a weapon, she thought. Reetha, unlike Barbara Van Buren, was a big, heavy-set woman. No one was going to manhandle her and throw her to the floor without a fight. And there was no evidence of a struggle. The attacker had to have struck her with something heavy.

Joanna opened her eyes. "It happened this way. Reetha was standing at the incubator, looking in. That's why the door was open. The attacker used some type of weapon, probably a blunt object, to hit her on the back of the head. She fell to the floor, striking her head on the steel. That's why there's blood on the floor near the incubator. Then the attacker dragged her over to the desk by her shoulders. The floor is rough and rubbed the skin off her heels."

"But she had her shoes on," Hawksworth said, thinking aloud.

"Not while she was being moved to her desk," Joanna explained. "Her loafers must have come off as she was dragged across the corrugated floor. The attacker saw them and put them back on Reetha's feet. It was a nice touch. Then he tried to scrub away the blood on the floor, but he didn't get it all. Our guy is being very careful now. He's not stupid, but he's not as bright as he thinks he is."

Hawksworth shook his head wearily. "It does look a lot like attempted murder, doesn't it?"

"Beyond any doubt," Joanna said and closed the incubator door. "Someone on this ship, for some reason, is trying to kill off your scientists."

"But who? And why?"

"If Reetha survives, maybe she can help us answer those questions," Joanna said.

"Let's hope she pulls through," Mark said, visibly shaken.

"Amen," said Joanna.

Thirty-two

"There is an urgent call for you," Hawksworth said. "It's Dr. McKay in Los Angeles."

Joanna looked up from the microscope. "Do you know what it's about?"

"She would only say that it was personal." Hawksworth held the door of the laboratory open and followed Joanna out. "We have a secure line to Los Angeles waiting."

"Thank you."

Joanna felt a hollowness in the pit of her stomach. In her experience urgent personal phone calls always carried heart-wrenching grief with them. She could still remember word for word the three most awful phone calls she had ever received. The first broke the news of her father's death in an airplane accident at age forty-two, the second her mother's death at age fifty-five of some strange neurologic disease, and the third her sister's near-fatal bout with an ebolalike virus she had contracted in Guatemala. Only her sister was left now, and she was on an archaeology dig somewhere in Central Africa. Although Kate was almost thirty, Joanna still considered her to be her baby sister, someone she had to look out for. She took a deep breath, praying that Kate was all right.

"I'm told Reetha Sims is not doing very well," Hawksworth said, breaking into her thoughts. "Her blood pressure and pulse are fluctuating erratically."

"That sometimes happens in head injuries," Joanna told him.

"But at least there's no skull fracture," Hawksworth said. "And according to Dr. Garrett, that improves her chances."

Not necessarily, Joanna thought. She had done autopsies in which only the skin was broken, but the force of the blow was so great that the brain bounced around inside its bony cavity like a tennis ball. The end result was massive irreversible brain damage. "Is Reetha moving at all?"

Hawksworth shook his head. "Not even a twitch."

They turned down the long passageway and went past doors with no markings. Up ahead Joanna saw a marine guard come to attention.

"Dr. Garrett is going to need some help in the sickbay," Hawksworth said. "She can't possibly look after Reetha day and night by herself."

"I thought a new corpsman was being flown in."

"He is." Hawksworth nodded to the guard, then came back to Joanna. "And he should be of considerable assistance. But he won't arrive until tomorrow."

"And even if a new medic were here," Joanna said, thinking further on the matter, "you'd still want a bona fide physician close at hand."

"That's Doctor Garrett's view as well," Hawksworth said.

"It's been a long time since I've cared for patients, but I'd be glad to help out," Joanna offered.

"Good," Hawksworth said approvingly as they emerged from the research complex. He punched the elevator call button. "Perhaps you and Dr. Garrett and Dr. Alexander can work out some kind of schedule in which one of you is always with the patient."

"That should be no problem," Joanna said. "I'm certain Mark will agree."

Hawksworth nodded. "He's already volunteered."

A marine guard snapped to attention as Hawksworth opened the door to the control room. The room was square-shaped and surprisingly large, with giant video screens on the walls. One of the screens showed an outline of the coast of the Gulf of Alaska. There were small blinking dots in the open sea to the west of *Global Two*'s current position. They represented the tagged icebergs, Joanna thought, now following Hawksworth past rows of desktops where men wearing headphones stared at banks of glowing consoles and monitors and spoke in nautical terms, some of which were obviously coded. A young sailor was giving instructions to something called Snow Eagle.

Hawksworth pointed to a desktop with a headphone set atop it. "As soon as you put those on you'll be connected to Dr. McKay. Please do not talk about any activities aboard this ship."

Joanna reached for the headset, her mind going back to Kate. *Lord, please let her be all right.* "Lori?"

"Hi, Joanna."

"Are you okay?"

"I'm fine," Lori said. "But that choleralike bug is spreading like wildfire. It's now crossed another ocean. They've just reported outbreaks in Paris and Rome. Everybody is scared shitless."

Joanna sighed heavily. It was indeed turning into a true pandemic. "How many cases have been reported?"

"Over five hundred. And that's not counting carriers."

"What do you mean, *carriers*?"

"I mean people who have the bacteria in their bodies but show no symptoms." Lori cleared her throat nervously. "You know, like Typhoid Mary."

Joanna thought back to the case of the peripatetic cook named Mary who, in the early part of the century, carried the *Salmonella typhi* organism in her intestines, blithely unaware, and infected dozens, perhaps hundreds of people over a period of seven years. "Have many carriers been identified so far?"

"A bunch, but only one at Memorial," Lori said. "Our carrier is a pediatric nurse who came down with viral gastroenteritis. Her symptoms cleared in a few days, but they cultured her stool to be sure, and it grew out the choleralike bug. Now everyone is frightened that she's infected others."

"Jesus," Joanna groaned, "this is getting worse by the minute."

"The people from the CDC want everybody who had immediate contact with the Chinese baby tested for the bacteria," Lori went on. "And that includes you and me. Do you have access to a bacteriology lab?"

Joanna heard a click, and Hawksworth's voice came on the line. "You may answer yes, but give no particulars."

After another click Joanna said, "Yes, we have very good facilities."

"Then have them culture you up from stem to stern. And if you develop any symptoms of the disease, isolate yourself from everybody."

"The first signs are fever and diarrhea, right?"

"That's how it presents in infants," Lori told her. "In adults it's different. They start out with fever and cough, then go on to develop hemorrhagic lesions on their lower extremities as well as pneumonia and sepsis."

Joanna leaned forward and pressed the phone to her ear. "Are you sure about the hemorrhagic spots?"

"Oh, yeah. The CDC says it occurs in over seventy percent of adults with the disease."

"And they're not having any difficulty growing out the bacteria, huh?"

"None at all. It grows great in culture dishes and even better in humans and experimental animals."

"And it kills just about everything it grows in?"

"Yeah," Lori said grimly.

There was a long pause. Joanna heard only low-grade static in the background.

"Joanna?"

"Yes?"

"I'm getting scared," Lori said, her voice breaking for the first time. "Really scared."

"Me too, but we'll be fine. I'll be back in L.A. soon."

Joanna took off her headset and left the control room, Hawksworth a step behind.

Once they were well down the passageway, Hawksworth said, "Do you think the bacteria in the iceberg and the bacteria causing the epidemic are one and the same?"

"They can't be the same," Joanna said thoughtfully. "The choleralike bug can be easily grown out. We can't get ours to grow at all."

"But the symptoms are so similar," Hawksworth argued. "The fever and the cough and particularly the hemorrhagic spots."

"The two bacteria could be first cousins," Joanna conceded.

"Why not the same?" Hawksworth persisted. "Perhaps our culturing technique is somehow lacking."

Joanna shook her head. "That's not even a remote possibility. We have world experts aboard this ship. They wouldn't miss that."

"But other than the ability to grow them out, what separates the two bacteria?"

"Geography," Joanna said promptly. "Our toxic iceberg is off the coast of Alaska. The epidemic started in China."

"May I remind you that we are on the Pacific Ocean?"

"So?"

"So that's all that separates us from China," Hawksworth said. "And I know for a fact that Chinese fishing vessels frequent Alaskan waters."

Joanna nodded slowly. "And if a fish infected by our

iceberg found its way onto a table in Shanghai, you've got the start of an epidemic."

"Exactly," Hawksworth said. "Now, are you still certain the two bacteria aren't the same?"

Joanna shrugged. "I'm not sure of anything anymore." She walked away, trying to come up with common denominators between the two microbes. Suddenly she turned back to Hawksworth. "The CDC will almost certainly have made a specific antiserum against their bacteria. See if you can obtain some for us."

"What will the antiserum tell us?"

"Everything, if we're lucky."

Thirty-three

At the sickbay entrance a marine guard stopped Joanna and motioned her to go through a metal detector that had been set up at the door. On the other side of the detector a second marine guard was sitting at a table watching a small television monitor. The screen showed Reetha lying motionless with an oxygen mask over her nose and mouth. She looked more dead than alive.

Joanna saw Doreen standing near the supply room and walked over. "How's your sister doing?"

"Not good," Doreen said worriedly. "She's still totally unconscious."

"Sometimes it takes days for people with head injuries to come around."

"I know, I know," Doreen said, and nervously nibbled on a fingernail. She glanced over at the marine guards and the metal detector. "Is all this security really necessary?"

"Unfortunately, yes," Joanna said. "The person who attacked Reetha might try again."

"Why?"

"Because she may have seen him."

"The bastard," Doreen growled under her breath. "Look what he's done to my sister." She pushed herself away from the wall and peered into the sickroom. It was windowless and barely large enough for two beds. Paula

Garrett and Mark were squeezed in between the beds, examining Reetha.

Doreen took a step forward as if to go into the room, then turned away. "I hate going into small, closed-off rooms. They terrify me."

"You're claustrophobic?"

"For as long as I can remember," Doreen said, and looked away before a panic reaction could start. Her claustrophobia had begun as a child when she accidentally locked herself in a closet. To this day the closets in her home had sliding curtains. Doreen swallowed audibly and glanced over at her sister's image on the television monitor. "Reetha has claustrophobia too, but it's not as bad as mine."

"Being enclosed in the *Global Explorer* must be very difficult for both of you."

"We tried to deal with it by going topside a dozen times a day."

"Did it help?"

"Not very much." Doreen took a deep breath, then shook her head sadly. "We came aboard this ship because it was going to be the adventure of a lifetime. And it turned into a goddamn nightmare. At exactly nine p.m. everything turned into a nightmare. That's the moment Reetha was attacked."

"How do you know the exact time it happened?"

"Because identical twins have ESP for one another," Doreen told her. "We know when something bad has happened to our twin. I got a cold, awful feeling at exactly nine o'clock. I tried to ignore it, but it stayed. That's when I went looking for Reetha."

Joanna made a mental note to requestion everyone about their whereabouts at exactly 9 P.M.

The women turned as Paula Garrett and Mark came out of the room. Both physicians had dark circles under their eyes.

"Is she any better?" Doreen asked.

"I'm afraid not," Garrett said. "She's still unresponsive."

"Does she show Babinski's sign?" Joanna asked, referring to a reflex in which the big toe extends when the sole of the foot is scratched.

Garrett shook her head. "There are no abnormal reflexes."

"What does that mean?" Doreen asked anxiously.

"The absence of abnormal reflexes suggests there hasn't been a great amount of brain damage," Garrett explained. "But we'll just have to wait and see how much."

"At least her vital signs have stabilized," Mark commented.

"That's good, huh?" Doreen asked, looking for any ray of hope.

"I'd say so," Mark said.

Garrett rubbed at her eyes, then turned to Joanna. "Did Hawksworth talk to you about setting up a night watch schedule for Reetha?"

"Yes, but I now think it best I not be involved."

"Why not?" Garrett asked, an edge to her voice.

Joanna told them about the phone call she'd received from Lori McKay. She described in detail the status of the epidemic, the symptoms and signs the patients were now exhibiting, and the appearance of carriers of the bacteria among health professionals who were exposed to the victims. "So I may be a carrier. And until I know for sure, I shouldn't get close to people in general and patients in particular."

Garrett's eyes narrowed. "And the patients in this epidemic are now showing hemorrhagic skin lesions, just like the ones we've seen here?"

"They sound identical," Joanna said.

"Strange business," Garrett said, furrowing her brow

in thought. "Two different bacteria causing the same signs and symptoms."

"Maybe these two bacteria are not so different," Joanna suggested. "Maybe they are somehow related. I've asked Hawksworth to obtain some antiserum to the choleralike bug from the CDC. We can test the antiserum against our microbe and see if it's similar to the one causing the epidemic."

"I thought we were having trouble growing out our bug," Garrett said.

"We are," Joanna told her. "But we don't need a large number of bacteria to do the test. All we require is a few colonies and we can obtain those in the first hour's growth before the bacteria die." Joanna thought about the testing procedure again, then nodded. "It'll work. Don't you agree, Mark?"

"It's worth a try," Mark said, but he didn't sound very enthusiastic. "In the meantime, let's get Joanna cultured and make sure she's not a carrier."

He turned to Doreen. "Do you feel up to doing the cultures on Joanna?"

"Sure," Doreen said. "I need something to get my mind off this nightmare."

"If you need any help, you let me know."

"I can handle it," Doreen assured him.

"And I'll keep a close eye on Reetha," Mark said.

Doreen saw the strained look on Mark's face and sympathized. "Don't worry, Mark. Reetha is going to pull through. I just know it."

Mark nodded solemnly, then glanced over at Garrett. "How do you want to set up the night call schedule?"

"I'll take tonight," Garrett said, "you take tomorrow. We may have help after that."

Everyone turned as Ann Cormier came through the metal detector and into the sickbay. She looked pale and weak, every step an effort.

"I don't feel well," Ann moaned.

"What's wrong?" Joanna asked.

"I'm so sick." Ann walked over slowly and showed them the inner surface of her lower lip. Everyone saw the big black spot on it. "Please help me!"

Thirty-four

Paula Garrett looked down at the body of Ann Cormier. The young woman's mouth was agape, with crusted blood around her lips and nostrils. There were large hemorrhagic lesions over both legs. Above the head of the bed a cardiac monitor showed a straight line.

Garrett covered the corpse with a sheet and stepped back. "I've never seen anything like this. The bacteria literally ate her alive."

"Maybe she would have done better if we had started treatment earlier," Mark said.

"I don't think it would have mattered a damn," Garrett said. "This bug is vicious as hell, and antibiotics don't affect it in the least. She was dead the moment she got infected."

"I guess you're right."

Garrett discontinued the IV drip the patient had been receiving. It contained massive doses of Rocephin, vancomycin and gentamicin. Despite the infusion, the patient had gone into irreversible septic shock and died. They had even tried cromolyn inhalation as Joanna had suggested, but it had no effect whatsoever. Garrett sighed wearily, wondering if there was anything else she could have done.

"And all because she had a little fever blister that let the bacteria into her body," Mark said, breaking into her thoughts.

Garrett shrugged. "A small blister, a scratch on your

tongue, a harmless paper cut. Any one of those, and the bug gets in and you're dead."

"We're all vulnerable," Mark said. "It's just the luck of the draw who gets it and who doesn't."

"We've got to somehow grow out this organism and test it against antibiotics in vitro," Garrett said. "Otherwise it's all guesswork, and a lot of people are going to die while we're guessing."

Two crewmen, pressed into duty as orderlies, came in and began preparing the body for transport to the morgue. They were in a rectangular-shaped room adjoining the sickbay. The largest compartment in the area, formerly used for storage, it had been hurriedly converted into a hospital room with two beds.

Garrett leaned against the wall as the orderlies unfolded a large plastic body bag. "If we get a lot of cases, we'll have to quarantine a section of the ship," she said to Mark. "That way we can keep the patients and medical personnel isolated from everybody else."

"I don't think Hawksworth will go for that."

"He won't have any choice."

The two orderlies glanced at Garrett, then at each other, obviously not liking the idea of being quarantined with dead and dying patients.

One orderly asked, "You want everything in here burned?"

Garrett nodded. "Incinerate everything but the body. Put that in the sealed room."

"Going to autopsy her?"

"Maybe. We'll see," Garrett said. "Dr. Blalock will let you know if she needs your assistance."

Fuck that, the orderly thought. Let the lady pathologist in her space suit do it by herself. He didn't want to get close to the girl's blood and guts. He didn't want to end up being another Bobby Shea. No way.

Garrett turned to Mark. "We've got to keep Reetha

protected from any infected patients. We'll have to be very careful with our isolation techniques."

"Absolutely," Mark said.

"Reetha really needs to be in an ICU at a trauma center," Garrett went on. "They're experts in head injuries, and that's the kind of care she requires. But Hawksworth says no. He wants everyone to stay on this ship until our problem is solved."

Or until we're all fucking dead, the orderly thought miserably. He zipped up the body bag and made sure it was secure.

Garrett looked over to the two orderlies. They were wearing caps, masks, gloves, and gowns. "You should clear the entire passageway of personnel before you move the body to the sealed room."

"We won't use the passageway," the orderly told her. "We'll transport her on the monorail."

Garrett squinted quizzically. "What monorail?"

"There's a tunnel with a single track right under us," the orderly said. "It runs just about the length of the ship."

Garrett now remembered the trapdoor that Hawksworth had pointed out inside the Plexiglas cylinder. "I thought the tunnel was limited to the area between the cylinder and the sealed room."

"No, ma'am. It's a lot longer than that."

"Are there more than two trapdoors leading into it?"

"For sure."

Garrett shuddered inwardly as she thought about the tunnel used to transport pieces of the toxic iceberg. It was a closed-off, dark, damp space that probably went from one end of the ship to the other. It was a perfect place for the bacteria to grow. And the tunnel could spread the deadly microbe to every part of the ship.

"Is something wrong with the tunnel?" the orderly asked.

Everything, Garrett wanted to say. "It's fine. But for now use the passageway to transport the body."

"But the colonel—"

"Just do what I tell you."

The orderly nodded submissively, but he was thinking, fuck you, lady, the colonel ordered us to use the tunnel to move dead bodies and that's what we'll do until he says otherwise.

The orderly grabbed the front of the gurney and guided it out of the sickbay.

Thirty-five

The helicopter began its descent. Commander Mike Mallory struggled with the controls, trying to keep the aircraft steady, but the crosswinds were too strong and he had to climb back to a thousand feet. Outside freezing sleet was coming down in horizontal sheets. Mallory could barely make out the deck of the *Global Explorer II* below.

"Is the weather always this bad?" the corpsman sitting next to him asked.

"In winter it is," Mallory said. "That's when the real storms start."

"Can you land in this?"

"It's not the sleet that bothers me," Mallory said and pointed straight ahead. "It's the fog."

The corpsman looked out the window at the opaque gray mass. At first he thought it was clouds, but now he could see it went all the way down to the surface of the sea. "Oh, shit!"

Mallory glanced over at the corpsman. "We'll get you in all right, Harmon. Don't worry about it."

But Clifford Harmon was plenty worried. He was frightened of flying and his fear was heightened by the bad weather. He didn't like where he was going, either. To a death ship. That's what everyone was calling it.

Harmon was having second thoughts about his decision to volunteer as a corpsman aboard the *Global Explorer II*. Who the hell needed it? But it was too late to back out now. And besides, the navy had offered him plenty of inducement. They had promised he would spend the last four years of his military service at a naval station in San Diego. That was only a stone's throw from Oceanside where his girlfriend lived. Oh, yeah! Sunny California!

The precipitation suddenly increased and the windshield wipers had trouble keeping up. The helicopter took an abrupt dip before leveling off. Yeah, Harmon thought miserably, sunny California—if I live through this shit.

"That's a roger," Mallory was saying into his headset. "I can see your landing lights now."

Here we go, Harmon told himself, and held on tightly to the armrests.

As the helicopter slowly descended, Mallory felt a strange coldness. He thought that perhaps a window had opened. Quickly he glanced around the cabin. Everything was secure and there was no draft. Then the chill came, a hard shaking chill that caused his teeth to chatter.

"What the hell is wrong?" Harmon asked, alarmed.

"I—I—don't know," Mallory stammered. "I can't st-sto-stop shaking."

"Mother of God!" Harmon hurriedly made the sign of the cross, certain he was going to die.

The helicopter was jerking from side to side erratically. Mallory fought to gain control, but his hands felt weak and clumsy. He forced himself to concentrate, to make his hands work. With great effort he managed to steady the aircraft. Then he leaned back and pulled at his collar. "Damn, it's hot in here."

Harmon studied the pilot's face. It was visibly flushed, with beads of perspiration breaking out. He reached over and touched the pilot's forehead. "You've got a fever, man. You're on *fire*."

"What the hell is causing it?" Mallory asked, mustering all of his strength for the final descent.

"Some kind of infection," Harmon guessed, then realized what he'd said. He quickly covered his nose and mouth with a hand and moved as far as possible from the pilot. Holy mother! The man had the bug that was killing everybody.

"This is Snow Eagle," Mallory said into his headset. "I'm sick and I've got a high fever." He listened for a moment, then said, "Negative that. I'm coming in. Better have your fire crew on deck."

The helicopter rapidly descended as the crosswinds increased. Mallory strained at the controls, trying to keep the aircraft on course. His collar was drenched with perspiration.

Harmon stared out the window at the fog and sleet. He could barely see the landing lights on the deck below. One moment the lights were there, the next moment they were gone. Closing his eyes, he made the sign of the cross again and thought about his girlfriend Caroline and the white sand beaches of San Diego, both of which he would never see again. This was a godawful way to die, he told himself. Then everything went quiet. Even the sound of the rotors was muted.

Opening his eyes, Harmon saw only thick fog. He couldn't make out anything below. No ship, no lights. It felt as if they were suspended in some sort of tunnel. Then he began to discern blinking lights, dim at first, then brighter.

The helicopter jerked abruptly, buffeted by a sudden gust. Then it jerked again, harder this time.

Harmon closed his eyes and prayed, begging God to let him live. The sound of the rotors suddenly increased as the helicopter came down very hard, bouncing twice and collapsing a wheel before settling on the deck in a tilted position.

Mallory had just enough strength to switch off the engine. Then he slumped over the controls.

Harmon opened his eyes and saw men in fire-retardant suits running toward them.

It was Eddie Walsh's turn to guard the sickbay and, like all the other marines, he didn't like it one damn bit. He imagined deadly bacteria hiding in the drawers and cabinets, just waiting for some dumb son of a bitch to get too close.

He sat at the table outside the sickroom and watched the Sims woman on the small television monitor. His eyes moved to the other, newly equipped room, focusing in on the bed where Ann had died. He wasn't going into *that* room, and he didn't give a damn if the President himself gave the order.

Walsh heard footsteps approaching and leaned back to look down the passageway. It was his friend Russell Kirby.

"What's up?" Walsh asked.

"The helicopter has just landed and the pilot is sick as hell with a high fever," Kirby said hurriedly. "They're on their way down."

"Holy shit!" Walsh reached for a mask and latex gloves. "I guess I'd better put these on."

"Damn right! And don't touch the guy. Stay the hell away from him."

Walsh snapped on the gloves. "You figure he's got it?"

"What do you think?" Kirby glanced quickly down the empty passageway. "Find out everything you can about the pilot. The boys will want to know all the details."

"Right."

Kirby looked down the passageway again. "Did you find out anything about Ann?"

"I tried to read the chart, but the doctors' notes were too scribbled."

"She didn't say anything about fucking you, did she?"

"I don't think so," Walsh said, uncertain. "If she had, the colonel would have been up my ass like a buzz saw."

Kirby pulled back the bandage covering the wound on his hand. It was red and swollen. "Did you get some of that antibiotic cream for me?"

Walsh nodded and reached into his pocket for a small tube. "It's called polymyxin B. It's supposed to be real strong. At least that's what the manual says."

Kirby pressed down on the wound and some greenish pus came out. "Fucking thing is still infected."

"Maybe you ought to have it lanced again."

"Down here? Shit! You'd have to be crazy."

At the far end of the passageway there was the sound of an elevator door opening.

"Got to go," Kirby said, and disappeared down a side corridor.

Walsh heard them coming and glanced around to make certain everything was in order in the reception area. He saw a sheet of paper on the floor and quickly picked it up. It was a page from Ann Cormier's chart that he had been reading. Someone with terrible handwriting had scribbled *Vancomycin started at* . . . The rest of the sentence was indecipherable.

Walsh crumpled up the sheet and put it in his pocket, thinking about Ann. She was cute and funny and nice, and now she was dead. And she had really, really liked him. He could tell. She did things for him in bed that felt so great, things she swore she'd never done for any other man. Only for him. Damn, it was so good. But not good enough to die for, Walsh thought nervously, remembering how the condom had slipped off, and hoping for the hundredth time that she hadn't transmitted the bacteria to him.

He looked down the passageway and saw the group hurrying toward the sickbay. There was a sailor he didn't recognize at the front of the gurney, pulling it. Behind the sailor were two doctors, both wearing gowns and masks and gloves.

Walsh opened the door to the sickbay and stepped aside, giving the gurney plenty of room to pass. He glanced perfunctorily at the television monitor, then watched the sailor go into the supply room, emerge in gown and gloves and mask, and follow the others inside.

It must be the replacement medic, Walsh thought, now positioning his chair so he could overhear the conversation in the larger sickroom. The female doctor began to talk. Walsh moved his chair a little closer to the door.

"Get his vital signs, please," Garrett said.

Harmon helped the pilot strip down to his shorts and eased him onto the bed atop the sheets. The pilot began to shiver as Harmon took his pulse. Overhead the ventilation system came on and the air stirred, but the room still smelled like stale sweat.

Mark asked, "Do you know if the pilot was exposed to the previous victims?"

Garrett nodded. "He flew the helicopter that took Henderson to Juneau. But he didn't touch the patient, and he was wearing a mask. Of course, that's no guarantee against getting infected, is it?"

Mark thought for a moment. "What about the body of the coastguardsman? How was it brought aboard?"

"In my helicopter," Mallory mumbled around the thermometer in his mouth. "But he was in a body bag."

"That's two possible exposures," Mark said, turning away as the patient coughed.

"But the coastguardsman's body was flown in at least two weeks ago," Garrett said. "That's too long an incubation period, isn't it?"

"Not necessarily."

Garrett lowered her voice to a whisper. "All the evidence points to a shorter incubation period. Think about what happened to Bobby Shea."

"The bacteria got into Shea through an opened carbuncle," Mark said quietly. "Maybe the incubation period is a lot longer if the bacteria entered via a more indirect route."

"You can talk louder," Mallory said as the thermometer was removed from his mouth. "I know what I'm up against."

"You may not have the infection we're talking about," Garrett said openly.

"Right," Mallory said tonelessly. "That's why everybody is bundled up to the eyeballs and walking on eggshells."

He stared up at the ceiling, wondering if he was about to meet death in a shitty little sickbay. He had always believed he would die in a helicopter crash, like so many of his pilot friends. His mind flashed back to Vietnam, just before the fall of Saigon. The cockpit was filled with smoke and fire, the aircraft spinning out of control. Then they were down and everybody walked away from the burning helicopter. "Lucky Mike Mallory" they had called him. But now he knew his luck had run out.

He thought about his wife and son, waiting for him at home, never knowing when he might not return from one of his missions. And he thought about the happy times they had when he did return. He missed them so much. He wanted to talk with them one last time.

"Did you feel perfectly well until all this started?" Garrett asked.

"I felt a little achy, like I was coming down with a virus," Mallory said as he shivered. The chills were returning and he reached for the sheets. "Then the shakes began. I was cold as ice one moment, burning up the next."

"Any other symptoms?" Garrett asked and went through a long list. Did Mallory have a headache? Sinus discomfort? Painful urination? Sore throat?

The pilot shook his head at each question until Garrett asked about coughing. "Some," Mallory said. "But I'm not getting up much phlegm."

"Do you have any sores or open wounds?" Mark asked.

"No."

Mallory pushed the sheets back. Now he was flushed and sweating profusely. "I'm starting to burn up again."

Garrett studied the pilot for a moment. Mallory looked awful and was getting sicker by the minute. Just like the others who had been infected. She asked, "Have you been around anyone else who's been ill with a fever?"

"Nobody," Mallory said, his voice raspy. He coughed with effort.

"Are you sure?"

Mallory thought back, trying to concentrate. "Well, I was around Ann, but that was before she got sick."

Garrett's eyes narrowed. "Ann Cormier?"

"Yes."

"When were you last with her?"

Mallory wetted his dry lips, thinking. "A day or two before she started feeling bad."

"Did you sleep with her?"

Mallory hesitated, then nodded. "Yes."

"How many times?"

"Two."

"And the last time was a couple of days before she became ill, right?"

"Yeah, I guess so," Mallory said, now regretting he had told them about Ann. That could cost him his commission. If he lived.

Eddie Walsh was fuming, barely able to control his rage. His hands were balled up into tight fists, nails digging into his palms. The bitch! The whore! She was screwing someone else at the same time she was screwing him. He dug his nails in deeper, now wondering if she did the same things to the pilot that she did to him. Sticking her tongue up everywhere and laughing while she was doing it. Bitch!

Then fear flooded through Eddie Walsh. If she gave the disease to the pilot, she could have given it to him too. He moved his chair even closer to the door and listened intently.

"Did you wear a condom?" Garrett was asking.

"No," Mallory said.

Dumb bastard, Walsh thought; at least I had enough sense to wear one. But then he remembered that the first time they didn't. And the next time the condom had slipped off. Shit!

Garrett asked, "Do you know if she was sleeping with anyone else on this ship?"

Mark looked at Garrett admiringly. It was a question he would never have thought to ask. Never in a million years. Women had a sixth sense for matters like that.

"There was one other guy," Mallory said.

Walsh's anal sphincter tightened. Oh, shit! Oh, shit!

"She told me it was a one-night stand," Mallory went on. "This other guy meant nothing to her."

Whoring bitch! Walsh wanted to scream out.

"Who was this other man?"

"She didn't say."

Walsh breathed a sigh of relief. So nobody knew except for Ann Cormier and Russell Kirby. And she was dead and Kirby wouldn't talk.

Garrett quickly examined the pilot and looked for possible routes of entry the bacteria could have taken. There were none. No sores or lesions on the skin or in his mouth. Mallory's tongue was dry and coated but showed no black spots, and his dental hygiene was excellent. A few fillings here and there, the gums nice and pink. Mallory coughed briefly as Garrett examined his lungs. They were clear, the air moving in and out without producing any abnormal sounds.

"Nothing," Garrett said, stepping back from the bed. She reached down for the pilot's hand and examined his neatly clipped nails. There were no nicks or cuts or abraded areas on the cuticles. Then she saw the discrete little pits on the surface of his nails. "He's got psoriasis," she pronounced.

"Why do you say that?" Mark asked. "He has no skin lesions."

"His fingernails have small pits on them. That's seen only in psoriasis."

"But he should have cutaneous lesions somewhere," Mark argued.

"My scalp," Mallory said, and coughed.

Garrett quickly examined the pilot's scalp. At the frontal hairline were several thick psoriatic plaques. One of them was partially split open and oozing a little. "How long has this one been bleeding?"

"Off and on for months," Mallory said, and started to shiver again. "Every time I comb my hair I crack it open."

Garrett and Mark exchanged knowing glances. The pilot had been exposed to three victims, and on each exposure he could have had an open lesion on his head.

Mark turned quickly to Harmon. "Did you bring the new antibiotics with you?"

"Yes, sir," Harmon said. "We've got a big supply of everything."

"Unpack them and get an IV line started with five percent dextrose in water." Mark turned back to Garrett. "If we start the antibiotics now, perhaps we can control the infection."

"Maybe," Garrett said absently, now staring out into space.

Mark studied her expression for a moment. "What are you thinking?"

"I'm thinking we have to find out who was the other guy Ann Cormier slept with."

"You're worried she could have given it to him too?"

Garrett nodded. "And maybe to others as well. For all we know, she could have slept with half the men on this ship."

Thirty-six

Doreen slowly moved the slide back and forth under the microscope. She saw clusters of rod-shaped bacteria that glowed bright green against a black background. To be absolutely certain, she studied the slide a second time and again saw the same staining pattern. Taking a deep breath, she pushed her chair away from the microscope and looked over at Joanna. "I've got bad news."

Joanna stiffened. "Don't tell me I'm infected."

"I'm afraid so," Doreen said softly.

Joanna felt as if her legs were going out from under her. She sat down quickly. "Is there any chance you're wrong?"

"None," Doreen said. "Your organism is identical to the choleralike organism at Memorial Hospital. It's a gram-negative, nonhemolytic, catalase-positive bacillus. And it reacts specifically with the antisera sent from the CDC."

"Jesus," Joanna murmured under her breath.

"Well, at least you're just a carrier."

"But some of the carriers come down with the disease."

"Maybe you won't."

"And maybe I will."

Joanna stared out into space, letting the shock wear off. "Just my luck," she said. "A new, antibiotic-resistant bug appears and I get it."

"I'm not so certain it's new," Doreen said.

"Have you seen it before?" Joanna asked quickly.

"I can't say I've seen this particular organism, but I've seen more than a few gram-negative bacilli that no one could classify." Doreen lit a cigarette and blew smoke into the air. "You see, it's the gram-negative bacilli like klebsiella and pseudomonas that are becoming the doctor's worst nightmares. Patients get infected with these organisms and antibiotics don't work against them. So every major research center everywhere has on hand a stable of resistant gram-negative bugs—a few of which have never been classified—to test against their newly discovered antibiotics. If you can find an antibiotic that kills these bacteria, you've got yourself a multi-billion-dollar drug."

"But this still might be a totally new organism," Joanna said. "I mean, no one has ever described it."

"That's true," Doreen conceded. "But most of the time, new bugs turn out to be old bugs that nobody recognized in the past."

Doreen puffed on her cigarette as she thought of Legionnaires' disease. The "first" outbreak had occurred during an American Legion convention in Philadelphia in 1976. Everybody said it was a new disease caused by a new microorganism. But studies on tissue and serum from the past showed that cases had occurred at least as far back as 1947. "Why are you so concerned with whether it's a new bug or not?"

"Because if it's new it may well be a mutation from another organism. And mutant forms tend to be even more resistant to antibiotics than their parents."

"That doesn't always hold true."

"But it usually does," Joanna said. "Hey, there are plenty of examples. When penicillin became widely used, the staphylococcus mutated and learned how to make penicillinase to inactivate the antibiotic. So then we invented Keflex to kill these penicillin-resistant staph, but the bacteria mutated again, now making beta-lactamases to neutralize Keflex and the other cephalosporin antibiotics." Joanna took a deep breath and slowly exhaled. "Mutants are bad news and you know it."

Doreen crushed out her cigarette. "You're not painting a very good picture for yourself."

"All I want is the truth," Joanna said. "I want to know what I'm up against."

"Who's heading the investigation at Memorial?"

"The CDC."

"They'll be able to tell you whether it's a new bug or not," Doreen said. "If it's a brand-new bacillus, it won't react with any of their antisera. If it's a mutant, it will retain some of its parental antigens and will still react with a specific antiserum. The CDC are very good at identifying this sort of bacteria."

"Are they any good at coming up with an antibiotic to kill it?"

Doreen shrugged. "That I can't answer."

Joanna got to her feet. "I may have some questions later on."

"Anytime."

Joanna walked with Colonel Hawksworth past the banks of glowing consoles and monitors and took a seat while her call was being placed. She tilted back in her chair and looked up at the giant video screen on the far wall of the control room. It showed an outline of Alaska. To the north there were heavy splotches of red and orange.

Joanna pointed to the screen. "What does that red mean?"

"It's a big storm coming out of the Arctic," Hawksworth said.

"It looks like it's heading our way."

"It is," Hawksworth said, unconcerned. "But our

weather people tell us the storm will lose most of its punch before it reaches us."

A radioman signaled to Joanna. "Your call is ready, ma'am."

Joanna quickly adjusted her headset. "Lori, how are things?"

"Worse."

"What's happened?"

"Eight more carriers have been identified at Memorial," Lori said dejectedly. "And half of them have developed the full-blown disease and died, including the pediatric nurse. They grew the bacteria out of her stool when she was still asymptomatic."

"Are they certain that's what she died from, then?"

"Beyond any doubt," Lori said. "They also grew the bacteria from her blood taken at autopsy."

Joanna suddenly found it hard to swallow. "Do they believe all carriers will eventually get the disease?"

"That's what they think."

"How long does it take to convert from carrier to disease?"

There was a long silence. The line was crystal clear with no static.

"No one knows for sure what the incubation period is," Lori said in a monotone. "In most cases so far, it seems to take at least a week from the time of exposure."

"And we were exposed more than two weeks ago," Joanna said softly.

"Yeah."

Joanna looked over at Hawksworth, who was listening to the phone conversation on a headset. His face was closed, without any expression on it. And why should there be? Joanna asked herself. He wasn't the one infected. And as long as it wouldn't interfere with his mission, he didn't give a damn. She went back to the phone call. "What about treatment? Have they come up with anything?"

"Well, there's an experimental antibiotic called Panamycin that shows some promise."

Joanna abruptly sat up. "How promising?"

"It's experimental, Joanna. The drug is just entering the initial phase of its clinical trials."

"How promising is it?" Joanna persisted.

"It seems to kill the bacteria in a test tube, but no one knows if it'll work in an infected patient," Lori said unenthusiastically. "And it might have hellacious side effects. A CDC investigator told me that the last time they jumped in with an untested antibiotic, it caused severe liver necrosis and killed more people than it helped."

"Any port in a storm," Joanna said, more to herself than to Lori.

"Forget that! I'm not going to take some untested drug."

"I'd take it if I came down with the disease."

"That's easy for you to say," Lori said, her voice sharper. "You're not the one who is infected."

"But I am infected," Joanna said. "My cultures came back positive. You mean—you mean yours did too?"

"Oh, Joanna!" Lori wailed. "What are we going to do?"

Joanna stared into space for a long moment. Then she reached for an index card and quickly reviewed the questions she needed Lori to answer. "Do they know how the pathogen is transmitted?"

"Probably via the gastrointestinal tract," Lori told her. "So wash your hands a lot, use disposable plates, and don't kiss anybody."

Joanna suddenly thought about Mark and the fact that she had slept with him twice since coming aboard the *Global Explorer II*. She had to talk with him about the possibility that she had infected him. "I wonder how we caught the bacteria from the baby. We were both wearing gloves and masks."

"I've thought about it a hundred times and still don't have an answer. Who the hell knows?"

There was a loud burst of static that came and went and then came again before finally disappearing.

"Lori, if anything happens to me, I want my sister Kate notified. My secretary has her number."

"I'll take care of it," Lori said and waited for another burst of static to clear. "I don't mean to sound morbid, but maybe you should return to Los Angeles. You know, just in case something does happen."

"I'll cross that bridge when I get to it."

"We may already be at the bridge, Joanna."

"I know," Joanna said despondently.

"Let me hear from you if anything happens on your end."

"I'll keep in touch." Joanna set the headphones down, her mind going back to the antibiotic that showed some promise. But if it had never gone through human trials—

Hawksworth broke into her thoughts. "This bacteria you were discussing, does anyone who is infected survive?"

Joanna stood up and shook her head. "Everyone who is infected dies."

Thirty-seven

"Can you hear me, Commander Mallory?" Garrett yelled into the pilot's ear. She waited a moment, then tried again. "Can you hear me?"

The pilot's head moved slightly. Ten seconds passed before he muttered, "Yeah."

"Do you know where you are?"

There was a long pause. Then his head moved again. "The *Explorer*," he said, his voice low and hoarse.

"And where's the *Explorer*?"

The pilot's eyes closed. He seemed to be drifting off to sleep.

"Where's the *Explorer*?" Garrett asked once more.

"A-Alaska," the pilot whispered.

Garrett touched his forehead and could feel his fever through her latex gloves. His face and arms were now covered with hemorrhagic spots.

She stepped back from the bed and looked over at Mark. "When did this start?"

"About three hours ago," Mark said. "He began to complain of a headache. Then he became obtundent. It's gotten progressively worse."

"Do you think he has meningitis?"

"Either that or he's bleeding into his brain."

Garrett shook her head sadly. "And we began treatment with antibiotics as quickly as we could." She sighed wearily. "What in the world are we dealing with here?"

"A sixty-five-million-year-old microorganism that's resistant to the most potent antibiotics we have," Mark said matter-of-factly.

"Are we missing anything? Is there some other antibiotic we should add?"

"From a bacterial standpoint we've got the field covered. There are damn few bacteria that can survive a mixture of Rocephin, gentamicin, and vancomycin." Mark nodded to himself. "Damn few."

The pilot suddenly began shaking and the bed shook with him. It went on for nearly a minute. Then the chill ended abruptly. Mallory groaned softly.

"So we just watch and wait," Garrett said helplessly.

The pilot struggled weakly and tried to turn, but the sheets restrained him.

Garrett looked at him, shaking her head. "I feel guilty as hell, Mark. We're just sitting here watching him die."

"Nobody could do more."

"Maybe if he were in an ICU somewhere."

"They'd do the same things we're doing," Mark said. "And probably treat him with the very same antibiotics."

"But ICUs are equipped with life-support systems."

"Which would be useless in a patient with widespread sepsis due to antibiotic-resistant bacteria."

"I guess," Garrett had to agree. "But wouldn't their laboratory facilities be better?"

"Not for isolating the bacteria," Mark answered. "Our facilities here are pretty good. But just to be sure we're not missing anything, I've asked Hawksworth to send some of the specimens to USAMRIID."

"What did he say?"

"He's thinking about it. He's worried about any specimen infected with the bacteria getting off the ship."

Garrett nodded. "It's a tough call."

"That's why Hawksworth is here," Mark said. "To make the tough calls."

They left the room and stripped off their surgical garb,

depositing everything in a hazardous material bin. Garrett led the way across the reception area and into Reetha's room. She waited for Mark to close the door, then went over to the bed. The monitors showed Reetha's pulse to be 88/minute, her blood pressure 108/70.

"Her vital signs are great," Garrett said, pulling back the sheet. "But otherwise she's a vegetable."

"No movement at all, huh?" Mark asked.

"None." Garrett pinched the skin on Reetha's arm as hard as she could and got no response. Then she lifted up the flaccid arm and let it drop. It fell without resistance, bouncing twice on the bed before becoming still again. "She's totally unresponsive."

Garrett checked for abnormal reflexes and found none. Next she examined Reetha's pupils. They were round and regular and reacted briskly to light. Garrett let Reetha's eyelids close, then opened them again. Again the pupils reacted rapidly.

Mark leaned in. "Did you find something?"

"I can't be sure, but I think her pupils are reacting better."

"What do you think that means?"

"It may mean nothing," Garrett said. "But yesterday her pupillary response to light seemed very sluggish."

"Maybe she's starting to turn the corner," Mark said, trying to sound optimistic.

"Maybe," Garrett said noncommittally. "We'll know for sure if she begins to respond to pain. That'll be a clear indication she's coming out of her coma."

Mark nodded solemnly. "I can take call again tonight," he offered. "It'll give you a chance to catch up on your sleep."

"I'm fine," Garrett said. "Let's keep rotating. I'll cover tonight."

There was a sharp knock on the door.

"Yes?" Garrett asked loudly.

"Ma'am," the corpsman called back, "we've got another marine out here with a high fever."

"Oh, please, no!" Garrett groaned. "Not another one."

They hurried out of the office and followed the corpsman Harmon to the reception area. Russell Kirby was seated at a table waiting for them.

"What's wrong, Corporal?" Garrett asked.

"My hand, ma'am," Kirby said, coming to attention. "I think it's infected."

Garrett waved the marine back down and examined the hand. On the dorsal surface was an obviously infected area the size of a half-dollar. It was red and tender and filled with pus. "How did you do this?"

"Scraped it on an iceberg, ma'am," Kirby said sharply.

Mark's eyes narrowed. "The iceberg in the Plexiglas cylinder?"

"No, sir."

"The other iceberg now aboard?"

"No, sir," Kirby said at once, but he wasn't sure. It could have been.

"It looks like either staph or strep," Garrett said, turning to Mark. "See the slender red streaks beginning to move up his arm? That's characteristic."

"Is that bad, ma'am?" Kirby asked.

"No. Antibiotics can take care of it," Garrett told him. "But why didn't you come in earlier for treatment?"

"I did, sir. The medic lanced it."

Garrett looked over at Harmon. "When did you incise this?"

"Not him," Kirby said. "It was Henderson who drained it."

Somehow Garrett managed to keep her face even. "When did Henderson lance it?"

"Last week," Kirby said, still unconcerned. "Then we put some polymyxin on it."

"Was Henderson ill when he treated you?"

"Yeah," Kirby answered. "He looked like hell, ma'am. You know, coughing and feverish and all."

An open wound, Garrett was thinking, and Henderson coughing less than a foot away.

Kirby suddenly started shaking, a giant chill sweeping through him. "Wh-what's wrong with me, ma'am?" he asked, teeth chattering. "What's wrong?"

"I'm not sure," Garrett said. But deep down she knew she was looking at a dead man.

Thirty-eight

Joanna had carefully scrutinized every bacteriology textbook and manual aboard ship, trying to learn more about the organism she was infected with. She knew that gram-negative bacilli made up most of the gastro-intestinal flora. Organisms such as klebsiella, proteus, and serratia abounded and caused no trouble under normal circumstances. But if the host defense mechanisms weakened, these bacteria could become vicious. Salmonella and cholera, on the other hand, were not normal inhabitants of the gut and were always pathologic. They were invaders from the outside, like the bacteria now infecting Joanna and Lori and God knew how many others.

"I'm thinking about putting myself on antibiotics," Joanna said to Mark after they'd discussed her infection for the umpteenth time.

"I wouldn't—"

Joanna held up a hand. "Let me give you my rationale. Then I'll listen to your objections."

She went over to the coffeemaker and poured herself a cup, then came back to the conference table. "This bug is multiplying inside my gut and it's just a matter of time before I come down with the disease. That's a given. If I allow the bacteria to multiply, the increased numbers will eventually break through my defense mechanisms. And then suddenly I go from being a carrier to having the disease. I want to treat myself while my defenses are still intact and the number of microorganisms is not over-whelming." Joanna sat down. "That's my plan."

"Stupid," Mark said simply.

Joanna ignored the comment. "I think I'll take neo-mycin orally in high doses. It's not absorbed out of the gut and it destroys most of the gram-negative bacilli."

"It's not a smart move," Mark said. "Let me tell you why. First, there's no evidence neomycin works against this organism. To the contrary. Even at high concentra-tions, it barely affects the bacillus. Secondly, you could be doing yourself real harm. You take neomycin and it might well induce the bacteria to become more resistant to other antibiotics, even the newer experimental ones. Don't hurt yourself, Joanna. Wait."

"For what?" Joanna asked tersely. "For this goddamn bug to kill me?"

"For us to find the answer."

Mark rocked back in his chair, his eyes still on Joanna. "Perhaps you'd feel safer if you were to return to Los Angeles."

Joanna thought for a moment, then nodded. "Perhaps I would."

"I've already suggested it to Hawksworth."

"And what did he say?"

"He said he'd think about it."

"Which means no," Joanna said. "Hawksworth won't allow anyone to leave this ship."

"I think we're getting closer to a solution."

"How close?"

"Maybe just a couple of weeks or so."

Joanna sighed deeply. "I may not have that much time left. It's already been three—"

There was a sharp knock on the door.

"Yes?" Joanna snapped at the interruption.

A marine guard entered and walked quickly over to the conference table. "Dr. Blalock, ma'am, the colonel would like to see you."

Mark said to Joanna, "Maybe Hawksworth has changed his mind."

"Don't bet on it."

Joanna followed the marine down the long passageway, wondering if she would leave the ship, given the chance. She wanted to stay aboard until the studies were completed, but in her current state she wasn't much help to anyone. And there was no question she'd feel safer in Los Angeles. It was home and there were wonderful specialists at Memorial for her to consult with. And if she had to die, better to do it among friends. Maybe she'd even get to see her sister one last time. A death ship— that's what everyone was calling the *Global Explorer II*. And that's what it was.

It was time for her to leave, Joanna decided as the elevator bore her upward. She would demand it from Hawksworth.

The marine guard opened the door to the control room and stepped aside as Joanna entered. The room was busier than usual. All the monitors and consoles were brightly lit, with men hunched over them and talking into headsets. Hawksworth was staring up at the giant video screen on the far wall. He gestured Joanna to a seat, but his gaze stayed on the screen. "Our weather people are having a field day," he said.

"What's happened?"

"For starters, the storm is moving toward us and picking up speed."

Joanna studied the video screen with its red and orange splotches. There was more orange than before. "It looks less intense."

"It is, but it still has gale-force winds."

"Are we in any danger?"

"Not really. We can easily ride this one out. We'll stay well outside the archipelago."

Joanna now saw a pulsating circle off the coast below Anchorage. "What does the circle signify?"

"Earthquake activity."

Joanna tensed involuntarily. Earthquakes scared the hell out of her. She'd been living in Los Angeles when the Northridge quake hit. It had been powerful enough to toss her out of bed. "How strong is it?"

"Three point two."

Joanna breathed easier. An earthquake of 3.2 was just a little shake when compared to the Northridge disaster, which registered 6.9 on the Richter scale. "That shouldn't cause any concern."

"Perhaps not on land," Hawksworth said. "But this one was under the sea, and we have to watch those carefully."

The ring stopped pulsating and gradually disappeared. The noise level from the conversations in the room dropped off noticeably.

"You've got another call from Los Angeles," Hawksworth said, and motioned to a nearby radioman.

The sailor turned a dial and pushed two buttons before handing a headset to Joanna. "It's Dr. McKay on the line."

Joanna quickly adjusted the headset. "Lori, what's up?"

"Remember the antibiotic that looked so promising?"

"Of course. What about it?"

"Well, it's working, and it's working damn good."

"Great!" Joanna yelled, and shook her fist in the air.

The men looked up from their consoles and stared over at the sudden outburst. Joanna waved apologetically to them and took a deep breath, savoring the moment. *Oh, Lord, thank you!*

"And the antibiotic wipes out the bacteria after only six doses."

Joanna took another deep breath and waited for her heart to slow down. "Does it have any side effects?"

"A little diarrhea, but who the hell cares?"

"Tell me all about the drug."

"It's called Panamycin. It's a new type of cephalosporin, and it's made by a company called BioMega,"
Lori said.

BioMega. Joanna smiled to herself. Mark's company.
It was as if everything had come full circle.

"How should we send the drug to you?" Lori asked.

Hawksworth motioned to Joanna and gave her
instructions.

"I'll arrange for someone to pick up the antibiotics at
my office," Joanna said. "And please send as much as
you can spare. Are there any special instructions to follow while taking the drug?"

"Just take it twice a day for four days," Lori replied.
"And don't take any other antibiotics at the same time.
Most important, don't take any neomycin. For some reason, neomycin induces the bacteria to become very
resistant to everything, including Panamycin."

Mark was right on target, Joanna thought, when he
advised her not to take neomycin. She could have done
herself real harm.

Lori laughed on the other end of the line. "Well,
Joanna, how does it feel to be back among the living?"

"Wonderful."

"When do you think you'll be coming home?"

"Soon. As soon as I can."

Joanna handed the headset back to the radioman, who
had overheard all of her conversations with Lori. He was
smiling, giving her a thumbs-up signal. She returned the
smile and the signal, then left the room.

Joanna hurried down the passageway, humming a tune
under her breath. She suddenly felt young and light of
foot, as if a giant weight had been taken off her back. One
phone call and she had gotten a new lease on life. All she
had to do was to take a drug called Panamycin. Mark had
been right. The disease could be cured with a new experimental antibiotic. She now wished she had listened to

him and believed him. It would have saved her a lot of worry and aggravation.

Joanna entered the bacteriology laboratory and saw Doreen studying a slide under the microscope. She walked over. "Is Mark around?"

"No. He had to go to the sickbay." Doreen looked up and noticed Joanna's smile. "I see a happy face. What happened?"

"They've found an antibiotic that's effective against the bug I've got."

"Wonderful!" Doreen reached for Joanna's hand and gave it a quick squeeze. "Sit down and tell me about it."

"You must know more about the antibiotic than I do," Joanna said. "It's made by BioMega."

Doreen furrowed her forehead, puzzled. "Are you referring to Megamycin?"

"Nope. It's called Panamycin."

"But that drug is still experimental," Doreen said. "They're just beginning the clinical trials on it."

"Well, it works, and it works damn well," Joanna told her. "Now tell me everything you know about it."

"I've only studied it in a roundabout way." Doreen lit a cigarette and leaned back in her chair. "Panamycin was originally developed at our plant in China."

"How long ago?"

"Two years or so," Doreen said. "They found it to be effective against almost all gram-negative organisms, with no toxicity in animals. Then we tested it in our Cambridge lab to verify the results."

"I take it the drug lived up to expectations."

"And some. Boy, that drug was really something! It even killed off the difficult-to-classify gram-negative organisms I told you about earlier. That's when we knew we had a hot ticket."

"It sounds like the perfect drug."

"So it seemed. But it had some peculiarities too."

Joanna moved her chair in closer. "Such as?"

"Well, if we used Panamycin against one particular organism, it worked fine—unless that organism had been exposed to neomycin, in which case the damn bug rapidly became resistant to Panamycin." Doreen puffed on her cigarette. "I mean really resistant."

Joanna nodded, thinking that was where Mark had gotten the information on neomycin inducing bacteria to become resistant to another antibiotic. He'd seen it in his own lab.

"And the neomycin barely affected the organism, even at very high concentrations." Doreen went on, "Yet it still induced resistance to Panamycin."

Joanna nodded again. Mark had said that the neomycin barely—Joanna's eyes narrowed suddenly as she thought back to her conversation with Mark. She concentrated, trying to remember his exact words. He had said that there was no evidence the neomycin worked against this microorganism. *Even at high concentrations, it barely affects the bacillus.* How could he know that? They were talking about the bacteria that had infected Joanna, the choleralike microorganism. And supposedly he knew nothing about that organism.

"Did Mark do a lot of the actual lab work when Panamycin was being tested against the various bacteria?"

"He was in the lab night and day," Doreen said. "Except when he was in China."

"I see," Joanna said, keeping her expression even. She got up and paced around the lab, trying to arrange her thoughts. The choleralike bacteria had come out of China. All evidence pointed to that. And Mark spent a lot of time in China. BioMega had a big plant there. And Mark had lied. He knew about the bacteria and its behavior in the presence of neomycin. Why would he lie?

"Do you still work with these neomycin-odd bacteria?" she asked.

Doreen shook her head. "But I heard we had sent some to our China plant for them to study. It turned out to be not such a hot idea. It seems that one of their technicians got infected with the bug and became very, very sick. And before she died she spread the bacteria to half her neighborhood. A lot of people apparently died. They hushed the whole thing up. I mean, couldn't you just see the headlines it would have generated? 'American bacteria kills scores of Chinese.' " Doreen flicked her wrist. "I say good riddance to the damn bug. I'm glad we gave it a one-way ticket to China."

And maybe they gave that ticket back to us, Joanna thought. She sank heavily back into her chair, considering the likelihood that the Cambridge bacteria and the choleralike organism at Memorial were one and the same. If what Doreen had heard was true, the culture sent from Cambridge to China had already gotten loose once and started a miniepidemic. Now it could be happening again, but on a larger scale. Or maybe the outbreak Doreen described had never been thoroughly stamped out.

"I'll tell you this," Doreen said, thinking aloud. "You're lucky as hell somebody thought of testing Panamycin against this bug. Only a limited number of specialists know about Panamycin. As I said, it's still experimental. It's just going through the first phase of clinical trials."

"And how long will it take?"

"At least two years and a hundred million dollars."

Joanna's eyes widened. "A hundred million?"

"Maybe more," Doreen said. "Horrible as it may sound, this little epidemic could be good for BioMega if it's forcing the medical community to use Panamycin without requiring it to complete its clinical trials. Conservatively, that will save BioMega a hundred million bucks."

Joanna stared at Doreen. Could Mark have intentionally started the outbreak of the choleralike organism? He had the perfect setup to do it, and a lot of motivation. A hundred million motivations.

"A hundred million," she said softly.

"A fortune," Doreen said, nodding. "And it couldn't come at a better time for BioMega."

"Has BioMega had financial problems?"

"It's had more ups and downs than an elevator," Doreen said. "But Mark always manages to pull a rabbit out of his hat at the last moment. He's a real magician."

"Yeah," Joanna said, pushing her chair back. "A real magician."

Thirty-nine

Eddie Walsh felt awful. His muscles and bones ached. Every part of him was sore and tender to touch. He could barely undress himself and crawl into a bed in the sickbay. Under the covers, he began to shiver.

"When did all this start?" the medic asked.

"The day before yesterday."

"Why the hell did you wait until now to check in?"

"I—I thought it might pass," Walsh said weakly. "You know, like a cold or something."

"Man, you ain't got no cold."

Harmon quickly studied the sick marine. His skin color was pale and there were small hemorrhagic spots on his legs. Just like the others infected with the toxic bacteria.

Walsh coughed, then swallowed hard. "I got it, don't I?"

"Maybe. I don't know for sure," Harmon said, and pulled up his mask.

"I got it," Walsh said again. He thought about Ann Cormier whom he had slept with twice, just twice. And it could end up costing him his life. She was like a black widow spider that killed every male she fucked. "I know I got it."

"Let's wait for the doc to examine you."

Walsh held out his arm while the medic took his pulse and blood pressure. He wondered if he should tell the medic how he contracted the disease. Maybe it would help in his treatment. "I want to tell you how—"

In the next bed Russell Kirby made a loud snorting sound. He twisted between his sheets, moaning and snorting again. Then he turned onto his side and became silent.

Walsh watched Kirby and decided to follow his best friend's advice. Don't say anything to anybody, least of all to the medic, who would tell the doc, who would tell the colonel, who would throw Walsh's ass right out of the Marine Corps. Fuck that!

"What did you want to tell me?" Harmon asked.

"Nothing," Walsh said curtly.

Harmon looked down at Walsh, sensing that the young marine was holding back information. "If you think it's important, you'd better let me know."

Walsh hesitated.

"If you're hiding something and they find out, your ass is history," Harmon warned.

Walsh coughed and tried to clear the phlegm from his throat. Finally he hawked some blood-tinged sputum and spat it into a cup at the bedside. He glanced over at Kirby and lowered his voice. "I think I caught the disease from Ann Cormier. She was the technician who got sick from doing the autopsy."

Harmon's eyes narrowed. "Is that the same broad who was screwing the pilot?"

"Yeah."

"And you slept with her too?"

Walsh nodded slightly. "Only once."

"How many other guys did she screw?"

"Just the pilot and me."

"Uh-huh," Harmon said, not believing that for a moment. The female tech sounded like she had hot pants, and she was on a ship filled with horny sailors and marines. Harmon would have bet a month's pay that Ann

Cormier had screwed more than two of the crew aboard the *Global Explorer II*.

"Of course," Walsh said on further reflection, "she could have slept with some other guys too."

"Yeah," Harmon said tonelessly, "she could have."

Walsh coughed hard, then swallowed back the phlegm. "Are you going to tell the doc about this?"

"I have to," Harmon said. "But I'll try to make sure it doesn't reach the colonel."

"Man, you've got to do that for me."

"I'll try my best," Harmon said, wondering if he too would have slept with the technician, given the chance. No way, he decided at once, not even if she was a movie star. Harmon had sixteen years in the navy and needed only four more to reach retirement. He wasn't going to risk that for some piece of ass.

"Well, let's get you set up," Harmon said, and stepped into a nearby supply room.

Walsh quickly leaned over to Kirby in the next bed. "Shit, man! I had to tell him."

Kirby was breathing shallowly under the top sheet. He wasn't moving.

Walsh reached over and shook Kirby's arm. "Did you hear what I said? I couldn't help it. It was the right thing to do, huh?"

Kirby didn't answer.

Walsh shook him again, harder this time. "Hey, Russ! Wake up, man!"

Kirby snorted loudly, his eyes now half-open and glazed. He began mumbling incoherently, then called out for his mother.

Walsh bolted up in bed. "Medic! Medic!"

Harmon came back out of the supply room and hurried to the bedside. "What?"

Walsh pointed to Kirby. "Something is wrong with Russell. He's talking funny and not making any sense."

Harmon quickly examined Kirby and saw the glazed-over look in his eyes. The marine's skin felt like it was on fire. "Kirby!" he said into the marine's ear.

Kirby didn't move.

"Kirby!" Harmon yelled.

Kirby snorted and began mumbling incoherently again.

"What's wrong with Russ?" Walsh asked, wide-eyed with fright.

Harmon didn't answer. He ran for the phone.

Neiderman nervously paced the floor of his room. He was fully awake now, but still sweating from the terror of his nightmare. It was the same nightmare he'd had in the past. He was up on a brightly lit stage and two men with clawlike weapons were attacking him, ripping off his clothes and tearing into his skin. The audience roared its approval. In the front row, his ex-wife was laughing, enjoying every minute. Then the clawed weapon came down again and took off his testicles. That was the moment he always awakened, groping for his balls to make sure they were still there.

Neiderman opened a packet of salted peanuts and poured the contents into his mouth, still thinking about the nightmare and what had precipitated it. He had gone to sleep dwelling on his failures. It was always his feelings of inadequacy that brought on the terrible dreams.

His psychiatrist had told him the cure was simple. No pills, no hypnosis. All he had to do was conjure up pleasant, happy thoughts at bedtime. But that was difficult for Neiderman to do, particularly since his life was rapidly turning into shit. None of his hopes and plans was working out. Not one.

The deadly microbe that he planned to sell was for all intents and purposes nonexistent. Oh, it was there all right, they just couldn't grow it out. None of the cultures showed any growth, not even the ones done with extracts from the prehistoric plants. Everything was a total washout. A big nothing.

Neiderman felt his stomach growling. He checked his pockets and suitcase for more packets of food, but his supply was exhausted. He glanced at his watch. It was after midnight and the galley would be locked. His stomach growled louder, the pangs of hunger growing. Remembering the candy bars he had stored away in the lab, Neiderman quickly dressed and stepped out into the passageway.

The quarters that had been reserved for the ETOX team were small and cramped, but by navy standards they were spacious. Each cabin had its own bathroom, giving a welcome degree of privacy. Neiderman hurried past the closed doors, first Joanna Blalock's, then Ben Kagen's.

As he passed Kagen's door, he heard a bumping sound within, then laughter. Neiderman moved closer to the door and pressed his ear to it. The bumping sound was louder, and now he could hear moaning and groaning and Doreen saying, "Oh, yes! Oh, yes!" It took him a moment to realize he was listening to Kagen and Doreen screwing their brains out. Whore! Neiderman thought miserably, and walked on, hating her and the ship and his life in general.

In the laboratory area a marine guard eyed Neiderman warily as he walked into the bacteriology lab.

Neiderman went through the communicating door to the toxicology lab and opened his desk drawer. Quickly he devoured a giant candy bar, followed by a bag of potato chips. Then he washed everything down with a can of warm soda.

He leaned against the desk and again thought how miserably his life had turned out. Nothing was working for him. There would be no great fortune, no one to come into his life and make him happy. He would end up going back to his government laboratory where he would remain until retirement. He would live a boring life, trapped in the same place and job with no hope of going anywhere else. He would live his life out doing the same thing over and over again.

Neiderman walked back into the bacteriology lab with its incubators containing the cultures that weren't growing out anything.

Opening the door of the largest incubator, he stared resentfully in. His eyes suddenly widened. Something was growing! Holy shit! Something was growing!

Neiderman quickly glanced over his shoulder, making sure no one else was around. His heart was pounding and perspiration was forming on the palms of his hands. He wiped them dry on his trousers, then reexamined the cultures. It looked like bacteria, and maybe there was a fungus there too. Neiderman couldn't be sure what the organisms were. He wasn't an expert, but he knew enough to recognize bacterial growth. And he knew enough to recognize his window of opportunity.

Now was his chance. It would not come again.

But how to do it? How to steal some of the bacteria without anyone knowing it was missing? How?

Neiderman paced the floor, his mind searching for the best solution. He couldn't just steal a culture. Plates didn't suddenly disappear on their own. Everyone would know it had been removed or stolen. He discarded that option. Too obvious. Too risky.

Neiderman went for another candy bar and hurriedly gulped it down. He thought better with food. Now he was pacing again. There had to be a way to steal the bacteria without leaving any incriminating evidence behind.

Neiderman furrowed his brow, concentrating, looking for an answer. Then he smiled. Do a subculture. Just take a culture from one of the petri dishes and plant it onto a new plate. Yes! That would work, and nobody would know. He quickly donned protective gear.

Carefully he took out a furred culture plate and, using a wire loop, scooped up some of the bacterial growth. He streaked it onto a new petri dish, sealed it, and put it into his pocket. That should do it, he thought.

But then, as he carried the original plate back to the incubator, he was assailed by uncertainty. Suppose the damn thing didn't grow? Suppose it was filled with contaminants like some of the cultures Neiderman had done? He knew he would never get another chance. It was now or never.

He examined the culture plate again and now saw the label on the bottom: *magnolia extract* #14. It was the plant, after all! The damn bacteria needed something in that prehistoric plant in order to grow.

Neiderman went to the cabinet that housed the plant extracts. Opening an airtight container, he poured small samples of the magnolia extract into test tubes with screw caps. Then he added the bacteria to the tubes. Three would be plenty, he thought, but he took a fourth for good measure.

Moments later he was walking back to his quarters, a happy bounce to his steps. As he passed Ben Kagen's room, he heard the sounds of two people whispering. But now it didn't bother him. With the money he would make he could afford a dozen women. Anytime he wanted them.

Forty

Hawksworth stared down at the sealed culture dish atop the illuminator. He could clearly see the white dots that indicated bacterial growth. "Now we've got the little bastard," he said, permitting himself a rare obscenity.

"Not quite," Mark said.

"Why not?"

"Because we still haven't proved that this is the bug that's producing toxins and killing people," Mark told him. "All we can say at this point is that some bacteria are growing in our culture plates."

Hawksworth grumbled under his breath. "How do we go about proving this bacteria is our killer?"

"By seeing if it produces the toxin found in the ice," Mark said. "The studies are being set up now. We'll have the answer in a few minutes."

"Good, good," Hawksworth said, pleased with the progress of the experiments. "When will we know which antibiotics can destroy the bacteria?"

Mark spread his hands. "I'm not sure. We can do the in-vitro tests with antibiotic discs in a matter of days. But whether the drugs can actually kill the bacteria is another question."

"And suppose they can't?" Kagen asked.

"Let's cross that bridge when we get to it."

"Suppose none of the antibiotics work?" Kagen persisted.

"Well," Mark said slowly, "if none of the currently available antibiotics work, we'll have to send the cultures to the CDC and USAMRIID for further testing. That could take weeks, or even months."

Doreen quickly looked over at Hawksworth. "We won't have to stay aboard this ship waiting for *that*, will we?"

"We'll see," Hawksworth said evasively. He would call Washington for instructions, although he already knew what they would say: Stay put until an effective antibiotic is found.

"Oh, we'll find the right antibiotic," Joe Wells said, coming over from the Plexiglas window where he'd been watching the guinea pigs in their cages. "We're already on the right track."

Mark asked, "How do you know that?"

"Because the last marine to come down with the disease—you know, the guy with the hand wound—is holding his own with triple antibiotic therapy."

"He's not holding his own," Mark said gloomily. "He's now delirious and he's dying."

Wells sucked air through his teeth. "Christ! I didn't know."

"And another marine was admitted last night," Mark went on. "We started him on antibiotics immediately, but he's still sick and getting sicker."

Hawksworth sighed wearily to himself, wondering if he was going to end up with a ship full of dead people. Too many deaths already, and more sure to come. The morgue was now packed to overflowing with bodies. Another morgue would have to be constructed, he told himself. For a moment Hawksworth considered burials at sea, but then he remembered that all the bodies were infected. Dumping them into the ocean would virtually guarantee that the bacteria got into the food chain.

Hawksworth detached himself from the ETOX group, now discussing the plant extract that was so essential for the bacteria to grow. They were talking about isolating and identifying the growth factor using mass spectometry and gas chromatography. It was all mumbo-jumbo to Hawksworth. All he wanted was an antibiotic to kill the goddamn bacteria. How they got it didn't matter to him.

His gaze settled on Joanna Blalock. She was sitting at a desk, apparently just finishing and folding a letter. As she slipped it into an envelope, he walked over.

"You do realize that no mail can leave this ship?"

"Of course," Joanna said, and handed him the envelope with the name Kate Blalock printed on it. "This is a letter for my sister. I want you to make sure that, if anything happens to me, it gets to her."

"I'd have to read it before approving transmittal."

"I understand," Joanna said. "It's only a goodbye letter to someone I love."

Hawksworth gave her a long look. "But I thought there was an antibiotic to take care of the bacteria you caught at Memorial."

"That's not the pathogen I'm concerned about," Joanna told him. "It's the one aboard this ship that has me worried."

"And you think it's going to kill you?"

Joanna nodded. "I think it's going to kill all of us."

"But we now *have* the bacteria."

"And it's still spreading throughout your ship, Colonel," Joanna said grimly. "Everybody who gets it dies. There's no treatment, none whatsoever."

"But eventually they'll find an antibiotic that works," Hawksworth argued.

"I think so too," Joanna agreed. "But by then we'll all be dead."

Hawksworth rubbed at the back of his neck nervously. "I wish I could come up with a way to protect the people who are not yet infected."

The door opened and Paula Garrett entered. There

were dark circles beneath her reddened eyes. "I've got good news and I've got bad news."

"Let's have the bad news first," Hawksworth said at once.

"Mallory just died."

"Ooh!" Doreen winced.

"Such a nice man," Kagen said softly.

Neiderman made the sign of the cross.

There was a silence as they thought about Mike Mallory. Everyone was fond of the handsome pilot who had been so helpful and reassuring while he was ferrying them over the icy seas to the *Global Explorer II*. They all knew and liked him. His death hurt.

"Did he have a family?" Joanna asked.

"A wife and young son," Hawksworth said.

"Jesus." Joanna sighed as the mood in the room became even more somber.

"Yeah," Hawksworth said. Suppressing thoughts of how many more would die, he turned to Garrett. "What's the good news?"

"Reetha Sims is responding to painful stimuli," Garrett said. "She's slowly coming out of her coma."

"Thank you, God," Doreen said in a whisper, and closed her eyes to say a prayer of gratitude.

Ben Kagen came over and gave Doreen a restrained hug. "See? You told me she'd make it."

Joe Wells grinned broadly. "Wonderful, just wonderful."

Joanna was watching the expression on Mark's face. She saw the half smile, but there was no joy or happiness. And his eyes were narrowed, troubled. Something was bothering him, Joanna thought. Everyone seemed overjoyed, but not Mark. Why wouldn't he be happy at Reetha's recovery? They had worked together for so many years and— *Oh, God! He doesn't want her to wake up because he was the one who tried to kill her. She must have discovered something—something that showed he started the epidemic.*

Joanna stared at Mark, almost certain she was right, yet casting about for any other explanation.

There were two pieces in the puzzle that didn't fit. The first was the death of Barbara Van Buren. Mark would have to be responsible for her death too. But why would he bother to kill her? She was a toxicologist. She couldn't have posed any threat to Mark. And the second problem was the epidemic itself. How could Reetha find something aboard this ship that related to an epidemic taking place thousands of miles away? That made no sense at all.

A buzzer sounded loudly, then abruptly stopped. The group walked over to the Plexiglas window and looked in. Two guinea pigs were already in the clear plastic tubes that led to the chambers containing the bacterial cultures.

"The chamber on the right contains room air," Mark explained. "The one on the left has a concentrate of the presumed toxin made by the bacteria. It's already been heat-activated."

Now the guinea pigs were at the end of the plastic tubes. They pushed through one-way doors and entered the chambers. The animals sniffed the air.

"Are you sure there's enough toxin in there to produce a lethal effect?" Hawksworth asked.

"More than enough," Mark answered. "The guinea pig is very sensitive to a small amount of toxin, just like man."

One of the guinea pigs suddenly tensed and rolled over, shaking and gasping for breath. It was dead in forty seconds. The guinea pig in the other chamber was still sniffing the air, obviously unaffected.

"The bacteria we're growing out is the killer," Mark said. "We've got our bug."

"Good," Kagen said. "Now let's find out how to kill *it*."

"That's our next step," Mark told him. "We'll set up the cultures with antibiotic discs first thing."

Kagen rubbed his hands together slowly. "I think we may be seeing the light at the end of the tunnel."

"Lordy, I hope so," Doreen said.

Kagen stepped forward to address the group. "I want all of our efforts to focus on the experiments Mark and Doreen will be doing. If they need your help or assistance, you're to drop what you're doing and lend a hand. Does everyone agree with that?" Kagen looked at the others and saw only nods. "Good. Now I think we should adjourn to the bar and raise our glasses to Reetha's recovery."

Kagen took Doreen's arm and led the way through the adjoining laboratory and along the dimly lit passageway.

As he reached for the door to the dining area, he felt a sudden vibration. Everyone else felt it too. It was accompanied by a series of soft thuds coming from the bow of the ship. A moment later all was quiet again.

"What the hell was that?" Garrett asked worriedly.

"We've been going through a storm in the open sea for the past hour," Hawksworth explained. "It won't be long before we're through the worst of it."

Doreen looked at him skeptically. "Are you telling us a storm makes thuds that come and go?"

"No," Hawksworth said tonelessly. "Those thuds were probably caused by the ship plowing through some ice floes. They present absolutely no danger to us."

Doreen gave Hawksworth a long look, not trusting him or his smooth talk. Anything that caused a big ship to vibrate presented a danger. Any fool knew that.

"Come, come," Kagen said as he ushered the group into the dining area. "We'll be out of this storm within two martinis."

"Better make that three martinis," Doreen quipped.

The group chuckled, but everyone remained on edge.

The bar steward began mixing drinks, knowing exactly who drank what. He handed Kagen two large goblets. "Double martinis, dry, one olive."

Kagen passed one goblet to Doreen. She took a small sip and glanced nervously across the room. Hawksworth was reaching for the wall phone, his back to them. She took another sip, larger this time. "I'm still nervous about that damn ice we just hit."

"I'm certain everything is under control," Kagen said reassuringly. "If there was any real danger Hawksworth would have informed us."

Doreen shook her head. "I'll bet he's checking damage control right now."

"So?"

"A moment ago he was telling us how sure he was that everything was fine."

Kagen studied the concerned look on her face. "Would you like me to speak with Hawksworth again?"

"Would you mind?"

Doreen watched him walk away, thinking about Reetha and wishing her twin were fully recovered and standing next to her. Reetha knew how to handle situations like this. If Reetha were here now, she'd be right in Hawksworth's face, demanding he tell the truth and knowing if he wasn't.

Doreen's gaze went to the paneled walls of the room. There were no pictures or windows, not even a mirror behind the bar. She hated the ship and the claustrophobic feeling it gave her. Never again, she vowed. They'll never get me on the bottom of a damn boat again.

Doreen saw Joanna approaching and put down her empty glass. "Well, Joanna, you're going to be a cured woman soon."

"As soon as the Panamycin arrives."

"You've very lucky," Doreen said. "I hope Reetha's luck is as good."

"So do I," Joanna said fervently.

Doreen glanced over at the bar where Kagen was engaged in an animated conversation with Hawksworth. She liked the way he stood up to the colonel, never backing down. "It's extra nice that a drug we developed at BioMega is going to save your life. Now if only it turns out that Panamycin works against our bug too."

Joanna's brow went up. "Have you tested the toxic bacteria against Panamycin?"

Doreen shook her head. "We don't have any Panamycin aboard yet."

"So you're just hoping the antibiotic works?"

"It's more than hope," Doreen told her. "Remember the antiserum against the Memorial bug you asked Hawksworth to get from the CDC?"

Joanna nodded.

"It reacts strongly with our bacteria too," Doreen said. "The two microorganisms are very, very similar. Hell, they could pass for the same bug. So it's a good bet Panamycin will kill both of them equally well."

Joanna's eyes suddenly widened as all the pieces to the puzzle fell into place. She was now certain that Mark was responsible for the epidemic that had spread across three continents. And she now knew why Mark had to kill Barbara Van Buren. All for money. All so BioMega could again become a money-making machine.

"Are you all right?" Doreen asked, studying Joanna's face.

"I'm fine," Joanna said, regaining her composure. "Does Mark know about the antiserum reacting so well with our bacteria?"

"Not yet."

"I'll tell him," Joanna said. "I'm sure he'll be fascinated."

Joanna walked over to a small couch and sat across from Mark. She looked straight into his eyes and said, "I know."

"You know what?" Mark asked.

"That you started the epidemic that came from China to America."

Mark stared back at her. "Are you insane?"

"Not at all," Joanna said evenly. "You sent the cholera-like organism from your lab in Cambridge to BioMega's plant in China. Then one of their technicians got infected and started a miniepidemic. Is that where you got the idea?"

"This is absolutely ridiculous," Mark said, his temper rising.

"And you already knew that Panamycin was the only antibiotic that worked against the infection."

Mark's jaw tightened. "Just because Panamycin was effective doesn't mean I—"

"Sure it does," Joanna said easily. "It means you had the strongest motive and the most to gain. And your company was going down the tubes again, so you came up with this brilliant idea. Start an epidemic with bacteria that are sensitive only to Panamycin. That forces the medical community to use an experimental antibiotic that hasn't even gone through the first phase of its clinical trials. You save a hundred million dollars for openers. Your drug is now in the marketplace, and it'll earn you a zillion dollars in the future."

"You're so full of crap it's unbelievable," Mark spat out. "You've concocted this wild story without a shred of proof."

"Oh, you've already given me all the proof I need."

"Like what?"

"Like when I told you of my plans to treat myself with neomycin. You immediately said that the organism was barely affected by neomycin, even at high doses. How could you know that? The epidemic started after you came aboard the *Global Explorer*. You shouldn't have known anything about the mysterious bacteria. Yet you did. And don't tell me Doreen tested my culture against neomycin, because I checked, and she didn't. So how could you know?"

Mark hesitated for a moment, then shrugged. "I was just guessing. We usually test gram-negative organisms against neomycin and I assumed it was done in this case as well."

"And did you 'just guess' that the neomycin would induce resistance to Panamycin?" Joanna glared at Mark, her eyes boring into him. "Does that happen a lot?"

"We've seen it—"

"Once," Joanna interjected. "Because it has only occurred in one very unique microorganism. It was a characteristic of the bacteria that you shipped from Cambridge to China, the same bacteria that just caused a major outbreak in America and Europe. You know all about this organism, don't you?"

Mark glared at her. "And where did I get this unique organism? Did I just dream it up? Or did I invent it in my laboratory like some mad scientist?"

"You didn't have to invent it," Joanna went on. "I think you discovered it on your previous mission on the *Global Explorer*. That was when it first appeared, wasn't it? I suspect you grew it out of one of those dead sea creatures and studied it extensively without telling anyone. And it was right here, aboard this ship, that you learned the organism was resistant to all antibiotics except Panamycin."

"Do you realize how ridiculous you sound?" Mark asked, shifting around in his seat. "Now you're telling me I started the epidemic with some strange bug I uncovered on my first mission out here. Am I hearing you correctly?"

Joanna nodded. "And it's the same bug that's in our iceberg. They're all one and the same."

Mark threw up his hands. "This gets more outrageous by the minute."

"Not really," Joanna went on. "The story goes something like this. After you got the epidemic from China started, you were called to join our mission off Alaska. You were in a panic. You figured the bug in the iceberg was the same one you'd found on your first mission, the same one you'd just used to set off the epidemic in China. Once you confirmed it, you did your best to ensure we wouldn't grow the bacteria from the iceberg, didn't you? You knew if we did, someone would put all the pieces together. They would learn that the organism in the iceberg was identical to the one that caused the epidemic. And then they would order new studies of the tissue specimens from all the sea creatures that died up here a year ago. And they would find the exact same bacteria." Joanna nodded to herself. "Everything would point to you. You were the common denominator, Mark. You were on both missions, you had a pharmaceutical house with bacteriology laboratories in Shanghai, and you would make billions from the epidemic because your company produced the only antibiotic that could kill the bacteria." Joanna nodded again. "Everything would point directly at you."

"You're assuming the bacteria in the iceberg and the one causing the epidemic are the same," Mark said calmly. "There's no evidence to back that up."

"There's plenty," Joanna told him. "Hawksworth received the antiserum to the Memorial bug from the CDC and Doreen tested it against the bacteria from the iceberg. It fit like a glove."

Mark's face hardened and Joanna knew she had him.

"Which brings us to the attack on Reetha and the murder of Barbara Van Buren," Joanna continued. "I suspect Reetha found out something peculiar was going on in the laboratory. Since you tried to kill her, it had to be something very important. I'd guess it had to do with how the cultures were being set up."

Joanna stared at Mark as his eyelids fluttered involuntarily. She remembered Jake Sinclair once telling her that fluttering lids were a sign someone was lying or guilty or both.

"With Barbara Van Buren it was different," she continued. "You weren't worried about her. It was her husband who posed the threat. He was in China investigating the origin of the epidemic, and she was going to contact him when he returned so he could tell us how to make an antiserum against our bacteria. And he would have surely sent us some of his antisera against the bacteria causing the epidemic, as well as some of the live bacteria, just to see if the Chinese bacteria and ours were related. All of that would have clearly shown that the iceberg bacteria and the Chinese bacteria were one and the same. In addition, her husband's team may have already tracked down some of the first cases of the disease in China and learned where they contracted the bacteria and how. You couldn't let the ETOX team here in Alaska and the epidemiologists in China put two and two together. And Barbara was the link between them. You had to kill her."

"This is utterly preposterous," Mark said evenly. "You've based your entire theory on the assumption that the organism in the iceberg is identical to the one that caused the epidemic."

"It is."

"Then explain to me why one is so easy to grow and the other so difficult. If they were the same bug, they should have grown the same in cultures."

Joanna smiled thinly. "That was the beauty of it, wasn't it? All specimens from both missions came to your lab. It was no problem for you to manipulate the cultures and make certain nothing grew out. What did you use to do it? Panamycin?"

"Obviously, nothing, since the bacteria *are* finally growing out."

"Yeah, you must have gotten careless and let one slip through."

"That's a weak explanation," Mark said calmly. "You'll have to do better than that."

"Or maybe you were doctoring the cultures with Panamycin and ran out of it."

Mark's eyelids fluttered again.

"You don't give up, do you?"

"Why should I? Everything points to your guilt."

"You still have no proof," Mark scoffed. "And even if I knew something about the bacteria, there's no reason to think I was involved in starting an epidemic."

"Sure there is," Joanna said, hating him and what he'd done. "It was your silence. You knew all about the infection and how it could be cured, but while people on this ship were dropping one by one, you remained silent. You had to. If Kagen and Hawksworth found out you were an expert on the bacteria, the trail would have led right back to the epidemic via your China connection. Even when you learned I was a carrier, you still said nothing. Not a word."

Joanna took a deep breath and tried to control her anger. "You were willing to let me die, weren't you?"

Mark got to his feet. "This conversation is o—"

There was a loud, sickening thud amidships. The entire ship began to vibrate, the floor most of all. Glasses and bottles rattled noisily on the shelves, some toppling and smashing into pieces. Everyone froze in place, waiting, listening.

Gradually the vibrations subsided. Then another sound came, a creaking, straining noise, again amidships. Slowly the *Global Explorer II* tilted to starboard. A beeping alarm went off.

Everyone grabbed for bolted-down chairs and fixtures as the ship listed even more. The lights in the dining area dimmed, then went out altogether.

Joanna was on the floor, holding on to a leg of the

dining table. She heard others around her crying and screaming. Doreen was nearby, praying at the top of her voice.

The ship shuddered and the floor seemed to move, but Joanna couldn't tell which way it was moving. Everything was pitch black. Panic and fear flooded through her. She wanted to get up and run, but there was nowhere to run. And even if there was, she could never find her way in the darkness.

Again the ship vibrated. Joanna wrapped her arms around the table leg and held on for dear life. Her body began to shake with fright and she held on even tighter. *I'm going to die! And this ship will be my grave!*

In her mind's eye, pictures of her life flashed before her. She saw herself as a child playing with her dad in a garden. Then she was graduating from medical school with her now dead mother proudly looking on. Then she saw Kate, the sister she loved more than heaven and earth. *Oh, Kate! I'll never see you again.*

Now Joanna could feel wetness on her feet. Abruptly she jerked them up. *Water! We're taking on water!* Once more the floor seemed to move. As before, Joanna couldn't determine the direction of the movement. But she could still feel the wetness on her legs.

The lights flickered for a moment, giving the room an eerie, ghostlike appearance. Everything was a greenish-yellow color, even the bodies of the people lying close to Joanna.

The lights flickered again, then came back on. The beeping alarm stopped, and all was dead quiet.

Hawksworth quickly got to his feet. There was a small gash on his forehead dripping blood. He ignored it. "Is anyone hurt?" He glanced around the group. Everyone was now standing, shaken but relieved to be alive. There were bumps and bruises, a few cuts here and there. Nothing serious. "Stay put while I check with damage control."

Kagen was testing his ankle. He had twisted it and it hurt like hell, but he could still move it. He limped over to Doreen and studied the laceration on her arm. "That's a bad cut."

"I'll be fine," Doreen said, her heart still pounding. She had never been so close to death.

"Dr. Garrett," Kagen called. "Could you take a look at Doreen's arm?"

Garrett carefully examined the wound. It was clean and two inches long with jagged edges. "You'll need stitches. Just keep it covered for now."

Kagen took out a fresh handkerchief and bound up the wound. "How's that?"

"Perfect," Doreen said, taking his arm and feeling safe next to him.

Joanna looked down at her legs. Her knees were abraded from crawling. Glancing back to the table where she'd clung during the darkness, she saw the wet area. The water had come from a broken bottle, not from the sea. And the ship was almost upright now. The floor was still tilted, but less than ten degrees.

The bar steward came over to Joanna and pointed to his back. A big sliver of glass was sticking through his shirt near the shoulder blade. "Could you pull this out for me, Doc?"

Joanna extracted the sliver and stemmed the flow of blood with bar napkins. "You'll need stitches, too."

"If these goddamn icebergs don't kill us first," the steward said hoarsely. "They've got a mind of their own and they mean to kill us, make no mistake about that. And they won't stop until they've finished what they set out to do."

Kagen patted the steward on the shoulder. "Come now, you don't mean to imply that icebergs intentionally kill people, do you?"

"Professor, you know the stars and I know the sea," the steward said darkly. "And I know there are certain things in the sea you don't mess with. Icebergs are one of those things. You stay clear of them, they'll stay clear of you. You mess with them, and they'll kill you. As sure as there's a God in heaven, they'll kill you."

Kagen shook his head at the seafarer's words. "One can explain everything these icebergs have done on the basis of concrete physical principles. There's nothing supernatural about it."

"The iceberg that just hit us was waiting for us," the steward said. "It was waiting for a gale-force wind to drive it into our hull and sink us."

"Why would it do that?"

"Because we have something it wants."

"And what's that?"

"The iceberg we took out of the sea and shouldn't have."

Hawksworth had been listening from a distance. He came up to the steward and gave him a hard look. "That's enough nonsense about icebergs having minds."

"It's what the men believe, sir."

"You save your sea stories for another time. Got it?"

"Aye, sir."

Hawksworth turned to the group. "Moments ago an iceberg rammed into one of our starboard compartments. It tore a six-foot gash in the hull. Fortunately, this ship has a double hull, and the inner one is still intact. We're afloat, we're seaworthy, and we'll be under way in just a few minutes."

Wells asked, "If we're so seaworthy, how come we're still listing?"

"Because there's a fair amount of space between the hulls, and water has flooded the breached compartment. So, one side of the ship is heavier. But we have ways to balance that out."

Hawksworth wrinkled his nose as he detected a strange odor. "Is something burning?"

"God Almighty!" The steward pointed to the galley

door. Black smoke was seeping out. He ran over and felt the door. It was warm, but not hot. Quickly he opened the door and stepped back. Dense smoke poured out, followed by a narrow tongue of flame.

While Hawksworth lunged for the phone, the steward hurried behind the bar and put a wet towel over his head, then grabbed a fire extinguisher. Spraying the fire repellent in front of him, he made his way into the galley.

The smoke was so thick he could barely see. The floor ahead of him was a sea of flame, and the smell of burning cooking oil mingled with the smoke.

He stumbled badly over a large object and looked down. It was the cook, burnt to a crisp, his face blackened and charred and almost unrecognizable. The flames sprang up higher, singeing the steward's arms. He quickly backed out of the galley, coughing and choking.

"Well?" Hawksworth asked, hurrying over.

"It's bad, sir," the steward said, gasping for air. "Flames to hell and back."

"What about the men?"

"Only the cook, and he's dead."

"The fire crew will be down here pronto," Hawksworth said. "You stay out of the galley until they get here. Understood?"

"Aye, sir."

Hawksworth wheeled to the others. "You must all leave the area immediately. Please follow me."

He led the way aft along the passageway that led past the laboratories.

"How bad is the fire?" Kagen asked.

"It can be controlled," Hawksworth said.

But he didn't say it could be put out, Kagen was thinking. He let the women go ahead and motioned to Mark and Wells and Neiderman.

When the colonel was out of hearing distance, Kagen said, "I don't trust him. I think we've got big trouble. We may have to abandon ship."

"If we do, we do," Wells said fatalistically.

"I'm not leaving all our work behind," Kagen said quickly. "It's too important."

"We can't take everything," Wells said.

"Only the essentials." Kagen turned to Mark. "You get samples of the most vigorous cultures. Don't bother with anything else. Put them in unbreakable plastic tubes."

As Mark hurried away, Kagen looked at Wells and Neiderman. "Malcolm, you and Joe collect all the magnolia plant extracts. If you can, get some of the whole plant as well."

Wells hesitated. "The whole plant may be loaded with bacteria."

Kagen thought for a moment. "Snip off small pieces of the roots and branches and put them in screw-cap tubes. And be careful doing it."

Neiderman asked, "What about the fern?"

"Leave it," Kagen said immediately. "Now go!"

Kagen hobbled to catch up with Hawksworth and the others, trying to ignore the pain in his ankle. He concentrated his mind, searching for anything he might have overlooked. The important things were taken care of. They would have everything they needed to grow the bacteria ashore.

Kagen entered the large area where the giant iceberg was housed. He saw Hawksworth and the women standing next to the Plexiglas cylinder and limped over.

"What's wrong with your leg?" Doreen asked worriedly.

"I sprained my ankle," Kagen said, waving away her concern. "But it's mild. I'm fine."

Joanna could see he wasn't. He was favoring the ankle with each step, and it would only get worse with time. "I'd sit and take the weight off the ankle if I were you."

"I'm fine," Kagen said again, but he leaned against Doreen for support.

Hawksworth looked around and frowned. "Where are the oth—"

A loud bang came from the bow, and the *Global Explorer II* lurched. The group grabbed for the metal scaffolding and held on tightly as the entire ship rocked and shuddered.

Within the Plexiglas cylinder the huge iceberg too rocked and shuddered. Mooring cables at its crown snapped, leaving only the metal struts at its ponderous base to hold the iceberg in place. Again the ship lurched, and the iceberg with it. The metal struts bent under the shifting weight of the ice, then gave way altogether.

Gradually the ship stabilized, though it still listed to starboard. And now the iceberg listed with it, moving with each motion of the ship, all of its restraining cables and struts dangling uselessly in the Plexiglas cylinder.

Hawksworth ran for the phone and spoke briefly, then listened. His expression turned grimmer and the color left his face.

The inner hull of the *Global Explorer II* had been penetrated. Water was pouring in.

Forty-one

Executive Officer Elliott Matts was receiving conflicting information. Initially he was told the compartment that the iceberg had penetrated was sealed off. Now the sensors said it wasn't.

"Is the damn area sealed off or not?" Matts snapped.

"It was, but it's not now," Seaman Radcliff reported. "We've got a leak."

"Location? Size?"

"I can't tell for sure." Radcliff pushed a button on his console and a picture appeared on a small television screen. It showed men trudging through water. "But the water in the adjacent compartment is knee deep."

Matts wheeled to his right. "Lieutenant," he ordered, "seal off the whole section."

"Sir, that would include the sickbay. And we've got men in there."

"Get them out and seal it off," Matts said quickly. "And do it now."

"Aye, aye, sir."

Matts turned his attention back to the monitors in the control room. There were still plenty of icebergs in the area, some close by. None was very big, yet they all required watching. Even the smaller ones could cause real damage. Usually icebergs were slow-moving and easy to avoid. But in a storm all bets were off. The icebergs moved as fast as the wind and tide, and could be on top of a ship in the blink of an eye.

Like the last son of a bitch that rammed us, Matts thought bitterly. There had been no warning, no sighting on the monitors. The iceberg simply appeared and caught everyone unawares. Especially the captain, who at the time of the collision was between decks. The impact threw him down the companionway and smashed his head onto a steel step, fracturing his skull so badly that his brains spilled out. Upon his instantaneous death the Executive Officer automatically took command.

Matts had always wanted his own ship. He had lived for the moment. But he hadn't wanted it to happen this way.

"Sir, we've got earthquake activity to the north," Radcliff reported.

"How far north?"

"Ten miles."

Matts looked up at a giant screen that showed the out-line of the Alaskan coast. The pulsating circle, which indicated the site of the seaquake, intensified briefly and then faded. "Keep a close watch on that area."

"Aye, sir," Radcliff said, knowing Matts was concerned about tsunamis, the fast-moving "tidal waves" set off by underwater earthquakes. They were huge and mean and destroyed everything in their path. Radcliff had heard about them but had never seen one and hoped to God he never would.

Matts's gaze went to another large video monitor on the opposite wall. It gave a panoramic view of the ocean surrounding the *Global Explorer II.* The first light of dawn was breaking, the sea still rough and stormy but less so than before.

Another hour, Matts thought, and we'll be out of it. We'll steam south and make port in Seattle for repairs. Then a hot tub and a massage and a nice steak with a good bottle of French wine.

His eyes drifted over to the captain's chair, and he wondered if they would let him keep his command once

they made port. Maybe, maybe not. He had enough experience, and his sea record was excellent. But he was
only thirty-six. They would count that against him. Still,
if he could pilot the disabled ship safely through the
storm and bring her into—

"Sir, they're having trouble controlling the fire in
the civilians' galley," Radcliff reported, breaking into
Matts's thoughts. "It's spreading aft."

"Get more men down there."

"Both crews are fighting the fire now, sir."

Matts tapped his finger against a table, thinking, trying to come up with an answer. "Tell the lieutenant to
make sure all hatches are secured and to prepare to flood
the area."

Radcliff pushed a button, and a diagram that showed
the watertight compartments of the ship appeared on the
screen. "If we do that, sir, we'll take out the laboratories
and everything in them."

Matts stared at the diagram. Destroying all the laboratories wasn't an option at this point. He would do that
only as a last resort. "Tell them to continue fighting the
fire. I want updates every five minutes."

"Aye, sir."

Matts looked away, cursing under his breath, unhappy
with himself. He was making snap decisions without
first thinking them through.

His gaze went back to the diagram on the screen. He
should have realized that flooding the galley would wipe
out the laboratories and the vital data they held. Stupid!
Stupid! Get your head out of your ass, Matts berated
himself. Stop thinking about home port and fancy din-
ners. Keep your mind on the ship, and the storm and the
icebergs that threaten it, and the fire that may consume it
from within. Think, man, think! Or you lose your first
and last ship, and all hands aboard her.

The fire was the most threatening problem, he decided. If the flames continued to spread and overwhelm

the automated extinguisher systems, the ship would explode like a bomb. No one would survive. And even if there were time to put lifeboats into the sea, the storm would quickly devour them.

Matts looked over at the screens showing the ocean outside. The storm was worsening.

Two men in space suits were working feverishly inside the cylinder, trying to stabilize the iceberg before it did even more damage. There were already fissures in the Plexiglas, and Hawksworth knew that one more solid hit could split it wide open.

He ran his hand over a vertical crack and felt refrigerated air escaping. The inner layer of the cylinder had shattered through and through. Tapping on the Plexiglas, he got the attention of a worker inside and pointed to the crack. The worker quickly sprayed sealant over the area.

As Hawksworth walked back to the group of scientists, a loud clanging sound came from the elevator shaft. The banging continued for a full minute before it stopped and its echoes faded. "We'll have the elevator fixed shortly," Hawksworth said.

"That's what you told us ten minutes ago," Doreen said, an edge to her voice. "Why can't they get it to work?"

"Because the door is stuck."

Hawksworth looked over at the elevator as the noise started again. The door was more than stuck. It was jammed, and it couldn't be pried open. They were now going through a steel wall to get to it. "It'll only be a few more minutes."

"We're trapped down here, aren't we?" Doreen asked nervously, trying to control her claustrophobia.

"Not at all," Hawksworth assured her. "We can always go through the sickbay to stairs that lead topside."

Doreen pointed to Kagen. "And how will Ben get up those stairs, Colonel?"

Kagen had his ankle propped up on a chair. It was black and blue and badly swollen. "I'll make it all right."

"You can hardly take two steps," Doreen said.

Hawksworth thought for a moment, then said, "We'll carry him if necessary."

Doreen glanced around the gigantic chamber, feeling closed in despite Hawksworth's assurance that there were stairs they could still reach. Her heart began to race at the very thought of being trapped.

Doreen squeezed Kagen's shoulder and turned to Paula Garrett. "Would taping the ankle help?"

"It's a bad sprain," Garrett told her. "The only thing that would help is a walking cast."

"Maybe we should try some ice," Doreen suggested.

"I'll be fine," Kagen said, moving his ankle slightly and clenching his teeth against the pain. "See, it's already better."

"I think some ice—" Doreen began to say as the banging noise returned, even louder this time.

Kagen patted her hand. "We'll be out of here before you know it." He smiled at her, but inwardly he was cursing his bad luck.

Pushing his pain aside, Kagen glanced at the other scientists and made sure he hadn't overlooked anything. Mark had the plastic vials of the cultures as well as the lab books containing all the experimental data. Wells and Neiderman had the plant extracts and snippings from the whole plant.

The banging noise stopped abruptly. Everyone turned and looked at the elevator shaft, hoping to hear the sound of the car moving. They heard nothing.

"Shit!" Doreen grumbled, knowing that the longer it took to fix the elevator, the more likely she was to freak out. She took deep breaths through her mouth and tried to calm herself.

The door from the laboratory complex opened and the

corpsman Harmon hurried out, carrying a sack of medical supplies over his shoulder. He gave Hawksworth a sharp salute, then swallowed as he caught his breath.

"Why have you left the sickbay?" Hawksworth asked.

"Sir, water is coming in from the forward compartment," Harmon reported. "They've sealed off the entire sickbay area."

"What about the patients?"

"Kirby is dead, sir," Harmon said. "I moved Walsh and the Sims woman to separate secure rooms one deck above."

Doreen stared at the medic. "Are you saying we can't get to the sickbay area from here?"

"That's correct, ma'am. All the hatches are locked and sealed."

Doreen's eyes suddenly widened as she began to hyperventilate. Her heart was pounding in her chest. "We're trapped! We're trapped in here!"

"What?" Garrett quickly came over to the nearly hysterical woman. "What are you talking about?"

"The stairs, the stairs," Doreen said, breathing shallowly. "The stairs are the only way out, and to get to them we'd have to go through the sickbay."

Garrett turned to Hawksworth. "Is she right?"

"We have other options," Hawksworth said calmly, and pointed to the ceiling. "The roof of this chamber opens onto the main deck. We can climb up the metal scaffolding around the cylinder and reach daylight."

"What about Ben?" Doreen asked at once. "He can't even stand, much less climb."

"We'll lower a chair for him and winch him up with ropes and pulleys."

Doreen looked up, stretching her neck back. "That's eight stories high. The chair would swing and sway and—"

"If it comes to that, he'll have no choice," Hawksworth said brusquely. "He can go up in the chair or he can stay here and die."

"Sir, I'm picking up something approaching from the north."

"What is it?"

Radcliff squinted at the screen. "I can't be sure, but it's big." He studied the image carefully, watching it move. "Estimated height is forty feet and it's real broad."

"How far away?"

"Eight miles."

"It sounds like a big iceberg."

"Sir, I think it's moving too fast for an iceberg."

"Sailor, I've sailed these waters more times than I care to count. And believe me when I tell you they can move fast in a storm, every bit as fast as the winds and tides that carry them."

"But, sir, it's—"

"It's an iceberg," Matts said sharply.

Radcliff stared up at the executive officer, wanting to tell him that the storm winds were subsiding and the icebergs were moving slower and slower. And all the icebergs were moving in a westerly direction now. But not the object he was seeing on the screen. It was big and fast and coming out of the north. "Sir, with respect—"

"The discussion is over," Matts said tersely. "Get me the engine room."

"Aye, sir." Radcliff made the connection and handed the Executive Officer a headset. Then he looked back at the screen. The image off to starboard was now bigger and moving even faster.

It was only seven miles away.

Mark pushed himself up and came over to Harmon. "Are you certain Kirby was dead?"

"Yes, sir," Harmon said. "He had no pulse and no

blood pressure, and his pupils were big as saucers and fixed."

"And Reetha Sims is still stable?"

"Yes, sir."

"Did you make sure her IV was still running?" Mark asked.

"It's going good. But, sir,"—Harmon gestured at a red, angry area on the side of Mark's face—"I think you've got an infection on your cheek. It's by your sideburn."

"It's just an ingrown hair," Mark said, unconcerned.

"It's more than that, sir. You'd better let one of the other doctors look at it."

"Come over here where the light is better," Joanna said, and moved closer to the Plexiglas cylinder. She quickly examined the infected area on Mark's face. It was the size of a nickle and filled with pus. His forehead was also very warm. "You've got a carbuncle. It needs to be incised and drained."

"I'm on erythromycin," Mark said. "That should take care of it."

"You know better than that."

"Oh?" Mark asked, lowering his voice so the others couldn't hear. "Are you a specialist in infectious diseases too?"

"You don't have to be a specialist to treat a carbuncle," Joanna said. "And you've got a fever, Mark. That thing needs to be drained."

"So now you're interested in my well-being, huh?"

"I don't give a damn about your well-being," Joanna said, her voice tight and angry. "Every time I look at you, I think of a beautiful Chinese baby you killed. An innocent child. The first of a long line of victims. All for money."

"You're making things up as you go along, aren't you?"

"Like hell I am!"

"We'll sort this out later."

"You're damn right we will."

The ship suddenly rocked. Outside the cylinder, everyone froze in their tracks. Inside, the men slowly moved around the iceberg and headed for the open trapdoor.

Abruptly the ship lurched again, setting the iceberg in motion directly toward Joanna and Mark. They reflexively backed away, holding their arms up protectively.

Then the ship tilted, now listing even more severely to starboard. The caged iceberg changed direction and plowed into the two men wearing space suits, lifting them up and crushing them against the Plexiglas cylinder. Their torn space suits turned bright red as their limp bodies fell to the floor.

The iceberg seemed to back off for a moment. Then it rushed forward and smashed through the Plexiglas cylinder with a loud pop. Joanna and Mark ran for their lives, the iceberg right behind them.

They dove for cover just as the iceberg changed course again, now bearing down on the medic Harmon. It picked him up and carried him like an ornament on the hood of a car. With a dull thud it smashed him into a steel wall. Harmon slid down, blood gushing out of his nose and mouth.

Again the ship rolled and the iceberg rolled with it, pinning the sole remaining technician against the console and crushing him.

Everything grew still. Nothing moved. Not even the iceberg.

Joanna jumped to her feet, looking around desperately for an escape route. The iceberg was pressed against the doors to the already sealed-off laboratory wing and the nonfunctioning elevator. The Plexiglas cylinder was demolished, its metal scaffolding now a tangle of useless metal climbing to nowhere.

Her gaze went to the open trapdoor. She pointed and yelled out to Hawksworth, "What's down there?"

"A tunnel with tracks," Hawksworth called back.

"How big?"

"Six-by-ten feet."

In an instant Joanna was beside the trapdoor, easing her way down into the tunnel.

Hawksworth hurried over and grabbed her arm. "The tunnel may be filled with toxic bacteria," he warned. "We used this tunnel to transport pieces of the iceberg to the laboratories."

"I'll take my chances," Joanna said and jerked her arm away. "If you want to stay up here while that iceberg mows you down one by one, that's your business."

Hawksworth thought for a fraction of a second, then nodded. "You're right."

He quickly motioned to the others. "We're going into the tunnel."

Hawksworth helped Joanna down, then Mark, Garrett, and Neiderman. Carefully he lowered Kagen, the others below in the tunnel lending a hand. Then he extended his hand to Doreen. "Come on, come on," he urged.

Doreen hesitantly stepped forward, then stopped, frozen with fear. She tried to overcome her fright, but her heart was pounding so hard she couldn't breathe.

"Come on," Hawksworth urged again.

Doreen suddenly bolted and ran for the metal scaffolding, tripping over it and falling. She scrambled to her feet, petrified, looking for a door or a window.

The ship rocked ever so slightly. The iceberg rocked with it, moving an inch or two before again pressing against the wall.

From the tunnel Joanna called up to Hawksworth, "Where's Doreen?"

"She's gone mad," Hawksworth said, getting on his knees to enter the tunnel. "She doesn't want to come with us."

"She's frightened," Joanna told him. "She's claustrophobic."

"There's nothing we can do about that," Hawksworth said, now sitting on the edge of the trapdoor.

"Pull me back out," Joanna said. "We can't just leave her to die up there."

Hawksworth grumbled under his breath and got to his feet. He hurried across the floor littered with broken pieces of plastic and metal and wet with melted ice, glancing from side to side, looking for Doreen.

He stepped over the dead men in space suits, almost slipping on their exuded blood. To his right was the technician, crushed up against the console, eyes wide open.

The ship vibrated for a moment, then quieted. Hawksworth walked on, searching but finding nothing. Another minute, he told himself, another minute and no more.

Then he heard someone crying faintly ahead. Stopping, he listened intently for the direction the sound was coming from. He heard it again, ahead and to the right. Bending down, he spotted Doreen huddling under a table.

"Get out here!" Hawksworth barked.

"No! Leave me alone!" Doreen backed away farther under the table.

Hawksworth grabbed her arm and pulled her out. She lashed out at him with her nails, scratching and screaming.

The ship rocked, the iceberg moving to and fro with it.

"Leave me alone!" Doreen screamed hysterically. "Leave—"

Hawksworth punched her on the jaw. Doreen went down like a dead weight.

The ship suddenly lurched again and the iceberg began moving toward them.

Hawksworth picked Doreen up by her shoulders and dragged her across the floor and around the bodies of the dead men in space suits.

Water was everywhere, and the tangled metal on the floor made the going dangerous. He tripped over a large chunk of jagged plastic, cutting his arm but not feeling it. Quickly he got back up and slung Doreen over his shoulder. Then he ran.

The iceberg was still skidding toward them, now picking up speed.

Hawksworth reached the trapdoor and pushed Doreen in, head first, to waiting hands.

The ship abruptly shuddered, knocking Hawksworth off his feet and away from the trapdoor. He scrambled for the opening, but the iceberg got there first, slamming into the trapdoor and closing it tightly. Hawksworth heard the latch snap into place as the iceberg ran over him, crushing his bones.

In the tunnel they huddled together in the darkness, listening and waiting.

"Do you think the colonel is all right?" Paula Garrett asked.

"Maybe," Joanna said. "But we've got to lift the trapdoor to find out. Any volunteers?"

"I'll do it." Joe Wells stood up and felt along the top of the tunnel for the trapdoor. He found the latch and sprang it. Then he pushed on the lid. It didn't budge, not even a little.

"Well?" Joanna asked.

"It won't open," Wells said. "The door might be stuck, or maybe the iceberg is sitting on top of it. Either way, we're trapped."

Forty-two

"The fire is out of control, sir," Radcliff reported. "The civilian dining area is now gone, and the flames are reaching the laboratories."

He quickly pushed a button on his console and a picture came up on a television screen. It showed a dark, smoke-filled passageway. In the dimness Radcliff could see firemen fighting the blaze.

"We have to flood the area," Matts said. "We have no choice."

"Aye, sir."

"Can our firemen get out?"

Radcliff pressed another button and a diagram of the ship's compartments flashed up. He could immediately see that the firemen's escape route via the sickbay was completely blocked off. The entire area was flooded. And they couldn't escape by going through the laboratories either. The elevator still wasn't working.

"Yes, sir." Radcliff pointed to a small room off the passageway. "They can cut an opening in the ceiling here and make their way up to the next level."

"How long will it take?"

Radcliff spoke into his headset and waited for a reply. Then he said, "Five minutes."

Matts's gaze scanned the diagram of the laboratories and the huge area that held the Plexiglas cylinder. "Are there any people still in the laboratories?"

"No, sir," Radcliff said. "I've tried to contact them, but I get no response."

"Put the area up on the screen."

Radcliff pushed more buttons and waited for the pictures to come up on the monitor.

The smaller labs were all empty and clouded with smoke. There were objects strewn about the floor, a few chairs overturned, but no people. Anything flammable—papers, books, chemicals—was now catching fire.

The next picture showed the huge area where the Plexiglas cylinder had once stood. Bodies were lying on the floor, crushed and bloodied. There was tangled metal and plastic debris everywhere. The iceberg was stationary. Radcliff shook his head. "No one is alive in there, sir. Maybe some of them got out."

Matts nodded. "Secure the hatches and prepare to flood the area as soon as the firemen are out."

"Aye, aye, sir."

Radcliff turned a key on the console and pressed two switches simultaneously. All doors and hatches leading to the laboratories closed and sealed automatically. He watched a blinking light go from red to green. Then he sat back and waited for the signal that the firemen were clear.

He looked up at the screens showing the ocean outside. The bow camera showed the storm still raising heavy swells, but less so than before.

In a half-hour, he thought, it'll be over. Then we can limp back to Seattle, listing like hell to starboard but still afloat. We'll make it.

His eyes shifted to the starboard monitor. Because the ship was listing so much, the cameras and sensing equipment outside were looking down at the water rather than at the horizon. The image blurred for a moment with zigzag lines.

Radcliff turned a dial slowly, and the picture sharpened. Small icebergs were floating by, the sea still rough and foamy.

The picture went out again and Radcliff refocused the image. Now he saw swells that seemed suddenly, dramatically larger. Maybe it was just an illusion, he thought, an illusion caused by the downward angle of the camera.

Radcliff activated remote controls and the camera slowly elevated. He still couldn't see the horizon, but he saw a lot more of the ocean.

Then it came into view. A huge iceberg. A mountain of ice coming out of the mist.

Radcliff reached up and pulled at the executive officer's arm. "Sir! Sir!"

"What?"

Radcliff pointed to the starboard television screen.

Matts immediately saw the gigantic iceberg. It took another moment for him to see the immense tsunami wave behind it, pushing the iceberg dead ahead and directly at them.

Matts had just enough time to scream before the iceberg slammed into the *Global Explorer II*.

Forty-three

There was a tremendous bang.

Suddenly Joanna was flying through the air, suspended in space. She felt nothing in the darkness, only a sense of motion and weightlessness. Then she hit something very hard with her hip and shoulder. The pain was intense and she screamed, but the sound of her voice was drowned by the screams of others.

Now Joanna was tumbling, bouncing off walls and people, pain and hurt everywhere. Instinctively she balled herself up, arms covering and protecting her head. She slammed into a rock-hard wall and dropped straight down, landing atop someone who yelled out in agony.

The ship shuddered violently. Then for a moment all was quiet. Joanna reached out in the darkness, feeling her way, searching for something to hold on to.

Suddenly the ship shifted and lurched and again Joanna was flying through the air, hitting people and things, bouncing up and down in the pitch blackness. The only sounds she heard were her own screams.

Then the quiet returned, the ship now rocking very gently.

Joanna lay still, dazed and trying to gather herself. Every part of her hurt. Slowly and carefully she moved her extremities, then felt her elbows and knees. They were badly abraded, the skin rough and torn and bloodied. But nothing was broken. She waved a hand above her and made sure there was no obstruction, then stood.

Her legs were shaking, and it took her a moment to get a firm footing. All around her she heard moans and groans, more to her right than her left. There was no light, not even a ray.

"Is everyone all right?" Joanna called out.

Everybody seemed to answer together. Mostly moans. A few feeble "okay's."

"I'll call your names," Joanna told them. "Let me know if you're hurt or not. But don't move. Stay where you are."

The ship shuddered again with a sinking motion. Everyone waited, holding their breath. After a few seconds, calm returned.

"Paula?" Joanna asked. "Where are you?"

"Here," Garrett replied. "I'm all right. I've got a lot of bumps and bruises, but nothing is broken."

"Where's Doreen?" Joanna asked.

"Next to me," Garrett said, holding on to the unconscious woman as she'd done throughout the tossing and turning. "She's still out, but she's breathing."

"Good."

Joanna envisioned the darkened area they were in as the face of a clock. If she was at six o'clock, the direction of Garrett's voice indicated that she and Doreen were at ten o'clock. "Ben?"

"My ankle is killing me," Kagen groaned. "And I've got a lump on my head that's bleeding."

"How much bleeding?"

"I—I don't know how to tell in the darkness," Kagen said.

"Is it pouring out or just dripping?"

Kagen felt the lump. "It's like a steady drip."

"Press your shirt sleeve against it," Joanna advised, noting his position. Kagen was at one o'clock. "Mark?"

"Here," Mark said, "closer to you. I'm fine except for some bruising and a very stiff neck. I think I pulled a muscle."

"Let's hope that's all it is," Joanna said, and noted Mark's position. Four o'clock. "Neiderman?"

"Over here," Neiderman answered. "I'm okay."

Joanna looked at the three-o'clock position. "You don't have any pain or injuries?"

"Hardly any," Neiderman reported. "When the ship started to really shake, I held onto the track on the floor. I guess that kept me from bouncing around. I only lost my grip on that last big jolt."

"You're lucky," Joanna said, gently stretching her knees and elbows, not wanting them to stiffen up in the damp cold. Everyone was accounted for but Joe Wells.

"Wells?" Joanna called out.

There was no answer.

"Wells?" Joanna called again and waited. The only sound she heard was her own breathing.

"Joe?" Kagen asked anxiously. "Joe? Where are you?"

There was only silence in the blackness.

Neiderman quickly reached into his coat pocket. "I'm going to flick my lighter and give us some light."

"Don't do that!" Joanna said at once.

"Why not?"

"Because we're in a closed-in space down here," Joanna told him. "There could be gas fumes or oil leaking. One spark and this place could blow sky high."

"But I'm not going to just sit here while Joe may be dying."

"Hold on for a minute," Joanna said. "Don't do anything until I've checked around."

Joanna sniffed the air carefully. It was stale and musty, but there were no fumes or gas odors. She ran her fingers over the floor and wall. They were damp but without a trace of oil. Like the air, they smelled musty. Joanna reached up to the ceiling just above her head. Again she felt a cold dampness. She shuffled forward and encountered a horizontal metal bar protruding a few inches from the ceiling. It was shaped like an I-beam and seemed to be very long.

What purpose would a longitudinal beam along the ceiling have? Joanna asked herself. Maybe it augmented the transverse supports. But she couldn't remember seeing it when she first climbed into the tunnel. And besides, the beam would have blocked the trapdoor and—

Then it struck Joanna. It wasn't a beam she was feeling. It was a *track*. A track that should have been attached to the floor. "Oh, my God!"

"What?" Kagen asked in the darkness.

Joanna took a deep breath and steadied herself. "Listen, everybody. I am now standing in an upright position and touching the ceiling. I just felt a very long metal beam. But it isn't really a beam. It's the monorail track which should be on the floor."

"How did it get up there?" Kagen asked.

"I think the ship is now upside down," Joanna said, trying to control the nervousness in her voice. "Whatever hit us made the *Global Explorer* turn turtle. What was once the floor of the tunnel is now the ceiling. That's why I can feel the track above me." Joanna took another deep breath. "And since we're upside down, the tunnel we're in now represents the topmost level of the ship."

"Wh-where's the rest of the boat?" Garrett asked.

"Underwater, mostly, I think."

"Oh, God!" Garrett murmured as she tried to control her fear. "We're going to sink and drown and there's no way out."

"Joanna, are you sure you're not jumping to conclusions?" Mark asked evenly. "There may actually be metal bars on the ceiling to serve as supports."

"Yeah," Neiderman said. "That would explain it."

"It sure would," Joanna agreed. "Now all you have to do is find the track on the floor to back up your argument."

Neiderman quickly moved his hands over the metal floor, going wall to wall. "There is no track down here."

"We've capsized," Joanna said, her pulse racing, her voice a hundred times calmer than she felt. "So let's put our heads together and come up with a way out."

Everyone was quiet, all contemplating their own mortality and the hopelessness of their situation. There was the sound of water dripping close by.

"Well?" Joanna asked. "Where should we begin?"

Kagen said, "Our first order of business is to find Joe."

"Right," Joanna said. "Now, we'll need to conserve the lighter fluid. So let's make the most of the light while we're searching for Joe. In particular, check the walls for equipment or first-aid boxes or anything else we may be able to use."

Neiderman said, "You sound like you've been in a similar predicament before."

"Yeah, you could say that," Joanna said, remembering the time she was trapped in a dark freezer at Memorial Hospital. There had been no alarms to set off, no one to come to her rescue. She had thought her way out of that one, but her present plight seemed so much more difficult, if not impossible. They were trapped in an upside-down ship with a fierce storm raging outside. Even if they found a way out, what would they get out *to*?

"Flick your lighter," she said.

The little flame illuminated things poorly. Joanna quickly surveyed the tunnel. It was rectangular, approximately six by ten feet, just as Hawksworth had said. And the track ran along the ceiling. The walls were bare except for a coiled-up fire hose and a pickaxe. She heard a groan in the darkness ahead.

"Oww!" Neiderman cried out as the flame died. "The damn lighter burnt my fingers."

"Let it cool for a moment."

As she edged forward, Joanna was thinking about the fire hose and the pickaxe. Even if the pumps were working, the fire hose wouldn't supply the fresh water they would need to stay alive for any length of time. The hose would deliver only salt water. And the pickaxe wouldn't begin to dent the thick steel hull.

Joanna felt her foot come up against something. Reaching down, she carefully touched it. It was round and immobile. It resembled an overturned dish.

"Can you flick your lighter again?"

The flame came back.

Joanna looked down at the plastic light fixture she was feeling. It was still firmly attached to the ceiling. On its rim was a switch. "Put your lighter out."

It was dark again, even darker than before.

"There's a ceiling light on the floor," Joanna told them.

"Forget it," Neiderman said. "There's no electric power. All the generators are under water."

"Maybe it's run by batteries," Joanna said and pressed the switch.

Abruptly the tunnel flooded with light. Joanna looked away from the intense brightness and waited for her eyes to adjust.

She saw Joe Wells's body ten feet away and hurried to him. He was lying face down and not moving. Gently she turned him over. There was blood dripping from his nose, and his right wrist was bent at an awkward angle. She moved the wrist and felt bone grating against bone. Wells groaned loudly.

"How is he?" Neiderman asked anxiously.

"He's got a broken wrist and a bloody nose," Joanna said, now seeing an angry bruise on Wells's forehead. "And maybe a skull fracture."

"Is he awake?"

"Semiconscious," Joanna said, and glanced back at Mark. He was leaning against the wall, a dazed look on his face. Blood streamed out of a nasty gash on his temple. In his hand were broken plastic tubes, their screw caps still on. Beside him was a cardboard-covered laboratory data book. Joanna came over to him.

"I'm okay," Mark mumbled.

"I need your tie."

"For what?"

"A splint."

Joanna took his necktie off and picked up the softcover book, then went back to Wells. She rolled the book around Wells's wrist and secured it there with Mark's tie. Wells was groaning louder now and moving all of his extremities. "I need another tie."

Kagen crawled over and gave her his.

Joanna knotted the tie around Wells's neck, using it as a sling for the broken wrist. "That should hold him for now."

She turned to Neiderman. "You stay by Wells and make sure he doesn't thrash about."

Neiderman watched her move away to attend to the others. Wells groaned and mumbled, his eyelids fluttering, then closing again. Stay by him, my ass! Neiderman thought. The guy had a badly broken wrist and a skull fracture and maybe internal injuries as well. He was as good as dead already. So were all of them unless a way out could be found. Like a secret passageway or something. Get real, Neiderman told himself. Everyone was going to die in this goddamn tunnel.

He glanced over at Mark and saw blood streaming down from a forehead wound. One side of Mark's face was covered with bright red blood. Neiderman took out a handkerchief and pressed it firmly against the wound. "Hold it there."

"Thanks," Mark said.

"Anytime."

Neiderman's eyes narrowed as he saw the broken test tubes in Mark's hand, their greenish contents spilled out. *The cultures! The bacteria cultures Mark retrieved!* Quickly Neiderman covered his nose and mouth and backed away to the other side of Joe Wells. Shit! The whole area would be contaminated with those damn bacteria.

He wondered if he should warn the others. Yes. Of course he should. But not right away. He still had time, because those bacteria needed special conditions and media to grow. And as long as no one touched the cultures, the stuff would just lie there dormant.

Wells groaned again. Neiderman wanted to tell the paleontologist to shut up and be quiet so he could think. He tried to recapture his train of thought.

He stooped and felt his leg under his sock. The three small vials of the plant extract taped to his skin were intact. For a moment his spirits soared. Now only he had samples of the extract with its growing bacteria, and they were worth a fortune. Then he remembered where he was and the predicament he was in. Trapped in a capsized ship. He and his valuable cargo would never see the light of day.

Joanna moved to where Doreen lay, still cradled in the arms of Paula Garrett.

"Doreen!" Garrett was saying into the woman's ear. "Can you hear me?"

Doreen moaned, slowly coming out of her unconsciousness. She moved her head from side to side as if she were trying to avoid something. She spoke briefly, but her words were unintelligible.

Kagen hovered at her side with evident concern. "Is she going to be all right?"

"I think so," Joanna said, feeling Doreen's pulse. It was strong and steady.

"What's this?" Kagen pointed to the red swelling along Doreen's jawline.

"I'd guess she fell and hit her jaw," Paula Garrett said.

Joanna guessed otherwise. The traumatized area had all the characteristics of a punch by a fist. Hawksworth had probably knocked her out so he could save her life, and in the process lost his own.

"She'll be awake in another minute or two," Garrett said.

"When she does come out of it, she's going to go wild," Joanna warned. "She's claustrophobic and we're trapped in a tunnel. You keep her calm. We don't have time to waste on her."

"I can't just talk her out of it."

"Sure you can," Joanna said. "You tell her that if she can't control herself, she won't be able to help Ben, and he needs her. She'll understand that."

Garrett sighed, holding Doreen close. "I'll try."

Joanna sat down next to Kagen and leaned back wearily against the damp wall. She glanced around at the others, bruised and bleeding, all wearing dazed expressions. "Do you have any bright ideas, Ben?"

"You're doing remarkably well so far," Kagen said.

"Well, 'so far' just ran out."

"No, it hasn't," Kagen said, and patted her hand gently. He wondered why the most terrible of situations always seemed to bring out the best in certain people. They stayed strong and grew even stronger, somehow able to push aside their own fears and carry on while others faltered. He wished he had those qualities. He was glad Joanna did. "You lead and we'll follow."

"I don't even know where to start," Joanna said honestly, staring up at the track on the ceiling. Everything was upside down and she was having trouble orienting herself. "Maybe if I understood how we ended up in this position, it might offer a clue as to how to get out." She turned to Kagen. "Do *you* know what caused this to happen?"

"It had to be a tremendous force," Kagen said. "Something so powerful it could lift us up and flip us over."

"Like what?"

"Like an iceberg pushed by a strong wind."

Joanna thought for a moment. "But wouldn't that just rip a hole in the ship and sink us?"

"Not necessarily," Kagen said. "Think of it like a speeding car hitting a stationary one. If the force is great enough, the stationary car flips over."

"But an iceberg doesn't move that fast."

"It doesn't have to. Remember Newton's second law of motion? It says that force equals mass times acceleration. What that means is that a thousand-ton iceberg moving at ten miles an hour could knock down a skyscraper."

Garrett asked nervously, "How can you be sure we're not already under water? We could be on the bottom right now."

"I can assure you we're not," Kagen said evenly. "The ocean floor in this area is more than a thousand feet deep. The pressure at that depth is considerable. If we were on the bottom, water would have flooded in through all the seams and hatches, and we'd have been dead long ago."

"What's keeping us afloat?" Joanna asked.

"We're afloat because the center of buoyancy has shifted. In other words, there's probably a big air pocket beneath us." Kagen took a deep breath and looked into Joanna's eyes. "That's the good news. The bad news is we're in a very unstable situation. We could flip over on our side at any time."

"How much time do you think we have?"

Kagen shrugged. "That depends on the size of the air pocket and how rapidly it dissipates."

"Is there a way to gauge the size of the air pocket?"

"Open the trapdoor and take a look," Kagen said simply.

Joanna hesitated. "There may be water right up to the top. I don't want it gushing in here."

"It won't."

Joanna still wasn't sure. She picked up the axe and tapped it against the floor, like a physician percussing a patient's chest. She felt a tympanic sensation. There was air on the other side.

She had to push down twice on the trapdoor before it

opened. She got on her knees and looked down into the darkness. The air smelled salty and she could hear water lapping against something. "Give me the fire hose."

Neiderman uncoiled the hose and put the nozzle in Joanna's hand. She slowly lowered it into the blackness below. When she heard the nozzle hit water, she pulled the hose back up. "The water level is six feet from us."

Kagen sucked air between his teeth as the trapdoor was slammed shut. "We've got even less time than I thought."

Forty-four

"We can't stay here," Joanna told them. "If we do, we'll all die."

"Where do you suggest we go?" Kagen asked.

"I think we should follow the tunnel and head for the bow of the ship."

Everyone tried to voice an opinion at the same time, each talking over the other, their words producing echoes that reverberated back and forth in the tunnel.

"Please! Colleagues! Let's think this through," Kagen urged. "Don't make a hasty decision that could cost us our lives."

Everyone began talking at once again, no one hearing or listening to the others. The noise level grew, compounded by the echoes.

"One at a *time*!" Joanna shouted above them. "One at a time! Let's hear what everyone has to say."

For a moment the group quieted. A creaking sound came from down the tunnel, then subsided.

"I'm staying here," Garrett said firmly. "If the rest of you want to go, go." She stroked Doreen's hair and held her close. Doreen had her face buried in Garrett's shoulder, fully conscious now but not saying a word. She was trembling, petrified with fear. "Doreen and I stay."

"So do I," Neiderman said. "It's dry here and we've got light. Who the hell knows what's down the tunnel?"

"I'm for remaining here too," Mark said, holding a handkerchief against the gash on his temple. It was still bleeding. "I'm certain they sent out an S.O.S. signal before we were hit. We should just wait here for the rescuers."

"There's no guarantee an S.O.S. went out," Joanna argued. "And even if one did, I doubt we have the time to wait for rescuers."

"You feel free to do whatever you want," Mark said. "I prefer to take my chances here."

Joe Wells was sitting up, dazed, leaning back against the wall. He was awake, but he hadn't spoken except for a few mumbled words. "I think we should move out," he now said tonelessly.

"Why?" Garrett asked.

"Because Charlie knows our position and we have no cover here."

"What!"

"The Cong," Wells said, his eyes darting around the tunnel. "They're here. They're everywhere."

Garrett shook her head sadly. "He thinks he's back in Vietnam."

"It's from his head trauma," Joanna said. "This type of reversion is always transient. He'll snap out of it."

"When?"

"That I don't know."

"Christ," Garrett said dejectedly. "This place looks like a MASH unit. We've got Doreen paralyzed by claustrophobic fear, Wells thinking he's back in the jungle, and Ben with an ankle so painful he can't even walk. And you want us to follow you into a black tunnel to nowhere? Forget it."

"If you stay here, you'll die," Joanna said, her expression even. "This ship is slowly sinking. The water level is now only six feet away from us. It's only a matter of time before the water reaches us and floods this tunnel. When that happens, we're all dead."

"The water will get to us anywhere," Mark countered.

"When the water floods in, it won't matter whether we're here or a hundred yards down the tunnel."

"I'm afraid Mark is right," Kagen said, gently stretching his ankle. Pain shot up his leg and he waited for it to pass.

"Yeah, it's hopeless," Neiderman agreed. "There's no way out of the tunnel except through the trapdoors, and those only lead to compartments that are already under water."

"Maybe, maybe not," Joanna said. "Keep in mind that iceberg probably punched a big hole in the side of this ship. And that hole could be our opening to the outside world."

Garrett looked at Joanna strangely. "Are you crazy? That whole area is filled with water."

"No, it's not," Joanna told her. "You're forgetting that this boat is now upside down. The flooded part is below us, and the hole in the hull would have settled to water level. Anything in the dome above that is dry—for the time being."

"But the hole in the hull could already be well below us and under water," Kagen said thoughtfully.

"It could be," Joanna conceded. "But there's only one way to find out for sure. And that's to march down this tunnel."

Everything became silent as the others considered Joanna's plan. They probed for flaws, defects, and miscalculations. No one really wanted to go with her. The risks were too great. Why go looking for more danger? they all thought. Things were bad enough already.

"We don't even know which direction to go," Garrett said, breaking the silence. "Which way?" she asked Joanna. "Left or right?"

Joanna thought for a moment, remembering back to when the iceberg hit. The noise had come from the front of the ship. "We'll go to the bow."

"And which way is that?" Garrett demanded.

"I—I don't know," Joanna said hesitantly.

"Great!" Garrett droned. "You're all in favor of going. You just don't know which direction to take."

Joanna clenched her jaw, now losing patience. "We'll try one goddamn way and if that's not the right way we'll go in the opposite direction. How does that grab you?"

"It grabs me fine," Garrett said, not backing down. "Because I'm not going anywhere."

"I'm staying here too," Neiderman said, and looked up at Joanna. "But if you want to make a trial run and then come back and tell us what you found—well, that's okay with me."

"Maybe a trial run *would* be in order," Kagen suggested.

Joanna shook her head firmly. "If I find the opening and a way out, I won't come back for you."

Kagen glanced up at Joanna, surprised. "You don't mean that."

"Oh, *yes* I do," Joanna said.

"But why not come back for us?"

"Because there might not be enough time," Joanna explained, her voice very serious. "It's going to be very difficult to locate that opening. It'll take hours, for sure. Maybe more. If you think I'll then try finding my way back here for you and take the very real risk this ship will sink while I'm doing it, then you're dead wrong."

Joanna stared hard at Doreen and Garrett. "One man has already lost his life because he had to go back for somebody else."

Again there was a deep silence.

Joanna kept her face even, wondering if she would come back for the others if she found a way out. Probably, she decided. Like a damn fool.

She took a deep breath, trying to think of ways to convince the group to follow her down the tunnel. It was their only hope. Staying put meant certain death.

Her gaze went to Mark. She was surprised he chose not

to come with her down the tunnel. If anything, she had always considered him overly aggressive, surely not one to stand by passively and let events take their course. But obviously she had misjudged him in that. And in a lot of other things too.

Now she noticed the broken test tubes next to Mark. She saw green-colored culture media on the floor and some on the sleeve of Mark's blue blazer. Maybe that would coax the group to follow her out, she thought. "It might be best if we moved down the tunnel," Joanna said, and pointed to the spilled culture. "Away from the bacteria cultures."

The others looked over and quickly backed away from the greenish material.

Mark remained where he was. "The bacteria in the culture won't grow in here. They need fresh media or an open wound to multiply in."

"We've got plenty of open wounds down here," Joanna said at once.

Mark nodded and moved away from the broken test tubes. But it really didn't matter a damn, he was thinking, because they were never going to get out of there.

Kagen sighed deeply, staring at the spilled cultures. "All of our scientific data are gone, all of our efforts wasted. The only thing we know for certain is that a very ancient microbe produces a toxin so lethal it kills people instantly."

"But not little kids," Joanna added. "And we never really found out why."

Neiderman burped quietly. "The last group of experiments I ran could hold the answer. It seems that the toxin becomes less potent as the temperature drops. As I recall, you said the kid was in the coldest part of the cabin. That plus the cromolyn he inhaled might have saved his life."

Kagen nodded, still staring at the spilled cultures and thinking about their wasted efforts. They had nothing to show for their work. Absolutely nothing.

There was a new sound in the tunnel. They all heard it. A tapping sound coming from beneath the floor near the trapdoor.

Someone was knocking on the trapdoor.

"Somebody is there," Joanna said, her voice barely above a whisper. "Somebody is down there."

The knocking sound came again, firmer this time.

"Maybe it's divers who have come to rescue us," Garrett said hopefully.

"Or maybe it's Hawksworth," Kagen said. "Maybe he somehow survived."

They heard another series of knocks from beneath the trapdoor. It seemed to have a rhythm to it. Joanna reached over and pushed down on the trapdoor. It opened slightly, then closed forcefully. Joanna pushed down again. This time it didn't move. Something on the other side was blocking it.

"What's wrong?" Kagen asked.

"It opened a little, but then it closed, and now it seems stuck." Joanna listened carefully for knocks or other sounds coming from below, but didn't hear any. "Let me give it another try."

She pushed down as hard as she could, and the trapdoor flew open. She peered into the darkness and heard nothing. "Hello! Anybody there?"

They all waited and listened intently.

"Hello!" Joanna called out again.

Everything remained still and silent.

Joanna got to her feet. "What in the world could have—?"

The tip of the iceberg suddenly jutted up through the trapdoor opening. It was pointed and sharp-edged and filled half the tunnel.

Joanna jumped back and pressed herself against the wall. The iceberg was so close, she could feel its cold-ness. Its knifelike tip was curved and seemed to be pointing right at her. She pressed herself even closer to the wall and screamed.

The others backed away quickly, pushing their bodies along with their feet, crying out and cringing with fear. Only Joe Wells stayed where he was and stared at the mass of ice. He kicked at it, cursing loudly, as if he thought it was a new Viet Cong weapon of some sort.

The tip of the iceberg jutted up even higher, now almost touching the track on the ceiling. Then it began to dip, slowly lowering itself through the trapdoor opening. It bobbed up and down for a few moments, then disappeared into the blackness without a sound.

They all stared at the opening, holding their breaths and waiting. Everything stayed still and dead quiet.

"The steward was right," Garrett said, her voice trembling. "The iceberg is trying to kill us. The son of a bitch wants us dead."

Kagen waited for his heart to stop racing. He swallowed audibly. "That's nonsense. The iceberg doesn't have a mind of its own. It was the rising water level that pushed it up at us."

"Oh, yeah?" Garrett said derisively. "And it just happened to push up through the trapdoor, huh?"

"That was random chance, and a lucky one at that," Kagen said. "Had it come up through the floor under us, we might all be dead now."

"You just don't get it, do you?" Garrett asked, fear still in her voice. "The son of a bitch is playing with us."

"There are other, more rational explanations for this iceberg's movements," Kagen told her. "Simple physical forces explain everything. We don't have to invoke the supernatural."

Garrett looked over at Joanna. "What do you think?"

"I don't know," Joanna said, taking deep breaths to calm herself. She had always scoffed at the supernatural, had always considered it pseudoscientific nonsense. But this iceberg's behavior was eerie. It killed people who tampered with it or came too close. And it did it with viciousness.

In her mind's eye she could still see the iceberg breaking out of its Plexiglas cylinder and heading directly for the medic. But it didn't crush him immediately. Instead, it picked him up and carried him across the room and slammed him into a steel wall. Harmon had plenty of time to know what was happening. It had to be a terrifying death. Then the iceberg got the technician at the console, picking him off like a sitting duck, and went for Hawksworth. It was eerie as hell, she thought once more. But as Kagen had said, everything could be explained without invoking some supernatural—

The iceberg suddenly came up through the trapdoor again, ripping metal and splitting the floor wide open. Joanna jumped over the opening and ran down the tunnel and into darkness.

The others were right behind her.

Forty-five

Joanna felt her way along the tunnel. The wall seemed damper and colder than before, and there was a wet sensation inside her shoes. Water was leaking in from somewhere, she thought, hoping it was from above. She wondered how close the water level below them was. It was six feet when she tested it last. It was probably closer now. Behind her she heard people stumbling and bumping into one another.

Joanna turned and said, "Let's stop here for a minute." She waited for the footsteps to come to a halt. "We'll do better if we stay close to the wall and walk in single file. I'd like each of you to extend an arm and keep your hand on the shoulder of the person in front of you. That way we'll all be in contact and not trip over one another."

"It's like the blind leading the blind." Garrett was standing just behind Joanna.

"You can take the lead if you'd like," Joanna said.

"No, thanks," Garrett said. "I've got my hands full with Doreen."

"How is she holding up?"

"Not worth a damn," Garrett said sadly. "She's scared out of her senses. All she does is mumble and bury her face in my shoulder."

"Who's behind her?" Joanna asked.

"Ben Kagen."

"How's your ankle, Ben?"

"I can't put any weight on it," Kagen reported. "I'm just dragging it along, and even that hurts like hell."

"We'll keep the pace slow for you," Joanna told him.

"You go as fast as you can," Kagen said at once. "If I can't keep up, that's my problem."

"We'll go slow," Joanna said again. "Who's behind Ben?"

"Me," Mark called out. "And I'm in front of Joe Wells. He still thinks he's in Vietnam. There's no way he'll hold on to my shoulder."

"Sure there is," Joanna said and raised her voice. "Lieutenant Wells, it's dark in this jungle, isn't it?"

"Yeah," Wells said hoarsely. "It's nighttime, the worst time. You can't see Charlie, but he can hear you."

"We're getting out of here," Joanna told him. "Put your hand on the shoulder of the man in front of you. He has excellent night vision."

"Got you," Wells said.

Mark felt a heavy hand grab his shoulder. "I'll be damned. He did it."

"Neiderman, are you there?" Joanna asked.

"Bringing up the rear."

Joanna tried to look past Neiderman's voice and down the darkened tunnel. There was no light at all, not even a ray. She wondered how much distance they had put between themselves and the iceberg. It could have been fifty feet or fifty yards. She had no way to tell. The blackness was so intense, it was disorienting.

"Would you flick your lighter on briefly?"

Neiderman pushed down on the wheel of his disposable lighter and a small flame appeared. It flickered and became smaller.

"Can you turn it up some?" Joanna asked.

"That's as high as it'll go," Neiderman said. "It's running out of fluid."

Joanna quickly looked up and down the tunnel. In both directions the floor was bare except for a few puddles of water. She stepped to her right, still examining the floor and searching for light fixtures. There weren't any. Her gaze went to the walls. They were wet, and something was dripping nearby. The light died out.

"Damn," Neiderman grumbled, and tried to flick the lighter on again. All he got was a few sparks.

"Let's move on," Joanna said. "I'm going to position myself more to the middle of the tunnel so I can feel with my foot for light fixtures."

Joanna walked slowly, running her hand along the wall. The steel felt much colder, and the temperature in the tunnel was dropping as well. That was to be expected, she thought. All of the heat in the tunnel came from the compartments beneath them, and those compartments were now filled with icy water. Joanna shivered, wishing she had on a parka rather than a thin white laboratory coat.

The ship began making noises again, mainly creaking sounds from below. There were no knocks or thuds to indicate that the captive iceberg was still close by. But it could be, Joanna told herself, remembering the size of the area where the iceberg had been contained. The chamber was more than fifty yards across. She wasn't at all certain they had traveled that far.

Joanna shivered again, feeling the cold even more. She buttoned up her laboratory coat, now wondering if the massive iceberg was just below the floor, slowly sucking all the heat out of the tunnel. Maybe Paula Garrett was right. Maybe the goddamn thing was playing with them.

Abruptly Joanna's hand left the wall. She felt only air.

"Hold it!" she called out.

The others stopped in their tracks, hands still on the back of the person in front of them.

"What's wrong?" Garrett asked.

"I'm not sure."

Joanna waved her hand in front of her and off to the sides. There was only empty space. She reached back to the wall and felt its corner. Then she carefully stepped forward, arm outstretched, until she came to another wall and another corner. "We're at an intersection."

Garrett asked, "Which way do we go?"

"Straight ahead," Joanna said, and waited for the others to cross. There was no wind or draft in the intersection, which might have told Joanna they were close to the hole in the hull. And to make matters even worse, there were intersections with crossing branches of the tunnel. That meant there was a maze of tunnels and not just one. It would be very easy to become confused and lose their way. Travel in a straight line, Joanna told herself. Keep going straight.

They were moving again, everyone touching the wall with a hand. Behind her Joanna heard Doreen whimpering and mumbling and Kagen groaning loudly with each step. His ankle would get worse, Joanna thought, much worse. Soon it would be so tender that Kagen would be unable to walk on it at all. Then he would try to hop on one foot, but that would require too much energy. Kagen wouldn't last five minutes. They would have to leave him behind and come back for him later.

The ship suddenly shifted and Joanna had the sensation they were sinking. She stopped and held her breath, her heart pounding wildly.

There was a loud creaking noise from below, followed by another. Then the ship shuddered briefly and settled.

Joanna breathed again and tried to control the panic flooding through her. It would be the worst kind of death, she thought, the very worst. A slow drowning while trapped in a black tunnel. It would be beyond terrifying.

"Jesus," Garrett muttered, her voice shaking. "We'll never get out of here."

"We have to push on." Joanna waited to feel Garrett's hand on her back. "Everyone stay close and make certain you're touching the person in front of you."

Joanna led the way farther down the lightless tunnel,

her pulse still racing. If anything, it seemed even darker than before. She took slow, careful steps, fearful of what might be ahead of her. Jagged pieces of sharp metal that stuck out worried her the most. They could inflict painful wounds and incapacitate a person.

She kept close to the wall, probing, again wondering how far they had traveled. And, more important, how far they had to go to reach the hole in the hull. It was their only way out.

But to *what*? Joanna asked herself. To a fierce Arctic storm and more icebergs?

Garrett broke into Joanna's thoughts. "Do you feel it?"

"What?"

"The heat."

Joanna quickly placed her palm on the wall. It was warm, and the floor was warm too. Even her shoes seemed dry. "Where do you think it's coming from?"

"I have no idea."

Joanna went through a mental checklist for the causes of heat. There were no heaters in the tunnel and no lights. That was for sure. And no fire either. They would have smelled the smoke. What about a fire below them? She shook her head. There was nothing but icy water down there. Where the hell was it coming from?

Joanna looked over her shoulder. "Ben, we have some heat up here and can't determine its source."

"Is it very hot?" Kagen asked.

"No. It's quite pleasant, actually."

Kagen pondered the problem for a moment. "My guess is we're near the engine room."

"Wouldn't everything be covered with icy water?" Joanna asked.

"Not necessarily. Remember the ship is upside down, so the bottom of an engine could be just beneath us."

Joanna moved her foot over the floor. "I don't feel any vibrations from any engine."

"It's probably out," Kagen said. "But the bottom of the

engine might still be hot, since the water level hasn't reached it yet. It could be transferring heat into the tunnel."

Joanna rubbed her foot over the floor again, trying to detect vibrations. There weren't any, and there weren't any water puddles either. Her foot hit a solid object that didn't move. She reached down and felt its hard texture. *A light fixture!*

"I've found another light," she called out, and pushed down on the switch.

Joanna turned away from the brightness and waited for her eyes to accommodate. When she looked back, she realized the light wasn't all that bright. It was weak, like a dying flashlight. But she could still see the others as they slumped to the floor and leaned against the wall, exhausted.

Joanna knelt beside Doreen. "How are you feeling?"

Doreen didn't answer. She stared straight ahead, face expressionless, eyes dazed and not blinking.

Joanna tried again. "Can you hear me?"

Doreen just stared into space.

Joanna turned to Garrett. "Has she spoken at all?"

"She only mumbles and cries some, but there are no tears," Garrett said. "I hope to God she comes out of this soon."

"Maybe when she sees the daylight," Joanna said, but she was thinking otherwise. Doreen's intense fear had caused her to retreat into a catatonic state. And sometimes catatonic patients stayed that way.

Joanna moved over to Kagen. "How's your ankle?"

"Worse." Kagen reached for his shoe.

"Leave your loafer on," Joanna advised. "If you take it off, you'll never be able to put it back."

She rolled down his sock and examined his ankle. It had a purplish color and was badly swollen. Just touching it caused Kagen to grimace. Joanna was amazed that he had been able to walk on it at all. "Do you think you can keep up with us?"

"I'll do my best," Kagen said. "But if I fall by the wayside, you go ahead without me. Save the others." He reached over and touched Doreen's face. "Save the others."

Joanna crawled over to Mark. He looked awful. The infected area on the side of his jaw was now the size of a silver dollar. She palpated his neck and felt tender, enlarged lymph nodes. "You've got a huge carbuncle and it's spreading."

"I know," Mark said wearily. "And my antibiotics are back in my cabin."

Joanna examined the area again. The light was poor, but she could still see pus near the skin surface. "It needs to be incised and drained, but I don't have anything to do it with."

"Here." Mark reached inside his coat and took out a small pocket knife. "Do it with one quick stab—in and out. Okay?"

Joanna opened the blade and tilted Mark's head back. Deftly she punctured the carbuncle. Yellow pus gushed out and down onto Mark's collar. "Let's hope that helps."

"Thanks." Mark leaned back, now feeling very warm. He wondered if this hot sensation was due to the heat in the tunnel or if his fever was returning. He cursed himself under his breath for not keeping the antibiotics in his pocket.

Joanna was examining Joe Wells's wrist. The make-do splint was coming undone, and Wells's hand was hanging down at an angle. She rolled the slim softcover book around his fractured wrist and tightened the tie holding it in place.

Wells let out a howl of pain, then quickly regained his composure. "A shrapnel wound, huh?"

"Yeah," Joanna said. "It's just superficial, though."

She glanced over at Neiderman, who was tearing the top off a packet of salted peanuts. "I wouldn't eat those."

"Why not?"

"Because those peanuts are loaded with salt," Joanna told him. "In an hour you'll be dying for water, and we don't have any."

Neiderman nodded and put the packet back in his pocket, keeping his face serious. But inwardly he wasn't concerned. Drinking water wouldn't be a problem for him. Inside his parka he had bottled water. A big bottle. He had picked it up when he retrieved the cultures. It was to be used to wet his sock and maintain a high humidity for the vials taped to his leg. He would still use some of the water for that purpose, but only an ounce or two. The rest he would save for himself. The others could die of dehydration for all he cared. Then he would be the only survivor and maybe he would get rescued. Yes, rescued. The bacteria cultures along with him. Holy shit! The money they would bring.

Joanna moved back to the front and sat next to Paula Garrett. "We'll rest here for a while."

Garrett leaned over and lowered her voice. "If the engine room is below us, then we're in trouble."

"Why?"

"Because I think the engine room is located to the rear of the laboratories," Garrett said. "And that means we're walking toward the stern of the ship. We're headed in the wrong direction."

"Are you sure?" Joanna asked, keeping her voice down.

"Not absolutely," Garrett said. "But I think I'm right."

Joanna thought for a moment. "We still have to follow it to the end and make certain."

"I guess."

Joanna stared at the trapdoor next to the light fixture and tried to think through the problem. If she was leading them in the wrong direction, she was using up valuable time and energy, neither of which they could afford. And she was condemning Kagen to death. He couldn't walk that far, from the stern back to the bow.

"Maybe we're not above the engine room."

"What else would give off heat like that?"

Joanna shrugged. "I don't know."

Garrett wrinkled her brow, concentrating, looking for other ways to explain the heat. It almost had to be the engine room.

"Maybe we should take a look," she suggested. "At least it'll give us our bearings. And besides, since it's still a dry area, it may have things we can use. You know, first aid kits and things like that."

Kagen was overhearing the conversation, listening intently. "I agree with Doctor Garrett. It's worth a look. And maybe—just maybe—it'll give us another way out."

Joanna thought at length, then said, "If we go downwards, we're heading for water, and that's the last thing we want to do."

"But it's a dry area beneath us," Kagen argued. "Maybe the water hasn't reached it because it can't."

Joanna slowly nodded, now seeing what Kagen was driving at. "You think there's an enclosed space below us? Like another tunnel?"

"Could be. The engine room might have its own tunnel system."

"Let's find out," Joanna said, and crawled over to the trapdoor. She carefully felt its surface. It was very warm, but not hot. She pushed down hard and the door sprang open. A puff of black smoke came up and quickly dissipated.

Joanna leaned over and peered down into the blackness. The smell of diesel oil was heavy, and there was another odor too, one she couldn't identify. She heard a soft hissing sound then an explosion.

A bright red flame suddenly shot up through the darkness. Joanna had just enough time to put her hands up to her face as the flame went by, hot and searing. Frantically she kicked herself away from the opening. Smoke and fire were everywhere. Joanna's arms felt scorched, like they were burning. It took her a brief moment to realize that her white laboratory coat was on fire. She quickly pulled it off and threw it aside. Then she crawled over to the others and pressed herself against the wall, her hands up and protecting her face.

Abruptly the flame subsided and went back through the opening into the darkness below.

Everyone stared at the trapdoor, waiting, their hearts in their throats. Black smoke curled out from below, but less than before. The smell of diesel oil was still heavy.

"Holy shit!" Neiderman said, and looked over at Joanna. "Are you all right?"

Joanna waved the smoke away and examined her arms and felt her eyebrows. "I got singed pretty good, but otherwise I'm okay."

Kagen shook his head, angry at himself. "We fed the damn fire oxygen and that's why it came back to life. I should have thought of that. Goddamn it! I should have thought of that."

"We all should have," Joanna said, now looking at her arms. They felt as if they had first-degree burns. She didn't see any blistering.

"We have to shut the trapdoor," Kagen said. "We have to cut off the flow of oxygen to the chamber below."

He tried to push himself to the opening with his good leg, but even that motion caused his twisted ankle to throb with pain.

"I'll do it," Joanna said, pushing herself in front of him. "I can move faster if need be."

She crawled over to the opening, cracking the scabs that had formed on her knees. She ignored the pain and peered down into the darkness, ready to jump back instantly. There was no fire or flame, but the smell of diesel oil was now overpowering. She heard a lapping sound, like waves gently hitting the shore.

Slowly she reached for the handle of the trapdoor and abruptly jerked her hand away. It was hot, very hot. "I need a potholder."

"Here." Mark gave her his handkerchief.

Joanna went for the handle again, grabbing it with the handkerchief. Then she heard the hissing sound again, the same sound that had preceded the explosion. Quickly she slammed the trapdoor shut and scrambled to her feet. "Up! Everybody up!"

"We need rest," Garrett said. "Just a few minutes more."

"Now!" Joanna screamed at her. "It's going to blow again. I heard the same hissing noise that I heard just before the flames came up."

They all scrambled to their feet and formed a single line, each touching the back of the person in front.

They hurried down the tunnel and into the darkness. The walls again became cold and damp, and the temperature in the tunnel began to drop noticeably.

Joanna slowed and glanced over her shoulder, wondering if she had acted precipitously. Maybe the hissing sound didn't mean an explosion was about to happen. And besides, she had closed the trapdoor securely, cutting off the flow of oxygen to the compartment below. If there was no oxygen, there'd be no explosion.

She came to a full stop, her knees throbbing, the skin on her arms burnt and stinging. She was so tired, so very tired, each step an effort. Perhaps they should go back to the warmth and light, and rest. Just a few minutes of sleep, she thought. A brief nap and they'd be able to go on.

There was a sudden rumble beneath them. The floor

shook and vibrated. Then the ship began to make loud creaking sounds. Behind them they could now smell smoke and oil fumes.

The group hurried deeper into the tunnel.

Forty-six

The mood in the satellite room at CIA headquarters in Langley, Virginia, was somber. Admiral Thomas Pearl, vice chair of the National Security Council, sat grim-faced and listened to the bad news. The *Global Explorer II* was missing and presumed lost at sea.

"Are you saying we don't know where she went down?" Pearl asked his aide, Charles Gordon.

"That's correct, sir," Gordon said, and pointed to a large video screen showing the coastline of Alaska. "She last made contact with us here, a hundred miles northwest of Juneau. That was twenty-four hours ago, shortly after she collided with the iceberg."

"And we've received absolutely no signal from her since?"

"None, sir."

Pearl carefully unwrapped the cellophane from a Jamaican cigar. "What about air search and rescue?"

"Nothing," Gordon said. "We've had a dozen aircraft up, and no one has seen anything. We even sent up a high-altitude reconnaissance plane. Again, nothing. Not even a clue."

"What about infrared?"

"The infrared camera on the U-2 malfunctioned."

"Christ," Pearl growled unhappily. "Get the damn thing back up."

"That may not be necessary," Gordon told him. "We have a satellite that will be passing over the area shortly."

Pearl slowly lit his cigar, hoping against hope that the ship was still afloat and that his friend Guy Hawksworth was still alive. Son of a bitch! The man survived two tours of duty in Vietnam and came home a decorated hero, only to get killed by an iceberg.

Pearl thought about Hawksworth's wife, a lovely woman, always optimistic, always saying nothing bad would ever happen to them because she was Guy's good-luck charm. Well, Pearl thought darkly, something bad had happened. The *Global Explorer* had gone down with all hands. When the sinking was confirmed, he would have to break the news to Mary Hawksworth.

Gordon pushed a button on the console, and a screen came down from the ceiling. "The satellite will be passing over the Alaskan coast in ninety seconds."

Pearl shifted his gaze to the screen and waited for the images to come up. The pictures would appear in real time, because the newest generation of satellites used television-type scanning cameras instead of photographic film. The images were transmitted and projected onto the screen as they occurred. But the weather was still bad, and it would be difficult to get high-resolution pictures. That's why the infrared images were so important. The infrared devices on the satellite detected anything below that generated heat. Man, animal, even ships. If the *Global Explorer* was still afloat, it would give off heat. It would appear as a white blob on a solid black background.

"Is the weather clearing any?" Pearl asked.

"Some," Gordon said. "But there's still a lot of cloud cover."

"That shouldn't hinder the infrared studies, right?"

"Correct, sir. But there's a new Arctic storm coming in." Gordon handed the admiral a recent weather update. "It's big and mean, with gale-force winds. And that could interfere with our cameras."

"How much of a window do we have?"

"Ten hours at the most."

Pearl grumbled under his breath. Nothing about this mission was going as planned, he thought miserably. A team of brilliant scientists dead, a valuable ship gone, and the mystery of the toxic iceberg still unsolved. How did it kill people? And where the hell was it now?

He quickly looked over at his aide. "Was the toxic iceberg still secure after the collision?"

"As far as we know."

"Yes or no, damn it!"

"Yes, sir," Gordon said firmly. "The last message said all was secure and they were preparing to steam south for Seattle. The iceberg in the hold posed no threat."

"As long as it stays in the hold."

"Why wouldn't it?" Gordon asked.

"Because ships sometimes split apart as they go down." Pearl puffed impatiently on his cigar. "Once the next storm has passed, send down the underwater people. Use the robot subs if necessary."

"Yes, sir."

"I need to know if the *Global Explorer* is intact on the bottom of the sea."

The screen began showing irregular dots and lines. Then blurred images appeared and gradually sharpened. High-resolution pictures revealed rough water and medium-sized swells. Icebergs and ice floes were everywhere, all moving south with the wind and current. There were no ships.

"We'll have this tape examined by the CIA analysts," Gordon said. "Sometimes they pick up small things we miss." The screen went dark. "We're now switching to infrared."

Pearl leaned forward and intently watched the black screen. He was looking for any white blip, any heat, any signs of life.

The screen stayed cold and black.

Forty-seven

They went through two more intersections before the tunnel came to an end. There were no doors or hatches, no buttons to push or handles to turn. Joanna reached up and felt the cold ceiling. The track was no longer there.

"We've reached a dead end," she told the others. "I've led you in the wrong direction."

"Goddamn it," Garrett growled. "I knew it."

"We've got to go back the other way."

"Nobody is going anywhere," Garrett said defiantly. "We're staying right here."

Joanna heard the others murmuring, agreeing with Garrett.

"If you stay here," she said curtly, "you'll die here."

"And what do we face if we go back the other way?" Garrett asked. "Have you thought about that?"

"It's our only chance," Joanna said.

"A chance for what?" Garrett snapped. "To walk through an area that's been ripped apart by an explosion?"

"Maybe we can get through there," Joanna said.

"That'll be great," Garrett scoffed. "Then we get to meet the crazy iceberg again."

"I think Dr. Garrett is right," Neiderman said from the rear. "The rescuers have as much chance to find us here as at the front of the ship."

"There won't be any rescuers," Joanna told him. "We either get out by ourselves or we die here by ourselves."

"If you want to go," Garrett said, "then go by yourself."

"I will," Joanna said, her fatigue now overwhelming. With effort she pushed herself away from the dead end. "If you decide to follow me later, remember to stay close to the wall."

She reached out for the side of the tunnel and took a careful step into the darkness.

There was a hushed silence, broken only by the sounds of Joanna moving away.

"Please wait, Joanna," Kagen called out, feeling her presence close by in the darkness. "We're all very tired and very frightened, to say the least. And the last thing we want to do is to make rash decisions. Let's rest for a while, then reconsider our position."

"We don't have that luxury," Joanna said. "This ship is sinking and could go down anytime."

"Just an hour's rest," Kagen urged. "We'll be refreshed and we'll move faster."

"And probably think better, too," Garrett added, now reconsidering their situation. There were no leaders among them, no one willing to take control. Only Joanna. Without her the group would flounder. "A little nap will do us all good."

It might also kill us, Joanna thought. But her legs were so weary, they had difficulty supporting her weight. Slowly she eased herself down to the floor. "All right," she said reluctantly. "But only for an hour."

She leaned back against the cold wall and tried to keep her eyes open. To sleep was to die, she thought, because they would sleep on and on unless there was someone to awaken them.

I'll stay awake, she told herself. *Just sitting and resting will be enough for me.* But her eyelids felt so heavy, so very heavy. She fought her drowsiness and fatigue, but it kept coming back stronger and stronger. *I'll close my eyes, but only for a moment. Then I'll get up and stretch and move around. I'll stay awake,* she told herself again, *I'll stay awake*. But her eyelids slowly dropped, and she drifted off into a dreamless sleep.

Joanna was abruptly awakened. Doreen was screaming in the darkness, frightened by something she saw in her mind. Her yells reverberated back and forth across the tunnel.

"Shhh," Garrett hushed softly, holding Doreen close and stroking her hair. "You'll be fine. It was just a bad dream."

Doreen began to mumble incoherently. It sounded as if she was saying, "Open, please open."

Slowly Joanna got to her feet. Every muscle in her body was sore, and her arms still felt as if they were on fire from the burns. Around her she heard the others stirring and groaning as they came out of their sleep.

Joanna shivered in the cold, wondering how long they had slept. Too long, she guessed, much too long. No one had a luminous watch, so she couldn't tell the time, but the stiffness in her joints meant that she had been in one position for a considerable while. At least a few hours.

She yawned widely, and even that caused pain. Her lips were parched and cracked, her throat very dry. Lack of water would soon become a big problem for them.

"We have to move on," Joanna told the group.

She heard people struggling to their feet, then a yelp of pain.

"Who was that?"

"Me," Kagen said. "My ankle is big as a balloon, and it's so tender I can't even touch it."

"Try to gently stretch it out," Joanna advised.

But a moment later she heard him cry out again. "It's no use. I can't move it, not even a little. It's too painful. I want you to go on without me."

"I'm not leaving you behind."

"You have no choice."

"We'll see," Joanna said, concentrating as she tried to

come up with a solution. He needed crutches or a cane, something to take the weight off his badly sprained ankle. She cursed herself for not bringing along the pick-axe they'd found next to the fire hose. It could have served as a cane for Kagen.

"Mark, can Ben lean on you while we walk?"

"I don't think I can support him," Mark said, his voice weak and weary. He coughed briefly, then swallowed. "The carbuncle on my face is swelling again. And I've got some fever now."

"Will you be able to keep up with us?"

"I guess so," Mark said. "But I don't know for how long."

Joanna looked to the rear and raised her voice. "That leaves you, Neiderman. You'll act as Ben's support. You're big and he's not. It should be no problem for you."

Shit, Neiderman thought sourly, and tried to invent an excuse. He didn't want to use up any of his energy helping Ben Kagen. Fuck him! It was every man for himself down here. "But if I have to support him with one arm and feel the wall with the other, how can I keep in touch with the person in front of me?"

"You won't have to," Joanna said promptly. "Ben can lean on the person in front too. It'll give him some extra support."

"All right," Neiderman said, and everyone sensed the reluctance in his voice.

"Let's form a single line," Joanna said. "Make sure you stay in contact with the person in front of you."

Joanna led the way, intentionally slowing the pace so that Ben Kagen could keep up with the others. In her heart of hearts, she wondered if she should have left Kagen behind. His hobbled state would reduce the chances of the others surviving. He would slow them down. He would take up valuable time. But she couldn't leave him behind. She just couldn't.

The blackness in the tunnel was now overwhelming her. Joanna felt as if she were in a closet and the walls were closing in on her. And to make matters worse, the temperature was dropping rapidly.

Up ahead she heard the sound of water dripping, and it reminded her of her thirst. Her throat was so dry that she had trouble swallowing. She moved on, now wondering whether the dripping water was fresh or salt. But it really didn't matter, because it would be crazy to drink water from a tunnel that had housed infected bodies and pieces of the toxic iceberg. No one in their right mind would drink it. But then again, if one became thirsty enough . . .

They passed through an intersection and walked on. The walls were becoming wetter, and so was the floor. Joanna's feet splashed as she stepped in and out of several puddles. The sound of dripping water was very close, but Joanna couldn't tell where it was coming from.

Behind her Ben Kagen was groaning with each step. She knew he couldn't last much longer. Then she'd have no choice but to leave him where he dropped.

They went through another intersection, now detecting the odor of smoke and diesel fumes. Joanna peered into the darkness, hoping that the light by the trapdoor would still be on. She saw only black.

"We'll rest for a minute," Joanna said and leaned back, taking the weight off her feet. The wall was warmer, definitely warmer, and so was the floor.

"We're getting near the engine room," Garrett said.

"I know." Joanna moved her foot around the floor. The puddles were gone.

"How are we going to get across that area?"

"Very slowly, I would think."

"Right," Garrett said, then lowered her voice. "But you heard the explosion. There may not be any floor left in there."

"Well, we'll just have to find that out, won't we?"

"Jesus," Garrett hissed. "You're going to get us all killed."

"I'm only trying to get us out of here."

"Up to now, the only thing you've done is lead us in the wrong direction," Garrett said. "That doesn't inspire a lot of confidence."

"All I've heard from you is bitching," Joanna snapped, her patience gone. "If you don't like what I'm doing, then go your own way. See how far you get."

Garrett backed down. "I—I just meant it's risky as hell."

"Of course it's risky," Joanna said, trying to control her anger. "And it's riskiest for me because I'll be in the front of the line. And if there's a big hole in the floor, I'll be the first to drop through it."

"I hadn't thought of that," Garrett said.

"I have," Joanna said tersely. "Every step of the way."

There was a rumble beneath them, a gentle rumble lasting only a few seconds. It came from the direction of the engine room.

"Kee-rist!" Garrett muttered nervously.

Joanna pushed herself away from the wall. "We have to move on," she called out. "Stay as close to the side of the tunnel as possible."

They walked on, the smoke and fumes so thick it irritated their eyes and lungs. Joanna wondered where it was all coming from. She remembered shutting the trapdoor to the engine room and hearing its latch snap into place. Maybe the explosion blew the lid off. Or maybe it took out the entire floor. If that was the case, they were trapped with no way out and no chance of survival.

Joanna peered into the darkness ahead. It was so black. She hoped the light they had left on was still functioning. Just a little light. That's all they needed.

Joanna thought she felt the air move. It was warm, very warm, and coming directly at her. What was its source? Where was it coming from? she asked herself.

The engine room. It had to be the engine room, still hot from the flames. Or maybe it was still on fire! Jesus, she hoped not. One more explosion and the entire ship would go down.

The heat was coming up through the floor as well. Joanna could sense it through her shoes. Her steps were more measured now as she tried to feel her way with one foot in front of her.

Ahead she saw a flicker of light. At first glance it looked like light from the floor fixture. Then she noticed its tonguelike shape. It was a flame coming out of the floor. The engine room was still burning.

Carefully Joanna led the way forward, the smoke and flames even thicker than before. But now there was light and she could see the tunnel ahead. The floor was badly buckled, more on the right side than the left. The trapdoor was also bent and cracked open, and this allowed black smoke to escape from below.

Joanna waved her hands and cleared the air for a better look. The floor to the right of the trapdoor was badly warped.

Suddenly a tongue of flame shot out from the left side of the trapdoor, scorching the tunnel wall. And then in an instant it was gone. The glow from the engine room below still lit up the tunnel.

"How the hell are we going to get through *this*?" Garrett asked.

"I'm not sure," Joanna said and studied the tunnel again. The floor to the right was so twisted they'd never get through. And if they tried and tripped, they'd fall onto red-hot metal. The floor on the left side bulged as well, but it was passable. "We might be able to get by on the left."

"But the flame shoots out in that direction," Garrett said quickly. "It'll make toast out of us."

"Maybe, maybe not," Joanna said, staring at the trapdoor and waiting for the flame to reappear. "Let's see if the flame comes up at predictable intervals. You know, every twenty seconds or every forty seconds, and so on. If it does, we'll know the times we can get through safely."

"Why would the flame have a periodicity to it?"

"I'm not saying it would," Joanna said. "But it might. Why don't you check it out for us while I tend to the others?"

Garrett nodded and glanced down at her watch. The crystal was broken and it wasn't running. Shit! She started counting in her head, her eyes glued to the trapdoor.

Joanna knelt down beside Ben Kagen and examined his ankle. It was grotesquely swollen with a deep purple discoloration. "How's the ankle holding up?"

"I've never felt this kind of pain in my life," Kagen said. "Even when I just sit here, it hurts like hell. It feels like someone has a knife in there and is twisting it."

"You're doing fine," Joanna told him. "I'm amazed you've been able to keep up with us."

Kagen smiled weakly. "The will to live is quite remarkable, isn't it?"

"Quite," Joanna said, admiring the man's courage. She moved over next to Mark. "Let's see how that carbuncle is doing."

Mark coughed hoarsely, then swallowed. With effort he tilted his head back. "I think it needs to be incised again."

Joanna was shocked by Mark's appearance. He looked so much sicker now, his face drawn and flushed. The carbuncle was even bigger and extended up to cover most of his cheek. Mark was obviously septic.

"It's still draining," she said. "It's probably best to leave it alone for now."

Mark coughed again and tried to clear his throat. Then he coughed harder, bringing up a small amount of sputum. He wiped at his mouth with his sleeve.

Joanna wondered if Mark had pneumonia too. The infection could have easily spread from his face to his lungs via the bloodstream or lymphatics.

A bright flame suddenly came up through the trapdoor. It licked at the left wall of the tunnel, blackening the metal. Then it abruptly disappeared.

"A minute and ten seconds," Garrett called out.

"Keep timing it," Joanna said, and turned back to Mark. He was coughing more and having trouble clearing his lungs. Yes, it was pneumonia, Joanna thought, and the smoke and fumes were making it worse. His cough was now coming in paroxysms, dry and hacking, and what little he got up stuck to his lips. He brought his sleeve up to wipe away the spittle.

Joanna stared at the sleeve of Mark's blue blazer and focused in on the greenish culture media that clung to it. *Oh, Lord! It's the bacteria culture. He's infected himself.*

Mark brought his arm down and saw Joanna staring at his sleeve. He took a quick look, then nodded. "Yeah, I think I've got it."

"From the cultures," Joanna said, keeping her voice low.

"Or from one of the patients," Mark said as he coughed once more. "Who the hell knows?"

"I'm sorry," Joanna said softly.

"It really doesn't matter," Mark said evenly. "Because none of us is getting out of here alive. Not you, not me, not any of us."

The flame shot through the trapdoor again, not quite as intense as before. But it lasted longer. Then it was gone.

"Forty-eight seconds," Garrett called over.

Joanna leaned back against the wall, her fatigue returning, the smoke burning her eyes and making them water. Mark was right, she thought dejectedly. No one was going to get out. Even if they stayed afloat for a few more days, Mark was surely going to die. And she might too. The choleralike bacteria were still inside her and could break loose at any time and kill her. But that wasn't her major concern. In all likelihood the frigid waters would kill her long before the bacteria did.

She pushed herself away from the wall and moved down to Joe Wells. "Joe, do you know where you are?"

"Out to sea," Wells said blankly.

"What's the name of our ship?"

Wells stared straight ahead and didn't answer.

"Are we in waters off Vietnam?" Joanna asked.

Wells shook his head. "Off Alaska."

Joanna readjusted the splint on Wells's wrist and made sure it was secure. His senses were starting to clear, she thought. At least he no longer believed he was in the jungles of Vietnam. Things would now begin to come back to him more quickly.

Joanna glanced over at Neiderman. "Are you all right?"

"I'm okay," he said.

Joanna took a deep breath and stood. "It's time for us to move on."

Neiderman got to his feet and stretched. As he turned, the plastic water bottle fell from his pocket. It bounced on the floor, making a hollow sound.

Everyone stared at the empty bottle, then at Neiderman, knowing what he'd done and hating him for it.

"It—there was only a little bit in it," Neiderman lied. "I was using it to keep my pocket moist for the plant extracts. My body heat might have dried them out."

Joanna noticed that Neiderman's lips weren't parched and cracked like the others'. And there was some salt still stuck to his chin. The greedy pig had eaten the salted peanuts and washed them down with a pint of bottled water. Five hundred milliliters of badly needed water. Divided among the group, that would have come out to more than two ounces a person. Enough to ease their thirst and keep them going for a while.

She felt like screaming at Neiderman and scratching

his eyes out, but instead she walked to the front of the line.

"There is no periodicity to the flame. We'll just have to take our chances. I'll go first, then Paula will lead Doreen across. Neiderman, you get behind Wells and guide him."

Joanna took a deep breath and gathered herself, then walked toward the trapdoor. The floor was hot, the wall even hotter. Her hand accidentally brushed against the metal and she jerked it away. "Don't touch the wall. It's very, very hot."

She glanced down at the trapdoor and the red glow coming from beneath it. Taking another deep breath, she dashed across safely to the other side. "All right," she called out and heard her voice shaking. "Move fast, but don't touch anything metal."

Without hesitation, Garrett came across with Doreen in front of her. Then Mark staggered over, Kagen behind him and using Mark's back for support.

Joanna looked down at the red glow beneath the trapdoor. It seemed brighter to her. She waited and watched. Its intensity didn't change. She called over to the two on the other side of the trapdoor. "Neiderman, let Wells put a hand on your shoulder and guide him across."

"I think he can do it himself," Neiderman said.

"Goddamn it! You guide him," Joanna bristled.

"Okay, okay," Neiderman said nervously. He placed Wells's hand up on his shoulder and slowly started across. He tried to stay in the middle between the wall and the trapdoor. But the walking space was only two feet wide and he could feel the heat coming through his clothes.

"Come on," Joanna urged. "Come—"

A red tongue of flame shot out at them, just behind Neiderman. It caught Wells on the leg, setting his pants on fire. He cried out in horror and pain and tumbled across on top of Neiderman. Both men were screaming and thrashing their limbs.

Quickly Joanna stripped off Mark's blazer and used it to snuff out the flames about Wells's leg. She found Mark's pocket knife in the coat and carefully cut away the charred pant. The skin on Wells's leg from the knee down was very red and already beginning to blister. There would be second-degree burns at best, maybe even third degree.

"How bad is it?" Wells grimaced with pain.

"You'll live," Joanna said, knowing the area was going to become infected. If he lived long enough.

Neiderman was busily examining himself. His pants and shoes felt hot, but he saw no fire or smoke coming from them. They had only been singed. He breathed a sigh of relief, then remembered the vials taped to his leg. He quickly put his hand inside his sock and ran his fingers over the vials. They were still intact.

The floor began to vibrate. Then they heard an ominous rumble coming from below.

"Quick!" Joanna called out urgently. "We've got to move."

In an instant they formed a single file and hurried down the tunnel as best they could. The darkness returned, denser than ever. Behind them the rumbling grew louder.

Joanna glanced back over her shoulder. There were no flames, no sparks, no light. But the diesel fumes were still with them, and so was the smell of smoke.

The walls became cold and wet. Good, Joanna thought, feeling her way along the tunnel. They were away from the engine room and approaching midship.

Now the air seemed fresher, and she took deep breaths, clearing her lungs.

Her fingers trailed along the wall—and then along no wall.

"We're at an intersection," Joanna called out. "Make sure you're touching the person in front of you."

As she took her first step across, she heard the sound of a muffled explosion behind her. Suddenly the ship rocked, then listed acutely. Joanna lost her footing and hit the floor, tumbling away from the others. In the darkness she heard their screams. And her own.

Forty-eight

"This is the infrared image the satellite picked up," Gordon said, handing a photograph to Admiral Pearl. "As you can see, it's very small."

"Is it the *Global Explorer*?" Pearl asked.

"The CIA analysts don't think so," Gordon said. "It's too small and its heat pattern is very erratic."

"What do they think it is?"

"They don't know, sir."

"So this could still be the *Global Explorer*?"

"They couldn't rule out that possibility."

Pearl leaned back in his swivel chair and puffed gently on his cigar. Some hope was better than no hope, he thought. "Have we got a fix on its location?"

"Yes, sir. But this photograph is three hours old and our image has moved." Gordon handed on a weather sheet showing winds and tides and currents. "Assuming the ship was powerless, we—"

"Why do you assume the ship was powerless?" Pearl interrupted.

"Because it's not giving off much heat."

Pearl nodded. "Go on."

"Assuming the ship was powerless, we estimate the tide and currents would have moved it twenty-eight miles due south of its earlier position."

"Get our reconnaissance planes to that area," Pearl said. "I want them to crisscross every square mile of it."

"They're already up, sir," Gordon told him. "We also

have a U-2 taking off in thirty minutes. It's equipped with a scanning camera that will transmit the pictures directly back to us."

"Good, good," Pearl said approvingly. "Well, at least the news isn't all bad."

"There's more, sir."

Pearl's eyebrows went up. "What?"

"Remember that Arctic storm that's brewing to the north?"

"What about it?"

"It's moving down much faster than predicted. It'll be over our search area in under two hours."

Pearl sighed heavily. "That's not enough time for us to get it done, is it?"

"Probably not, sir."

Pearl shook his head sadly. His friend Guy Hawksworth was dead. And if he wasn't, he soon would be.

Forty-nine

In the blackness, Joanna heard the others moaning and groaning. She slowly stood, using the wall for support. Her knees were throbbing and bleeding where the scabs had been torn away. And she could taste blood as well. Her lip had been split by the fall. The groans were louder now and seemed to be coming from the front, but in the darkness she couldn't be sure.

"Where is everybody?" Joanna called out.

"Here."

"Right here."

"Over here," the voices called back.

"Stay put and I'll come to you."

Joanna carefully moved forward, running her hand against the wall. She felt something warm dripping down her chin. Warm and sticky. It took her a moment to realize it was blood coming from her lower lip. She came to an intersection and bumped into someone.

"It's me," Garrett said.

"Are you okay?" Joanna asked.

"I've got a few more bumps and bruises, but I'll live."

"What about the others?"

"Doreen is all right," Garrett answered, and kept her arm tightly around the dazed woman. "I don't know about the rest."

"I'm okay," Mark said, his voice so weak it was hard to hear.

"My ankle is killing me," Kagen muttered in the darkness. "But it's no worse."

"What are we doing in this black hole?" Wells asked loudly. "Why don't we go topside?"

"Because we can't," Joanna said. "There's been an accident, and this tunnel is the only safe place on this ship. Ben will fill you in on the details."

"Owww!" Wells cried out. "What's wrong with my wrist?"

"You broke it in the accident," Joanna told him. "I put a splint on it, and it should hold if you keep your arm still."

She looked past the location of Wells's voice. "Neiderman, where are you?"

"Here."

Not too thirsty, are you? Joanna wanted to ask, but she held her tongue. "Let's get in single file and move on."

Joanna led the way through the intersection and down the dark tunnel. Her knees were stiff and sore, but at least the bleeding had stopped. Behind her she heard Mark coughing his guts out. And with each cough, she thought, Mark could be infecting all of them with the deadly bacteria. He was spraying it all over the tunnel, filling the air with it. And every one of them had cuts and abrasions that the microorganism could land in and grow.

Stop worrying about the damn bacteria, she told herself, and worry about getting out of here.

The temperature in the tunnel was dropping rapidly. Joanna felt goose bumps breaking out everywhere except on the burned areas of her arms. And frigid water was seeping up through her shoes. Her feet were now splashing in puddles that seemed deeper than before. She shivered with the cold and wondered how much farther they had to go.

The group stopped abruptly, all hearing the noise at the same time. It was a thumping sound, a soft thumping sound.

"Oh, Christ! It's the iceberg!" Garrett said breathlessly. "The bastard is going to kill us."

Fear flooded through Joanna and she had to force herself to move forward. Desperately she searched the blackness for light but saw nothing. Behind her, Garrett was holding on so tightly that her nails were digging into Joanna's skin. Mark coughed hard, and the noise from his cough echoed down the tunnel. Then all was still and silent.

Joanna could hear her heart pounding in her chest. Nearby water began to drip and hit the floor.

"Maybe it wasn't the iceberg making that noise," Garrett whispered.

"Don't bet on it," Joanna said.

The thumping sound came again, louder this time.

Garrett pulled on Joanna's shoulder. "Let's go back and try one of the side tunnels."

"This is the only way out," Joanna said, pushing herself on.

Ahead was a dim light, so dim it seemed to come and go. But the closer they came to it, the brighter it became. Now Joanna could see it was the floor light, still on but not nearly as strong as before. Its batteries were running out, she thought. They would have to move quickly. Without the light, they stood no chance at all.

The floor was very wet and slippery, and they all were watching their steps. They were now amidships, standing over the laboratory section of the *Global Explorer II*. Joanna pricked her ears and listened intently. She thought she heard the sound of water lapping against something.

She moved on cautiously, her eyes scanning the area in front of her. The floor was even wetter now, at least an inch of water on it. And the sound of waves lapping against something became more pronounced.

She stopped abruptly and pointed. "There it is."

The others came up alongside her and stared down at the floor. The trapdoor was wide open. Its lid was gone, its edges split apart with large gaps extending to the walls. There was no more than a foot and a half of walking space on each side. Joanna peered down at the opening. The water level was clearly visible.

"The iceberg is probably looking up at us right now," Garrett said.

"There's more than one down there," Wells reminded her. "Don't forget about the second iceberg we took aboard, the one that damn near sank us."

"The second iceberg is gone," Kagen told them. "It shattered into hundreds of pieces when it fell into the hold, so Hawksworth decided to vaporize it at a thousand degrees Fahrenheit. It no longer exists."

"Good goddamn riddance!" Garrett said.

The tip of the iceberg suddenly appeared, just the tip. It bobbed up and down gently in the water.

"Look at that!" Garrett hissed. "It's just waiting for us, waiting for one of us to make a move."

It did look evil, Joanna thought. It just sat there waiting. It seemed to be daring them to cross over.

Behind her, Joanna heard a long groan and turned to see Mark easing himself down the side of the tunnel. As he reached the floor he began to shake. In an instant Joanna was by his side.

He looked terribly ill, his face swollen and distorted by the raging infection. She touched his forehead. He was burning up.

"I can't go any farther," Mark said, his voice barely above a whisper.

"I know," Joanna said softly. "But we'll come back for you."

"No, you won't." Mark leaned his forehead against the wall and coughed weakly. "You'll have enough trouble saving yourself."

"We'll come back," she repeated.

Mark tried to clear his throat, then swallowed. "I

wouldn't have let you die from that infection, you know. I would have given you the antibiotic."

"I know," Joanna said, not at all sure he would have. She moved closer and lowered her voice. "Why did you do it? Why start a global epidemic? Was it just the money?"

"It got out of hand," Mark murmured. "They were supposed to control the—" He started shaking again, his entire body convulsing with chills. "Ge—ge—get out of here. You're wasting time."

"Just one more question. The bacteria that came out of China was the same as the one in the iceberg. Yet the bug from China was so easy to grow and produced no toxin. How could that be?"

"The bacteria mutated in my Cambridge laboratory," Mark said, catching his breath. "The mutant was far easier to grow and made virtually no toxin, but it was still resistant to everything but Panamycin." Another chill swept through Mark. "Now get . . . get the hell out of here."

Joanna pushed herself up, pitying him and hating him at the same time. "Mark can't go on," she announced to the others. "We'll have to come back for him later."

Everyone nodded. But they all knew they would never return.

Water splashed up through the trapdoor and spread over the floor, drenching their feet. It was ice cold. Slowly the water seeped back down into the compartment below.

"We'll cross over one at a time," Joanna told them. "Move quickly and don't look down."

Joanna took a deep breath, gathering her strength, and dashed for the other side. She made it in less than three seconds. "All right," she called back, her heart pounding wildly. "You're next, Paula."

Garrett hurried across, pushing Doreen in front of her. The iceberg barely moved.

Then Kagen limped past the trapdoor, dragging his leg like a dead weight. He almost tripped on a warped section of the floor. He slowed and grimaced but kept coming.

Just two more, Joanna thought as Kagen passed her. "Come on, Joe."

Wells moved quickly until he reached the trapdoor opening. He stopped and stared down at the iceberg, its tip barely above the waterline. "Fuck you!" he said and spat at it. Then he walked on.

The iceberg moved slightly. Wells ignored it.

Garrett grabbed Wells's good arm as he came across. "I wish I had that kind of courage."

Wells shrugged. "It's not courage."

"What is it, then?"

"It's the simple fact that I should have died a dozen times over when I was in Vietnam. I've looked at every day since then as a bonus. If I were to die right now, I'd have no complaints. I've gotten twenty-five years more than I should have."

"Come on, Neiderman," Joanna called out. "Get a move on."

Neiderman felt for the vials taped to his leg and made certain they were secure, then took a tentative step. He stopped and nervously looked down at the tip of the iceberg.

"You can do it," Kagen encouraged him. "Just put one foot in front of the other."

Neiderman moved slowly, now approaching the open trapdoor. The floor was warped in this area and he slowed even more.

"Move it!" Joanna urged.

Neiderman was almost across. He glanced down again at the tip of the iceberg. *Fuck you! Another step and I'm—*

The iceberg suddenly jutted up through the opening and pinned Neiderman to the wall. He heard the plastic containers inside his parka crack. Then he heard another cracking sound as the iceberg crushed his ribs. He tried to scream the pain away.

The others recoiled, horrified. The iceberg now filled most of the tunnel and was slowly mashing and grinding Neiderman against the steel wall. They couldn't tell if he was dead. Bloody bubbles were still coming out of his mouth, but that could have been the iceberg pushing the very last pockets of air from his lungs.

Gradually the iceberg descended through the opening and into the black water, taking Neiderman with it.

"Oh, my God!" Kagen muttered.

Wells stared down at the dark water, his mind flashing back to Vietnam. A land mine up ahead had exploded under an armored vehicle, flipping it over and atop a young black corporal, crushing his chest. He died blowing bloody bubbles.

Wells felt Garrett tugging on his sleeve and looked over. "Just bad luck," he told her.

"Bad luck, hell!" she blurted, trying to swallow her fear. "That bastard iceberg is going to get us all, one by one."

"It will if we stay here," Joanna said, now remembering the words of the steward. *This iceberg has a mind of its own,* he had said. She still thought it was nonsense—but saw no reason to test it.

Glancing around the tunnel, she saw the pickaxe on the floor by the uncoiled fire hose. She reached for it and handed it to Ben Kagen. "Use this as a cane. It'll help support some of your weight."

"Thanks," Kagen said gratefully.

Joanna looked back to the trapdoor. Water was again splashing up from below and flooding into the tunnel. She looked down at the floor. The water was up to her ankles. "We have to move," she said quickly.

"Where to?" Wells asked.

"Toward the bow."

"You lead. I'll bring up the rear."

In a single line they started down the tunnel, moving faster without Mark to slow them down. The light began to dim, but it was still bright enough to see by.

Joanna felt water streaming over her feet and looked down. It took a moment for her to realize what was happening. The stern of the ship was beginning to sink, lifting the bow. That caused the water on the floor to flow toward the stern. Jesus Christ! She looked at the floor again. There was no doubt. They were walking uphill, and water was streaming by them.

They moved on, the water less abundant than before. The light was fading, but at the next intersection Joanna saw a light fixture protruding up through the wetness. She hoped to God that the water hadn't shorted it out. Reaching down, she pressed the switch. The light came on brightly.

"Great!" Garrett shouted out.

"Not so great," Joanna said, and pointed directly ahead of them. The tunnel was blocked off by a steel wall. "It's a dead end."

"Oh, shit!" Garrett said dejectedly and sank to the floor, Doreen at her side.

"All this way for nothing," Kagen muttered to himself.

Wells came up to the steel wall and examined it. He saw a grouping of small rivets halfway up from the floor. "It's not a wall. It's a hatch that has been closed and secured."

"Can you open it?" Joanna asked at once.

"Probably," Wells answered. "But remember, there's a reason why this compartment is closed off. I suspect it's filled with water."

"From the hole in the hull," Joanna said gloomily.

Wells nodded. "Exactly."

"How much water?"

"Tons and tons of it, I would guess."

"It'll wash us away."

"Not if we have something to hold on to."

Joanna glanced around the tunnel, her gaze finally going to the ceiling. "The monorail! We can hold on to the track."

Wells thought for a moment. "It'll be chancy. But we don't have any other choice."

"Everybody hold on!" Joanna told them. "Hold on to the beam as tightly as you can!"

Everyone reached up and grabbed hold, even Doreen—with Garrett's guidance.

"Here we go."

Wells took the pickaxe and began to bang away at the area where he guessed the lock mechanism was located. The first few blows barely scratched the metal. Then it began to give. Even though he was holding the axe with his good hand, every swing caused his fractured wrist to throb fiercely. Wells pushed the pain aside and hammered away.

On the tenth blow the pickaxe broke through the metal and into the lock mechanism. Wells jerked the axe handle up and felt the lock spring open. "Hold on for your life!" he shouted, and slid the door back.

A wave of water gushed into the tunnel, pounding against them and sweeping them off their feet. In an instant they were all under water, gagging and choking as the salty sea filled their noses and mouths. The current seemed to grow even stronger and pulled at their arms, but everyone held on, knowing that to let go meant certain death.

Gradually the tidal force diminished and the water level began to recede.

Joanna's head popped up above the surface and she sucked in lungfuls of fresh air. Around her she saw the others. Garrett, Doreen, Kagen, and Wells, all were holding on and gasping for air as the water level dropped ever lower. Now it was at their waists.

Joanna looked around again. She could see everybody and everything so clearly. The water, the walls, the shining metal track above her. Then she saw the light streaming in from the hole directly overhead. "Daylight! Daylight!" she yelled out.

The others saw the light too and rushed toward it, cheering and shouting with joy.

Doreen stared at the hole in the hull and a faint smile came to her face. "It's the sky," she said softly.

Paula Garrett grabbed Doreen and hugged her. "Oh, dear God! Oh, dear God!" she said over and over.

Joanna shook her fist triumphantly. They were going to win! They were going to survive! They had beaten the odds, she told herself, now thinking about her sister Kate and Jake Sinclair and the life she was happily going back to.

Then she looked again at the hole in the hull and her spirits suddenly sank. "Oh, no!"

"*What?*" Wells asked.

Joanna pointed to the hole. "Look!"

The ship had a double hull. The iceberg had ripped open the outer one, leaving a huge gash ten feet across. But it had made a much smaller hole in the inner hull, a foot in width at the most. None of them could squeeze through that.

The ship abruptly shifted again, rolling from side to side before it settled. The bow had lifted further, the tilt of the floor now more obvious.

"What do we do next?" Garrett asked, knowing there was no "next."

There was a still silence as the group sank to the floor and waited for the inevitable.

The ship creaked and groaned, and Joanna could sense the floor tilting more. They had been so close, she thought, so close to surviving. But now they were trapped with no way out, the ship sinking faster with each passing minute.

She took a deep breath, totally exhausted and resigned

to her fate. So close, she thought again. Had the iceberg just been playing with them, as Garrett had said? Maybe it had let them live, pushing them on and on, giving them false hopes, knowing that even when they reached the hole in the hull there would be no escape.

Joanna shook her head. That was nonsense. An iceberg couldn't act with intent. It had no brain or will power. It was a floating block of ice. Yeah, Joanna thought miserably, a floating block of ice that had outsmarted them every step of the way.

In the distance she heard a faint popping sound. She couldn't tell if it was coming from within the tunnel or not.

Garrett sat up. "What's that?"

"Shhhh!" Joanna hushed her quietly and leaned forward, concentrating her hearing. The noise was coming closer.

Then they all recognized it. The putt-putt sound of a helicopter.

They jumped up, yelling and screaming at the top of their voices. Garrett was dancing, one arm around Doreen, the other around Wells. Kagen hurried over and hugged Joanna, kissing her cheek.

The sound of the helicopter began to fade.

The group quieted abruptly.

"What's happening?" Garrett asked, her face now serious.

Joanna furrowed her brow, thinking. "They may not know we're alive. All they can see is an upside-down ship with a big hole in its hull."

"Oh, God! They are going to leave us here to die."

Joanna reached over and ripped a sleeve from Kagen's shirt, then tied it securely to the end of the pickaxe. She handed it to Wells, the tallest of the group. "Stick this through the outer hull and wave it for all you're worth."

Wells put the pickaxe through the hole and waved it vigorously back and forth.

The sound of the helicopter faded even more. Now it was barely audible.

They sank back down to the floor, their hopes gone. Paula Garrett was crying softly, Wells at her side trying to comfort her. Doreen and Kagen were holding hands quietly, thinking their own thoughts.

Joanna was thinking about her sister Kate—the younger sister she had always looked after and cared for. She'll always be my baby sister, Joanna thought, hoping Kate would have a good life with no more heartaches. And then she thought about Jake Sinclair, still the best man she'd ever known and loved. She now wished that . . .

Joanna suddenly pricked up her ears. She heard the sound of a helicopter, still distant but closer than before. Joe Wells jumped up again and thrust the makeshift flag through the hole and waved it frantically. The sound grew louder and louder. Now it seemed to be almost on top of them. Everybody was standing again, yelling and shouting.

They heard soft thumps on the hull above them, followed by male voices barking out orders. For a brief moment the stream of daylight was blocked out. All eyes went to the hole in the hull.

A navy frogman was peering in through the hole. "Hello!"

"Hello!" the group yelled back.

"How many are you?"

"Five," Joanna called. "But we've got a problem. The hole in the inner hull is too small for us to get through."

"We'll take care of it," the frogman said and disappeared.

They heard people moving around above them, then a clanking sound of metal dropping onto metal.

The frogman reappeared. "Are there any oil or gas fumes around you?"

"None," Joanna yelled back.

It took the acetylene torch less than three minutes to slice a large opening through the inner hull. One by one the group were helped to the outside, then placed in harnesses and hoisted to the helicopter hovering above the sinking ship.

Joanna was the last one out. The cable slowly carried her upward. Below, the *Global Explorer II* was rolling over, now sinking for the final time.

Joanna glanced up at the heavily overcast sky. In the distance to the south she could see traces of blue and even a few streaks of sunlight. She smiled broadly. The sky had never looked so blue, the sun never so bright.

Epilogue

Jake Sinclair knocked tentatively on the door to Joanna's condominium, then stepped back and waited. He tried not to look at the peephole, thinking that she was probably looking out at him while she decided whether or not to let him in. He now wished he had picked another time to see her. It was late and raining and she might already be in bed. And she would be mad as hell that he came by without being invited.

The door opened slowly.

"Hi, Jake," Joanna said, her voice hoarse.

Jake was taken aback by her appearance. She looked thin and tired, with deep abrasions over her forehead and cheeks. "Jesus! What happened to you?"

"It's a long story," Joanna said. "Do you want to stand out there or would you rather come in?"

Jake entered and shook the rain from his head. He was carrying a wrapped package under his arm.

"What's in the box?" Joanna asked.

"I'll tell you later." Jake set the package down and went over to the fireplace to warm his hands. "I tried to call you all evening, but your phone was busy."

"I was calling Africa," Joanna told him. "It took forever to reach Kate in Kenya."

"Is she all right?"

"She's fine."

Jake studied Joanna in the fire's bright light. The abrasions on her face were deep, but healing. Now he could see a small split in her upper lip that was scabbed over. She looked like a battered woman.

"I could have used your help," Joanna said quietly.

Jake's face suddenly hardened. "Don't tell me some son of a bitch did this to you."

Joanna nodded. "A son of a bitch called Nature."

"You want to tell me about it?"

"Not really," Joanna said, then glanced over at the wrapped package. "What's in the box?"

"Nothing important."

Joanna sat on a large pillow in front of the fireplace and stared into the blaze. For a moment she thought about the fire aboard the *Global Explorer II* and how it had nearly killed them. She forced herself to think of something else. She looked up at Jake, now recalling the last case they'd worked on together. "What happened in that Brentwood murder case?"

"We got a confession," Jake said. "The cat hair in the ski cap did it."

Joanna nodded. "Did you have to do DNA testing to match up the cat hair?"

"Lori McKay did it for us," Jake said. "She did a hell of a job on this case."

"You really think so?"

"Oh, yeah. She's a little short on experience, but she's damn good when she puts her mind to it."

"Did you tell her that?"

"Sure did," Jake said, grinning slightly. "I told her she was my favorite forensic pathologist—after you, of course."

"Of course." Joanna continued to stare into the fire as her mind went back to the nightmare aboard the *Global Explorer II*. "I was so near to death. I'm still thinking about it."

Jake sat beside her and looked at the blazing logs. "Was death close enough for you to touch and smell?"

"Yeah."

"That takes a while to wear off."

"How long?"

"Weeks. Sometimes longer."

"So you just have to wait it out, huh?"

"Right."

"Shit," Joanna said, and reached for a poker to stoke the fire. "When I really thought I was going to die, I kept thinking of two people. You and Kate. Even after our big fight, I still thought about you." Joanna put the poker down and sighed wearily. "I never seem to learn, do I?"

A log in the fireplace popped loudly and split into two, sending up a shower of sparks. The blaze came back, brighter now.

"I missed the hell out of you," Jake said softly. "I came by every night to see if your light was on or I called and always hung up just before the answering machine clicked. Hell, I even looked for flimsy excuses to stop by your laboratory to see if you were back or maybe learn how you were doing."

Joanna smiled at him. "You did all that?"

"Yeah."

Joanna placed her head on his shoulder and leaned against him. "I'm never going to learn."

"Lord, I hope not." Jake kissed her head. "Did I tell you you're beautiful?"

"I look like hell," Joanna said.

"You're beautiful."

Joanna glanced over at the wrapped package. "Are you going to tell me what's in the box?"

"See for yourself."

Joanna quickly unwrapped the package and opened it. On top was a Waterford crystal glass, an exact replica of the one she'd broken when she and Jake had their fight.

Joanna smiled broadly. "Thank you, Jake."

"There's more."

Joanna dug through the styrofoam packing and uncovered two exquisite brandy snifters. "They're lovely. But why two?"

"One for you, one for me."

Joanna pecked him on the lips. "Want to try them out?"

"Oh, yeah."

Joanna bounced to her feet and went into the kitchen, leaving a trail of styrofoam packing behind her. She rinsed the snifters and poured double brandies, glad to be alive, glad to be back with Jake. Even with his flaws, he was still wonderful. She returned to the living room and handed Jake a brandy.

She raised her glass. "Cheers!"

"Not yet," Jake said, and gave her a slender velvet-covered jewelry box. "Happy birthday."

Joanna opened it and gazed down at a string of Miki-moto pearls. They were gleaming and perfectly matched. "They're gorgeous."

"So are you," Jake said, then saw the bright pink areas of skin over her forearms. In some places the skin was peeling, exposing a reddened subepidermal layer. "What happened to your arms?"

"There was a fire." Joanna sipped her brandy absently and snuggled up to him in front of the hearth. Outside, the last storm of the winter was moving in from the ocean. The wind was howling, the rain pounding against the sliding glass doors in Joanna's living room.

She pushed up the sleeves of her terry cloth bathrobe. "The skin on my arms is still sensitive from those burns."

Jake ran a gentle finger over her forearm. The skin was soft and smooth. "You've healed pretty good."

"Most of me has," Joanna said softly.

"You were cured of that Chinese-cholera bug that Lori told me about, right?" Jake asked.

Joanna nodded. "Me and everybody else. But the dose of Panamycin originally given the patients wasn't effective in me. The microorganism began to reappear in many of us. While the people at the CDC were debating what to do, I decided to re-treat myself. But the second time around, I doubled the dose of the antibiotic and took it for a full ten days. That regimen cured me, and I told the CDC about it. It's now being used on all infected patients and working very well. For all intents and purposes, the epidemic is over."

She took a deep breath. "At least that part of me is okay."

"Which means there's a part of you that isn't?"

Joanna shrugged.

"You still don't want to talk about it, huh?"

"They've asked me not to."

"That's never stopped you in the past."

"This one is different," she said, now thinking about the scientific expedition and all those who had died and the few who had survived. So many of them were on the bottom of the sea. Lord knew how many sailors and marines went down along with Hawksworth and Reetha and Mark and Neiderman.

The survivors were still recuperating weeks later. Kagen's ankle was badly fractured and required surgery, as did Wells's wrist. Doreen was recovering with the help of intensive psychotherapy, but the progress was slow. When Doreen was able, she had promised she would visit Los Angeles. But Joanna knew that would never happen. Everyone would want to put the horrors and the people involved behind them and get on with their lives.

Jake pulled Joanna close to him and stroked her hair as thunder boomed outside. The rain pelted down even harder, rattling the sliding glass doors. "Do you want some advice?"

"No."

"How about some very good advice?"

"I might consider it."

"It would help if you talked about it."

Joanna lifted her head and smiled at him. "You really want to hear the story, don't you?"

"Hell, yes," Jake said promptly. "I may not be the smartest cop in Los Angeles, but I'm certainly not the dumbest either. Now, when a colonel dressed in civilian clothes comes to Memorial and whisks you away with no explanation and with no bitching on your part, it doesn't take a genius to figure out something big is happening. And add to that the fact that we could only reach you by dialing some unlisted government number." Jake touched her nose with his index finger. "Oh yeah, this is a story I want to hear."

"You won't believe it."

"Try me."

Joanna put her head on his chest and gazed into the fire. "It's about icebergs."

Jake looked at her oddly. "Get out of here."

"I told you you wouldn't believe it."

"Is it really about icebergs?"

"Really."

Jake reached for his Greek cigarettes, his eyes never leaving her. "Tell me the story."

"No interruptions while I'm speaking," Joanna said. "Not even a peep. Understood?"

"Understood."

Joanna sat up and leaned forward for her snifter of brandy. She took a sip and stared at the blazing logs. "Once there was this iceberg, an incredibly beautiful iceberg . . ."

Jake listened intently to every detail, not uttering a sound. When the story was over, he said, "The news media are going to have a field day with this one. They'll turn it into a real circus and scare the hell out of everybody."

"I don't think it'll ever see the light of day."

"You'd better think again," Jake said. "This story is red hot. It's got to leak out."

Joanna smiled thinly at him. "The only possible source will be the ETOX team, and none of them will talk about it. Do you know why?"

"Why?"

"Because there's no proof that this ever happened. No proof at all. No pictures, no tapes, no lab books, no data. No nothing. And if by chance the story did leak out, the NSC and the navy would have all the answers to cover it up. They'd say a toxic organism was identified, but we now have antibiotics that kill it easily. It presents no threat. You try to disprove that."

"What about the *Global Explorer* and the crew that went down with her?"

"A tragic accident."

Jake flicked his cigarette into the fire. "Well, at least the iceberg served some purpose."

"What was that?"

"It took the bacteria to the bottom of the sea, safely away from us."

"I'm not so sure we are safe."

"But the iceberg was the only source for the bacteria, right?"

"That we know of."

"And we know this new antibiotic kills the bacteria, right?"

Joanna hesitated. "We may have a problem there. Do you recall what I told you about treating myself with Panamycin? That I had to double the dose in order to eradicate the bacteria?"

"Yeah," Jake said, nodding. "I remember that."

"Well, it's now taking more and more of the antibiotic to kill off the bacteria in patients," Joanna told him. "In other words, the bug is rapidly developing a resistance to Panamycin. It won't take very long before it's totally resistant. So that iceberg down there is a ticking time bomb, waiting to go off."

"Son of a bitch," Jake muttered. "What about the *Global Explorer*? Did it break apart when it sank?"

"Nobody knows," Joanna said quietly. "And if anybody does, they're not talking about it. I had to call Washington three times before they would give me an answer."

"What did they say?"

"That the situation was being contained and posed no threat."

Jake squinted an eye. "What the hell does that mean?"

"I think it means that the iceberg is still trapped inside the *Global Explorer*."

"Permanently?"

"God, I hope so!"

In the spring of the following year a seaquake occurred northwest of Juneau. The ocean floor shook for a
full ten seconds. The quake caused the sunken hull of the
Global Explorer II to vibrate violently and split apart. All
its contents were released.

Passengers and crew aboard a nearby cruise ship felt
the quake and lined the deck to watch the rippling effect
it had on the sea. When the last swell had come and gone,
a huge iceberg suddenly surfaced. It was blue and gold
and it sparkled in the sun.

It was the most beautiful iceberg they had ever seen.

If you enjoyed DEADLY EXPOSURE,
you won't want to miss Leonard Goldberg's
next scalpel-sharp medical thriller,
LETHAL MEASURES!

Forensic pathologist Joanna Blalock and
homicide detective Jake Sinclair return in this
explosive novel of medical suspense!

Turn the page for a special preview
of LETHAL MEASURES . . .

. . . a Dutton hardcover on sale now!

Simon Murdock stared at the television screen, shocked by the devastation he saw. The explosion had leveled a half block of houses and turned them into rubble. Sixteen people had been killed, twenty-eight injured seriously enough to require hospitalization. And the numbers were rising. Now the television screen was showing a fireman as he emerged from a pile of bricks and wood. He was carrying a young child, no more than three years old. The toddler with his nightie still on was obviously dead. Murdock winced and looked away, thinking that only a madman would do something like this. *A bomb! In the middle of Los Angeles! Jesus Christ!*

Murdock glanced around his office at Memorial Hospital. Potted plants and flowers were everywhere, gifts delivered yesterday to celebrate his twentieth year as dean at the medical center. They gave the room a cheerfulness that seemed so inappropriate at the moment. His gaze went back to the television set.

The intercom on Murdock's desk buzzed loudly. He quickly pushed a button and spoke to his secretary. "What?"

"Mr. Kitt from the Domestic Terrorism Unit of the FBI is on line one."

Murdock hung up the phone and left his office. Passing his secretary, he said, "I'm not available."

He took the elevator to the B level and hurried down a long corridor, organizing his thoughts on how to carry out the FBI's instructions. Putting all the blast casualties into beds at Memorial shouldn't be a problem. Those already admitted were either in the Orthopaedic or Surgery ward. The new admissions should go there as well. It would be a tight squeeze, but it could be done. He'd call the nursing supervisors and have them begin rearranging beds. Then he would talk with the hospital spokes-personnel. No press releases unless cleared by the FBI or whoever took charge of the investigation. No press conferences on the victims until told otherwise. A goddamn bomb, he thought grimly. Something specially constructed to kill and maim. In his mind's eye he again saw the fireman carrying the dead child out of the rubble. With effort he pushed the picture away.

Murdock went through a set of double doors with a sign that read POSITIVELY NO ADMITTANCE EXCEPT FOR AUTHORIZED PERSONNEL. A secretary looked up.

"Is Doctor Blalock around?" Murdock asked.

"In the back."

Murdock pushed through another set of swinging doors and entered the autopsy room. Joanna Blalock's back was to him as she was speaking to Dr. Lori McKay, an assistant professor of forensic pathology. Both women looked so young, he thought, particularly Lori McKay. She could pass for a medical student with her long auburn hair and green eyes and scattered freckles across her cheeks. Murdock sighed wearily, wondering if she was really that young or if he was just getting old. Probably both, he decided.

"I'll be with you in a moment, Simon," Joanna called over to him.

His gaze went to a piece of fleshy tissue Joanna was holding up to the light. The specimen was covered with skin and had two appendages hanging down. It took Murdock a moment before he realized he was looking at part of a human hand.

He moved in for a closer look. "Accidental dismemberment?"

"That's one possibility," Joanna said.

Murdock glanced down at the clean stainless steel table. "Where is the rest of the body?"

"This was the only part found," Joanna said, now examining the fingers with a magnifying glass. "Some hikers stumbled onto it in a secluded canyon in northern Los Angeles County."

Murdock rubbed his chin, thinking back. "Could it be

a murder victim who was chopped into pieces to prevent positive identification?"

Joanna shook her head. "That's not what happened here. When a body is purposely chopped up, the perpetrator almost always uses a sharp instrument, like a hatchet or an axe, and that leaves a clean, even wound. Here the wound edges are ragged and shredded, the bone splintered." She shook her head again. "This hand was ripped off by some very powerful force."

"Well, at least you have a few remaining fingers to give you some prints."

"Not really," Joanna said and pointed to the gnawed-off fingertips. "You can see a number of bite marks here. I suspect the ends of the fingers were nibbled off by coyotes or other scavengers."

Murdock swallowed back his nausea, thinking that the dissecting tables at Memorial would soon be filled with dismembered body parts. "I need to talk with you about a matter of some importance."

"I'll be right with you," Joanna said. She examined the specimen once more, then gave it to Lori. "I'd like you to study the hand, paying particular attention to the skin. Then look at the X rays. When I come back I want you to tell me about the person this hand belonged to. You should be able to determine the victim's age, size, marital status, ethnic origin, and his past and most recent occupations."

Murdock studied the fourth finger on the hand. He saw no wedding band. "Single," he guessed aloud.

"Married," Joanna told him. "You can see a distinct pale area on the fourth finger where the ring blocked out the sun's rays."

"Where's the ring?" Lori asked.

"Probably ripped off by the same force that tore off his hand," Joanna said. "Or perhaps nibbled away by a coyote. The finger has been gnawed down to its middle joint."

Lori looked at Joanna skeptically. "He could have been divorced a while back and removed his ring."

"Possible, but unlikely," Joanna said. "The sun would

have re-tanned the area, and it would have done it quickly in Southern California. The man worked outdoors."

"Doing what?" Lori asked.

"You tell me," Joanna said and handed Lori the magnifying glass with a grin and a wink.

"Are you going to give me any clues?"

"I already have."

Joanna stripped off her latex gloves and went over to the wall where the individual refrigerated units were located. She leaned back against the metal and felt its coolness come through her scrub suit. The autopsy room was warm and humid because the air-conditioning system was malfunctioning again.

"I need a large favor from you, Joanna."

"Fine," Joanna said. "As long as I can do it between now and five o'clock tomorrow afternoon."

"What happens at five tomorrow afternoon?"

"I leave on a two-week vacation."

"I'm going to have to ask you to reschedule."

"No way," Joanna said at once. "My sister, whom I haven't seen in over two years, is flying in from Paris to visit me. And she's bringing her son, whom I've never seen."

"I think you'll change your mind when you hear the nature of the request."

"I doubt it, but go ahead."

Murdock took a deep breath, wishing it was twenty years ago when deans gave orders that were followed and never questioned. "This is not for me, but for the FBI. They want you to perform the autopsies on the victims of the explosion that occurred last night."

"There are other forensic specialists who could—"

"They specifically asked for you," Murdock interrupted.

Joanna sighed weakly. "I'm not an expert in blast injuries."

Murdock shrugged. "They must have their reasons for requesting you."

Joanna looked over at Lori, who was now standing by the X-ray view box. "Damn it, Simon," she said softly. "I've never seen my little nephew. I've never seen the next generation of Blalocks."

"I know," Murdock said, thinking about the son he'd lost to drug addiction and all the time he should have spent with the boy and hadn't. He was too busy building Memorial into a world-class medical center. Murdock brought his mind back to the problem at hand. "If you refuse, I'll have no choice but to bring in forensic specialists who will take over your laboratory for as long as needed."

Joanna nodded slowly, understanding the subtle threat. The outside people would covet Joanna's position at Memorial and would do anything to get it. From amongst them Murdock could find a replacement for Joanna if he wished. "Perhaps I could do it part-time for the first week," she suggested.

"It'll be a full-time job," Murdock said. "You'll be working sixteen hours a day on it. And even at that pace, the FBI believes it will take months to get the work done."

Joanna nodded again. The autopsies would be straightforward and could be done in a matter of weeks. But examination and identification of the body parts would take months and months. Joanna thought about resigning on the spot. But that would be stupid. She had the best of all worlds. She directed the division of forensic pathology at Memorial most of the time, but she also had an outside consulting practice that allowed her to take whatever cases she wished. It gave her the independence so few had. It really would be stupid to resign, she thought again, but the urge to see and spend time with her sister and her little nephew kept pulling at her. And so did the thought of missing a weekend in Montreal with Paul du Maurier, the new love in her life. It would have been so perfect. She and Paul in Montreal, then back to Los Angeles to see Kate and her baby boy. Joanna quickly searched for a way out of her dilemma. She glanced over at Lori and wondered if her young assistant could lead the investigation, at least initially.

"I'm having trouble reading these X rays," Lori called out from the view box. "There's mashed-up bone all over the place."

Joanna walked to the view box, Murdock a step behind her. Lori was pointing to the metacarpal heads, which were larger than they should have been. And there was heavy calcification in the soft tissue around the shafts and heads of the metacarpal bones.

Joanna asked, "What do you make of that?"

"It looks like he broke his hands on more than a few occasions," Lori answered.

"And in what occupation do men repeatedly break their hands?"

Lori wrinkled her brow, concentrating. "Boxers!" she blurted out.

"Exactly," Joanna said. "And the extensive changes on X ray tell us he had a lot of bouts, so he was probably a professional."

Lori's eyes suddenly narrowed. "How do you know he wasn't just some punk who was involved in numerous street fights?"

"That would account for the repeatedly broken bones perhaps, but not for the marked soft tissue calcification." Joanna used a red crayon to circle a dense calcium deposit. "This is the result of frequent continuous trauma, such as occurs when boxers hit punching bags over and over again."

Murdock listened attentively, his interest piqued. Boxing was the only sport Murdock followed. In his teens he had been a Golden Gloves champion.

Lori stared at the X ray, unhappy with herself for not deciphering the obvious clue. Dummy! Use your brain! "So the victim was a male professional boxer who was married. And the color of his skin indicates he was probably Hispanic."

"Excellent," Joanna said. "What about his age?"

Lori went back to the dissecting table and pinched the skin on the dorsum of the hand, checking its elasticity. There were no lines or wrinkles. "I'd say late twenties or early thirties."

"And his size?"

"Small," Lori said promptly. "I'd guess he was just over five feet tall and weighed in the vicinity of a hundred and ten pounds. Those are just approximations based on the size of his hands and bones."

"You're getting pretty good at this," Joanna said.

Lori smiled widely, basking.

"Now tell me whether he spoke English and what his most recent job was."

Lori gave her a puzzled look. "We just determined he was a boxer."

"But not recently." Joanna used a tongue blade to turn the hand over, palm-side up. She pointed to thick calluses. "Boxers don't have calluses on their palms. These are seen in men who do heavy manual labor."

"And you think he could speak English because he might have to in order to get such a job," Lori concluded. "You know, at a big construction site or someplace like that."

Joanna shook her head and turned the hand over to a palm-side-down position. "On the backs of the fingers are very pale tattoos."

Lori took a magnifying glass and carefully studied the bases of the fingers. "On the fourth finger I see a faded *V* and on the fifth I believe I can make out the letter *E*."

"Tell me what you think of that."

Lori thought for a moment, then shrugged. "I think I'm out of my depth."

"You should talk with Jake Sinclair about tattoos," Joanna said, her mind now on the homicide detective who had been her lover off and on for ten years. He was good-looking and fun to be with, but he was also a confirmed loner and always would be. He drifted away when he felt like it and came back when he felt like it. And she had put up with it. But no more.

Lori tried to read the expression on Joanna's face. "What would Lieutenant Sinclair tell me about the tattoos?"

Joanna brought her mind back to the hand. "He'd tell you that the most common tattoo seen on the hands of Hispanic males are the words 'Love' and 'Hate,' with one letter per finger. And most people won't have themselves tattooed with something they can't read. So it's fair to say this man could read and speak English."

"But why are the tattoos so faded?" Lori asked.

"Now I'm just guessing," Joanna said. "But I suspect he had the tattoo put on when he was a kid. And, as so often happens, he regretted it later on and wanted the tattoo removed."

Lori nodded. "Probably with a laser."

"And that's expensive to have done," Joanna went on, "so I would guess he was successful in the ring."

"But if that's true, why did he become a common laborer?"

"Maybe he came on hard times when he left the ring. That's the usual story with boxers."

Murdock nodded ever so slightly. That was the story with most boxers, even the great ones like Joe Louis and Sugar Ray Robinson. He continued listening to the interchange between the women, amazed at how Joanna Blalock could make so much from so little. But then again, he reminded himself, that's what forensic pathologists do. No wonder the FBI wanted her.

"But we still have no idea what ripped his hand off," Lori was saying.

"Chances are, once we learn his identity the other things will begin to fall into place," Joanna told her. "So far, we're dealing with a young Hispanic, married, former boxer who was probably successful in the ring. We approximate his weight at a hundred ten to a hundred twenty pounds. He speaks English, so he's lived in this country for a while. He may even be native-born. His last job involved heavy manual labor."

"Well, that narrows it down some," Lori said without enthusiasm.

"That narrows it down a lot," Joanna said. "And with some digging, you're going to find out who this fellow was."

"How do I go about doing that?"

"Through the Boxing Commission," Joanna explained.

Murdock interjected, "He'd be either a flyweight or a bantamweight."

"Are you sure?" Joanna asked.

"Positive," Murdock said.

"Good," Joanna said, but she made a mental note to look it up. "So he fought in the bantamweight or fly-weight division sometime during the past ten years. He had a fair number of fights and I suspect he won more than he lost. And he had the word 'Love' tattooed across his fingers."

Lori exhaled loudly. "You're talking about a lot of work. If only we had some distinguishing feature to go on."

"You do. He recently disappeared and nobody knows where he is."

"His wife will really be worried," Lori added.

"She may have even filed a missing persons report," Joanna said, thinking aloud. "Once you've narrowed your list down, we can cross-check it against the people reported as missing over the past week or two."

Lori scribbled a note. "Anything else?"

"That'll do for now." Joanna glanced at her watch. "Let's hustle down to Radiology. If we get there before nine, they'll do a CAT scan on the hand for us. Maybe there's something in the soft tissues that we missed."

Murdock looked up at the wall clock and cursed himself for wasting so much time. It was 8:50 A.M. He was late for his meeting with the chief of Pathology to discuss a temporary morgue. There would be at least sixteen bodies. They would need a big room.

Murdock cleared his throat loudly and waited for the women to turn. "Joanna, I've got to run. Please carefully consider my request. I'll need your answer by noon, one way or the other."

Lori watched him leave, then said to Joanna, "What was that all about?"

"It's about being boxed in with no way out."

"By Murdock?"

Joanna nodded. "He's an expert at it."